“Attention to detail is the Shell

rates us from the masses. If I select be

guests, know it’s for a reason. Everything I do for this family is for a reason. I shouldn’t need to remind you how important this event is to your father’s career.”

No, she didn’t need a reminder of the dinner’s importance. How could she forget, when her own future depended on its success? Cal’s imminent departure to manage her father’s upcoming political campaign would give her an opportunity, one she’d waited for since pigtails were her hairstyle of choice. For Rayne, the promotion to oversee Shelby Lodge after Cal stepped away from his post had nothing to do with a boost in salary or a flashy new title. She’d never desired status or prestige. She’d simply craved a place to belong—within her family and within the community her grandfather had loved until his dying breath.

Shelby Lodge was such a place. Not only had it been her childhood home, but it remained the heartbeat of her dreams.

Cal tapped the toe of his Italian loafer against the polished hardwood, and the knot in her chest tripled in size. “Is there anything else I should be made aware of?” he asked.

Unable to meet his gaze, she paired a slight shake of her head with a lie that burned all the way up her throat. “Everything is in perfect order.”

“Good. That’s what I like to hear. These guests are your father’s biggest supporters. They’re worth every extra effort on our part.” With a half pivot toward the exit, he glanced back over his shoulder. “I’ll be meeting with the mayor tonight to go over security protocol. If your father’s secretary contacts you, make sure you reroute her to my cell.”

“Certainly.”

Cold dread flooded her abdomen as she watched him leave. Her time was up. She had two choices: One, chase after Cal and confess she’d forgotten to place the order he’d specifically requested. Or two, chase after her dream, cross into forbidden territory, and somehow convince her family's enemy to keep their exchange a secret.

Like in the Garden of Eden, there was only one place that had been off-limits to Rayne since childhood: Ford Winslow's Orchard and Farm.

The property neighboring Shelby Lodge.

Rayne angled her head, hoping to catch a clearer view of her neighbors—*one* in particular. She rubbed slick palms down the seams of her skirt and waited for old Ford Winslow to make his exit. The exhaust from his work truck puffed out in thick black plumes, much the way she'd pictured the inside of his soul to look.

She spied the farm from the gravel turnabout on Ramsey Highway, just a quarter mile out from the shared property lines. The golf cart she'd commandeered for her mission seemed less conspicuous than her Audi and much easier to conceal under the generous maple tree overhead.

From this vantage point, her family's forty-three-room redwood estate resembled a fairy-tale illustration. Storybook beauty shadowed by the Rockies and surrounded by two hundred acres of grassland. The prize-winning ambience of Shelby Lodge, located in Shelby Falls, Idaho, had made the lodge one of the most prestigious getaways in the Northwest. Their clientele ranged from business executives and politicians, to the wealthy and retired, to international aristocrats looking for a quiet place to holiday amid nature's finest. But Rayne's plans for the future of Shelby Lodge were less about catering to pampered travelers and more about bridging the gap within their local community.

Rayne clamped her bottom lip between her teeth, hoping the sting might dull the stab of guilt in her chest for what she was about to do. No, what she *had* to do.

If she didn't come up with one hundred and thirty-six thoughtfully unique, locally made, and perfectly packaged gifts for her father's guests,

But a tiny spark can set a great forest on fire.

—James 3:5

To Tammy Gray,
my favorite truth-teller.
I love you.

This is a work of fiction. Names, characters, organizations, places, events, and incidents are either products of the author's imagination or are used fictitiously.

Published by Waterfall Press, Grand Haven, Michigan

www.brilliancepublishing.com

ISBN-13: 9781503937703
ISBN-10: 1503937704

Cover design by Jason Blackburn

Printed in the United States of America

the promise of rayne

Nicole Deese

ALSO BY NICOLE DEESE

Love in Lenox Novels

A Cliché Christmas

A Season to Love

Letting Go Series

All for Anna (Book 1)

All She Wanted (Book 2)

All Who Dream (Book 3)

Other Titles

A Summer Remade

the promise of rayne

CHAPTER ONE

Desperation undermines wisdom. Her grandfather's legendary words crash-landed in the space between Rayne Shelby's heart and head, though they did nothing to combat her frantic thoughts.

Before today, she'd prided herself on her ability to remain level-headed in a crisis. She'd learned how to pacify self-righteous politicians, calm disgruntled lodge guests, and regularly appease a man who could flatten her future with the snap of his micromanaging fingers.

But this particular crisis had pushed her internal panic meter from a steady five to an off-the-charts fifteen.

She'd exhausted every option possible to fix her mistake.

Except for one.

The one that would brand her a traitor to her family name.

Event preparations inside the Great Room at Shelby Lodge were in full swing, a production she'd witnessed since early childhood, long before her role as event coordinator, and years before her father had won his first election. Pressed linens, patriotic decor, and shipments of gourmet foods had all arrived on time and without issue, which made the missing delivery—the special order she'd forgotten to place—all the more glaring.

Rayne's gaze flickered between the clock on the mantel and the shadowy tree line of the farmland beyond the parlor window. The countdown to Governor Shelby's fund-raising dinner mocked the rising staccato of her pulse and pummeled her good-girl conscience into submission. She had only minutes to make a decision that could result in a domino effect of undesirable repercussions.

If she got caught.

A distinct cadence of footsteps echoed in the hallway off the lobby, the acoustics almost as unforgiving as her uncle Cal. *Almost.* Her father might govern their state, but it was her uncle who governed their family. Rayne fastened a smile on her face just in time to meet his disapproving scowl.

"Why wasn't I notified that Delia changed the dessert menu for Saturday night?" Cal's charcoal eyebrows pinched together. "Who signed off on that?"

"I did." Rayne's quiet assertion did little to slow her skipping heartbeats. "Delia felt apple cobbler would be a better choice than mixed berries because—"

"You know I abhor apples."

Admittedly, the thought had crossed her mind, but Delia had been cooking at the lodge for twenty-seven years, a year longer than Rayne had been alive. The woman knew food the way Rayne knew every nook and cranny of her late grandfather's estate. "I apologize if I overstepped. It seemed like such a small detail to bother you with."

He clasped his hands behind his back and stiffened his broad shoulders. Cal's salon-retouched onyx hair, russet eyes, and pointed features looked as authoritative as his daily three-piece suit. But it was the dominant cleft in his chin that reminded Rayne of her grandfather, and of the dime-size dimple in her own chin.

her uncle would have one hundred and thirty-six reasons to kick her promotion to the curb.

Swift movement to her right snapped at her attention. Someone with faded gray hair and a dog on his heels ducked inside the pickup truck. Ford Winslow: the man responsible for scheming against a grief-stricken widower eighteen years ago.

Thankfully, the solution to her blunder didn't need to involve him—not directly anyway. Trespassing couldn't really be equal to treason, could it? Even if the patriarch of her family would rip her argument to shreds, she hoped God operated on a more case-by-case basis.

Ford pulled away from the Second Harvest warehouse at the rear of the farm and rolled up the long drive and then turned in the direction of town.

Rayne waited until the glow of his taillights faded out completely before creeping her tires onto the quiet highway. When she was just a few car lengths away from the entrance, her potential redeemer sauntered into view.

She smashed the brake to the floorboard.

With the exception of a rebellious August night long ago, Rayne had steered clear of everything and everyone associated with Ford Winslow and his farm. Yet the sight of Levi Harding never failed to poke a few holes in her family allegiance. In nine years, her memory of the one and only time she'd broken the rules and interacted with the lonely-eyed boy hadn't faded. But neither had the memory of her uncle's controlled fury when he'd hauled her into his study at nearly three in the morning and lectured her on every transgression Ford had committed against her family—against her grandfather.

And despite the depth of connection she'd felt for Levi at the Falls in those stolen moonlit moments, her grandfather's legacy would always come first in her heart.

She followed him with her eyes and wondered yet again how Levi could willingly partner with a man like Ford for all these years—working as his apprentice, building a home on his property. She'd never understand it. Sure, her uncle Cal was difficult to work for—even on his best day—but he wasn't a crook.

He wasn't a con man.

Levi peeled off his overshirt and blindly tossed his plaid button-up into the air, briefly exposing the hard, tanned planes of his stomach. Her throat went dry as the crumpled fabric landed on a workbench midway between the warehouse and the barn. A slight shake of his head pulled her attention upward, and she zeroed in on his summer-streaked hair. Sweat and sunshine bounced off a perfect blend of shimmery golds and bronzy browns and ignited a memory long ago buried.

She blinked it back.

"You can do this," she muttered to herself. "You *have* to do this."

Without another moment to second-guess, she punched the accelerator.

Hot dust billowed from underneath the tires as she cranked the steering wheel to the left and hoped her grandfather's proverb held an exception . . . that sometimes wisdom meant making the most of a desperate situation.

Especially when her greatest dream was at stake.

CHAPTER TWO

The crunch of unfamiliar tires rolling down the drive caused Levi to pause his mental checklist. But it was the driver of the glorified Power Wheels who had him questioning his sanity. Even before her face came into focus, her hair exposed the secret of her identity.

Shelby hair was as distinct to the eye as a gasoline leak was to the nose. A shade so dark it haloed blue. Like a bruise. With the sleeve of his shirt, he wiped the sweat from his brow and moseyed in her direction.

Usually he had enough sense to keep his distance from flammable substances, but something told him Rayne Shelby was about to challenge his look-but-don't-touch policy. She parked her toy a few paces away from where he stood, his work boots planked as wide as his shoulders.

The raven-haired beauty slid to the edge of her open-air seat, and for a fraction of a second, her heels hovered above the ground, her flowery skirt rising to midthigh as she slipped off the bench onto his land—as good as his land, anyway. He didn't avert his gaze, not even when a stiff breeze threatened the integrity of her skirt length for a second time.

After a quick tug to her hemline, she caught his eye and walked toward him—no, not walked, glided. And then, as if the two were perfect strangers, she stretched out her hand.

"Um, hello. You may not remember me, but I'm Ray—"

"I know who you are." The sting of rejection was funny that way. It left a lasting impression—much like the aftermath of their first encounter.

"Oh . . . right, I wasn't sure if . . ." Thin fingers tucked an unruly strand of hair behind her ear as her words trailed into silence.

"What can I do for you, Ms. Shelby?"

"I was hoping we could . . ." Her gaze roamed his property as if searching for a safe place to land. "Talk business."

Though her statement surprised him, he kept his face as neutral as his tone. "I'm afraid Ford's out for the rest of the day. Care to leave a message for him?"

Even from three feet away, he sensed her shudder at the mention of Ford's name.

"Actually, I was hoping I might speak with you. About Second Harvest." She glanced over her shoulder like a lost puppy looking for her pack leader.

"Second Harvest?" *Interesting.* His refined farm-to-table co-op generally contracted local merchants and farmers from the area. Not Shelbys. And though he wouldn't mind reaching into the wallets of some of her deep-pocketed friends, his leeriness prevailed. "What is it you'd like to know?"

"I'm looking to purchase a bulk order of local items." Her cognac-colored eyes scanned the sign near the warehouse doors. "Maybe some lavender-infused soaps? Or perhaps some specialty lotions?"

Oh, how he enjoyed guessing games. "How many do you need?"

Again with the over-the-shoulder glance. Hopefully there weren't more of her kind on their way. He wasn't exactly prepared for a Shelby ambush. "A hundred and thirty-six."

He blinked, waiting for her to correct herself.

She didn't.

"Do you understand how a co-op works, Ms. Shelby?"

"Please, call me Rayne. And yes, I understand. I'm prepared to pay for whatever inconvenience my purchase may cause your customers."

He cracked a smile. "You having a bathing crisis?"

Her eyes snapped to his. "Excuse me?"

"A hundred and thirty-six bars of soap seems extreme."

"I'm not having a bathing crisis."

"Just a regular crisis, then?"

"Are you not going to sell me the soap?" The falter in her sweet voice snagged his attention.

"Still deciding." He crossed his arms and debated how long she'd stick around to find out. Although, if her track record of avoidance held true, he could be looking at another nine years of silence.

"Please, I have to . . ." On the tail end of a sigh, she sucked in her bottom lip and seemed to reconsider her plea. "I *need* to purchase them." The way she emphasized the word unnerved him. Whatever her crisis, it wasn't nearly as shallow or vain as he'd first suspected.

"I don't make business deals in the heat, or while standing in the middle of my driveway."

Her eyebrows arched and dipped succinctly. "So where do you—"

"There's three offices on this property, but my laptop's in there, along with my current inventory figures." He hitched a thumb in the direction of Ford's house, and her reaction upstaged his imagination. Whatever brave front she'd pulled on before Power-Wheeling it over here had vanished, along with the pretty flush of her cheeks.

"I won't bite, but if you'd rather take a seat over there on the shaded porch swing, I'll make a compromise."

Her gaze dragged back to his. "No, we can go inside. It's fine." Though her tensed upper body and hard swallow told a different story.

She hiked her duffel bag of a purse onto her shoulder and strolled toward the house, navigating each porch step in her heels as if to avoid a scattering of hidden land mines. Once at the top, she waited for Levi to hold the door open and invite her inside.

Good thing he was 80 percent gentleman.

He held the screen and allowed her to pass into the cluttered living area ahead of him. Ford's books and mechanical trinkets lay strewn over every shelf, table, and chair. His boss might not be the tidiest man alive, but he was definitely one of the wisest.

"Don't be shy about shoving that stuff over. Ford wouldn't mind." Not that she cared what Ford would or would not mind.

Rayne bent to push a pile of Ford's treasured theological reference books aside, and then froze. Her gaze seemed to fixate on a cedar frame propped on the fireplace mantel—a twenty-year-old photograph of William Shelby, his hair the same shocking black as his granddaughter's. But Levi doubted Rayne's interest was on her grandfather's hair, not when his arm was slung around the shoulders of a midforties Ford.

Levi cleared his throat. "You want something to drink?"

"No, thank you." As stiff as her voice, she perched on the dusty sofa and smoothed a nonexistent wrinkle from the front of her skirt. "I really shouldn't stay long."

"Probably not." Levi chuckled at the obvious statement and shot her a sidelong glance. Though her once-girlish figure had transformed into subtle womanly curves that kicked his pulse several notches higher, it was clear she was no closer to escaping her chosen captivity than she'd been the first night they'd met. Hunching over the desk, he opened his laptop and scrolled through the Second Harvest spreadsheets until he found the information he sought.

"I imagine you've checked with other stores around town?" And by *other stores*, he meant *every store* in town. If Rayne Shelby had shown up asking him for help, then Second Harvest had to be her very last resort, an ironic twist of events considering her family wanted nothing more than to stomp on Winslow Farm like a wayward seedling.

Eyeing her, he closed his laptop and anchored his weight against the edge of the desk, crossed his ankles.

"Yes, I've checked with other stores," she replied.

"Even Gil over at Gilbert's Party Palace?" His lips twitched, thinking of the elfish man with the personality of a doorknob and merchandise fit for the inside of a piñata.

"He offered me a box of kazoos or a case of I-heart-Idaho shot glasses."

"Not quite up to the old Shelby standard, I suppose."

She tangled her hands in her lap. "Look, I realize my request seems strange, but this purchase is a critical part of an event I'm responsible for this Saturday night. I need one hundred and thirty-six unique, Idaho-made gifts to give to our patrons."

"For this Saturday, huh? That's forty-eight hours from now. Seems kind of last-minute to be ordering something so *critical* for the governor's party." Word spread quickly when Governor Shelby was due for an appearance in the town named after his lineage. Especially when Shelby headquarters was located only a few hundred acres away. "Sounds like somebody screwed up."

She rubbed her lips together and he anticipated some kind of save-face cover-up to launch off her tongue. After all, she was the niece of the slickest manipulator he'd ever encountered. And Levi had known his fair share of con artists.

"I did," she said. "I forgot to place the special order weeks ago, and I didn't realize the oversight until this morning."

He uncrossed his ankles and studied her with renewed interest . . . and perhaps something else too. Her unexpected honesty seemed to peel back the corner of a memory he'd chosen to repress. *An invitation to a moonlit party at the Falls during his first summer in town. A nameless girl with jet-black hair who'd strayed from her friends to follow a loner. A few stolen hours skipping rocks and swapping secrets and—*

He blinked hard, clearing the unwanted thoughts before they could travel any further down a dead-end road. "What will happen if you can't provide them—the gifts for your guests?"

She glanced down at her knotted fingers, her anxious stare revealing more about the consequence of her failure than she seemed willing to admit. But her silence only confirmed his suspicion: Rayne's harried arrival on his farm had little to do with pleasing patrons and everything to do with pleasing her overbearing uncle.

Fear had an uncanny way of motivating people.

"Does Cal know you're here?"

She stood without warning, her skirt swishing around her shapely legs. "If you're not going to help me, then please just say so."

When he said nothing, she started for the exit.

"I'll help you."

She pivoted to face him, and in reply he offered a lazy shrug. "Thing is, I don't have enough of those specialty soaps for all your guests. But I do have something else. Something better."

"Really?" Hope flashed in her amber eyes, and Levi's face broke into a grin he usually reserved for winning a hand of blackjack.

"I'd never tease a paying customer."

The sigh that escaped her was closer to a sob than a tension release. "You'll really help me—*anonymously*?"

"Princess, for the right price I'd help anyone." Even a Shelby.

"I'm desperate."

"You don't say."

For the first time since she arrived at the farm, Levi watched skepticism mask her dainty features. "If this is a trick, then—"

He stepped toward her, moving in so close he could smell the sweet scent of jasmine and honeysuckle on her skin. "Despite what your uncle may have told you, Winslow Farm didn't earn its good reputation by cheating anyone. We sell quality products. And we get paid for quality products. End of story."

She inched back but kept her lips tightly pursed. He wasn't dumb enough to accept her silence as belief, but this moment wasn't about erasing the past, it was about banking on the future.

"I'd need the order ready by Friday night—*tomorrow* night," she stressed.

Before her father's entourage arrived in town, no doubt. "So I take it your daddy has officially announced he'll be running for reelection?"

She gave a curt nod, her gaze suddenly absent from his face. "Yes, he announced last week. Saturday's dinner is a VIP fund-raiser for his biggest donors."

Figured. Governor Randall Shelby wasn't the type to step out of the limelight unless forced.

"Honey," he said.

"Excuse me?" Her hair bounced behind her shoulder.

"Honey. The product that's better than scented soaps and specialty lotions. Second Harvest just contracted some of the best beekeepers in the region. The honey is both local and unique."

Her delighted expression did more for him than he'd ever admit. "May I try a sample?"

He'd already woven his way into Ford's kitchen. The old man didn't keep many groceries around the house, but he always had farm honey on hand. The recent repackaging into short mason jars was quite an upgrade from the old snap-cap plastic bottle, an upgrade that would pay for itself soon enough.

She clasped her hands under her chin. "Oh wow. That will work perfectly. I can add a ribbon and a lodge logo to each jar—as long as you're okay with that, of course."

"Fine by me." He dipped the taste-tester stick into the jar, the honey stretching and twirling as he pulled it out and handed it to her.

She didn't hesitate to indulge him, and he didn't steer his gaze from her perfectly shaped mouth.

Maybe he was only 60 percent gentleman.

She rubbed her lips together after the last droplet of honey touched her tongue. "That's really excellent."

"I know." Levi set the jar aside and slid his phone from his back pocket. With his calculator at the ready, he formulated a plan and punched in a sequence of numbers.

He flipped the screen around, and her eyes ticked wide.

"That's nearly triple my budget."

"Plucking huckleberry honey from the hands of my most loyal customers comes at a premium."

The sag of her shoulders and wringing of her hands tore at him a little, but not nearly enough to thwart his strategy. She wasn't the first pretty face he'd done business with. She was only the first Shelby.

"I'll write a business check for the budgeted amount and cover the rest with a personal check."

He considered the enigma before him. Either she was the most devoted employee he'd ever met, or the consequence she feared really was as costly as she'd made it seem.

"Or perhaps I could cut you a deal." He recrunched the numbers and showed her the screen once more. "This better?"

Her relief was audible. "Yes, yes. I can do that. And I'll owe you a fav—"

"A ticket to the dinner."

Her brows shot skyward. "What?"

"Get me a ticket to the dinner, and you get the discounted price and my personal guarantee of the rushed delivery time. It's the best deal you'll find for a high-quality gift on such short notice."

"You can't be serious."

"I never joke about business." He winked. "Don't worry, I clean up well. Promise."

"That's not . . . that's not the problem. I mean, I'm sure you do clean up well, but there's absolutely no way I can get you a ticket."

"How many local vendors do you know who could provide you with one hundred and thirty-six Idaho-made gifts in twenty-four hours?"

She lifted her chin and he had to work at suppressing a smile. He knew exactly how many she would find. Heck, if he hadn't collected all those orders at the farmers' market last weekend, he wouldn't have the quantity to offer her either. But luck and opportunity were in sync today, and he wasn't about to pass up a chance at some of the deepest pockets in the state. Second Harvest needed investors, and that fancy dinner party would have them in spades. He'd gamble more than his pride for the chance to pitch his business plan to Tom Hutchinson, owner of a dozen Wellness Smoothie Shacks.

"My uncle will never let you through the door."

"Our deal won't be dependent on your uncle inviting me inside. I just need a ticket to the dinner. That's all."

As the worry lines in her forehead deepened, Levi held his carefully honed expression. Patience was a salesman's best weapon. And Levi knew just how to sharpen the blade. He'd worked with the can't-stand-a-moment-of-silence types many times.

He'd give her eight seconds.

She made it to four.

"Okay." A weighted sigh and then, "Tell me who to make the check out to and I'll get you the ticket, but *no one* can know about this. Do I have your word on that?"

A strange request coming from her. He had it on good authority that every member of her nepotistic family believed the farm to be ruled by thieves. And yet here she was, asking for his word.

"You have it." Levi held her gaze for a second more. "Money is money. I don't care where it comes from." Unlike her uncle. "You can make it out to SH Inc. It's a private account used only for Second Harvest deposits. It's not linked to Winslow Farm yet."

Math had always been one of his better subjects—especially when that math had a dollar sign in front of it.

She dug into her oversized bag and pulled out two checkbooks—one business and one personal. After a few quick strokes of her pen, their deal was done.

She handed the payment over to him. "The ticket will be in your mailbox by ten o'clock tomorrow morning."

She pushed out the screen door and Levi followed her down the porch steps.

"Just one piece of advice," she said over her shoulder as she slipped onto the golf cart's bench seat. "Stay clear of my uncle."

Levi wasn't sure if the four-figure payment in his hand or the estranged neighbor in his driveway was more appealing. "One piece of advice for you, Rayne Shelby?"

She twisted the key in the ignition and then found his eyes.

"Never tell a businessman you're desperate."

Fine, maybe he was only 40 percent gentleman after all.

CHAPTER THREE

Rayne swept her hair off her shoulders and twisted it into a knot at the nape of her neck while counting the chairs and place settings in the Great Room for a second time. With its vaulted A-frame ceiling, cedar trusses, and refinished last-century hardwoods, the room begged for social gatherings. A request Rayne loved to fulfill. Elegantly adorned tables and chairs dotted the hall's massive footprint. The presentation and decor sparkled with black-tie readiness.

One hundred and thirty-six VIP guests had RSVP'd—and though the setup had been finished for nearly twelve hours, she couldn't risk even the smallest oversight. Especially not with Cal's last-minute checks and white-glove demands.

Thankfully, though, the drama over the patron gifts was no more. The huckleberry honey had been delivered under the guise of night, just as Levi had promised. She'd spent the majority of the evening readying the jars and sprucing up the gift bags before finally surrendering to sleep.

By now, Levi had likely found the red ticket in the farm's mailbox. She just prayed he wasn't foolish enough to use it.

"Rayne—has your father checked in yet? He was supposed to be here an hour ago to go over tonight's agenda with me." Her uncle's intimidating stature blocked the entryway to the Great Room.

"No, sorry. I haven't seen him come in." She skirted around several tables to where he brooded. "You know what it's like when he comes back to town for a visit. He'll be here soon, I'm sure." She wore the practiced smile of a daughter who'd reassured herself of the same thing many a time.

Her father was a busy man. An influential man. A heavily sought-after man. Following in her granddaddy's footsteps, Randall Shelby had been elected as mayor of Shelby Falls before her tenth birthday, and then as state senator during her junior year of high school, and now he was running for his second term as Idaho's governor. But unlike her grandfather, who'd retired from politics during the pinnacle of his popularity, Cal had every hope her father's career would peak in the Oval Office.

"Well, if he thinks he can simply shake a few hands while tossing around that winsome grin of his without—"

"Rayne, please tell your uncle to keep his blood pressure in check—at least for the next eighteen months." Her father's hand clamped onto her uncle's shoulder, but his attention held on his only daughter. "Hello, darling."

He kissed each of her cheeks and then promptly turned to face his brother's abused scowl. "You know, I get enough flak in the capital. I would hope my future campaign manager might cut me a tardy break every once and again."

The creases around Cal's mouth disappeared. It seemed a flash of pearly whites and a head tilt had bought her father a temporary pardon. "Not if you want another victory, Governor Shelby."

Her father pressed a palm to his heart and chuckled. "From your lips to God's ears, brother."

Rayne looked between the two before focusing on the lobby behind them. "Didn't Veronica come with you?" Her father rarely traveled without her stepmother. In the ten years since the flashy couple had exchanged vows in the Bahamas, Veronica's role as a politician's wife had become an elevated priority. But Rayne didn't fault her for it. Veronica wasn't uncaring or mean-spirited, she just wasn't very . . . maternal. Not in the way Delia and Aunt Nina were, anyway. Even so, Rayne's stepmother fit her father well, a classy woman who was as devoted to him as she was to his lifestyle.

"Afraid she got caught up shopping with Marilynn Brightwater downtown. Turns out they have the same ridiculous obsession for refurbished junk," her father said.

"And hopefully we can use that obsession to persuade Marilynn's mule of a husband," Cal added dryly.

"*Rich* mule of a husband," her father corrected before turning back to Rayne. "I'm sure she'll be here in time to get all dolled up for tonight's dinner." He glanced up then, his eyes scanning the fully decorated room and then focusing on the stage near the large picture windows. "You do all this, Rayne?"

Before she could answer, Cal stepped in. "She flew on her own with this event, Randall. I think you'll agree her attention to detail has greatly matured."

As her father's eyes brightened on her, a memory of her granddaddy's kind gaze gripped her heart. She'd been much too young to remember moving into the lodge after her mother's sudden death on the ski slopes of Silver Mountain, but she would never forget her Grandpa Shelby's smiling eyes or his listening ear. She could easily recall the day she'd run into his office, cheeks flushed with excitement, and placed her best-ever lodge sketch into his inviting hands. His words had planted a seed in her heart that day—one she'd tended to every year after: *Dreams bloom when the time is right, Little Blue Jay.*

Her father's voice cut through her reminiscing. "It's a lovely setup, Rayne."

His compliment may have sounded more dismissive than delighted, but she wouldn't bypass the opportunity to remind them both of her proposal. "Thank you. I wondered, since you're here, if the three of us might discuss my business proposal for the lodge."

"Your proposal?" her father questioned.

Yes, her proposal. The one she'd mentioned a dozen-plus times over the last year. The one she'd spent nearly six months documenting. Had Cal not discussed her ideas with her father? Surely they'd talked about the details of her promotion; the campaign started in just four and a half months. What would he be waiting for?

"Yes. I have some ideas for how we can better utilize the empty common areas in the lodge and connect with our local community while creating—"

Her father slipped his phone from his breast pocket, his fingers firing off a text. "I can't promise I'll be able to fit that in on this visit, Rayne. It's a tight one. But I'll try." He shot his brother a wry look. "Okay, you have forty-two minutes to brief me on tonight's agenda before I meet Paul Sanderson for a round of golf."

"How very generous of you," Cal deadpanned, pivoting toward his study.

The men's determined steps pounded the hardwood in unison. She listened as they beat a path through the lobby and down the narrow hallway that bordered the side parlor. Rayne only allowed herself a minute—just sixty short seconds—to reminisce about a time before.

Before every conversation, smile, and head nod was measured in polls, popularity, and political gain.

Overlooking the Great Room from her secret perch on the second floor, Rayne shifted her weight from one toe-pinching stiletto to the other.

The arches in her tired feet cramped from the longer-than-normal wear, and her calves would never forgive her for the extra inch in heel height, but she would trade comfort for the perfection of this evening a thousand times over.

Her concern regarding a certain extra confident farm boy had died as soon as the first course of the night had turned into the third, and then finally, into dessert and coffee.

Levi wasn't coming.

Every tendon, muscle, and bone in her body sighed at the revelation.

Her floor-length pale-pink gown swooshed as she rotated her right ankle clockwise and leaned over the cedar railing. She scanned the tables and patrons below, enjoying what had always been her favorite part of a Shelby event: the afterglow at the end of the night, when pretenses were lowered and socializing with the masses felt far more comfortable than cumbersome.

Only tonight, her heart soared with a private celebration all her own.

The string quartet's rendition of "God Bless America" sailed high above the rafters to her hidden corner. The notes swelled in her soul and pricked at her most tender of memories—of stretching tall on tiptoes to set the butter and jam on the breakfast table, of managing the check-ins and checkouts at the front desk during her middle-school summers, of the hundreds of validations from respected guests who spoke life into her most sacred of hopes. That someday she might be the Shelby who would carry her grandfather's legacy into the next generation.

A tear escaped from the corner of her eye. So many moments had led up to this night. So many sacrifices for the sake of her dream. And all of it—every critical look, every tactless comment, every pitying pat on the back from family members who believed her daft for not going on to grad school or interning with one of her father's associates—had been worth it. Cal's rare nod of approval from the back of the room had diminished every last one of her doubts and reinforced her hope. He'd finally seen her. Not just the little motherless girl he'd tolerated at the lodge after her grandfather's death, but *her*, a woman capable of organizing an elite dinner party for her father's VIP guests. She wasn't an aimless Shelby in search of purpose. She *knew* her purpose—had always known it. And in only a matter of days, Cal would hand her the proverbial keys to her destiny.

"Weren't you warned never to lean over railings?"

The cool words were in direct contrast to the warmth feathering the hollow of her neck.

Rayne spun toward the husky baritone and blinked him in, breath seemingly trapped in the same unknown location as her voice. The man before her, the man who drank her in like duty-free liquor, wasn't the same dusty-blond farmhand she'd spoken with two days ago wearing worn Wrangler jeans and work boots.

No, this man looked far, *far* more devastating.

In a three-piece suit that could have been taken straight out of a politician's closet, Levi emanated status, prestige, and danger.

Heavy on the danger.

Words failed to form quickly enough, her thoughts breaking through like the faded dash lines of an old county highway.

Lazily, his gaze traveled the length of her gown. "I told you I cleaned up nice. I just wish you would have given me the same courtesy warning about you."

She sidestepped him. "Why are you here?" The question came out sharper than she'd intended, but her every nerve felt exposed under his shameless scrutiny.

"Your memory can't be that bad." He angled his head, raised an eyebrow. "You're the one who gave me the ticket."

An exasperated huff leapt from her lips. "But dinner started nearly *three* hours ago. So why are you here *now*? It's over."

"It's not over for me." He gave her a sly wink. "Make an impression at cocktail hour and they forget you by dessert. Catch them in the mingle at the end of the night . . ." Two bold parentheses indented each side of his mouth.

"*Please*, this isn't a game." She pressed two fingers to the center of her forehead, closed her eyes for half a beat, and recalculated. "This night means everything to me." Despite herself, panic broke through her rationale. "If Cal catches you here—"

"He won't." Levi shifted closer. "Because my word means everything to me." In the span of a single heartbeat the man's arrogance morphed into amusement. "How'd those gift bags turn out anyway?"

She swallowed. "Nicely."

"Good, that's what I like to hear." After a smug nod, he reached for her hand, brought it to his mouth, and planted a warm kiss just above her knuckles while he stared at her through hooded eyes.

For the briefest of moments, Rayne lost herself in those sea-green eyes, in the resoluteness of his voice, in the air of his unshakable confidence. The same way she'd lost herself on an August night long ago at the Falls.

Footsteps sounded on the stairs.

"*Please*, you have to go." She pointed and backed away, every part of her pleading with him to obey. "Take that staircase over there."

Levi turned much too slowly before he stepped in the direction she pointed.

A new voice, a familiar mix of sass and sarcasm, filled the space. "You know, someday you could stand to shed a layer or two of predictability, Rayne. I mean, I'm gone for a couple of months and I still know exactly where to find you during one of these fancy shindigs."

Gia!

With an overwhelming swell of joy, Rayne swiveled on her heels and rushed toward her cousin, nearly tripping over her hem as she neared the top of the staircase. She threw her arms around Gia's neck. "You didn't tell me you were home!"

"Technically, *I* didn't know when I'd get home. International travel tends to screw up my reference of time. Besides, you know there's nothing I enjoy more than upsetting the Shelby fruit basket with my punctual arrivals. I never like to miss a party." Gia tilted her head toward the elegant crowd waiting downstairs, a stark contrast to Gia's attire of ripped jeans and her "Fear The Artist" T-shirt. "But it seems you're the one who surprised me . . ." She wiggled her eyebrows and all at once Rayne's blood felt as thick as sludge. She followed her cousin's dark gaze and caught only a sliver of Levi's golden hair as he descended the far staircase.

Had he been watching her reunion with Gia?

"Who's the guy? And since when did you start using this spot as a secret rendezvous?" Gia poked Rayne in the rib cage.

"No one. And since never," Rayne said in her most convincing tone.

Her too-smart-for-her-own-good cousin cocked an eyebrow. "There's only two reasons you blush like that: One, a hot guy has you all flustered because you don't know the first thing about flirting." Gia held up her pointer finger. "Or two, when you're three seconds away from a full-fledged combustion. And let's face it, you haven't been angry like that since my brother tossed your pinned-butterfly collection into the burn pile. So yeah, Hot Guy has my vote for sure."

Rayne shook her head and linked arms with Gia, guiding them down the opposite staircase. "Of all the things I've missed about you, your imagination holds first place."

"Funny, I just got a call from an international art dealer who told me almost the same thing. Right before he bought two dozen of my pieces. Now"—Gia searched the downstairs lobby as the duo stepped into a cloud of overpriced perfume—"where's the wine? You and I have a lot to celebrate."

"Oh, that's wonderful news, Gia!"

"It kind of is, yeah. So what about you?" Gia nudged her. "Please tell me Cal finally acknowledged your undying loyalty to this place and promoted you."

Rayne couldn't help but smile at her cousin's backhanded compliment. "Not yet, but I have every reason to believe it's coming soon."

"What is he waiting for? You're practically the den mother of this joint."

Rayne laughed and steered her cousin down the hallway, hoping to avoid another surprise encounter with Hot Guy.

She gave her cousin a gentle push toward the kitchen door. "I need to go shake some hands, but there should be a bottle of red breathing on the counter. Want to stay at my cabin tonight? I can't wait to hear all about your trip. I shouldn't be more than an hour. Two at the very most."

"Are you trying to hide me from Cal? Because I really thought he'd get a kick out of my new shirt."

If Gia only knew who Rayne was really trying to hide.

"Somehow I doubt he'll find it quite as humorous as you did."

"True, but it's my way of quietly rebelling against the family image. It's an art form I've perfected. You should learn from me."

"I'm not nearly as skilled as you. If I tried to rebel, I'd probably end up like Cousin Milton."

Gia pinched Rayne's arm and then crossed herself. "Don't even joke like that."

Momentarily shamed, Rayne bit the inside of her cheeks. The fate of their great-cousin Milton had only ever been discussed in private. It wasn't a joke between them, or a joke anywhere really. His name wasn't so much as breathed inside the Shelby family, mostly because he'd been renounced. Excommunicated. Cut off from all Shelby privileges. The man had raised too many questions, pried too deep, and overstepped too many boundary lines, all while riding on the shirttails of his surname. Not surprisingly, Cal had been the one to lead the charge against him.

"Sorry," Rayne said. "That was a stupid thing to say."

"You're fine. Just be glad Cal didn't overhear you." Gia waved her hand dismissively. "Now, I need a glass of vino. Jet lag's a beast. It's like seven in the morning Rome time." Gia's exotic copper complexion matched her saucy Italian personality, a perfect blend of both her parents. Aunt Nina was a successful franchise owner of Italian cuisine bistros, with credit for the authenticity of her menu going to Gia's father, a full-blooded Italian who knew his way around the kitchen almost as well as he knew his way around their town. No one messed with her uncle Tony, Shelby Falls' chief of police.

Gia pranced past Rayne and pushed through the doorway of the kitchen, calling over her shoulder, "I'd offer to save you a glass, but you wouldn't know the first thing about appreciating a good Cabernet."

Rayne winked at her. "I might grab a sparkling water."

"Ooh, be careful not to overdo it there, cuz." Gia rolled her eyes and let the kitchen door swing closed.

On the way back to the lobby, Rayne narrowly escaped the grasp of two wine-wobbly couples, both wishing to compliment her on such a nice affair. She'd smiled gracefully, while her eyes continued to scan every last corner of the lodge for her neighbor.

Levi was nowhere to be found.

Her little secret was safe.

CHAPTER FOUR

The screen door to Levi's modest abode squeaked open, but he didn't have to spare a glance to imagine Ford's patient stance or the rancher hat curled inside his leathery hand. He knew the sight well, had seen it from his first day on the apple orchard nine years ago. It simply wasn't Ford's style to interrupt. The man gave respect the same way he earned it, by making others a priority above himself.

After entering one last figure into the spreadsheet on his laptop, Levi pushed back from the small kitchen table, which doubled as his work desk, and grinned at his mentor. "You get the backhoe up and running again? Travis said you were both up to your eyeballs in hydraulic fluid all afternoon."

"Your friend exaggerates." Ford's push-broom mustache danced as he chuckled. He strolled into Levi's kitchen and took a seat at the table. "Although I won't say I wasn't grateful for his help. Replacing the pump in Old Bess is not the easiest task to perform solo. But she's up again, diggin' like she was twenty years ago."

Levi shook his head and stood to grab a couple Cokes from his fridge. Ford's affection for his backhoe was borderline cause for concern, second only to his first love, Tabby the Tractor. "Glad to hear you two have been reunited." A rush of chilled air swept across his face as he reached onto the top shelf, grabbed the red-and-white cans, and then bumped the door closed with his elbow. "You digging that new irrigation line?"

Levi handed a sweaty soda can to Ford and then popped the tab on his own. After a long, and much-needed, fizzy swig, he searched the property through the side dining-room window overlooking the apple orchard, pumpkin patch, corn stalks, and Shelby Falls' favorite Christmas tree farm. If he strained, he could almost make out the seasonal gift shop and the storage barn. Too bad the profit on all those commodities combined had given them little more than sore backs and pennies on the dollar.

But that was all before the launch of Second Harvest, Winslow Farm's personalized farm-to-table collaboration.

"Well, I got it started at least." Ford spun the can on the tabletop, the undersides of his cropped nails a permanent stain of oil. "I promised Hauser I'd take him for a ride and now the dog won't move from his post."

Levi laughed when he spotted Old Bess parked to the west edge of the orchard where Hauser, Ford's golden retriever, was stationed next to the back tire, waiting for his master's return. "No one could ever discount his dedication, that's for sure."

Ford raised a woolly eyebrow. "Kinda reminds me of someone else I know."

Levi brushed off the remark with an easy smile. "A lesser man might take offense to being compared to a dog, but since I know Hauser, I'll consider it a compliment. For his sake. And . . . since you asked"—his voice dripped with sarcasm—"Second Harvest is having an excellent week."

Without warning, a pretty face with doe eyes surfaced to the forefront of his mind. He blinked and returned his focus to the window.

On the other side of the farm's two-hundred-acre parcel, the old storage warehouse had been fully transformed into Second Harvest's distribution center. Inventory was based solely on the goods contracted to them by local farmers, merchants, and vendors. Second Harvest not only distributed the custom orders to local residents and small businesses, but also contributed to an in-house food pantry for the community. Ford's decade-long vision had finally come to fruition, and Levi had been the one to make it happen.

Ford assessed him with knowing eyes. "Wouldn't hurt you to take a break every now and again. Have a life outside all these spreadsheets."

Levi hooked his foot around the wooden chair leg and dragged it away from the table before dropping into the seat. "You don't hear me complaining."

"No, I don't, although sometimes I wish I did."

An odd comment for Ford, yet Levi had a feeling he knew what was coming.

"You have more ambition than anyone I've known in my sixty-three years. But, Levi, I never want this farm to become a burden to you." The vibration of Ford's rumbly tenor knocked against Levi's chest. "All this will be yours one day, but an inheritance should be received as a gift, not tacked onto a debt you feel obligated to pay back. You've paid me back. A hundredfold in a hundred different ways. No matter how much you slave away on your laptop or network with the biggest and the best, you can't make a free gift any more free. Don't kill yourself trying to earn something that's already yours."

But while Levi appreciated the man's fatherly tone and valued his wisdom, he knew Ford was wrong. There weren't enough resources in the world to pay the old farmer back for all he'd given him over the last decade. Levi would never forget his kindness, the same way he would never forget that fateful June afternoon just three weeks after his eighteenth birthday.

Wearing the last clean T-shirt he owned, he'd knocked on Ford's front door and whispered a prayer to a God he wasn't even sure he believed in. With little more than a weak job lead and a quarter tank of gas, Levi had gone all in on a chance for seasonal farm work. Only, the paycheck Ford had provided him every month for the last nine years represented the least of the man's generosity. Ford had shared his food, his finances, and his faith, all in equal measure. But more than that, he'd given Levi the one thing he'd been certain he would never find: a family.

The intensity of Levi's gaze held a message as bold as his words. "I don't want an out—not now, not ever. This farm is a part of me, the same way it's a part of you."

"Okay." The old farmer regarded him with a single dip of his chin. "I hear ya, Levi." Ford crossed a dirty boot over his knee and allowed his top lip to curl into a lazy grin that wrinkled the skin around his eyes. "Now that we have that settled . . . do you care to explain why Tom Hutchinson called me this afternoon?"

Levi blinked twice, his mouth falling open seconds before sound followed. "Wait—Tom *called* you?" Not even his years of religious poker playing could mask his childlike enthusiasm. At the governor's party, Levi had been given less than five minutes with the rich entrepreneur to pitch his business plan for the expansion of Second Harvest, and he'd left with nothing more than a noncommittal, *Don't call me, I'll call you.* But he had. The man had called.

"What did he say? What did Tom say?"

Ford's expression gave away nothing. "A few things, actually. Told me the two of you met in person."

Yeah, yeah. Levi would deal with that part of it later. "But what did he say about Second Harvest?"

"He said he'd never met a more determined salesman in his life, and that we have a deal for ten of his Wellness Smoothie Shacks."

Levi could only gawk until the adrenaline pounding in his chest shot down to his calves and into his feet. With a leap, he pumped a fist to the ceiling. "Yes! Yes!" He spun around. "Do you realize what that means, Ford? That account is—"

"Substantial."

Levi laughed in full at Ford's humble translation. "There's only a few accounts larger than his in the entire state!" And someday he would crack into those as well. How he'd love nothing more than to make the Shelbys beg for his business after all the years they'd tried to choke them out.

"He also said he'd like to come on as an investor."

No words. Absolutely no words. Securing Tom as an investor would be the link he needed to secure others just like him. Levi would just have to work around the Shelby blockade to get to them.

Ford shifted in his seat to rest his forearm on the back of the wooden chair. "Yes, I was quite surprised myself. Especially when he told me *where* he'd had the pleasure of meeting you."

A tug—just a single tug of guilt. "It wasn't a big deal."

Ford sighed. "You and I seem to hold different definitions of that phrase."

"Cal never even knew I was there, trust me. I made sure to keep my distance. And just look what a little party crashing over at the Shelbys got us? First with the honey sale—" He caught himself before Rayne's name could slip out of his mouth the way she'd so easily slipped into his thoughts. But Snow White Shelby was nothing more than a fantasy. An adolescent crush. He cleared his throat. "And then landing the Tom Hutchinson account. Well worth it, I'd say."

"Poke at the hornet's nest and you're gonna get stung, son."

Levi held his arms out wide, palms up. "I was simply proving a point."

"And what point is that?"

"That Cal and his cronies might own the majority of Shelby Falls, but there are still businessmen smart enough to see past his deceptions." And most importantly, willing to contract with the farm.

"Do you really think getting a few of their big-name, big-walleted friends to contract with us will show them anything? It won't, Levi. If you mess with their world, they will mess with yours."

"You know, Ford, even after all these years, there are still times I don't understand you. Haven't you rolled over and played dead long enough? Because I have, and I've only been doing it for half the amount of time as you. Eighteen years is a long time to live under their lies, Ford. Too long. You are ten times the man Cal Shelby will ever be, and yet, you've never fought back. You've never challenged his threats or the way he's slandered your character all over this town." Levi took a breath, tempering his tone. "But no matter what that man thinks, this land was *always* meant to be yours—and if I'm being honest, you deserved a whole lot more than this farm after the position William left you in with his family."

"William Shelby was a good man."

Levi refrained from commenting.

Ford was a good man, but Levi had his own opinions when it came to the Great William Shelby. Unfortunately, he'd never have the chance to meet the man for himself. He'd been dead for eighteen years. "I'm tired of playing opossum around them."

"Be careful, Levi. Bitterness can compromise a heart the way fire-blight disease can consume an apple orchard. When you learned the truth all those years ago, my hope was not that you'd take on an attitude of vengeance but that you'd weigh the complexities of my situation before agreeing to our partnership. What's done is done. God's heard my prayers and He's been faithful to answer them. With peace."

"Peace is overrated."

"Peace is *never* overrated."

"Seems we'll have to agree to disagree on that one." Levi flashed a smile, and Ford conceded with a long sigh.

"I've gotta check the fences before nightfall." Ford secured his hat over his wiry hair and stood. "Good job with the sale, Levi. You did well, but in the future, I'd prefer it if you kept a much quieter profile around our neighbors."

"Is that a suggestion or a mandate?"

"If I tell you it's a mandate you'll only find a way around it, but if I tell you it's a suggestion, you'll let it roll off your back."

Levi grinned. "So you're saying I have a problem with authority?"

Ford shook his head as he pushed through the squeaky screen door, his tone teasing. "Eighteen years I've stayed clear of that lodge and you go and eat dinner with them . . ."

"Hey, I'll buy you that new tractor attachment you've been eyeing with our first check from good ol' Tom," Levi called after him. "Promise."

He could hear Ford's rumbly laughter well past the gravel drive that separated their houses. No sound in the world could possibly please Levi more.

CHAPTER FIVE

There was little Levi despised more than patching fences. Not only was the supply store a twenty-four-minute drive from the farm, but where there was one boundary breach, there were sure to be others. Like jackrabbits, fence holes seemed to multiply quickly. But better he be the one to patch them than Ford. As it was, the man overdid it on physical labor. Thankfully, Levi had only made the mistake in saying so once. Turned out, pride didn't fade with age.

With a stride that could have mowed down several small children, Levi exited the "Lawn and Garden" area, five metal T-posts stacked high on his shoulder. As he neared the self-checkout register, his gaze snagged on a loose black braid and then shifted to a pair of white cotton shorts and a set of Oscar-worthy legs.

Two steps more and he would have slammed straight into a display of wheelbarrows.

Rayne didn't flinch at the commotion of his sudden stop—though he couldn't have been more than ten feet from the woman. Her focus was so intent on the lined paper in her hand he was fairly certain he could spin doughnuts with a hijacked forklift and still not garner so much as a blink.

He ought to keep walking. Pay for his merchandise. Exit the store. Hightail it back to his Chevy.

And if not for her curious muttering, he would have done just that.

Either Rayne Shelby had an imaginary friend standing in front of her, or she hadn't a clue what she was doing in a hardware store. But why he made that his problem *he* hadn't a clue.

She lifted her head and searched the aisle banners, mumbling, "What the heck is a flapper?"

He ignored the "Do Not Proceed" sign flashing in his frontal lobe and approached. After all, she'd been the one to break the barrier of silence between them the day she'd rolled onto his farm. "Depends on who you ask. If this were Chicago in the nineteen twenties, you'd be in the wrong place altogether."

At the very least, he'd expected an awkward chuckle-and-nod combination, or maybe some kind of refined, high-society brush-off, the kind her father excelled at. But instead, the expression that crossed her face could have turned back the hands of time. A look of quiet restraint he'd saved to his mental hard drive nine years ago. A look that said, *We can't be seen together*.

Back then, as an eighteen-year-old Shelby Falls transplant, he couldn't understand the reason behind her overnight metamorphosis—how a kindhearted girl who'd befriended him, a girl who'd promised she'd return to the rocky shore the following evening, could morph into a girl who wouldn't stand within twenty feet of his shadow. From the time Rayne had climbed into the backseat of her uncle Tony's patrol car that night to when he saw her on the steps of the lodge the next morning, everything had changed. And she'd made it clear that whatever connection they'd shared at the Falls had fallen under the same immoral slogan as a sin-filled weekend in Vegas.

But Levi had grown up since then. And he'd made a few promises of his own, to an old man who'd chosen peace over payback.

With the slightest dip of her chin, and a poorly masked farewell in her eyes, Rayne smoothed out the list in her hand and started down the main aisle.

In the wrong direction.

Levi slid his gaze from the exit doors to Rayne.

No. It wasn't his job to rescue her. Their deal was done. Complete. He'd upheld his end of the bargain. This was in no way a damsel-in-distress situation. He wasn't leaving Rayne stranded on some old abandoned highway with a flat tire and a dead cell phone. He was in a hardware store where there were at least a half dozen employees roaming the floor in blue vests with the words "How May I Help You?" embroidered on their backs. Yet as he watched her retreat, the burn in his conscience intensified.

No matter what he felt about the Shelby family as a whole, Rayne had been single-handedly responsible for the most lucrative business contract he'd ever negotiated. He owed her. And he hated owing anyone.

"You're headed in the wrong direction," he called out after her.

Rayne kept walking.

"The flapper's the other way."

A pleasantly plump woman near the entrance giggled at his outburst, and he shot her a cheeky grin. "At least one person in this store has a sense of humor."

Levi leaned his fence posts against a patio table and jogged after the girl with the hypnotic hip swing. The clipped pitter-patter of her sandals against the concrete caused a laugh to stall in his throat. "Did you run track at that prep school of yours?"

She startled and glanced over her shoulder. "What are you doing?"

Funny, that exact question was currently beating up his common sense. "I need a flapper too."

She stopped full and raised both eyebrows. "Are you serious?"

"No, but I doubt the good employees of Hardware Depot have recently reshelved the toilet flappers next to the . . ." He cocked his head and pointed to the sign behind her. "Spray paint."

Pink blotched her cheeks. "I would have found it eventually."

"You seem in too much of a hurry for *eventually,* and interestingly enough, I have a few extra minutes in my schedule today, so . . ." He scanned her lowered list and held out his hand.

"You're offering to help me?" The suspicion in her tone ate at his resolve. "Why?"

So we'll be even. "Because I know this store the way you know your lodge." He peered at the perfectly scripted items. "But, hey, I'll leave you to tackle it on your own if you can tell me what an *aerator* is."

She handed him the list and didn't say another word until they reached the plumbing aisle.

This was exactly what her grandfather had warned her about as a child. If you told a lie, white or otherwise, well intentioned or not, repercussions always followed. Because truth always leaves a trail. And her trail was currently strolling the home-improvement aisle beside her.

"I believe this is what you're looking for." Levi pinched a rubber ring between his fingers and dropped it into the blue basket looped around her arm. He did the same with several more items on her list, swiping the objects off hooks and shelves nearby. And amid the randomness was a shiny metal sink piece called an *aerator.*

"Thank you." The words dried out her mouth like chalk—which she was quite positive Levi could locate in this oversized warehouse nightmare. Why was he helping her? Their deal was over. Finished.

They could both go back to normal now by pretending the other didn't exist.

On a sudden turn, her shoulder collided with his chest, setting both her feet and mouth in an awkward dance of stumbling apologies. But Levi merely smiled and continued down the aisle with her list in hand.

He shot her a sideways glance. "Doesn't the lodge have a handyman on payroll? What qualified you for flapper duty today?"

Careful to avoid eye contact, she kept her answer simple, though, in truth, she'd wondered the same thing this morning. "I don't mind running errands."

She'd been nothing short of surprised when Cal had requested she be the one to gather supplies instead of calling Teddy, their night clerk. But the maintenance list he'd handed her wasn't a random inventory of lodge to-dos. It was an itemized repair list for a fourth-floor suite she'd called the Blue Jay, chosen for the nickname her grandfather had given her years ago. The room was a whimsical space with sky-blue walls and an octagon window complete with stained glass panels. Her childhood haven.

"I'll be listing this room as available on the lodge website once you head off to college this fall," Cal announced on her eighteenth birthday.

She was stunned at first, caught off guard by the unexpected flood of grief at the thought of strangers sleeping in her space, their perfumes and aftershaves tainting the scents of her childhood: the smell of worn pages read from her favorite bedtime stories and the peachy leave-in conditioner Gia kept on Rayne's vanity. She didn't want the heart-shaped purple nail polish stain on the bathroom tile to be rubbed out, or the deep grooves from her grandfather's rocking chair under the window to be refinished.

"But where will I stay when I come home in the summers?" Her tone had been much too desperate, but she couldn't bear the thought of advertising a room crammed full of her favorite memories like some generic guest-room suite.

"You're not a child anymore, Rayne. Keeping that room for the sake of nostalgia would be a costly and foolish business decision on my part. You can move your belongings out to the cabin near the greenhouse." At the sight of her unshed tears, Cal released an irritated sigh. "Part of becoming a responsible adult is learning when to let go of juvenile desires. It's time you grew up."

Cal had said something eerily similar the night she'd been caught fraternizing with the neighbor boy—right before he'd demanded she cut ties with Levi completely.

A weighty deposit in her basket shook her back to the present.

"Where'd you go?" Levi asked, staring.

At the sight of him, a tempting sort of wistfulness tugged at her insides. "I . . . nowhere."

"Could have fooled me," he said with a wink.

Newly awakened nerves churned in her belly. How long had she been walking these very public aisles with him? *Too long to be safe.* She pointed to the college-ruled paper in his hand. "Um, how many more items do I have left on there? Maybe you could just point me in the right direction so I can grab the rest on my own?"

Levi folded his arms, her list crinkling in the crook of his elbow. "If I didn't know any better, I'd think you were embarrassed to be seen with me. But I'm sure that's just my imagination. It acts up from time to time." With a lazy grin he turned back to the merchandise.

As she watched him pluck another few items from metal hooks, her guard lowered just enough to wonder at the what-ifs she'd abandoned nearly a decade ago: What if she had been just any girl and he just any boy the night they'd met? What if she'd gone back to the Falls like she'd promised him? What if there'd been no fence lines keeping them apart?

A mental roadblock slammed into place, putting an end to her dangerous musings.

She needed to get out of this store. Now.

She glanced at her invisible wristwatch. "Well, hey, thanks for your help with all this." She raised her pregnant basket. "I appreciate it, but I really do need to get going. This is only my first stop of many today." She scooted past him, careful to avoid an accidental brush with one of his knotted biceps. Not that she'd noticed his biceps. Or any other part of his carved physique, for that matter.

"Actually, there's only one item left on here." He showed her the list. "And it's in the security hardware aisle, right across from the checkout lanes."

Of course it was.

Levi mistook her mental stumble as an agreement, matching stride with her before she could form an appropriate exit strategy. They strode in tandem until they arrived in a section almost as foreign to her as plumbing. Metal, glass, and wood doors hung on endcap displays, showcasing a variety of knobs, locks, and dead-bolt combinations. *Dead bolt* happened to be the only item on her shopping list she'd recognized.

Levi tapped his pointer finger on a few different lock combo packages. "Which finish do you need? Nickel, chrome, or gold?"

She tugged at the end of her braid, her anxiety building. "Oiled bronze."

Levi chuckled. "Of course."

"What's that supposed to mean?"

There was a tilt to his mouth when he spoke. "You realize that oiled bronze is double the price of every other option here, right?"

"That may be, but it's the finish we have throughout the lodge." Was she actually trying to justify a piece of hardware? To Levi Harding?

"Naturally." He didn't add the lock combo to her pile. Instead, he inclined his head toward the end of the aisle and reached for her basket. "Here, I can carry all this up to the front for you."

She stepped back. "No, that's okay, really. I can manage it." She switched the cumbersome basket to her opposite arm and held out her hand to take the lock package from him.

He did not oblige her.

A deep crease appeared in the center of his forehead. "So this is how it's going to be, then—like the other day never happened? Like I didn't save your bacon?"

She locked her knees in place and met his gaze. "We had a deal, Levi."

"Yes, we did."

"So why are you doing this? Why are you talking to me, helping me, following me around like we're—"

"Two people shopping at the same hardware store?"

"You know what I mean." She was certain he knew exactly what she meant, though the story he'd been told about Ford swindling her grandfather out of his land had most likely been twisted by fallacy and falsehood.

"Maybe I'm just being neighborly."

She nearly laughed at his uncouth joke. "We've never been neighborly."

"And whose fault is that?"

She shook her head. This had to stop. Now. "My family is—"

"Not like you." His words punctured the air and pierced the center of her chest. "That's the thing, Rayne. There's something about you that doesn't quite add up for me—never has. If not for that nightshade hair of yours, I'd question if you were one of them at all."

She raised her chin. "Well, I am. One of them." *Lamest. Reply. Ever.*

His eyes narrowed. "So which one are you? The Rayne who showed compassion to a drifter nine years ago at the Falls? Or the Rayne who cowers under her family's every wish and whim?"

She reared back a step. "Excuse me?"

"You may have grown up since that night at the Falls, but you're just as afraid of them now as you were back then."

Heat climbed her neck at the memory—their connected hands, their whispered words, and the endless horizon reflected in their eyes.

What she wouldn't give to slam one of the store's display doors on this entire interaction. "I am not afraid of my family."

"Sounds like a bad case of denial to me."

Doorknob package still in hand, he headed in the direction of the cash registers.

"I am *not* in denial." Despite herself, Rayne hurried after him, her sandals slipping on the slick concrete underfoot.

Ignoring her, he plopped the hardware package onto a conveyer belt manned by a cashier who looked half-asleep.

Levi slipped around the corner to retrieve five gigantic metal rods leaning against a patio set. Rayne placed her basket on the belt, hoping the college-age boy would ring up her items at a speed faster than drying paint. She tapped her foot, her gaze straying to where Levi stood at the self-checkout station. Was that really how he saw her? Like some scared little girl? Afraid of her own family? *Ridiculous.*

Her eyes drifted again as Levi collected his receipt and hefted the poles onto his shoulder. Without sparing her another glance, he gave her a two-finger salute and swaggered out the automatic doors.

Unreal.

Whatever fantasy she'd invented about him in a three-piece suit the night of the VIP dinner faded into the background. She'd been a fool to ask him for help and an even bigger fool to step foot onto Winslow Farm. What had happened between them—the honey transaction she'd been stupid enough to initiate—would forever hang over her head. His arrogance would make sure of it.

Stuffing her receipt into one of the crinkly paper bags, she exited the store with a purposeful stride. If she couldn't go back in time and erase her error in judgment, she could—at the very least—have the last word.

In the almost empty parking lot, Levi slammed his truck's rusty tailgate closed, just three spaces away from her silver Audi. And to her annoyance, she couldn't seem to ignore the staccato beat thrumming inside her chest as she neared him. Pressing the red button on her key fob, she popped her trunk and then tossed her bags inside. If she damaged her new flapper, so be it.

She spun around to see Levi watching her. "It's not true—what you said back there. I'm not in denial about anything."

"Really?" he challenged, hands on hips.

"Yes, really," she mocked. "But I don't expect you to understand the ins and outs of my role—at the lodge *or* in my family." She straightened her spine and narrowed her eyes. "I'm proud to be a Shelby."

His expression remained as unenthusiastic as her words had sounded. "Do you know that maintaining eye contact when trying to prove a point is *not* a sign of truthfulness?" He crossed his arms, his navy T-shirt tightening across his taut shoulders. "Really, that's a widespread myth. Completely false."

He moved in closer. Or had she been the one to move closer? The familiar blend of his scent—minty soap and something earthy and crisp she couldn't quite name—tugged at the recesses of her mind. In less than three seconds her entire body warmed.

His gaze dipped to her mouth. "You should really work on your tells, Rayne."

After a too-dry swallow, she licked her bottom lip and backtracked several feet to her car. "I don't have to convince you who I am."

But before she could slip into her driver's seat, before she could shut him out entirely, he spoke again. "You shouldn't have to convince anyone of who you are—but I have a feeling you've spent most your life doing just that."

CHAPTER SIX

Like the irritating buzz of an alarm clock set to a permanent snooze cycle, Levi's words slipped into her subconscious and disturbed her dreams. All night long. *You shouldn't have to convince anyone of who you are—but I have a feeling you've spent most your life doing just that.*

When her actual alarm sounded a happily familiar tune, she whipped her summer comforter off her body and swung her legs to the edge of her mattress, thankful for the reprieve of morning.

Yet it wasn't until after her second cup of coffee and her fifth bite of extra-crunchy peanut butter toast that she made the decision.

Today was the day she would meet with Cal about her proposal.

By the time she retrieved the broom from the closet under the staircase in the lobby, she'd formulated a plan. And with every vigorous sweep of the hallway, she rehearsed her speech.

Though she'd expected Cal's "a promotion is a responsibility" lecture during her father's visit last week, he hadn't scheduled a meeting with her. There'd been no announcement and no further mention of the thick blue folder she'd handed him nearly a month ago. But she wasn't a little girl content to hide in the shadows anymore. She was a grown woman, one who'd dedicated her life to the legacy of a man who'd cared as much about his community as he'd cared about her family.

She'd secured every precious memory of her grandfather into a special pocket of her heart for safekeeping. The piggyback rides through rows of apple trees after a summer rain. The ice-cream dinners when her father left town for business. The bedtime prayers that came with a gamut of questions about heaven and angels and the mother she could hardly remember. But it was his way of connecting with people, his generous offering of time and resources, his simple invitations to meet the needs of those around them that had marked her destiny. William Shelby had been a friend to everyone, and his lodge had once been the lifeblood of Shelby Falls.

Rayne wanted nothing more than to revive his vision.

The minute her shift ended today, Rayne would knock on Cal's door and share her ideas with him in person. He might be able to ignore her printed thoughts on paper, but he couldn't deny the passion that brewed inside her. She'd gathered dozens of contacts since college, researched hundreds of service opportunities, and read thousands of inspirational articles on growing community centers nationwide. Shelby Lodge had an opportunity—maybe even an obligation—to connect and serve the people of Shelby Falls the way her ancestors had done in generations past. She simply needed to convince Cal the efforts and change would be worthwhile.

Rayne propped her chin on the broomstick handle and peered out the front lobby window, her daydream lost when her gaze caught on a strange grayish haze hovering above the mountain range across the river. Yet unlike the cloud cover that slumbered atop their town during mid-autumn, this gloomy mass definitely wasn't fog.

"News said the wildfires are expected to spread as far as Blanchard by next week."

The broom sprang from Rayne's grip and clattered to the floor. "Blanchard?" she repeated, eyeing Delia. "That's only a hundred miles from here."

The head cook rubbed her fingertips down the front of her white apron. "Don't I know it." Delia's cropped locks played off the silvery hue of her blue eyes. "I can already taste the smoke in the air, which means it's gonna be wretched for us allergy sufferers. With the lack of snowfall last winter, I'm predicting this will be the driest summer we've had in decades." Her plump cheeks hollowed on a hard breath.

One of Delia's many talents included her uncanny ability to predict weather patterns. The woman was a walking, talking barometer, as fascinated by the changes in nature as she was by the spices in a new recipe. "You know, your sixth-sense detection skills could teach that meteorologist over at Channel 9 at thing or two," Rayne said as she bent to retrieve the broom.

"Don't think I haven't kept my options open for when this gig finally gives out." Delia winked. "Weathercasting is my plan B."

Delia had joked about a plan B since before Rayne moved into the lodge with her father. Over twenty-three years ago. Delia would no sooner leave the lodge than Rayne would submit her notice as a Shelby. Hospitality was too ingrained in them both to ever leave.

At nearly forty years her senior, Delia was one of Rayne's most treasured relationships. Their connection was unique, tethered by monotonous tasks and daily repetition, and yet the woman had waited on the sidelines during every awkward transition Rayne braved: glasses and braces, training bras and failed friendships, and of course, crushes on boys she'd never been bold enough to approach . . . except for one. Even still, the standing invitation into Delia's kitchen had remained open. And what they hadn't exchanged in conversation over the years, they exchanged in recipes and taste tests and dough punching.

Delia's brow puckered slightly. "Speaking of jobs . . . haven't you heard anything on your promotion yet? I figured you'd be begging me for some celebratory coconut cream pie by now."

"Not yet, but I'm going to meet with Cal later today." There. She'd said it out loud. No going back now. "I'm sure he's been preoccupied with the follow-up from my father's dinner."

"I'm sure you're right, but still, he ought not keep a smart girl like you waiting. Lord knows you've paid your dues to this place." Delia's lips eased into a maternal grin. "Your grandfather would be proud of the work you put into that proposal, Rayne. I wish he could see you now, the woman you've grown into. What he wouldn't give for a front-row seat in that meeting today."

And what Rayne wouldn't give to have him back.

Long after Delia had said her good-byes for the day and Rayne had finished her daily sweep of the main floor, Rayne glanced down the vacant hallway to Cal's closed office door. Strange that she hadn't seen him come out of his study all morning—not even for his usual coffee refill between ten and eleven.

She slipped her phone from her pocket and checked the time.

Thirty more minutes.

Might as well have been a year.

She clicked into the home screen on the front desk computer, deciding to better acquaint herself with upcoming events. The color-coded calendar grid was one she'd worked on for weeks.

The height of tourist season was just a month away, and even though several destination weddings, galas, and reunion events would max out the lodge near the end of summer, there was an emptiness she felt could never be filled by a full reservation calendar.

Just like the common areas that sat vacant during the majority of the year.

These quieter days made it hard for her to believe that her grandfather used to joke about replacing the main entrance to the lodge with a revolving door. Back then their clientele had been ordinary townsfolk, Shelby Falls residents who'd stop in for a peaceful view and a hot cup of tea or an ice-cold glass of lemonade. And while she could barely remember those days, something inside her ached for them still.

She clicked through July's reservations and took in the colorful grid of August—their busiest month, thanks to a town that tripled its population during tourist season. The smallest wink from the sun, the briefest flash of warmth, and every resident in Shelby Falls would be in full preparation for the coming burst of activity.

The lobby door pushed open, and she looked up from the screen.

"Dad? I didn't know you were back in town?" He'd headed home to Boise just twenty-four hours after last week's dinner. And he wasn't expected for another visit until early fall, before his official campaign kickoff.

Her father planted a light kiss on her cheek, and the biting smell of cigar smoke wafted from his jacket. She wrinkled her nose involuntarily.

"I'm only back for the afternoon. Had a few things I needed to attend to in town." He glanced down the hallway. "Have you spoken with your uncle today?" It was an odd question, not the words exactly, but the detached way in which he spoke them, like they'd been unhooked from emotion.

"No, he's been tucked away in his office since early this morning. Are you here for a meeting?"

"Unofficially, yes." Ever the groomed politician, her father met her confusion with a steady expression that was anything but comforting. He patted her on the arm. "Cal holds a lot of responsibility on his shoulders, Rayne. More than you see here. It's best not to forget that."

Without another word, he released her and strode down the hallway.

She hadn't forgotten anything. Cal was as busy a man as her father these days, more reason why he needed to pass the management baton on to her sooner than later. She was ready for the handoff—had been ready. Her father's unexpected visit wouldn't deter her plans; if anything, his visit confirmed her decision. Speaking to them at the same time would avoid the inevitable delay in their back-and-forth conversations.

She read the clock on her phone again.

In fifteen minutes she'd knock on that door and propose her dream.

On the release of an optimistic exhale, Rayne lifted her fist and knocked on Cal's study door. The masculine swell of voices on the other side of the polished walnut hushed, and her uncle's command to enter zipped through her insides with a flurry of nervous energy. Pushing the door open and her anxiety aside, she stepped into her grandfather's old study, a room she'd sought refuge in dozens of times. But where his office used to hold casual furnishings and a jar of Tootsie Pops for everyone who entered, Cal's expensive decor and dim lighting lacked her grandfather's warm welcome.

She blinked as her eyes adjusted to the change of light. "I was hoping, with my father here for the afternoon, this might be a good time to discuss my ideas for the lodge."

"Please." Cal motioned for her to take a seat. "Your timing is impeccable. We were just discussing the future of the lodge."

She lowered into one of the imported leather chairs opposite him, her gaze flitting from her uncle to where her father stood propped against the side of Cal's mahogany desk. When he made no attempt to meet her eyes, a cloud of confusion fogged her mental clarity. She searched the top of Cal's organized desk for her blue folder—the one her fifteen-page business outline was assembled inside of—but it was nowhere to be found.

She cleared her throat and Cal raised his hand, as if to quiet her unspoken thoughts. He pushed away from his desk a few inches, crossed his legs, and leaned his back into his brass-trimmed leather chair.

"I've always prided myself on putting our family first." Loosely, Cal threaded his fingers in his lap. "After growing and selling a successful business of my own, I've spent the last twenty-plus years pouring my resources and time into advancing your father's political ambitions, as well as continuing my father's honorable legacy."

Rayne tucked her chin, knotting her own fingers together. Cal often started their discussions this way—like he was standing at a podium about to give the State of the Union address.

"Do you remember a conversation we had in this office, say, roughly a decade ago, after Tony picked you up at some godforsaken hour and dropped you off to me in his patrol car?" he asked.

"Yes, I remember." How could she not?

"I thought you would"—he swiveled the seat of his chair side to side in a seasick motion—"seeing as that was the night you assured me of your desire to stay true to your family and follow in my footsteps at the lodge."

"Yes, it was—*is*—still my desire. And I can assure you that my vision for the lodge's future mirrors Granddaddy's, while also increasing our annual revenue."

Cal continued on as if she hadn't spoken. "Not only did I feel you were mature enough to learn the details of my father's last will and testament that night, but I answered every one of your questions regarding what had happened eighteen years ago after my father's wayward employee betrayed our entire family. I explained in no uncertain terms how Ford used my father's most private information against him, how he swindled a lonely, grieving old man into changing his will without a thought to the man's own children. How my hands—as the executor of my father's estate—were tied because Ford had covered his tracks like a seasoned criminal. How when we'd offered Ford a check for double the fair market value to buy our property back—to keep the farm our ancestors had tilled with their own hands inside our family—he refused, only to build his own home and business on Shelby land just to spite us." He stopped the twisting of his chair and leaned forward. "So how does a man who came from nothing, a man who has no family to speak of, no college education, and who worked a blue-collar job his entire adult life end up with a two-hundred-acre orchard and farm?"

Like in Sunday school, she knew the correct answer without having to dig deep. Repetition tended to store knowledge close to the surface. "Because Grandpa Shelby trusted the wrong man."

Cal hooked a finger under his top desk drawer and slowly dragged it open, reached inside, and produced a folded receipt. "And it would appear, Rayne, that so have you."

He slid the tissue-thin paper toward her using only the tip of his pointer finger, and then pressed it flat. And there, staring back at her, was a carbon copy of the check she'd written to Levi before the dinner.

This meeting between Cal and her father hadn't been happenstance. They hadn't been discussing polls or political agendas.

They'd been discussing her.

Rayne's throat tightened, muting her voice to a panicky rasp. "I can explain—"

"Why you ignored my warnings? Why you went behind your family's back? Why you negotiated a business deal with a farmhand employed by the man who conned your grandfather weeks after he'd lost his wife?" He slapped the flat of his hand on the shiny desktop and every organ inside her recoiled. "This is unacceptable, Rayne."

Her vision blurred but she refused to give in to her tears. Crying in front of them would only compound their list of grievances.

"Cal." It was her father's voice that sliced through the tension. His tone remained predictably calm, yet his arms stayed crossed. And despite the vacant chair beside her, he made no attempt to occupy it. "Let's allow her a chance to defend herself. Go ahead, Rayne."

Cal pressed his mouth into a grim line and nodded once. Only now that she had their undivided attention, her thoughts toppled over themselves, much the same as her racing heartbeats.

Suddenly, every excuse in the world felt wrong. Cal wouldn't care how many media questions she'd fielded, or how many food orders she'd placed, or how many party supply shops she'd called for the exact *burnt-crimson red* tablecloth he'd requested. There was only one answer to give: she'd screwed up.

She twisted her hands in her lap and forced herself to hold Cal's darkened gaze. "I forgot to order the patron gifts, and I didn't realize my error until it was too late. I just . . . missed it. It was an honest mistake. I knew how important this dinner was to you and my father, and because of the short turnaround time and the gift specifications you'd outlined, I felt my best and only option was to seek out a vendor associated with the co-op at Winslow Farm."

At the mention of the farm, Cal's coloring deepened, while her father, the ever-steady diplomat, remained taciturn.

She wouldn't give up Levi's name unless she was forced. "The vendor—"

"Levi Harding," Cal interrupted. "The same charity case you were canoodling with at the Falls the night I sent Tony after you."

She swallowed, a new sense of betrayal pressing against her conscience. "Yes, Levi assured me he could fill the large order and have it delivered on time for the event." She sought her father's understanding. "He kept his word and I've received nothing but high praise and gratitude from your supporters. They loved the honey, felt it both thoughtful and reflective of Shelby Falls." She pushed her thumbnail into her opposite palm and reminded herself to breathe.

But it was all too apparent that her explanation had missed the mark of her father's approval by miles. The thick stretch of silence that followed tugged at her intuition. Had they figured out the rest? Did they see Levi at the dinner? Did they know she'd given him a ticket?

Her father shifted his stance, accompanied by a resigned nod to Cal. Though her father's political standing held weight outside the lodge doors, on the inside, family politics were less democracy and more dictatorship. The ten-year age gap between her father and her uncle had never been more apparent than in family-business deliberations.

Cal clasped his hands on the desk, tenting his index fingers while his heavy gaze fell to the tarnished check once more. "You know as well as I do that this has little to do with a few cases of honey and everything to do with you seeking help from a farm that would have been a part of your inheritance one day if not for that crook." He shook his head. "If you were a new employee I'd fire you on the spot. But you're not a new employee, Rayne. You're a Shelby."

You're a Shelby. Her entire life had been defined by those three words.

"I take full responsibility for my actions. I should have come to you first. I'm sorry." She couldn't be more so.

Cal's stern expression held, but a flicker of fleeting remorse in his eyes pummeled her with fear. "Managing your father's campaign is my top priority. When I leave this fall to join him, I'll be handing over the lodge and all its responsibilities to a single individual. To someone I trust. To someone who shares our core values."

"I understand." She nodded in earnest. "I won't let you down again. I'll take care of everything—"

"You're not ready."

She lifted her head and stared at the man who spoke the word daggers straight into her heart. Not her uncle, but her very own father.

"Not *ready*?" She pushed to the edge of her seat and implored them both. "But I've grown up in this lodge. I've spent every summer of my youth working that front desk. I drove back to Shelby Falls the morning after I graduated college. This lodge is my whole life—my future."

"A week ago I might have been moved by such a loyal speech," Cal stated dryly. "But that was before I spent the last forty-eight hours tracking down the alias on this check after one of your father's largest donors requested the name of our local beekeeper so he could purchase more honey." He tapped a finger against the shiny mahogany. "Do you understand how destructive a tie with that man could be to your father's future? To his campaign? As a past employee of the lodge, Ford has had access to our family's most private accounts. He knows intimate details about your grandfather's political and personal life, information we've gone to great lengths to keep from the public. Information that could tarnish not only your grandfather's legacy but your father's impeccable reputation as well."

"But what could possibly be Ford's incentive now—after all these years? He already owns the farm."

Cal tipped his gaze toward his brother, as if giving him permission to chime in. "He wanted more, he felt *entitled* to more," her father answered. "What you have to understand is, from the day Ford came to the lodge seeking employment, Cal warned our father against him. He was only a few years older than your uncle, but we felt all along that the unassuming man he portrayed on the outside didn't match who he was on the inside. Unfortunately, we were right." Her father's eyes narrowed. "Ford saw an opportunity while Cal and I were busy building our careers, and he took full advantage of it. The truth of his jealousy didn't show in full until the day we buried our father. We've all been the victims of Ford's deception."

"And yet you handed him and his motley crew an invitation into our lives," Cal said.

Rayne could only hope her uncle didn't realize the full truth of his statement.

"Which is why," he continued, "I've asked your cousin Celeste to step into the position of lodge manager during my absence."

Rayne stood so abruptly her chair caught the edge of the Oriental rug and tipped over.

"What?" Shock numbed her senses.

A hand gripped her upper arm as if to steady her. Only, she couldn't be steadied, not when her world had just been yanked out from underneath her. She looked into her father's eyes and saw a truth that cut nearly as deeply as the day he'd told her Granddaddy Shelby had died of a heart attack. Tears climbed her throat and soured on her tongue. "You agree with this?"

"Your father spoke to her this morning before she left for the airport," Cal said.

"Rayne, your cousin understands the complexities of running a business of this caliber. We're fortunate she's between projects. She has some great insights to enhance the lodge's current structure of operation, and I believe she'll be a good business mentor for you . . ." Her father continued to speak, continued to fill the space with all the credentials her second cousin possessed. All the business plans she'd drawn up for profitable franchises. All the fancy degrees and letters trailing her name.

All the ways in which Rayne had failed to measure up.

Rayne turned back to her uncle, every ounce of her pride stripped bare before him. "Please, *please,* don't do this. I know I made a mistake, but you have my word I'll never step foot onto their property again. I can make this right, I promise you I can." She pressed a hand to her heart, the strong beat thrumming against her palm. "Don't give away my dream."

Cal rubbed his forehead as if to erase her plea from his mind. "The problem, Rayne, is that you already gave me your word. Nine years ago." He stared at her head-on. "Sometimes the best thing we can do for a person is identify their weaknesses. Your talent for hospitality has never been in question, but your naiveté and lack of business instinct have revealed you simply aren't mature enough to manage the lodge without supervision. Your most recent lapse in judgment is a case in point."

She closed her eyes briefly against the watery sting while the obedient side of her personality sidestepped her passion and surrendered to practicality. "When? When will she be here?"

"She starts tomorrow morning," her father answered.

Rayne couldn't bring herself to face him, couldn't bring herself to see his disappointment in raising a daughter who never seemed to spread her wings wide enough for his liking. "And what about my cabin?"

"You can keep it. We're prepared to continue your salary as a front-desk clerk and event planner. Celeste will take the Blue Jay Suite on the fourth floor."

Another blow Rayne couldn't dodge. All those repair supplies she'd gathered yesterday were for her replacement. Celeste was moving into her old bedroom.

"May I be excused?" Her voice thinned to a whisper.

With a stiff nod, Cal granted her leave.

Halfway out the door she heard her father mumble a question she couldn't quite decipher, and her hand stilled on the knob as if in wait for an undeserved mercy pardon.

Her uncle's reply was immediate. "Mistakes which don't teach us become habit. It's long past time she learned how to think like a Shelby."

CHAPTER SEVEN

Every pathetic drip of coffee through the makeshift paper-towel filter she'd concocted in Gia's tiny kitchen seemed to magnify Rayne's current view on life. She peeled the soggy napkin back and took a small sip before tossing the contents down the drain. Sometimes the quick fix ruined the whole pot.

"Why are you making coffee in the middle of the night?" Gia stumbled out of her bedroom, arm slapped over her eyes. "And *why* is every light in my apartment competing with the surface of the sun?"

"It's five thirty." Rayne's voice sounded as far away as she felt. "And you're out of coffee filters."

Gia lowered her arm just enough to test her squinty scowl before returning to her duck-and-cover stance. "You wouldn't need coffee if you were still sleeping."

Robotically, Rayne reached for her purse. "I work at six. Every day."

Gia flipped the light switches off in the kitchen and living room before slumping onto her sofa. "I still don't get why you're so bent on going in today. You need a mental-health vacation, especially after—"

"We talked about this, Gia." At length, until two in the morning. "I'm going in because it's my job." And her life. She could no sooner live without the lodge than she could without Gia.

Though, in her father's eyes, choosing to stay at the lodge wasn't even in the same stratosphere as those fancy internships he'd offered her fresh out of college.

"You realize you're not Cinderella, right? You're not the family slave. You could do something else."

Her eyes dragged to Gia's. "Like what?"

Gia's mouth hung open, and Rayne could practically see her cousin's brain cells overheating.

"I belong at the lodge as much as you belong with your art."

Gia huffed and rested her chin on her knees. "I wish I could have been in that meeting. One stupid mistake shouldn't wipe out a lifetime of loyalty."

One stupid mistake. One quick fix.

Rayne had dug her own grave the day she'd crossed the property line into Winslow Farm. She'd told Gia as much; although, she'd been careful to leave Levi out of the retelling. No good could possibly come from her cousin connecting the dots. Gia had her own issues with Levi Harding—or rather, with Levi's best friend. No, what Rayne needed most was the ability to rewind time, to leave the golf cart parked at the lodge, to tell Gil at Gilbert's Party Palace that she'd happily purchase a hundred and thirty-six plastic kazoos if it meant keeping her promotion.

But nothing in life ever worked out that easily.

"She's not better than you. You know that, don't you?" Gia's voice cut through Rayne's childish yearning. "Celeste might have all kinds of fancy degrees, but that doesn't make her more capable. It doesn't make her more deserving."

Her father and uncle had certainly believed so. The same way they believed Rayne to be too soft, too naive, too heart-strong.

Her role in the family had yet to be seen. It wasn't just her overall lack of political ambition that had dropped her to the bottom of the totem pole—it was her lack of credibility and purpose. Gia's artistic drive and talent were both respected and esteemed; the same could be said of Gia's brother, Joshua, whose honorable pursuits in service had ranked him an officer in the US Air Force. Outside of her great-cousin Milton, Rayne couldn't name a single relative who hadn't achieved some grandiose level of personal and professional success by twenty-five.

Levi was right when he'd said Rayne didn't fit into the Shelby family.

She never had.

"Rayne."

Rayne's forced smile wasn't enough to reassure her protective cousin, but it would have to suffice for now. If she didn't leave Gia's studio soon, she would add tardy to her list of offenses. Cal would expect her at the front desk at six o'clock sharp. Punctual, positive, and perky.

She buttoned her crop-sleeved pink cardigan. "Maybe Celeste has changed," Rayne added with a spark of hope she didn't feel.

"That's about as likely as chocolate being named a vegetable."

"We haven't seen her in years. Maybe . . . maybe this won't be as horrible as I'm envisioning. Maybe Celeste and I can build a cousin bond, a friendship, even."

"I really don't want to pop your positivity bubble, but before you float off into the clouds, I feel it's my duty to ground you. The woman's as self-absorbed as a Jersey Shore housewife."

Rayne made for the door. "Gia, you can't possibly know—"

"I stalk her on social media. I know."

Rayne had seen the posts as well, but not everyone was who they appeared to be online. She turned the knob.

"Want to stay over again tonight? I won't be home until sometime after nine since I have that private showing for the Art Institute, but I want to hear how your first day with the wicked witch from the east goes."

Even in Rayne's foggy mental state, the invitation to stay with Gia felt like a better idea than staying alone in her cabin. "Sure."

Gia smiled. "Good, then I'll buy the ice cream. And the wine."

Rayne gave Gia one last glance over her shoulder, then took three steps down the flight of stairs.

"Remember," Gia called after her. "Stay grounded, Rayne."

Stay grounded.

Words that hadn't quite registered until Celeste descended into the lobby at a quarter after eight, an electronic tablet pinched between her French-tipped fingers. "Hello, Rayne."

The natural-brunette-turned-platinum tipped her chin. Her metallic vented boot heels, black sleeveless blouse, and cropped white skinny jeans were a style Rayne had only seen on supermarket magazine covers. Slung over her tanned shoulder was an expensive-looking satchel.

"Good morning, Celeste."

An awkward impasse stilled the air between them. On any other occasion, Rayne would have hugged a family member she hadn't seen in almost a decade, but nothing about Celeste's body language looked hug inviting.

"I hardly recognized you without those nerdy purple glasses. Lasik?"

Lasik? "Oh—Lasik surgery? No, actually, I wear contacts."

Celeste paired her perfectly penciled eyebrow raise with an enigmatic *"Ahhhh."*

Whatever reunion optimism Rayne had previously mustered plummeted at breakneck speed. "And . . ." Rayne searched her mental database for possible small-talk topics outside of her poor vision. "You went blond?" Or white. Considering the lighting.

Celeste's peroxide locks seemed to swish involuntarily. "Yes, I did." She offered nothing else.

At the sound of Cal's distinguished gait in the hallway, they redirected their attention.

"Good." He clasped his hands. "Glad you two have been reunited."

Reunited was hardly the word for it. Celeste's pursed glossy lips and smug gaze left little room for reminiscing about childhood summers. There weren't many good memories to choose from.

"You haven't seen each other since you were, what, sixteen?"

"Seventeen," Rayne supplied.

"Which would have made me nineteen," Celeste added. "I remember that reunion weekend well. A memorable one for sure."

Considering Celeste had been the one to nark on Gia and Rayne's attendance of a certain party at the Falls—Rayne would have to agree with the memorable comment. And she'd also have to agree that Gia had been right. Their grandfather's great-niece hadn't changed much at all in the last nine years.

Cal angled his head toward Celeste. "I have to run into town for a meeting with the city. Rayne can give you a full tour of the lodge. Make sure she points out all the common areas you were asking about last night."

He snapped his fingers and pivoted on the polished hardwood. "And, Rayne, set up a staff meeting for next Monday afternoon. Celeste has some brilliant ideas we discussed over dinner last night. Turns out she worked with a bed-and-breakfast in Vermont last year—created a four-season business plan that really put them on the map by collaborating with some national travel sites."

National travel sites. The complete opposite direction of her proposal.

"Sure," was the only reply she could muster.

"I'll be back around one." He left them to bask in a trail of spicy cologne.

Celeste raised her shapely eyebrows. "Well, shall we get started? I'm ready if you are."

Nearly three hours later, they'd toured every vacant room, peeked inside every storage closet, and noted every common area, the last of which was the Great Room.

"And how exactly has this space been advertised?" Celeste's heels click-clacked onto the shiny hardwood.

"Well, it's pictured in our gallery on the website—"

Celeste chuckled. "That website is getting a whole new look, and soon. I already booked my tech guy for next week."

"The site was updated last year." Rayne had contracted a local web designer. She'd been pleased with the quality of his work and his professionalism.

"Might as well have been last decade. Trends change quickly, and this room . . ." Celeste slinked farther into the cavernous space and leaned her sharp hip bone against one of the breakfast tables. She bent to sniff the fresh lilac bouquet in the center. "Is exquisite. It's a waste for it to sit empty."

Rayne couldn't agree with her assessment more. "It's used for all our big events—weddings, parties, business dinners—but of course I'd love to see it used more often."

Celeste's pensive expression and thorough scan of the open space seemed to revive Rayne's dying hope. "It holds a lot of potential."

Rayne felt the same way. Even now, her heart tugged at the thought of opening this room up to the community again, hosting events for underprivileged children, preparing holiday meals, creating memories for young families who needed a hand up in life.

With tentative steps, Rayne moved in closer. "Actually, I've given a lot of thought to this space. I have some ideas if you'd like to—"

Celeste plucked a lavender petal from its stem and rubbed it between her forefinger and thumb. She flicked the smashed piece of flower onto the table, where it lay battered and lifeless. "I know all about your ideas, Rayne." She reached into her satchel and plopped a familiar blue folder onto the table.

Rayne's proposal.

Her voice released a broken, unrecognizable sound. "How did you get that?"

"Cal brought it to dinner last night, wondered if there was anything salvageable inside." Celeste tilted her head, a gut-stabbing pity staring out through her icy eyes. "And no, there definitely was not. This lodge is not a nonprofit organization. It's a business. A profitable business that has missed way too many opportunities for growth." For the umpteenth time since the tour had begun, Celeste tapped her digital screen. "But we'll talk more about that on Monday when we discuss the changes."

A poison-dipped promise that pierced Rayne straight through the chest.

CHAPTER EIGHT

Levi loaded the last box of early-harvest apples into the food truck. After a stiff yank of the roll-down door, followed by the satisfying sound of latching metal, he swiped his clipboard off the bumper and double-tapped the Winslow Farm logo on the side of the truck.

"You're all loaded, Marty."

"Thanks, man. And thanks again for the hours." Under the green Winslow Farm cap, Marty's baby face could hardly pass for seventeen, much less twenty-one, but his dark circles and two-day-old scruff were impossible for Levi to ignore. The kid had more going on than one could see at first glance.

"You can thank Ford." Levi lowered his clipboard and studied the new hire. "He's the man who signs your paychecks."

"Yeah, I'll do that."

Levi took note of the fresh memorial tattoo on Marty's forearm. "Your old man serve in the Marines?"

A slow lift of his chin and then a flash of recognition in his eyes. "Yours too?"

Levi held back a morbid laugh. "Nah." The only thing his father would ever serve was prison time. "You taking care of your family, then?"

"Working two jobs. Oldest of four."

Levi had suspected as much. "We'll keep you in the rotation as much as we're able to."

"I appreciate it." Marty turned back to the driver's side door.

"And Marty?"

"Yeah?"

"Make sure you grab whatever your family can use from the pantry. We appreciate your father's service and sacrifice."

With a hard swallow, Marty ducked inside the truck and then pulled away.

Before Levi made it across the gravel drive to Ford's front porch, his boss approached him, Hauser on his heels. The retriever wagged his tail three times faster than his legs carried him.

A battered smile lit Ford's sun-lined face. "I thought you'd be at BlackTail by now." A wisp of graying hair lifted from his head like a flag waving in the wind. "Is the winner's pot too small for your liking?"

"Not at all. I just had some things to finish up here first. The guys will wait."

"Oh, I'm sure they will—though why they show up to lose week after week I'll never know." The puzzlement in Ford's tone caused Levi to laugh.

"You have a standing invitation to join us, you know. Travis never gives up asking if you'll come."

"I gave up card playing a long time ago." Ford took the clipboard from Levi's hand. "You go have fun now. With all the business you've brought in over the last few weeks, you deserve a night off." There was an undercurrent of pride in Ford's deep tenor. Not the kind of pride the old man warned him about, but the kind of pride that rose up from some fatherly place deep within him. Levi had spent the first eighteen years of his life trying to find such approval.

Levi's gaze swept over the Shelby tree line. From this distance he could make out the side of the ridge and the corner of the oversized back porch off the kitchen.

Ford clapped a rough hand on Levi's shoulder. "They're not giving you any trouble, are they?"

Levi tore his attention away from the property. "No. No trouble." Although, if trouble meant seeing more of Rayne Shelby, he wouldn't be opposed to it. He'd replayed her half-truths from the hardware store parking lot a dozen times.

"I'll admit, when you told me you went over there, I was fairly certain I'd be hearing from Cal's lawyer."

Levi flicked his gaze back toward Ford. "Trespassing is one thing, but you know I'd never take it so far as to jeopardize the farm. Or you, for that matter."

Even after eighteen years, Cal's ironclad restraints still bound Ford and the farm to his rules. He'd made sure of that the day Ford signed the nondisclosure agreement.

"Too far is relative, son. One doesn't realize they're drowning until the water's filled their lungs."

In a town the size of Shelby Falls, there were only so many establishments that could host a weekly card game—especially when Levi's oldest friend, Travis Garrett, was among the crew. But despite Travis's obnoxious antics, not only did BlackTail Bar and Grill allow their standing Friday night game, they welcomed the lot of them.

Travis smacked his beefy hand onto the green felt, his cards fanning and flipping from the vibration. At a height of six foot six, with muscles stacked on top of muscles, his presence was hard to miss. His opinions harder still. "This was supposed to be my night." Travis knocked back in his seat, swiped his beer off the table, and drained it by half.

"I can hardly remember the last time you made such a claim," Levi deadpanned.

"I can. Last week," Devon said. "And only every week before that for the last three years."

"Shut it," Travis shot back. "It's not like I don't put up with your OCD freak-outs every single day."

"*My* freak-outs?" Devon spat the words. "Excuse me for thinking hand washing is an essential part of hygiene."

"Is that what you tell yourself all forty-eight times you pump that soap?" Travis prodded.

Levi shut the idiots out and accounted for his latest win before pushing the discard pile toward Eli, their fourth and quietest player. After nearly three years together, Levi had only educated guesses on what Eli did for a living. Something as technical as it was profitable. But one thing Levi did know for certain: Eli never brought his work—or his personal life—to the poker table. A trait Levi valued more and more each week.

Levi took a deep swallow of his Coke. Between the constant drivel of Travis and Devon and the blaring eighties rock music, he almost regretted his stance on sobriety. He was a hand away from calling it a night . . . when he saw her.

Wearing a pink short-sleeved cardigan that hugged the subtle curves of her chest and hips, Rayne moved through the restaurant with fluid grace, her trim legs accentuated by the swing of her skirt. Not bothering to spare a glance at her surroundings, she strode straight to the back counter and slid onto a barstool. And, as if on a single exhale, she offered an immediate reply to the bartender's query.

To the average onlooker, Rayne would appear to be a regular at BlackTail.

But Levi knew differently. He'd been coming here for almost as long as he'd been a resident of Shelby Falls, and never once could he recall the governor's daughter crossing the threshold of this blue-collar establishment.

He studied her.

Though her posture appeared relaxed, only a slight slouch to her shoulders, her profile looked anything but stress free. Even from his seat across the room, the pinched concentration on her face alarmed him. There was no reaction when the bartender slid her drink down the counter. Not a head tilt. Not an eyelash bat. Nothing. Something was definitely off. And no matter what he felt for the Shelbys as a whole, he'd failed to stuff Rayne into the same mental compartment as her family.

A hard slap to his back tore his attention from the lone beauty to the impatient glare of his best friend. "You in for another round or you gonna go talk to that—" Travis stopped short, eyes rounding. "Is that Rayne Shelby?"

"I doubt she appreciates the announcement." Levi turned to Eli and inclined his head at Travis. "Cut him off after this one, okay?"

With Eli's silent confirmation, Levi pushed back in his chair.

Travis clasped a clammy hand to Levi's forearm. "What are you doing? You can't talk to her."

"Why not?" He didn't actually care to hear Travis's opinion—especially Travis's intoxicated opinion—but the question matched the one circling inside his own sober mind.

Devon, the ever-faithful realist, tossed one of his chips into the air and caught it in his palm. "Uh, maybe because her kind hates your kind."

Levi focused again on the woman in question. Her drink sat untouched, her face still burdened by an expression that nagged at his insides.

He stiffened when the man who'd warmed the last stool on the left side of the bar lumbered toward her. Ernie's cheap taste in cologne matched his cheap taste in beer . . . and usually in women.

Levi shucked off Travis's clumsy hold and took a calculated step in Rayne's direction—willing her to dismiss the drunk's feeble attempts at flattery. Instead, when she lifted her chin to answer the creep's nonsensical babble, Levi's intensity and irritability multiplied.

The slight shake of her head didn't seem to faze Ernie. He dropped an elbow beside her, his chest brushing against her arm.

Levi tightened his fists and didn't slow until he stood at her back. As a big fan of the power of suggestion, Levi offered Ernie little more than an unimpressed stare, and given the man's intoxication level, Levi allowed for a slight delay in comprehension time.

"Oh . . . hey, Levi," Ernie slurred and swayed on his feet.

Rayne's back tensed as she turned her head. Something heavy sank in his gut at the sight of her rose-rimmed eyes blinking him in. He reached into his pocket, pulled out a ten, and dropped it beside her drink.

With a hand curled loosely around her bicep, he bent and spoke directly into her ear. "Come on, let's get out of here, Rayne."

"No." She tugged free of his hold.

Stupidly, Ernie snickered at her response. But only three seconds of a hard stare later and Levi's silent encouragement proved effective. Ernie picked up his watery beer and migrated to the end of the bar.

Rayne's blotchy cheeks darkened as she looked from Levi to the crisp greenback next to her drink. Without a word, she slipped her hand into her purse, removed a folded bill, and set it under her sweaty glass.

In a synchronized movement, she shoved his money down the counter and slid off the barstool. "Please. Leave me alone."

Clutching her purse, the dark vixen sped toward the exit.

He inhaled the scent of honeysuckle and wildflowers that lingered in the air. A scent, he realized, he'd committed to memory after only three brief encounters.

He exhaled.

Only a fool would chase after a girl who'd been bred to hate him. But Levi had been called much worse than a fool.

And by a Shelby no less.

CHAPTER NINE

Rayne hurried across the black pavement in her open-toed heels, wishing she could ignore the masculine shadow trailing after her. "Why are you following me?"

"I could use some fresh air." He trotted alongside her now. "Bar was a little stuffy tonight, don't you think?"

"I'm not doing this with you." She stopped. "You won, okay? You can go back to your buddies and have a good laugh at my expense."

"Is that supposed to be my prize for chasing a beautiful woman out of a bar? I get to laugh with my buddies over a beer? Pretty sure I could think of a thousand better ways to spend my evening."

"Then don't let me keep you." She twisted away and quickened her pace.

"Why have you been crying, Rayne?"

"If there's some kind of neighborly quota you're trying to fill, then, please, consider it filled. I don't need to be psychoanalyzed."

"I'm not psychoanalyzing. Just observing." He jogged ahead of her and reversed his stride. "If you don't want to tell me what brought you to this fine establishment tonight, then perhaps I'll make a few educated guesses."

She ignored him, nearing her parking space.

"Let's see," he began. "Maybe you dented your uncle's car with a golf cart. No? Okay, then. So maybe you stained your favorite ball gown and the cleaner couldn't get it out. No, again? Hmm . . . I got it—you lost your summer bonus to your father's greedy campaign fund."

"You don't understand anything about my life or what I've lost."

"Then help me understand. What did you lose?"

"Just my future." No louder than a breath, she tossed the words into the air as if they meant nothing to her at all. Only they did. They meant everything.

"That seems pretty dramatic coming from someone who's set to inherit the whole freaking state of Idaho."

"There you go again!" Like a bolt of lightning, fury flashed through her body. "I'm not your problem, Levi. And I'm not your friend."

"The first is true, but the second's only true if you want it to be," he said plainly. His muscled frame blocked her path. He leaned against the trunk of her car and tilted his head in that annoying I-can-pluck-the-thoughts-from-your-mind way of his. "And, as I see it, you seem in need of a friend tonight, and I seem to be the only one offering."

"Friend?" He couldn't be serious. "We can't ever be friends."

"Says who?"

She saved her breath; the answer didn't need to be voiced.

"Do you listen to everything your family says?"

"Yes." Her insides recoiled at the pitiful statement and she folded her arms, the clasp on her clutch purse digging into her rib cage as she prepared for another round of his deception detection.

He scanned her face and lowered his voice. "Did someone hurt you tonight?"

The question unsteadied her. "Why would you think—"

"Deflection doesn't work well on me."

Apparently, he wasn't going to let this go. "I hurt myself."

He sighed. "Try again."

"It's the truth! Unless there's something *you'd* like to admit?"

He reared back a step. "Me?"

"Yes, *you*." Surprised at her bold assertiveness, she mirrored his narrowed gaze. "Did you or did you not set me up the night of the party?"

A muscle at the base of his jaw jumped. "Set you up how?"

"My uncle traced your alias check. He knows it's connected to the farm."

"That's impossible—" His concentrated stare morphed into confusion. "We haven't linked it yet."

"He linked it."

Levi leaned in close, his face a whisper away. "I didn't set you up, Rayne. I played fair. Did exactly what you asked of me."

Her bottom lip quivered. "Well, then, it's like I said. I hurt myself."

"What did he do?"

Rayne knew exactly who Levi was referring to. The overreaching power of her uncle was known by all.

She worked to regulate her tone, mute her hurt for the time being, but the gravelly sound that escaped betrayed her. "I'm not your problem."

"No. You're not. I'm glad we can finally agree on that."

She shouldn't say anything more to him. She shouldn't even be standing here at all. This entire scenario was backward. Messed up. Wrong on every level imaginable. And yet, she couldn't seem to stop the words. "He gave my promotion to someone else." Her fingers skimmed the length of her braid. "I came here after . . ." She tugged at the rope's end until her scalp stung. "After my replacement showed up."

"Your replacement?" he asked. "Wait . . ." His discerning gaze intensified, and she glanced away a moment too late. "Did he give it to another Shelby?"

Tears built behind her eyes, the truth too raw to speak. Too exposing.

"Figures." But the way he said it—the tone, the undercut of resentment and disgust—unnerved her.

"You shouldn't look so surprised. That's what your kind does. They eat their young. Everything is image and polish and pretense—if something doesn't go their way, well . . ." He waved a hand at her face. "This happens."

As hard as she'd worked to keep her tears tucked inside during Cal's reprimand yesterday, and during Celeste's verbal beating today, the last of her Strong Independent Woman front had faded. She pinched her lips together and turned her head. Hurt spilled down her cheeks while a sensation like burning coals radiated in the pit of her stomach.

"Hey." With a feather-soft touch, Levi's fingertips grazed her elbow. "I'm sorry. I took that too far. I was honestly trying to make you feel better, not worse."

He dropped his hand, discomfort spanning their sudden silence.

Rayne had every reason in the world to leave this man behind, every reason to climb into her car and never look back, yet none of those reasons could compel her to go. And despite the progression of subtle expressions playing across his face, Levi didn't retreat either. He simply stood there, waiting, as if he, too, were trying to understand why his legs weren't moving away.

"I have this ritual," he said with a tug on the back of his neck. "When I have a crap day."

"Yeah?" She blotted her cheek with the back of her hand and warily met his gaze. "What's that?"

"I shoot stuff."

"What kind of stuff?"

He quirked an eyebrow. "Was that *interest* I just heard in your voice?"

"Possibly." It'd been far too long since she'd felt the weight of cold, hard metal pressed into her palm, or the rush that followed the pull of a trigger. Her fingers twitched in memory.

He smiled fully. "A girl in heels who likes to shoot. You're just one walking contradiction, aren't you?"

"You shouldn't sound so shocked. I did grow up on acreage in north Idaho."

He cocked his head and studied her. "Maybe you're due for a round or two tonight."

"You want to take me shooting?"

"Depends."

"On?"

"If you're willing to agree to a truce."

She blinked, letting his words settle into comprehension.

"For one night," he continued, "no talk of families or feuds or property lines. Just . . . a night to cure your bad day, and to redeem me for making a beautiful woman cry outside a bar."

She bit her bottom lip. "I was a mess before you followed me, remember? And I've been less than kind to you after what you did to help me—"

"Doesn't matter. I don't want to be responsible for a single one of your tears." He held her gaze. "What do you say, Rayne Shelby? Can we be friends for a night?"

She ignored her balking conscience—the wailing siren screaming inside her head. Hadn't she learned her lesson? Hadn't she already lost too much because of her association with Levi Harding?

And yet, not even the answer to that question could make her yearning for a reprieve disappear.

"For one night?"

"One night. We can go back to ignoring each other tomorrow if we must, but rest assured that I'm not stupid enough to go shooting with a mortal enemy."

He retreated several steps, and strangely, her cheeks burned hotter with every inch of space he relinquished, as if his nearness had lit a brush fire under her skin.

"You know you want to say yes." His half smile, half smirk unbalanced her in more ways than one.

She did. She did want to say yes. More than she wanted to say no. More than she wanted just about anything at the moment. But could she really do this? Let go for a single night—of her conscience, her position, her last name?

Levi opened the passenger door to his truck and waited for her to make a decision.

She looked from him to the cracked vinyl seat.

"Okay," she said. "One night."

CHAPTER TEN

With a relaxed grip on the steering wheel, Levi glanced at her again, sure that in just a matter of seconds she would come to her senses and order him to turn around and take her back to her car. But instead, she sat quietly, staring out the passenger-side window as their town faded from view.

After their truce was all said and done, he'd walk away with a clean conscience. His fascination with Rayne was nothing of substance—nothing more than a fantasy developed over nine years of untamed curiosity.

Tonight would cure him of her for good.

The full moon illuminated the old country road that cut through dense pine trees and pastures of grassland. Ramsey Highway was the only road that led to and from Shelby Lodge and Winslow Farm. He'd driven it thousands of times, passed the cedar-planked estate and pristine landscape without a second glance. Without care or consequence. But tonight, it was impossible to ignore. His awareness of the wealthy estate had become as real as the girl tensing beside him.

"It's not too late to change your mind, you know."

"You're positive Ford is asleep?"

"The man wakes before the roosters. I'm positive. He's usually in his second cycle of REM before nine."

His statement caused her head to turn, yet her attention remained far away.

"Then I'm not changing my mind."

"Okay, then." He took note of her bare legs and her delicate choice in footwear. "But you realize I can't take you out to the actual shooting range, right? It's too dark, not to mention the issue of your . . . uh, attire."

"My attire shouldn't be a deterrent."

Oh, it certainly wasn't a deterrent, but it was an issue. "You'd think differently after a hot shell casing burns the top of your foot."

"You seem very concerned with my feet."

"I'm more concerned with getting sued by a Shelby."

"You're breaking our truce," she said, her eyes fully engaged on his face. "No more mention of family ties."

He slowed the truck and signaled onto the gravel drive that stretched from the road to the farm. "Fine by me."

She sat up a little straighter and scanned the property. "If we're not shooting on a range, then what are we—"

"I've got a plan B." He always had a plan B. A life lesson he'd learned early on. He rolled past the houses on the property and then the warehouse, heading straight back.

"You're taking me to the barn?"

"Trust me."

"I'm trying to."

He laughed at her honesty, parked the truck, and then looped around to open her door. Her entire body seemed to relax as she stepped into the twilight.

Levi jogged toward the large red doors, yanked one side open, and called back to her through the dusky haze. "It will take about ten minutes for the overhead lights to warm up. Just stay here, I'll be quick."

But stay she didn't.

When he doubled back, she wasn't in the barn. Or his truck. Or—*wait.*

The faintest flash of her white skirt pulled his gaze to the far left. Heels in hand, she walked along the railroad ties that bordered the Christmas tree farm and the orchard. Her dark hair flirted with the moonlight. He fought the urge to call out to her as she teetered momentarily, but as quickly as she lost her balance, she righted herself again. A heartbeat later she stopped and tipped her head toward the darkening horizon.

His breath faltered.

Whether it was the star-speckled backdrop, or the rare innocence she exuded, Rayne Shelby was far and away the most enchanting woman he'd ever laid eyes on.

She didn't startle when he came to stand next to her; she simply sighed. "It's strange what your heart remembers when your mind's been told to forget."

What *had* she been told? Certainly not the truth. He'd bet the farm on that. "When was the last time you were out here?"

"My seventh birthday." She looked to him, almost eye to eye with the added elevation of the railroad tie. "With my grandfather. He bought me an apple tree."

"An interesting gift for a seven-year-old."

"He was . . . an interesting man." She nearly laughed. "He told me to choose anything I wanted for my birthday, and all I could think was how much I loved homemade apple pie. So I asked for my own tree. And sure enough, he bought me a starter tree and helped me plant it somewhere in this orchard." She took in a deep breath and then released it. "I can still remember the feel of his hands on mine as he helped me pack the dirt. He was so patient. So careful to make sure I understood every minute detail." She shook her head slightly, then swept her gaze across the darkened orchard. "It looks so different out here now, but . . . it feels the same. It's hard to explain."

"I get it." And he did. More than *he* could explain.

He took her hand, helped her down, but didn't release her. Not even after she'd slipped her shoes back on. Heels weren't suitable for the farm, no matter how graceful the wearer.

"Now, are you ready for my plan B?"

The glint of mischief in her eyes was answer enough.

Rayne stepped through the splintery doorway of the barn and nearly choked on a sharp intake of breath. The place was double—no, triple—the size she'd imagined. The half-obstructed view from the octagon window in the Blue Jay Suite had only revealed a small section of the barn's tin roof. But as Levi grasped her hand to guide her through the congested area, she realized her reference for scale had been way off base.

Harvest trucks with mechanical buckets, large blue barrels, and wood pallets stacked twenty feet high were just the beginning.

"Hey, what's that thing?" She tugged him to a stop and pointed to the strange machine parked behind a tractor.

"An apple conveyer belt. Never seen one of those before?" There was a hint of surprise in his voice, but she was too awed, too overcome by her surroundings, to think up a witty retort. Her senses were on overload. Her eyes could hardly take in all the tools and equipment, much less her nose take in the spicy scents of juiced apples and fresh-cut grass. All the while, overhead, the circular fluorescent lights flickered and buzzed like a swarm of angry bees.

Slowing her pace yet again, she ran her free hand along a stack of wicker baskets with rope handles. "And are these what you give to the U-pickers?"

Levi offered an easy half smile. "Yeah, Ford's big on nostalgia. Only a few of our acres are designated for U-pick, but for some families, apple picking has become a fall tradition."

There was something to those baskets—some memory stored away that she couldn't quite access. But hearing Ford's name quickly snapped her out of her own moment of nostalgia. If she allowed herself to dwell on what she was actually doing, allowed herself to *think* about what it meant for her to be here again, this whole night would be in vain.

Just don't think about it, a rebellious voice cooed.

She wasn't a Shelby tonight.

She was simply an average twenty-six-year-old woman. In a barn. With a man. A very good-looking man.

Levi squeezed her hand. "Hey . . . you okay?"

"Yep," she said much too quickly. "I'm just hoping your idea of fun isn't built around harvesting equipment."

"Not even close. Keep walking, princess."

And walk they did. To the very back of the barn, through a storage closet, and then finally into a large clearing. A room of sorts. No equipment, no tools. Just a massive roll-up door at the far end. Bark chips scattered the floor, and a few hay bales bordered each side wall.

"Wow . . . what is this space used for?"

His eyes danced with amusement. "Fun."

Goose bumps rose on her bare legs and arms. This area was several degrees cooler than outside, but it was the chill of anticipation that managed to get the best of her. She shivered when Levi let go of her hand.

He headed into the storage closet. "It will just take a minute for me to set up."

"How can I help?"

Again, his smile seemed to come easily. He pointed. "See that shelf on the far wall?"

She nodded as he slipped his pocketknife out of his jeans and placed it in the center of her palm.

"There's some twine on the bottom. Cut off a few strips—about five feet or so—and lay it on the ground between those two posts. We're gonna need some markers. Oh, and don't turn around until I'm set up."

"Okay," she agreed on a nervous laugh.

She didn't bother to ask questions. At the moment, she needed to *do*. Not ask. Because asking involved thinking, and thinking involved a level of complication she wasn't ready to deal with. But as she cut the strips of twine, her mind floated to a safe zone as she noted the expansiveness of the room. She couldn't help but imagine all the possible uses for a space like this. What it could offer the community. She'd organized several fund-raisers in barns and community centers half this size when she was in college. And though there was nothing posh or polished about this particular barn, nothing decorated or uniquely distinguishable, there was something so inspiring about the rustic feel.

Something homey.

A rush of guilt nearly swallowed her whole at the thought.

No. *Just don't think about it.*

While she'd been arguing with her internal opponent and laying out the strips of twine, Levi had been dragging out all kinds of—what sounded like—heavy objects from the storage closet. There was scraping and banging and then . . . she heard him behind her.

"I'm ready when you are."

She took just a second to temper her expectations before she turned. After all, *fun* was a relative term.

Yet once again, the man had exceeded the limits of her imagination.

No, he wasn't wearing a three-piece suit while crashing a high-society dinner party. Neither was he schooling her on the art of deception in the middle of a parking lot. This time, he was simply handing her a BB gun and telling her to shoot at his makeshift targets: two hay-stuffed scarecrows, five aluminum cans set on a wooden sawhorse, a crudely painted pumpkin, and a handful of other harvest-like paraphernalia.

The belly laugh that escaped her was so abrupt she couldn't wipe the tears clinging to her bottom lashes fast enough. "What is this stuff? And why—" She pointed to the pumpkin and tried again. "Why is that pumpkin so . . . creepy?"

"*Hey*—Pete's a jack-o'-lantern. And kids love him."

She'd almost calmed, almost dried her damp cheeks and righted herself, when Levi's flat-toned response put her in stitches all over again. That pumpkin had to be the worst rendering of a jack-o'-lantern she'd ever seen. Smeared black paint for eyes, a carved-out triangle nose, and a hideous curvature for a mouth that looked more like a grimace than a grin.

"Wait," she said. "That thing's for children? Levi, I've seen scary movies less horrifying—that pumpkin will give me nightmares."

"Give me that." He snatched the gun back from her hand. "You're gonna lose an eye if you don't stop flinging that barrel around. And for the record, *that thing* happens to be a work of art."

"Please don't tell me you were the one who painted it." Rayne sucked in her cheeks, pinching them tight to keep her laughter under control.

"Well, it's not like I had a lot of other options." The side of his mouth twitched as he spoke, but amazingly, he managed to keep a straight face. "I don't screen our seasonal employees for artistic ability."

"Perhaps you should start."

"And perhaps *you* should be grateful for this spectacular indoor shooting range I've created in less than ten minutes. Bet you've never had a date quite like this one."

She brushed aside his casual use of the word *date* and simply held out her hand to retrieve her gun. “Can't say that I have.” She eyed the crooked face of the ugly pumpkin once again. It didn't take much more than a squint for Rayne to replace Pete's twisted smile with the mocking grin and haughty eyes she'd endured only a few hours ago.

Rayne adjusted the target in her scope and pulled the trigger.

Pete went down on her first shot.

CHAPTER ELEVEN

If a picture was worth a thousand words, then Levi's mental snapshot of Rayne peppering two pathetically thin scarecrows with BBs was worth a million.

The girl didn't mess around. Every item he'd brought out of storage was either lying prostrate like Old Pete or no longer intact. So much for taking turns.

"You do realize you've made it impossible for me to shoot now, right?"

She assessed the damage. "Don't worry, I'll set everything back up the way you had it. Creepy pumpkin man and all."

"Jack-o'-lantern. And that's not the reason."

She lifted an eyebrow. "Then why—you afraid I'm a better shot than you?"

"Who taught you to shoot like that?"

She handed Levi the gun, crossed over the forbidden line of twine, and retrieved two of the scattered, hole-drilled cans. "My cousin Joshua."

Ah, Gia's brother. "He the family hit man or something?"

"He's an Air Force officer." She reset one of the cans and then the next, spacing them perfectly. "No family talk, remember?"

"Right." He studied her. "Is that the only topic off limits tonight?"

Even under the harsh fluorescent lighting, her dark-amber eyes sparkled. "I suppose so. Within reason."

"Good, 'cause reasoning happens to be my specialty."

She straightened the scarecrow's arm, bending the wire underneath to stay in place. "I believe that."

"So what do you say to a friendly get-to-know-you game?"

She shot him a look of suspicion. "Depends what you mean by *friendly*."

"Please, Rayne. Try and keep your mind out of the gutter."

She rolled her eyes. "Fine. How do we play?"

"For every target I miss, you get to ask me one question. And vice versa."

She wrinkled her nose. "But you already know I can shoot the tar—"

"You in or not?"

"Sure, I'm in."

"Perfect." He set the gun on a hay bale and headed for the storage closet.

"Where are you going?"

"To retrieve the target."

"But I thought—"

Levi rolled out a six-foot apple punched full of seed holes. "Be a dear and grab that red bucket of beanbags, will ya?"

"A beanbag toss? That's the game? You tricked me!"

Levi leaned the apple against the far wall. "No, you *assumed* I meant target shooting."

"Only because you led me to that assumption."

"Exactly." He winked at her. "Hope your arm's as good as your trigger finger."

She reached into the bucket, grabbed a beanbag, and threw it at him. It grazed the top of his shoulder.

"Oops, sorry." She shrugged. "Slipped right out of my hand."

Levi smiled. *So Rayne Shelby has some fire in her blood after all.*

He placed the line of twine ten feet away from the happy apple and then gestured to her. "Please, ladies first."

She kicked off her heels—something she hadn't bothered to do for target shooting—grabbed a handful of mismatched beanbags, and marched herself behind the line.

"Oh, and just the center hole counts," he added.

Like a slow-moving bullet, her gaze shifted from him back to the apple.

He stifled a laugh when she scrunched up her shoulders, rotated her hips in an awkward half-twist maneuver, and chucked the bag with a stumble-step forward, followed by an unladylike "Oomph."

She missed.

"Tough break. Looks like I get to ask you the first question."

She gave a long sigh and then conceded with a nod.

"So, Rayne Shelby, what's your hidden talent?" He lifted a finger. "And please, if at all possible, include a demonstration."

She tilted her head. "Is that another add-on rule? You just keep tacking them on—"

"You're stalling."

"Fine." She huffed. "I can sing all the names of the fifty states in less than twenty-five seconds."

"And to think, I didn't even have to pay for this kind of entertainment."

She cleared her throat while he took out his phone, found the stopwatch, and pointed at her to start.

She didn't miss a single state. Alabama to Wyoming. And all were said—or, *sung*—in twenty-two seconds flat.

She pointed to the bucket and then to him. "You're up."

Making sure to match her dramatic windup, he flung the bag straight into the center bullseye. "Guess I get to ask you another one."

"Only if you agree to move your twine back another ten feet. You have an unfair advantage."

"I know it might be hard to believe, but I don't spend my free time tossing beanbags into Apple Adam. But let the record show, I'm moving the line." He kicked the rope toward the opposite wall.

"Now"—he tapped his chin with his forefinger—"let's say a friend hands you a highly recommended novel. Do you read the ending first?"

She squished her lips to one side of her mouth.

"There's no right or wrong here." But he knew by the way she scrunched her brow, she believed otherwise.

"No."

"Why did you pause so long?"

She smiled. "Sorry, your question's up. My turn."

Opting for a different approach, Rayne went for the underhand toss. She missed again.

She let her head fall forward as Levi reached into the bucket.

He circled her, tossing a yellow square from hand to hand. "Must be something," he said, "operating that lodge day after day, surrounded by hundreds of strangers every month, all the while working for that—your uncle. I couldn't do it. The monotony and stuffy clientele would grate on my nerves. And all for the sake of what—good hospitality? Makes me wonder how you do it. *Why* you do it. Makes me wonder if there's some hidden purpose I'm not seeing."

"Is there a question in this monologue of yours?" she asked.

He stopped in front of her and softened his voice. "Why do you stay, Rayne? You could have your pick of any job in this town or in this state, for that matter . . . and yet you work there. Under *him*."

She swallowed and took a step back. "You're breaking the rules."

"And you're avoiding my question."

She also avoided his gaze. "You already answered it—hospitality. I enjoy it."

"Lie." He spun around, pitched his bag into the center of the bull's-eye, and turned back to her again. "Hospitality may be something you're good at, but it's not the reason you stay there. You didn't show up at that bar tonight afraid your gift of hospitality was going to be replaced by someone else." He puckered his lips. "You showed up there for the same reason you came here to ask for my help that day. Fear. You're afraid of losing something."

"And you're not afraid of prying into other people's business."

She skirted around him to retrieve her next pile of ammo. Levi caught her hand, trying hard to ignore the fact that it was so much colder than his own. "Another sad attempt at deflection."

"Then obey the rules and ask me a real question."

"Fine. Why did you follow me that night at the Falls?"

She blinked, clearly not expecting that, and dropped her gaze to her toes. "That was a long time ago."

"Why, Rayne?"

"I guess, because you seemed . . ."

He waited for the list of adjectives that would have described him then: pathetic, needy, neglected—

"Like you could use a friend."

Something splintered inside him at her revelation, something he wasn't quite prepared to examine. He chose a safer alternative. "You're right, especially after I got caught in those godforsaken weeds."

Her lips twitched. "I tried to warn you about the devil's club."

True. Those were the first words Rayne Shelby had ever spoken to him: *Watch out for that patch of devil's club!* "Too bad that was only after I'd starting tromping through those woods like an idiot. A little prewarning would have been nice." He winced at the memory of the hair-thin, noxious spines pushing into his flesh. "That demon bush is the most appropriately named plant on the planet. If not for your voodoo tricks, I would probably still have those needles poking out of my palm." He'd never forget the way she'd plucked a leaf from the same foliage that had attacked him and gestured him back to the river's edge. She'd created some kind of a puttylike salve to apply to his palm after she'd drawn out each nettle from his irritated skin.

"It's a useful tip to know."

"It was for me." While she'd worked on his hand, he'd studied her face under the stars—the slope of her nose, the rose tint of her lips, the dimple in her chin, and the compassion in her eyes. The same kind of unexplained compassion he'd been shown by a farmer only a few weeks earlier. "Well, before my unfortunate mishap with Satan's shrub, I'd wondered if you were ever going to say a word to me."

"I was shy."

"Not buying it." His grin was wicked. "After you were finished playing doctor, you practically begged me to kiss you."

Her mouth smacked open. "That is so not true!"

He barked out a laugh. "Oh yes, I remember it well. There you were, fluttering your eyelashes and speaking to me all soft and sultry in the quiet of the night."

"Oh? Like when I told you about all the other indigenous plants you should look out for?"

No, like when she'd told him she'd felt like an outsider for most of her life, like she was constantly letting people down, like she would never quite measure up. And when, in turn, he'd shared his own fears—of the unknown, of starting over in a new town, of a future he couldn't envision.

"Exactly," he lied.

The amusement in her eyes dimmed. They both knew what had come next: the sheriff's patrol car rolling up, Gia yelling for Rayne to come back to the campfire, Rayne's troubled gaze as she told him she had to leave, Levi following after her, asking her to meet him again the next night, Rayne promising she would.

"I don't know what my uncle Tony said to you after I got in his car that night, but I can imagine. He's protective."

Levi could still feel the man's finger drilling into his chest with a threat to stay away from his niece, the same threat he'd given Travis to stay away from his daughter, Gia. "I'd never fault a man for protecting a seventeen-year-old girl." But they both knew it was more than that. The sheriff's bent against Levi and Travis had less to do with good parenting and more to do with Tony's connection to Cal Shelby. "Although, it must have been some warm welcome back at the lodge that night, since I never saw you at the Falls again."

She crossed her arms over her chest. "It must be nice winning every round of this game so you can steer the conversation however you'd like while I've yet to ask a single question of you."

"Then ask me something." He moved in closer, disregarding every ounce of his common sense. "What is it you want to know?"

"Where did you come from—before you moved to the farm?"

"That's a tricky one to answer." Nothing about his past was simple.

"Try."

Something about the rich sincerity of her request made him want to.

"Before I knocked on Ford's door . . ." It would be so easy to spin a different tale the way he'd done for so many years, but the expectation he read in her eyes left no room for anything less than the truth. "I lived in my car. For nearly a month. And before that, a group home for teens in Washington. And before that, five different foster families in Oregon."

He watched the heavy weight of his words register, watched as she tried to reconcile a lifetime of rumors against the story he'd just told her.

"And before that?"

He was certain nothing less than a quick pulse of bravery had pumped the question out of her mouth. And if there was one thing he'd reward with honesty, it was courage—especially the kind that acted before justification could set in.

"Before that I learned all about the kind of man I never want to become. And I pray to God He never lets me forget those lessons."

"You have no family?" she asked.

"Not the kind connected by blood, no."

She seemed to think on that for a minute, let his answer soak in before she hit him with, "Your eyes look different now—than they did the night we first met, I mean."

"How so?"

"They're not lonely anymore."

He said nothing, yet his thoughts were far from silent. If she kept biting her bottom lip and staring at him with those same caramel-colored eyes of nine years ago, he'd have no choice but to pull her in and kiss her the way he'd wanted to before—

She released a heavy sigh. "I dropped out of political science my third year of college, much to my family's displeasure. I switched my degree to public relations instead and interned with a social worker for one of my service projects. She worked specifically with teens in transition and . . . I learned a lot."

He cleared his throat, rerouting his thoughts. "I imagine you did."

"What I mean to say is, if I'd met you for the first time tonight, I never would have guessed all that about your past. There's nothing easy about finding your way alone. And yet you did." Again, something crumbled inside him at the validation he heard in her voice.

She rubbed the upper arms of her pink cardigan and he noted the goose bumps on her forearms for the first time.

"You're cold." Levi unrolled the long sleeves of his plaid overshirt and shrugged it off. He placed it around her shoulders. "Take this."

"Thank you." She slipped her arms inside the too-long sleeves. The length of the blue-and-green plaid reached past midthigh, the width swallowing her small frame as she worked the buttons.

"So." She glanced over her shoulder at the giant apple. "Whose turn is it?"

"Think we should probably put your tossing arm to rest for the night." He stuffed his hands in the pockets of his jeans. "I figured you'd want to head back soon anyway."

"Not unless you're kicking me out."

"Don't tempt me." He winked. "But unless you have something else in mind, I've pretty much exhausted my resources in the storage closet."

"I do." She pointed to the loft above her head—to the rope, in specific. "Ever swing from there onto those bales?"

He folded his arms at his chest. Why couldn't this girl understand the limits of her attire? "Obviously you've never crawled on hay with bare legs before. It's not like a pillow-top mattress."

She tilted her head. "I'm not looking for a mattress. I'm looking for fun." She looked around the room and pointed at the closet. "There. That white sheet, the one covering up another unidentified harvest creature. I'll tuck it around my legs, like loose pants."

"You seriously want to swing from that loft and jump ten feet onto a manger of hay, wrapped like a mummy?"

She nodded vigorously.

He scrubbed a hand over his jaw. "And I know for a fact you haven't had a drop to drink," he murmured.

"Nope." She beamed. "Now, go take that sheet off Cory the Corncob and let me have my fun."

He saluted her. "Fine, but for the record, it's Connor. Connor the Corncob."

Only a few hours ago, Levi had had no doubt he could rid his mind of the memory of Rayne in his barn . . . but that was before she'd climbed into his truck wearing his shirt. And that particular image—the one with her hay-rumpled hair resting against his seat, the tail of his button-up draped over her crossed legs—had already seared itself into his subconscious.

It would take nothing short of a lobotomy to cut the memory out.

"I can't remember the last time I did anything like that," she said on a yawn.

"Doubt there are many who have taken a fifteen-foot plunge into a pile of hay dressed like Casper the Friendly Ghost and lived to tell about it."

Her laugh was relaxed, sleepy, even. "I just meant . . . I haven't really . . ."

Though her voice faded out, Levi understood her meaning well enough. "Taken a break." Coincidently, Ford had accused him of the same thing recently.

"Yes." She fingered the lock on her door. "It's been a long time since I've taken a break from responsibility."

From Shelby expectations was likely what she wasn't saying.

"You're twenty-six, Rayne. Not seventy."

"Yeah, I know." Yet her acknowledgment lacked conviction.

Rayne flipped the lighted visor down, slipped the elastic band from the end of her hair, and slowly untangled each woven plait of her braid. Heat sparked in the center of his chest and spread into his limbs. After a tight swallow, he focused again on the road, drumming a tuneless melody on the steering wheel.

If he wasn't careful, he'd drive his truck straight into a ditch.

Right along with his mind.

"How's the hip, by the way? You have some work to do on your tuck and rolls."

"Oh, it's fine." She let out a loose laugh. "I had a lot of fun, bruise and all."

"So did I."

He spared a glance in her direction as he pulled off Ramsey Highway onto the main drag of downtown Shelby Falls. The straggles of hair that had framed her face only minutes ago had been retucked, smoothed back into a fresh braid. And something inside him rebelled against the sight.

He wasn't ready for Repackaged Rayne to appear just yet.

When she snapped the visor shut and lowered her arm to her lap, Levi reached across the seat divide and captured her hand. To his utter amazement, she didn't resist. Didn't pull away.

She simply stared at the union of her hand folded into his.

"I'm not your enemy, Rayne. You realize that, don't you?"

The shift on her face was slight, but it was there. Enough for him to note she'd heard him—maybe even *believed* him.

Obnoxious laughter, followed by the raised voices of a crowd gathering outside BlackTail Bar and Grill, caused her eyes to tick wide.

She slid her hand out of his grasp and shielded her face in the shadows.

"Keep driving." A quiet yet firm command.

"Your car's parked in that lot."

"Keep driving. *Please*. You can drop me at the gallery on Sixth."

Irritation pitched his voice. "And how will you get to your car?"

"My cousin will take me."

"Rayne—"

She shook her head. "We said one night, Levi. One night. Let's leave it at that, okay?"

He clamped his mouth shut, his jaw straining under the pressure. Crazy how it only took seconds for her to complete the transformation back into a Shelby. Back into a woman who'd allow her family to dictate her life.

"Right here's fine." She pointed to the dark corner junction at Sixth and Sherman and then reached for her door. "I'll walk."

"No, you won't." He gunned it, speeding through a yellow light and over a curb. "I don't care what your last name is, I'm not dropping a woman off on a dark street corner alone."

"Levi, don't—"

He swerved into the parking lot of the gallery, the squeal of his brakes equal to the rage that spewed from her lips.

"That was completely unnecessary. You *knew* I didn't want a scene!"

"News flash, Shelby. *You are a scene.*" He shot her a smile that could melt metal.

Her fingers shook as they fumbled with the lock. She yanked back on the door handle and proceeded to ram her shoulder into the frame for leverage. "Why won't this thing open?"

He crossed his arms over his chest, his truck idling roughly in the quiet of the night. "I'd be happy to assist you. Just say the word, princess."

"Urgh!"

"Nope. Not the one I was looking for."

She rammed the door once more, and that time, it popped open.

"I'd offer to walk you inside, but I think this is the part where you start pretending I don't exist. I can't quite remember the protocol from last time."

A sharp tap of metal against his window stilled his hand on his driver's side door.

And then he went blind.

CHAPTER TWELVE

"Gia, turn that thing off!" Rayne rounded the front of Levi's truck, her heels clicking against the asphalt in a clipped trot.

With calculated ease, Gia lowered the police-issue Maglite from Levi's face and swung the beam onto Rayne—making a full and complete pass over her borrowed shirtfront. "*Really*, Rayne?"

"I'm . . . it's not what it looks like." Rayne's fingers stumbled over the buttons, plucking them free one by one.

Levi rolled his window down and leaned into the open air in his white cotton undershirt, resting his elbow on the doorframe. "Is this where I get read my Miranda rights?"

"Shouldn't you have them memorized by now?"

Levi dipped his chin. "Nice outfit, Gia."

She took a step toward him, her fringy jean shorts, paint-blotched T-shirt, and unlaced combat boots a sight to behold. She planted her feet shoulder width apart as if preparing for a street fight. "At least I'm wearing a real shirt."

"I'll be sure to pass that along."

"You do that, and while you're at it, tell your poker buddy to stop buying my pottery. My art is for connoisseurs. Not for bachelors in a need of a beer coaster."

"Oh, he's more inventive than you give him credit for. In fact, I'm pretty sure Travis uses one of your bowls for composting."

Gia drilled him with a glare that could have shot fire. "Stay away from my cousin."

Rayne clamped a hand at Gia's elbow. "Stop it, Gia."

His face darkened. "The last time I checked"—Levi cut his gaze to Rayne—"which was quite recently, your cousin's a grown woman. She can make her own decisions."

A chill feathered Rayne's exposed skin as she slipped out of the plaid garment and stretched her hand toward him. Her eyes pleaded with him to take the shirt and leave without further comment. She'd have enough to explain as it was.

He didn't oblige her; he simply stared at her face until her legs felt as weak as her pulse. "Keep it. See you in another nine years, Rayne."

She opened her mouth to argue, but he revved his engine, rolled up his window, and disappeared into the night.

The blue-static security light that stained the walls of the gallery reminded Rayne of a scene from *Ocean's Eleven*. Paranoia had her gaze bouncing from corner to corner as if expecting—maybe even hoping for—a group of undercover agents to pop out of hiding and drag her into an interrogation cell. They'd question her on tonight's whereabouts, ask her about the article of clothing still clutched in her fist, and eventually let her go.

But that kind of Hollywood drama would have been far too easy.

Rayne wove through a maze of randomly placed display pedestals and past endless shelves of Gia's glazed pottery. She sucked in a gasp after narrowly avoiding a head-on collision with a small table of handcrafted clay jewelry. Though her cousin had a perfectly usable flashlight on her small person, she hadn't offered to flip the switch. A decision that was most definitely purposeful.

Gia drew back the curtain near the red-lettered exit sign, took a sharp left, and tromped up the steep staircase to her living quarters. She didn't bother to check behind her. She didn't need to.

Rayne had been trailing after Gia since they wore multicolored bangles and played in Aunt Nina's makeup during Sleep-In Saturdays, careful to put every expensive lipstick and mascara tube back in its rightful place before Gia's mother was aroused from bed. They'd captured frogs in the pond near the lodge, made mud-and-grass stew for their imaginary clubhouse guests, and camped under the stars in the Shelby pasturelands.

They were cousins by blood, sisters by circumstance, and best friends by choice. Rayne would always follow Gia.

Her cousin pushed through the door of her one-bedroom apartment and marched into the could-hardly-count-as-a-kitchen kitchen. Rayne braced herself against a piece of furniture she knew almost as well as her own bed, the hide-a-bed sofa in Gia's living room.

"Do you have any idea how many times I called you tonight?"

Rayne hadn't bothered to bring her clutch purse into the barn, which meant she hadn't checked her phone since . . . before BlackTail. "I didn't have my phone on me, Gia. I'm sorry if you were concerned—"

"Concerned? No." She laughed like a cartoon villain. "*Concern* is when your pants feel snug after a long holiday season. *Concern* is when you see your first wiry gray hair at twenty-seven. *Concern* is not when your overly predictable cousin tells you she'll be waiting at your apartment that evening and then doesn't show up. For hours. I went to the lodge, Rayne. And you can imagine what a help sweet Celeste was when I asked where you were."

The gut-punch she'd felt earlier when Celeste had shot down her proposal hit her all over again, but Gia wasn't finished.

"I called the restaurant and had my mom lock up the gallery for me so I could look for you. I called and I called and you didn't answer. Nobody knew where you were. So no, I wasn't *concerned.* I was out of my mind with worry!"

"I'm sorry, Gia. I wasn't thinking."

Gia kicked off one boot at a time. The hard plunk vibrated the thin laminate floor. "I was going to give it one more hour before I called my dad for help. You better be thanking God that I didn't, because he would have found you." She crossed the room and pointed to Levi's shirt as if it were a dead animal. "With *him.*"

Rayne's skin chilled at the thought of her uncle Tony finding her at the barn with Levi. "I know what you think of him—what the family thinks, but he's . . ." *What?* What could she really say? "He's different than I thought."

Gia didn't move, didn't even blink. "He's a con man. Just like Travis. Just like Ford."

"No, he's not." Rayne had little to go off of but intuition, yet she felt more sure about that statement now than she had a few hours ago. Than she had a few weeks ago.

"Oh? And did he tell you that as he wrapped you up in his shirt?" Gia dropped her voice a full octave and added a husky drawl. "Rayne, sweetheart, don't worry. I'm one of the good guys, you can trust me. I'm definitely *not* a con man."

"Don't be mean."

"Then don't be naive." Gia spun toward her miniature wine rack and selected a bottle of red.

"It was an innocent night of fun."

"There is nothing innocent about playing with matches." She riffled through a drawer. "I don't even understand how you two—wait." Gia gripped the wood handle of the corkscrew, her eyes opening wide. "Is he . . . is Levi *Hot Guy* from the party?"

Rayne's expression was answer enough.

Gia plunged the spiraled tool into the cork, and Rayne would have sworn she felt the prick through her chest wall. "You have got to be kidding me. When I encouraged you to rebel, I meant, like, go get a wrist tattoo, not go have a fling with your family's enemy."

"It was one night. Not a fling. I went to BlackTail after work and he happened to be there. I just needed a mental break, but it's over now. So please, just drop it, okay?" The last thing on earth she needed was another lecture from a Shelby.

"You went to BlackTail?" Gia's stern tone slipped.

"Yes." Rayne sighed. "And yes, Travis was there too. And no, I didn't talk to him." Truth be told, she wouldn't have spoken to anyone if Levi hadn't chased her outside the bar. But in her rush to exit, she'd seen Travis. His imposing stature was hard to miss, even while he was seated. The relationship between Gia and Travis might have ended after their senior year of high school, but for reasons Rayne couldn't understand, the drama between them hadn't. "Can we move on from this topic now?"

After several seconds, Gia finally relented. "Fine. I'll drop it. For now."

"Thank you." Rayne slid onto the couch and pulled a pillow into her lap, allowing her head to rest on the back of the sofa, and closed her eyes.

Gia joined her a moment later, a glass of wine pinched between her fingers as she stretched her legs over the middle cushion between them. "So, I'm guessing it went pretty badly today with Celeste."

Rayne didn't want to think about how badly it had gone, but she couldn't put it off any longer. She'd had her reprieve, her escape, her . . . fun. It was time to be an adult again. To face the truth, no matter how ugly or painful. "You were right; she hasn't changed."

"If it helps, I wish I weren't." Gia nudged Rayne's leg with her socked feet.

"I keep thinking this is all a bad dream, ya know? Like the kind you try to wake yourself up from but can't." She toyed with the frayed edge of the pillow. "I really believed I could be the one to continue Granddaddy's legacy after Cal moved on."

Gia slumped her shoulders. "Nostalgia won't win this battle, Rayne." There was no malice or contempt in her voice, just bone-chilling honesty. "I know that's not what you want me to say. I know how hard you've worked, how hard you've tried to prove yourself to the family, but . . ." The corners of Gia's mouth turned down. "I asked my mom what she knew about this whole Celeste thing." She released a hard exhale. "I guess Celeste and Cal have been corresponding for months. She sent him ideas for improvement, marketing plans for growth and expansion, and basically told him she'd be his little trophy employee whenever he needed her. Of course Mom told him he couldn't do that to you, not after all the years he'd groomed you for management, but . . ."

But Cal had done it.

Just like she'd gone and proven herself unworthy of such an iconic Shelby position.

Rayne stared at the crumpled overshirt draped on the arm of the sofa, Levi's words ping-ponging inside her skull. *You shouldn't look so surprised. That's what your kind does. They eat their young. Everything is image and polish and pretense* . . . Four hours ago his statement had felt like a personal attack. Now it felt like a prophecy.

Rayne stood and paced the length of her cousin's apartment.

"What are you doing?" Gia asked.

"Trying to think like a Shelby."

"Care to clue me in?"

Rayne swiveled to a stop on her second pass. "Who is Celeste? I mean, really. What do we know about her?"

"That depends. How many expletives am I allowed to use in this conversation?"

Rayne pressed the heels of her hands against her temples as she carried herself back and forth. "I'm serious."

"So am I."

Everything felt clearer, sharper, fresher than it had moments ago. "Based on the brag letters at Christmastime from Great-Aunt Christine and all of Celeste's social media posts . . . she's in constant activity."

"Yeah, so—"

"Go with me on this. Everything Celeste does is a calculated step toward her next career goal. And you and I both know she doesn't crave small-town life, not when she's spent the last decade in New York City trying to make a name for herself. Shelby Falls isn't her scene. And she knows it." Rayne pivoted. "Which means . . . she's not planning on staying here long; she's only here now to soak up all the limelight she can."

"I think I'm going to need another glass of wine." Gia hopped off the sofa to pour herself another glass, while Rayne followed the winding trail of her thoughts.

"Think about it, Gia. Summertime is the liveliest season at the lodge—weddings, dinner parties, a full wait list for reservations. Very high-profile, especially during an election year. It's no wonder she wrote to Cal during the same time my father announced he was running for reelection. She's hoping to share the spotlight. But after Cal leaves for the campaign and our busy summer turns into a much slower fall and then into a practically dead winter . . ." Rayne secured her hands on her hips. "Don't you see? Celeste's marketing plan for the lodge is more of a marketing plan for herself. She's only here to rub elbows and soak up some publicity to add to her résumé. And when it's all over, she'll move on."

Gia took a small sip of her vino, her dark lashes peeking over the rim of the wineglass. "Okay, so let's say your Nancy Drew hypothesis is correct and she's only planning to stay as long as it benefits her. What will you do in the meantime?"

"I'll wait her out."

"You realize she's going to do everything in her power to snuff you out so she can soak up the glory."

"Yes." Rayne straightened, her face etched with steely resolve. "But you were right before; it won't be my nostalgia or my passion that wins this war. It will be my loyalty. I'm the tortoise in this race, Gia."

Gia lifted her stemware high. "Well, let's hope your shell is thick, Tortoise. Because this is going to be one loooong summer."

CHAPTER THIRTEEN

At a quarter to six, a single ray of sunlight pushed through the low-lying smoke cloud. The faint tap of Rayne's canvas flats against the rock pavers leading from her cabin to the lodge kept time with her steady pulse.

There was hardly a morning Rayne wasn't showered, dressed, and fully caffeinated before the sun's first yawn of light. Hardly a morning she wasn't prepared to face the challenges of managing a forty-three-room lodge. And today—day one of the proverbial tortoise-and-hare race—was no exception.

The practiced pep in her step was as purposeful as the positive self-talk on perseverance she'd rehearsed all weekend.

As she neared the expansive wraparound porch, she took in the withering herb garden under the back kitchen window and made a mental note to water twice a day. The forecast called for yet another week of dry heat and wind. No chance of rain.

The screen door sang a sweet welcome of familiarity, reminding her once again that her home and her heart resided nowhere else. There would be trying days, weeks, and months ahead, but there were certain comforts she could always find joy in: the hint of lilac in the summer air, the funny notes Teddy left her on the front desk every morning, and Delia's off-key humming as she manned the breakfast spread.

"Good morning, Delia."

The frosting knife in Delia's hand stilled over a particularly gooey batch of cinnamon rolls. "You can swipe the *good* right off that greeting and just say, *mornin'*. 'Cause that's what it is—a morning. Not much good I can see about it, and I'm not even the one who has to work with her."

Rayne heeded the "Approach with Caution" undercurrent in Delia's tone and added an extra beat of happy to her smile. If she could win Delia over to her positivity plan—encourage her to weather a few Celeste-size wind gusts, then maybe she wouldn't have to run this race on her own.

"It will be an adjustment." Rayne touched the back of Delia's cotton blouse. "But we can handle this. Together."

A glob of buttery frosting plopped onto the corner roll, and Delia's mouth dipped into a frown. "So it's true then. Cal gave her your promotion."

"Cal did what he thought best."

"And what about you?"

"I'm going to keep doing what I do best." The forced playfulness in Rayne's tone fooled no one. "Make sure you behave." She planted a rushed kiss on Delia's squishy cheek.

"Sometimes I think you're too nice to be under the thumb of this family."

Hadn't Levi said something similar? She shook her head, refusing to go down that mental rabbit hole again.

"You've worked here since before I was born, so we must not be that bad."

"I'm a creature of habit."

"So am I." Rayne winked and gave her a quick pat on the shoulder. "Just hang on, okay? I'll do my best to cushion the blows."

With a huff, Delia picked up the tray and waited for Rayne to hold the swinging door into the Great Room. "That's exactly what I'm worried about."

There wasn't a guest who refused Delia's famous breakfast table selections: homemade cinnamon rolls, apple-berry scones, and cheddar quiche with bacon. The gourmet buffet had been built into the cost of the rooms. Guests often claimed the lodge offered the best French press coffee in town. Rayne couldn't argue.

Entering the lobby, she halted before she reached the front desk to read whatever Teddy had scribbled for her. He'd been entertaining her with his Post-it note stories of mischief and mayhem for years.

But Teddy's usual sticky note trail wasn't waiting for her. Instead, a gridded yellow piece of paper lay on the shiny mahogany, Rayne's bolded name printed at the top.

SCHEDULE CHANGE—PLEASE BE ADVISED.

The rotation of front-desk clerks had been the same since Rayne had graduated from college. She oversaw the morning shift that stretched from six to two; the afternoon/evening shift was split between Clara Brinkman, a retired preschool teacher, and Barbara Hale, a volunteer librarian. And then there was Teddy.

And yet, it was her name typed in the column under the hours of ten p.m. to six a.m. Not his.

"Oh good, you found the new schedule."

The single-ply paper suddenly felt like a brick in her hand under the scrutiny of her new supervisor. Rayne moved her lips but failed to form any of the questions circling inside her head.

Celeste's manicured hand retrieved the schedule. "I figured the lodge doesn't need both of us working the day shift."

"You . . . you moved me to the night shift? To work with Teddy?"

"No, I let Ted go so you could keep your job. His last shift is tonight." Celeste's blue eyes pierced her through. "Guess I thought you'd be grateful."

Rayne was no stranger to dealing with difficult personalities. She'd worked in customer service since before she was of legal age, yet Celeste seemed to take *difficult* to an extreme. "And Cal approved this?"

"Of course, didn't I tell you Monday would bring change?" Her reply dripped with contempt.

"But what about Teddy? He's worked here forever. You can't just—"

"I'm sorry, was I wrong to assume you wanted to keep your position after the reconfiguration? Cal assured me you were teachable, willing to be mentored. There's only so much budget to be stretched." Celeste angled her head, giving Rayne the once-over.

Rayne bit the insides of her cheeks and reminded herself of her perseverance plan. She wouldn't answer that—wouldn't be a pawn in Celeste's twisted power games. What mattered now was Teddy. She'd call him the second her shift was over, figure out a way to fix this for him. "The overnight shift is mostly to man the desk in case of late-night emergencies. I don't see how working that shift could possibly benefit you or any of the duties I'm responsible for at the lodge."

"Perhaps that's exactly why you weren't consulted. It's over your head." She gave a pity-soaked smile and waved her hand as if to shoo a fly. "Stay close to the desk today."

"Wait—when is this schedule supposed to start?"

Celeste pivoted on her snakeskin heels, her white-blond hair swooshing over her shoulder like a shampoo commercial. "Tomorrow. Well, tomorrow night for you. Rest up."

Rayne pressed her lips together, refusing to speak the rebuttals that formed on her tongue.

Two things came to mind as Celeste sashayed out of the lobby: One, if Rayne was going to survive her cousin's jaunt at the lodge, she'd need to memorize a few more perseverance quotes. And two, she wasn't about to allow Teddy to fall victim to Celeste's heartless business decisions. She'd make it right.

As one hour at the lodge ticked into the next, Rayne's dread of what was to come grew. The thought of working through the night, losing her sunlight, losing her connection to the guests, losing her monthly tea dates with her grandfather's oldest friend, Vilma Albright, was hard to swallow.

Duster in hand, Rayne brushed the feathers over one of the brass frames mounted on the family history wall off the lobby. William Shelby stared back at her through the glass. In his lifetime, he'd held many prestigious titles. Yet she knew if he were here now, he would tell her his most treasured position wasn't serving their state as governor—but rather, serving his family as grandfather. She considered his striking face: his predominant cleft chin, his meticulous mustache, his keen hazel eyes that concealed a plethora of wisdom. She'd spent hours studying this picture after he passed away, wishing he could talk back, wishing he could answer all her questions about her family.

The phone clipped to her waistband rang.

"Shelby Lodge, how may I assist you today?"

"Yes, my name is Miles Higgins and my wife and I have the Hayden Suite booked for Friday and Saturday night."

"Oh yes. I made that reservation myself—that's a beautiful suite."

"Well, unfortunately, we'd like to cancel our stay. Due to the fires."

"Oh?" Rayne set the duster down on the desk and went to the laptop. After logging in, she pulled up the most recent report on the fires and the air quality. "I'm sorry to hear that, Mr. Higgins, and though I understand your concern, I'd like to assure you that the fires are still over seventy-five miles away, and with the river separating us, the threat to the lodge is minimal."

"We've been staying current on the reports, and to be honest, we just don't feel comfortable."

Rayne clicked away from the fire danger site and opened up the reservation calendar.

"Okay, I understand. Let me cancel this weekend out for you." She highlighted the reservation and deleted it. "May I reschedule you for a future date? Possibly for this fall? It's gorgeous at the lodge during the changing of seasons. I could even offer you a ten percent discount if you'd like to book today. We'd love the opportunity to have you and your wife as our guests."

"Absolutely. Thank you. Let me check with my wife on some dates and then call you back?"

"That would be fine. Thank you." Rayne clicked off the call and made a note to call the Higginses back if she didn't hear from them by the end of the week.

"Was that a cancellation?" Celeste stood before her, electronic tablet in hand.

Rayne let out a breath and straightened. "Yes, we've had several over the last couple weeks due to the smoke and proximity of the fires—"

"I didn't hear you mention the cancellation policy."

"Because I didn't."

Celeste pinched the framed red-letter policy on the desk and read it word for word. "All cancellations occurring within thirty days of the reservation between May first and September first are subject to a fifty percent cancellation fee."

"Yes, but the fires—"

"Should I read this to you again? It doesn't say *barring natural causes*. It's June twenty-sixth, Rayne. We are well inside the window to collect on those fees. Is this how you've been managing all our reservations?"

"Collecting fees should be secondary to repeat customers." Rayne pushed the words out, willing her quickening pulse to steady.

"Did you learn that while studying for your MBA—oh wait . . ." The perma pout on Celeste's lips quirked. "You never went to grad school." Her glower intensified. "Collect the fees, Rayne. And yes, consider this a warning."

The last two hours of her shift were much the same as the first six, excluding the thirty-minute noninteractive staff meeting held in the parlor at noon. Apart from that, everywhere Rayne turned, everything she did, was subject to Celeste's commentary and reprimands. And she hadn't been the only one. The hostile takeover had reached every corner of the lodge. While delivering a wine-and-cheese basket to a couple celebrating their thirtieth anniversary, Rayne overheard two of the housekeepers whispering behind a leafy plant—worried about their paychecks.

She wished she could reassure them, wished she could stop the gossip virus spreading through the staff like a flu bug. But how could she save them when she wasn't even sure she could save herself?

She was two steps away from the back door when Cal called her name. "I wanted to make sure you'd heard."

Dare she hope he'd fired the blond dictator so soon? Or maybe he'd changed her schedule back?

"I'll be heading to Boise tomorrow to meet with your father and his team. I need you to be available for Celeste—in case anything comes up. She's a sharp cookie, but I need to know I can count on the two of you while I'm away."

"The two of us?" It was the first time she'd heard the phrase. Did he really picture them working together—as in a partnership?

"You'll be the only Shelbys at the lodge. Don't disappoint me."

Whether from emotional exhaustion or unrestrained insurgence, the words slipped out before she could stop them. "I thought I already had."

Multiple times. In multiple ways.

His brow wrinkled. "There's no need to be childish."

Apparently he hadn't eavesdropped on any of Celeste's one-sided conversations today.

Rayne curled her toes in her shoes and plastered a Shelby-worthy smile on her face. "I'll be available if she has any questions."

He returned a fraction of the phony gesture. "Good. I'll check in by phone over the next few days. I plan to be back before the weekend. If things go well here while I'm away, I'll likely trek back and forth a few times over the next month."

As she pushed outside onto the path leading to her cabin, pressure built inside her lungs, smothering the remains of her positivity. The fresh air did nothing to cure her suffocating doubt, and it did nothing to release the tension coil of questions inside her mind. How long could she live like this? Had the race between her and Celeste even started? Were her tortoise legs even moving?

And worse . . . today was only day one.

There couldn't have been a lonelier realization in all the world.

She tugged open the door to her quaint cabin, seeking comfort—needing comfort. But the comfort she found inside wasn't attached to the familiar scent of lavender, the inconsistent drip of a leaky kitchen faucet, the couch she'd purchased with Gia last summer, or even the bookshelf of hardback classics she'd collected since high school. No, her gaze stilled on the plaid overshirt crumpled on the chair at her dining table.

Levi's shirt.

She'd pretended to ignore the shirt's tempting presence all weekend, the same way she'd pretended that their night together hadn't meant something significant. The same way she'd pretended to forget how Levi Harding had offered her a temporary respite from life's chaos.

She fingered the soft collar, remembering how the bottom corner had flipped up after he'd tossed the beanbag at Apple Adam. She'd wanted to smooth it—to fix it. Only, she hadn't been the one to fix anything that night. Ironically enough, she'd been the one to break things further.

She told herself it was just a walk. Just some time in nature to strategize and plan and maybe even pray. But her pace didn't slow when the grassy terrain shifted from manicured to untamed. She didn't look back, not at the ant-size lodge or the multitude of trees guarding her escape.

She simply kept walking until she reached the fence line of Winslow Farm. And for the second time in four days, Rayne crossed into forbidden territory.

CHAPTER FOURTEEN

"You have got to be kidding me," Levi said around a tart bite of apple.

Yet there was little humor to be found in him as he watched Rayne Shelby through his upturned blinds. Sundress hiked to her knees, she slipped between the fence boards onto his side of the property divide. For a girl who'd made him feel like the equivalent of a roach on a shower-room floor just three nights ago, she had some nerve showing up here again.

Based on their history, her visit was about a decade too soon.

She conducted a traffic check of the farm, her gaze sweeping from left to right, her bottom lip tucked firmly between her teeth. She was right to be hesitant. She'd be even more right to go back home where she belonged.

He took another bite of his sour apple, his eyelid ticking as he chewed the bitter fruit. What more could she possibly want of him? He'd invited her into his world, extended a peace offering, and she'd wadded it up and thrown it back in his face at the first sign of discomfort.

Crazily enough, he regretted not listening to Travis's inebriated advice. But his friend had been right. He shouldn't have gone after Rayne at BlackTail. He should have minded his own business. Let her deal with her family drama on her own.

He strolled into his kitchen and pitched the apple core into the trash can. And then he heard a knock.

He didn't move. Not a single muscle.

She knocked again.

He faced the sound.

On her third knock, he strode for the door and yanked it open. "Does your uncle know you're here?"

Instead of shrinking back the way he'd envisioned, Rayne squared her shoulders. "The last time I checked—which was quite recently—I'm a grown woman. I can make my own decisions."

The sound of his words spoken through her pert lips nearly sprang the lock on his resolve. Yet no matter her plight, he wouldn't give in to her. Not this time. He wasn't interested. He leaned against his splintery doorjamb, hoping to appear unmoved by her presence on his front porch—the exact opposite of the full-throttle awareness that thrummed inside him at her nearness.

"If you came for more honey, I'm afraid you're too late. Sold my last monthly subscription yesterday."

Her gaze softened as a sincere voice caressed his ear. "I'm sorry, Levi."

This was . . . not at all what he'd expected. He blinked her in. "For what?"

"For treating you the way I did the other night. You showed me compassion and kindness and I . . . I was ungrateful and rude and I'm very sorry for how I acted."

If this were a trick, he would sense it. Sniff it out the way he'd done hundreds of times in his youth. But whatever this was, it wasn't a game. At least not one he knew the rules for.

"Come in." He took a half step back to allow her room to pass, but still her shoulder brushed his chest upon entry. "I would have tidied the place up if I'd known the governor's daughter was coming for a visit."

Midway into the living room she stopped, her face crimped in confusion. She turned in a slow circle, eyes wide and scanning. "This . . . this is my cabin."

"Pretty sure I would have noticed a roommate. Especially if that roommate was you."

"No, I mean, this is so similar to the floor plan in my cabin. Like . . ." She ducked into his kitchen, skimmed her fingers along the maple cupboards, and then peeked into his walk-in pantry. "Like an exact replica."

Levi would have shrugged the statement off, but the gesture felt too careless compared with the awestruck expression on her face.

"Wish I could take the credit, but I only worked with the lumber, not the blueprints."

Either she didn't hear him or she didn't care for his explanation. She wandered the short distance to the back of the cabin, taking in every wall and window before placing her palm on his bedroom door. As if zapped by an electric charge, she dropped her hand and backed away. Apparently, according to Rayne Shelby, crossing into his personal space constituted a breach of intimacy.

He folded his arms. "I disarmed the trip wire if that's what you're worried about."

"I . . ." Her voice wavered slightly. "Sorry, I was just curious to see if . . ."

"It looked the same as yours?"

She nodded. "Yeah. I'm sure it's just a coincidence. I mean, there can't be too many ways to arrange a two-bedroom cabin."

He waltzed past her, pushed open the door, and threw on the light. Permission granted, she stepped into his room. Sure, there was a pair of work jeans tossed over a chair and his blankets rumpled on top of his unmade bed, but the same something that stirred in him the other night when she'd asked about his home-hopping childhood stirred in him now as he studied her.

Few people in life were brave enough to search for truth. Fewer still to accept it.

He'd always believed the Shelby family bred cowardice, but that was before he'd spent time with Rayne.

He remained in the doorway watching as she took in the corner bookshelves built into the far wall. When she approached the walk-in closet, Rayne gasped.

She tipped her neck back, scanning up the narrow stairway leading to a small landing at the top of the A-frame attic. "Is that an . . . octagon window up there?"

"Installed it myself." Even as he said it, he knew his answer would hardly satisfy her growing curiosity. Octagon windows weren't standard issue in homes in these parts. Especially not the kind with blue stained-glass panels.

"How?" It was a breath more than a word. Her fingers hovered near her lips. "My grandfather built the cabin I live in now over thirty years ago. And that window . . . that exact window is in my attic too and in the Blue Jay Suite on the fourth floor of the lodge. My old bedroom."

"Ford." The only answer he could give. "The plans were his."

"But why would he have the plans? And why would he even want to replicate the cabin on our property? I don't understand."

He wished he could say, *There are a lot of things you don't understand.* But while he'd love nothing more than to rip the Band-Aid off of her family history and expose eighteen years of festering wounds and secrets, his loyalty had already been pledged. To Ford.

Not all truth was his to share.

Besides, his fascination with Rayne was fleeting. Temporary.

Nothing he could say to her, or she to him, would change the past. Or their allegiances.

"I told you. I just built it." He pushed off the wall. "Now, do you want something to drink, or do you want to explore my dresser drawers too?"

Her startled expression nearly cracked his mouth into a smile.

"How is this not weird to you? We share a custom-built house, Levi."

"So do millions of people who live in suburbs all across America. Not weird. Just economical."

She craned her head to the side, narrowed her eyes. "I know for a fact that the octagon window up there was specially made by a craftsman in Coeur d'Alene. It's not something a person can just pick up at Hardware Depot. My grandfather loved those windows."

Rayne wasn't wrong. Levi had searched high and low to find the craftsman who sold the windows to William Shelby all those years ago. But the surprise on Ford's face when Levi showed up with the hard-won treasure had been worth the extra effort. "If you want to know more you'll have to ask Ford."

"Ask *Ford*? You can't be serious."

"Ya know, disgust isn't the prettiest expression I've ever seen on your face." Levi slipped out of the bedroom and headed toward the kitchen again. She followed.

"Like he'd even be honest with me if I did ask."

Levi gave a trifle laugh and opened the cupboard to remove two glasses. "You really don't know anything about him, do you?"

"I know enough."

At the odd inflection in her tone, he spared her a glance. "Code for you only know what you've been told from the Shelby nursery rhymes."

She released a long exhale, as if to clear all traces of Ford from their conversation, and then shook her head. "Believe it or not, I didn't come here to talk about Ford. Or my family."

He faced her fully. "Then why *did* you come, Rayne?"

"To apologize."

"Which you've done. So why are you still here?" He gripped the edge of the counter. "What is it you want from me?"

When she didn't answer, Levi shook his head and turned back to the sink. He flipped on the faucet. Cool water splashed into his glass, dotting his forearm. "If you're here to explore some late-onset rebellion from your repressed adolescence, you're out of luck. I'm not that guy."

At the press of her hand against his back, his muscles went taut.

"You weren't wrong when you said I could use a friend the other night, and the truth is, I could still use one."

Glass full, he bumped the tap with a closed fist. "You have Gia."

"Yes, and she's my best friend, but she's also . . ."

"A Shelby."

"Yes."

He handed her the glass and searched her eyes. "You want to extend our truce?"

"If your offer hasn't expired."

"So I would be what—an escape? Your personal 'Get Out Of Jail Free' card from that overpriced prison?"

Her cheeks blanched. "I wish I could deny it, but that's a pretty accurate assessment right now. All of your assessments have been pretty accurate." When she brought the rim of her glass to her lips, he tore his gaze away. Unlike the last two times she'd shown up on his property, there was nothing logical about today's visit. She shouldn't be here. Shouldn't be standing in his kitchen asking him for anything, least of all his friendship. And maybe that was exactly why her request appealed to him so much.

An uncomfortable silence rubbed against his conscience.

"You're debating why you should trust me, right?" She paused and scanned his face. "But you do. You do trust me."

"More than I should."

"The same can be said for me when it comes to you."

In Levi's world of bartering and bargains, the earning of trust was the one component that couldn't be faked. But there was no commodity for sale here. No contracts being signed or deals being made. Whatever was happening between them now, it definitely wasn't business.

"If we do this, if we become *friends*"—he emphasized the word—"there'll be some rules."

She bristled, her glass clinking on the counter beside her hip. "I have enough rules to follow at the moment."

"Relax." He ticked a finger in the air. "That's the first one. I don't want to pal around with high-society Rayne. I want the girl who was here the other night with me—laughing, joking, being real. The version of you that doesn't care about disheveled hair or pants made out of a barn sheet."

"Fine."

"And two, I won't keep secrets from Ford. If you want to sneak around your family, that's one thing, but don't ask me to hide you. I won't. That old man means everything to me. Which leads me to three." He moved in close enough to see the flecks of green and gold in her eyes. "You can believe what you want to about him, but I don't take well to disrespect, especially when it comes to the people I love."

"Yet it's okay for you to bad-mouth my family every five minutes?"

"How 'bout we simply agree to disagree. If we can't find other topics to discuss, then maybe this whole thing is as broken as it seems."

"We can," she said with a confidence that took him by surprise. "You're more than Ford's apprentice and I'm more than my last name."

The sudden desire to touch that adorable dimple in her chin had him retreating a step, and then another. Perhaps the scent of her hair—that honeysuckle-lilac combination—was messing with his brain waves. He needed a breather and quite possibly an impulse-control check.

"I need to head into town for a meeting." He'd be able to think clearer on a drive, analyze how this agreement could affect Ford, the farm, their bottom line.

"Alright," she said.

"Alright." Levi repeated the word for no apparent reason and spanned the living room in six steps to open the front door for Rayne.

At his prompting, she stepped onto the porch.

"What are you doing tomorrow afternoon?" he asked.

Her shoulders sagged a few inches. "Sleeping."

"Aren't you a little young to be scheduling nap times?"

"My hours changed at the lodge." She scanned the farm again, searching the orchard before stepping onto the gravel drive. "Starting tomorrow I'll be working the graveyard shift."

Even with her back to him it was easy to deduce the change hadn't been her idea. "Who changed your schedule? The blonde you told me about?"

"The *fake* blonde. And yes." She glanced over her shoulder at him, a weak smile tugging at her lips. "But it will be fine."

"You just broke rule number one."

She turned, eyebrows raised. "What—how?"

"That was a pathetic attempt to save face. You hate the new schedule. Admit it."

Her lips twitched and gave way to a grin that tugged at his gut. "I hate it."

"Better." He winked at her. "Now, hand me your phone."

"I think you mean, *May I please have your phone, Rayne.*"

He tried it her way, drawing out the word *please* until she let out a laugh.

"Better," she mocked. "But I don't have it on me. Not a lot of sundresses have pockets, if you haven't noticed."

Oh, he'd noticed. Every single seam and sunflower. Levi took his phone out of his back pocket, swiped into his contacts, and placed the device into her open palm. She tapped his screen with her fingertip and added her number into the blank space.

"Don't suppose you'd accept a lift home?"

Her you-can't-seriously-be-asking-me-that expression was funnier than he'd imagined. "I'm joking."

He waited for her to slip through the slats of the white fence and disappear into the pasture beyond before climbing into his truck. The instant his engine fired, he slumped against the seat and rubbed at his temples, wondering when the last of his common sense had escaped him.

CHAPTER FIFTEEN

Three days ago Rayne believed she knew everything there was to know about Shelby Lodge. But that was before she'd worked her first graveyard shift.

Shadows slinked along walls, windows reflected like fun-house mirrors, and every single sound that pricked her eardrums seemed to reverberate her paranoia. Not even the most inviting spaces in the daylight were immune to the drop cloth of night. Darkness had transformed her familiar haven into a haunted house.

At a quarter to four, she walked the length of the dim corridor toward the poorly lit lobby. She rubbed her arms, more to keep alert than to keep warm. No wonder Teddy had penned so many mysteries while working these unnerving hours.

The floor creaked underfoot as she neared the front desk. She debated making coffee, but her conclusion remained the same as it'd been since her first shift. Messing with Delia's programmed brew timer wouldn't be worth the effort, not even for a much-needed caffeine boost.

Truth be told, breaking a chronic morning person of their natural sleep cycle was like trying to force a bear to hibernate in summer.

Staying up all night and sleeping away the day proved far more of a challenge than Rayne had expected. She wasn't accustomed to spending so many hours alone. Even during her quietest day shift, there'd always been someone to talk to. Someone to assist. Someone to serve.

Gia had dumped a pile of international art magazines at the front desk yesterday, and Delia had given her a book of Sudoku puzzles to pass the long hours. But not even her nightly routine of reading her favorite nonprofit blog posts had managed to fast-forward the clock. Or transport her into the future. Turned out, there was no secret time machine waiting for her inside any of these mind-numbing activities.

Her phone was tucked in the back pocket of her jeans, but she'd long grown weary of checking the screen for missed calls and texts. Gia's seventy-two-hour rule had proved to be true. She'd always said, *If a man doesn't contact you within three days of asking for your number, he never will.*

Probably for the best. What had she been thinking to go to the farm in broad daylight, or better yet, to ask for Levi's friendship? What was she? In the sixth grade? Besides, what she felt when she was near him wasn't the definition of platonic. It was . . . it was something far more intense. Something she refused to name. Something she'd spent the last three days trying to forget.

The click, click, click of a slow-turning doorknob paired with the moan of brass hinges shot a bolt of fear down her spine.

She'd memorized the code for Cal's gun safe in her teen years—though that knowledge did little to help her in this moment. The study door had remained locked since he'd left town. She gripped the phone receiver on the front desk, her chest suddenly tight. The toe of a brown boot wedged its way into the gap and shoved the lobby door open.

"How's a guy supposed to know what you take in your coffee if you don't answer your texts?"

Levi.

Her face must have asked the question her stunned mind wouldn't form.

"I texted you fifteen minutes ago. No response. Figured you were asleep on the job."

There he stood. In the entryway. Wearing distressed jeans and a snugly fit, faded-gray T-shirt. His golden-tipped hair was slightly disheveled in a lazy, I-just-rolled-out-of-bed kind of way, yet it was the whole of him, his confident presence in her family's lodge, that was nothing short of disorienting. "What are you doing here, Levi?"

"Bringing you coffee." He handed her a red-capped thermos and tapped the door closed with his heel. "Light cream with a hint of sweetness."

She didn't know whether to laugh or to—

"I think the response you're searching for is *thank you, Levi,*" he said.

"Yes, thank you. It's just—"

"You should really keep that door locked through the night."

Wait—was this actually happening right now?

Levi's gaze dragged down her legs, and her toes tingled inside her flats. Yep. She was definitely awake.

"You're wearing jeans," he said.

"Yes?"

The side of his mouth quirked. "I approve."

"I wasn't aware I'd asked for your approval."

"You didn't. I'm just generous like that." He tipped his thermos to his mouth and meandered his way through the lobby and into the parlor. "Looks a bit different in here when you're not hosting a stuffy dinner party."

She trailed after him. "Are you always awake this early?"

"Nope." Offering no further explanation, he took another swig.

"So . . . ?" *Why are you here at four in the morning?*

He plopped onto a hunting-themed wingback chair and crossed an ankle over his knee. "So *what*? I thought we were supposed to be friends now."

Her eyebrows nearly touched her hairline. "I wasn't sure what you thought since you hadn't bothered to call." She regretted the I'm-a-needy-girl statement the instant the words fell off her tongue.

His gaze moved from where she stood fidgeting to the front door. "Are you expecting another visitor—a pack of zombies, maybe?"

"I don't think *pack* is the right terminology for zombies. You're thinking of werewolves. Or maybe it's vampires? I can't be sure. I never really got into the whole fantasy movement, although Gia was obsessed with the Twilight series for a while, so I had to hear all about Team Edward and—"

"Rayne." He dipped his head toward the chair opposite him. "If I promise to be gone before your cook shows up, will you stop rambling and sit down for a minute? Please?"

Face growing hot, she obliged, folding one leg underneath her in the chair.

"Hi," he said through a smooth smile.

One spoken word with ten thousand possible interpretations.

"Hi," she replied.

His triumphant expression vibrated her insides, and she lifted her thermos to cut the tension coiling in her belly. The taste of his coffee triggered a throaty *"Mmm."*

"What did you say was in this again?"

"You like it?"

"Very much. What sweetener did you use?"

"Honey."

"In coffee?" She took another sip as if to dissect the flavor this time. "But there's something else to it—"

"Vanilla bean. One of my vendors swears by it. Turns out she was right. It's pretty good, huh?"

"Good is an understatement." Rayne smiled and sank back a bit more in her seat. "Thank you for thinking of me."

"I'll try a different variation on you next time."

Next time. Two words that wiggled themselves into the space between hope and desire.

He held her gaze. "You up for a field trip after your shift ends? There's another cup of coffee in it for you."

"A field trip? As in somewhere outside of Shelby Falls?"

"I'm not stupid enough to ask you to go somewhere local with me, Rayne."

The bite of his words stung—or maybe it was the truth behind them.

"How long is your uncle away on business?" he asked.

"You don't miss much, do you?"

"Not if I can help it. Plus, we both know you wouldn't have let me through that door if he was in town."

True. She pressed her palms to the warmth of the insulated mug. "He'll be back sometime this weekend."

"So, I'm curious." He hiked an eyebrow. "When the cat's away does the mouse play?"

"That philosophy doesn't work when the cat has replaced himself with a pit bull."

Levi laughed and Rayne tossed a blue-and-red-plaid pillow at his face. "Be quiet. If Celeste hears you, you're on your own."

"Fine by me." He winked. "I seem to have a knack with Shelby women."

Rayne puckered her lips. "I'm going to pretend you didn't say that. Celeste and I may share a last name, but we are nothing alike."

"How is she related to you exactly?" He popped the top of his thermos and drank the last of his coffee.

"She's my second cousin. My grandfather's brother's granddaughter."

Levi's eyes bounced from left to right as if trying to picture the lineage. "Family trees have never been my strong suit. The upside to having no family, I suppose."

He chuckled at his joke, but Rayne didn't see the humor. "You really have no siblings, or cousins, or extended family at all?" Growing up in the system didn't mean he had no relatives; it simply meant there'd been no family of age or means to care for him.

He uncrossed his leg and planted his foot on the floor. "None worth mentioning, no." Such a foreign concept to her. She'd been surrounded by family her entire life, whether she wanted to be or not. "Ford's the only family who matters."

There was a slight challenge in his tone, as if he were baiting her to ask another question—about him or about Ford, she couldn't be sure. She chose to let the subject lie. After all, hadn't she been the one to suggest the two of them could find friendly conversation away from family contentions?

She set her thermos on the elk-head coaster she'd given Ted for Christmas two years ago. "What time were you hoping to leave today?"

"Could you be ready to go by six thirty? I can pick you up by the mailboxes."

"Sure," she said. "But do I get to ask where we're going, or is this another one of your guessing games?"

His lips twitched. "It's a delivery. To the fire camp an hour and a half west of us. You'll want to keep those jeans on. A pair of boots wouldn't hurt either."

A fire camp. She'd seen a picture on one of the forestry websites but had never imagined visiting one in person. "Is it safe for us?"

"Afraid things might get too heated?"

She rolled her eyes at his implication. "That's not what I meant."

"We'll be surrounded by a hundred-plus firemen and their gear. You'll be just fine."

She steered her gaze to the clock above the fireplace mantel. "You should try to catch the sunrise down at the dock since you're up so early."

"Is that your not-so-subtle way of kicking a man to the curb? I still have twenty-seven minutes left."

She bit the insides of her cheeks and managed to avoid a smile while Levi rose from the chair and pointed to the wall of pictures lining the hallway outside the Great Room. "Mind if I take a look?"

Thinking of his impromptu arrival at the lodge this morning, she found the question amusing. "You're not really asking my permission."

"Maybe not, but it seemed an appropriate time to exercise my manners." He winked and raked a hand through his morning hair. Rayne fought back the urge to smooth out a stalk-straight strand in the middle and instead stepped in front of him to point out the first frame on the left. Shelby history was a subject she excelled in.

"That picture was taken in nineteen ten." She motioned to the small boy with an ax over his shoulder. "That was my great-grandfather, Herbert Shelby. He was only thirteen years old when his parents built the first Shelby homestead on this property."

"The first homestead," he repeated. "How many have there been?"

"Five if you count the last remodel of the lodge in nineteen ninety-eight." She tapped the glass with her fingernail. "The very first one burned to the ground in a forest fire. They lost their home, their barn, their cattle, and nearly the life of their only son. My great-great-grandmother Nettie kept journals of the entire account. Her stories of survival are heartbreaking but incredibly inspiring. She credited her strength to her faith in God and the help of settlers nearby. The small community pooled their resources together, food and trade goods, and even shared lodging for a time while they worked to rebuild.

"It took them nearly two years to rebuild all they lost, but when they did, they added a single-room cabin to their lot, and then eventually, a small, two-story lodge with several rooms for boarding. Nettie said she never wanted to be in a position where she couldn't help someone in need." Rayne smiled as she looked at her favorite portrait on the wall. "My grandfather used to tell me it was his grandmother's vision that laid the foundation for our community. When she died from cholera in the thirties, the town changed its name from Pine Falls to Shelby Falls in her honor. Nettie's son, Herbert, went on to become the first mayor of Shelby Falls, and consequently, a generous businessman who poured his life into his town and his resources into Shelby Lodge. The same way my grandfather did many years later." Rayne loved sharing the story of her ancestors. An excellent reminder of her own vision and purpose.

"William Shelby," Levi murmured under his breath as he settled beside her and took in the details of her grandfather's portrait.

"There's no one I miss more." The comment slipped through her lips without reservation. "Sometimes I feel guilty about that."

"Why so?"

"My mother died when I was three—a skiing accident on Silver Mountain. And even though I wish I could have known her, wish I could have grown up with a mother, I had my aunt Nina and Delia and even my grandmother Betty before she got sick with Alzheimer's. In a way, those women reduced the maternal void inside me." She hugged her arms to her chest. "But there was nobody like my grandfather. No one to fill his role in my life after he passed. Our relationship was special. He was special." And he'd made her feel special in a way no one had since.

"He died when you were what? Eight?"

She shot him a surprised glance. "Yes, that's right. How did you—"

"I'm good with math." Levi tapped a finger to the dates etched in the gold plaque below the framed portrait. He worked his way down the picture wall, observing without commentary, until—"Tell me about this one."

His amusement turned her head.

Fifty-plus people smiled at the camera at the backside of the lodge. "Oh, that was a family reunion." And the last summer Rayne, Gia, and

Celeste had been forced to stand side by side. The photo was taken the day after their second cousin had ratted them out at the Falls.

Levi narrowed his eyes as if to zoom in. "Wow . . . How bad is your vision? Those glasses covered half your face."

"Pretty bad. I had prescription contacts by then, but my allergies were acting up that day." And so were her emotions, but she didn't dare bring up that infamous night with Levi again. She glanced back to the picture and cringed at the oversized purple frames. "Thank you, though, for pointing out the obvious."

He leaned in close and bent his mouth to her ear, his warm breath sweeping the curve of her neck. "I never said you weren't adorable."

She sucked in a shallow gasp as he pulled back just enough to study her face. She felt it again then, that glorious and frightening vibration inside her, the one that seemed to beckon him closer without bothering to ask for permission. Neither of them moved for several seconds, and she wondered . . . wondered if his mouth would taste like vanilla-infused honey. Wondered if his kiss would feel the way she'd imagined nine years ago, wrapped in starlight and possibilities.

He cleared his throat and glanced over her shoulder at the clock. "I should probably head out if I'm going to catch that sunrise."

She could only guess at her stupefied expression. "Yeah, you don't want to miss it. It's beautiful."

Her heartbeats stalled under his gaze. "Six thirty by the mailboxes. Don't forget."

"I won't." She couldn't, even if she tried.

CHAPTER SIXTEEN

A yawn escaped him as one minute rolled into the next. He stretched his neck to keep the idling rumble of his truck from becoming a lullaby. Early mornings on the farm were as much a habit as checking the fence lines around the orchard, but even "early" had its limitations. Waking before four o'clock seemed downright ungodly. He could only imagine how Rayne must be feeling right about now.

He glanced again to the right. *Where was she? Had she fallen asleep? Changed her mind?* If she didn't show soon . . .

Just then he saw Rayne zigzag around a rose bush and trot toward his truck. She flicked her wrist in a shy wave, and an unnatural and somewhat unsettling familiarity struck him at the gesture. Her jeans had taken him by surprise this morning, hugging her curves in all the right places, but it was her choice in footwear that had his pulse tripping: wheat-colored work boots, worn and mud-splattered, were absolutely the sexiest thing he'd seen on her yet.

He leaned over the seat and popped her door open.

"Thanks." She climbed inside and tucked her hair behind her ears before twisting to reach for the buckle at her shoulder. "Sorry I'm late.

Nothing like ending my work day with a Celeste lecture." She shut the door and leaned to secure her seat belt, her satiny hair swishing like a curtain over her face. "It's like she waits for the most inconvenient times to tell me everything I'm doing wrong, as if, I don't know, she's worked there for the past two decades and didn't just drop in from the East Coast a week ago. I mean, what makes her believe I have the power to control cancellations? I can't control them anymore than I can control the wildfires and the smoky air."

Rayne's whirlwind energy shook the last of his morning brain cells awake. He worked to process it all—her body language, her tone, her word choice. But the most surprising realization of the moment wasn't in her willingness to spill her frustrations to him. It was his desire to want to fix them for her.

She swung her head to the left and met his eyes for the first time. "What? Why aren't we driving?"

Oh. Right. "I was listening."

"I'm sure I sound petty, but if you met her you'd understand. It's just . . . she makes me feel like I'm going crazy."

"You don't sound petty." Levi put the truck into gear and rolled down the drive to signal onto the old country highway. "But I'll refrain from commenting on the crazy thing." He shot her a sidelong glance.

She pushed at his shoulder. "Don't think I won't jump from a moving vehicle."

"And that would do what exactly? Besides prove my point."

She let out a mix between a chuckle and a sigh and then spotted her thermos from this morning. "Please tell me you delivered on your promise?" She reached for the coffee and he trapped her hand inside his.

"Not so fast."

"Holding out on caffeine from a girl who just pulled an all-nighter is cruel and unusual punishment. I'm really not up for one of your trivia games if that's what you have in mind. I'm fresh out of hidden talents."

"No trivia today." He released her and leaned over her seat, continuing to steer as he flicked open the glove box and pulled out a tattered logging road map. He tossed it on her lap. "I need you to play navigator."

"I should've known you had a secret agenda—inviting me along. What if I told you I have no sense of direction and can't read a map?"

He quirked an eyebrow. "I'd know you were lying."

"Because"—she tilted her head to the side and squinted—"you figured anyone raised on as much wooded land as I was would know how to read a map?"

"That, and your tells haven't gotten any better. But don't fret, we'll work on that."

She unfolded the map and trailed her slender finger along the highway until she located their nearest exit. "Do you have directions for us?"

Levi lifted her thermos and handed it to her. Attached to the shiny red aluminum was a yellow Post-it note. She peeled the memo off, read his hastily written chicken scratch aloud, and uncapped the spout, taking a test sip.

"As good as you remembered?" he asked.

She took a longer sip. "Better, actually." Pursing her lips, she returned her attention to the map and reread his shorthand directions. "I really hope your map proves a better guide than your scribbles."

"There's nothing wrong with my handwriting. Or my directions."

"Except that they're incomplete."

"They are not." Levi snatched the sticky note from her hand. "I talked to Marshal Harris myself."

"You have two logging roads written down—but no road that connects them. They don't meet."

He frowned and reached for the map.

"Nuh-uh." She pulled it away. "This is my job, remember? *Your job* is to drive and trust your navigator. Give me a minute to study this.

You don't have to turn off for another twenty miles or so anyway." She flattened the wrinkly atlas on her lap once more.

Levi rubbed his chin and peered at her every few seconds from the corner of his eye. It was hard to reconcile his early encounters with Rayne—her timidity and hesitation weren't anywhere to be found now. He hadn't been wrong about her exactly, but she had surprised him. On multiple occasions. She'd proved to be one of the most unique people he'd ever known, special in a way he couldn't quite put his finger on.

"Okay, so I think I've figured it out. You wrote one of the forest service numbers down wrong. Inverted it. There wasn't a missing road, it was just that service road two-three-seven was really three-two-seven." She tapped the microscopic lines in triumph. "Bet you're thankful this legally blind companion of yours has her contacts in today."

"Good thing I like more than your eyes, Shelby."

She gave a halfhearted eye roll. "And it's a good thing I like more than your smart mouth."

Whatever had shifted inside of Rayne in the time between his unannounced lodge visit and their field trip to the fire camp, Levi wasn't complaining. She rested her feet on the dash, a slight bend to her knee and a look of comfortable tranquility on her face.

As they drove, she asked him question after question about Second Harvest—the concept behind farm-to-table deliveries, the clientele he marketed to, even his vision for the farm's future. And all the while, she remained rapt with interest.

At her command, he steered left, cutting his speed in half.

Hot dust plumed in clouds around them as he pulled onto a service road through the dense forest. Pine trees enclosed them at every angle, while thick smoke hung overhead, the stench of burning foliage venting through his air conditioner.

"We have one more turn up here in about seven miles," she said, studying the tops of the trees. "So this food pantry you started, tell me about it."

The fact that she'd chosen that particular topic to land on, after all they'd discussed, chipped at something inside his chest. "What do you want to know about it?"

"How it works? How you've set it up? Who you will reach out to?"

"Geesh. Maybe you should've been a reporter."

Her smile appeared gracious enough, yet he wondered at the reticence he noted in her eyes.

"Part of the expansion we've planned, bringing on investors and business partners as well as farmers outside of Shelby Falls, would allow Second Harvest to contribute a higher percentage to the pantry. Right now it's just an oversized closet in our warehouse filled with nonperishables, but our vision is to grow it into a warehouse of its own. To provide quality produce and products for struggling families, or even—"

"Teens in transition," she finished. "Like you were once."

"Yeah." He nodded.

Again with that indecipherable look, and then she said, "I'm jealous." She huffed a short laugh that lacked any trace of humor. "I've always wanted to be a part of something community focused, something that made a difference in people's lives the way you're describing."

"So what's stopping you?"

She tore her gaze away from him and seemed to ponder his question. He figured either she didn't have an answer, or if she did, she didn't want to share it.

Until she spoke.

"I've had a dream for a long time—to share Shelby Lodge with our community, use some of the common areas to serve. Believe it or not, finding a space to organize events is more difficult than you may think. But the lodge, in my opinion, is ideal." She released a slow exhale. "Over the years it's . . . it's become so segregated, so set apart from the rest of Shelby Falls. And as much as I love the lodge, as much as it's home to me, I hate the stigma it holds in our town. I hate how quiet it is, how closed off we are to people who've been nothing but supportive of my family for decades."

Her words settled between them like a fog, and for first time, he had nothing to say. No quip, no joke, no sarcastic comment. He could only think of one person whose heart matched the depth he'd heard in hers. The only person she claimed to despise.

"So who doesn't share your opinion?" he asked.

"What?"

"You said 'in my opinion' when talking about using the common areas of the lodge for community events. Does your family not agree with your ideas?" No big shocker there.

"With the . . . recent reconfiguration of staff it might be a while before my vision comes to fruition." She straightened as if to heave an invisible wall of positivity into place, and perhaps to block any more of his prying questions. "But I'm not giving up. Timing is everything, ya know?"

He simply nodded. He did know.

"Do you ever worry about the sustainability of Second Harvest?"

He laughed at her obvious diversion. "The farm is multifaceted and multifunctional for a reason. We'll never put all our efforts into just one branch of the farm. Wouldn't be smart."

Levi snuck a glance at his passenger, wondering how much she'd be willing to hear, considering Ford's increased level of involvement in this conversation. "Ford's old school. He values hard work more than trends, even if those trends can put a big chunk of money into his bank account. But we seem to have found a good balance, a rhythm that works."

She pondered his statement quietly and then said, "You know a lot about business."

"Guess I'm a quick study."

"No, it's more than that. Celeste has all kinds of fancy business degrees, but you have . . . instinct." He felt her gaze wander over his profile.

"I don't know if it's instinct as much as profiling an opportunity when I see it. In my experience, opportunity doesn't just come knocking."

"You mean, you're not afraid to search for it."

"Most people seek after the shiny Aladdin's lamp version of opportunity, waiting for a bout of good luck to come their way."

"And you don't?"

He eyed her. "Every opportunity worth pursuing comes with a price tag. Either sweat or sacrifice. Sometimes both."

She braced an elbow in the crook between the door and window to support her head.

He pumped the brake gently. "According to these fresh tire tracks, I'm thinking this is my turn here."

She jolted upright. "Yes, sorry. Turn here."

He reached for her shoulder and kneaded his fingers into her tight muscles. "Relax."

"Careful, I'll fall asleep if you don't quit that."

"Maybe that would be best."

"No way. I came to help you."

"You've already helped me. You navigated. Kept me company."

She perked her head up and stared at him through half-squinted eyes. "Don't underestimate me. I'm a hard worker."

He wondered at the edge of defensiveness in her tone. Was that how she'd been made to feel in the past? Underestimated?

"Though I have no doubt that's true," he began, "many of the crews here will be from local dispatchers. If you hope to keep a low profile around me, then you should probably chill out in the truck. It shouldn't take me longer than forty minutes or so to unload these boxes and check in with my contact here. It will give you some time to take a nap."

He took her lack of argument as agreement.

As they came to the start of the clearing, Rayne scooted to the front of her seat, her eyes flickering left to right. "Oh my goodness. It's like a minicity."

They'd reached the edge of the forest, which opened up to a large field housing hundreds of pop-up tents; a semitruck for showers; a dozen or more porta-potties; and several large canopy shelters for dining, food, and supply storage.

"Wow . . . I had no idea." Reverence laced her voice.

Levi rolled along, looking for a place to park when a crew of three sooty, fresh-from-the-wild firemen ambled from their nearby quad cab. Obviously exhausted from their last shift, they seemed to be heading in the direction of the shower semi.

Levi braked to let them cross, paying extra attention to the lopsided gait of the man at the rear. His steps were unsteady at best—clunky, heavy, unbalanced—and then he was on the ground, face-planted in the dust.

Levi jammed the gearshift into park and threw open his door. He called out to the men yards ahead of their fallen crew member.

He skidded to a stop, dropped to his knees, and rolled the unconscious fireman onto his side. Blood streamed from his nose, creating a trail through the dirt and grime. He was young. The guy didn't even look old enough to vote.

"He passed out," Levi told the two firemen who joined him.

The bulkier of the two cursed and chucked his helmet to the ground, the white of his teeth a blinding contrast to the soot mask on his face. His scowl mirrored that of a grizzly bear. "I told the kid this would happen if he wasn't monitoring his water intake. Probably dehydrated. Shed his gear, he'll need fluids over at medical."

"I'll help shoulder him," Levi said, stripping off as much of the bulk from the rookie's beaten body as he could.

"And I'll help carry his gear."

Rayne's voice caused Levi's head to swivel. Sure enough, every object the men tore off the kid, Rayne collected, soot and debris smearing her clothing and skin. She pulled on the suspender straps of the web-gear belt, draped his reflective jacket over her arm, and clutched the helmet and safety goggles to her shirtfront.

"On my count," the grizzly fireman bit out. "One, two, three."

They hoisted the kid up by his armpits and linked their arms around his back, maneuvering him like a wounded solider. The toes of his boots dragged behind him in the dust.

The moment they cleared the medical tent, the field doctor gestured toward an open bed.

"The kid's dehydrated," Grizzly announced to the doctor. "Smacked his face on the dirt when he passed out." He shrugged the coming-to fireman onto a stiff cot. "I swear, I'm not paid enough to babysit a newbie."

"His name?" the doctor asked.

"Pascal. Kevin, I think," the fireman behind Grizzly stated.

"It's likely heat exhaustion as well as dehydration. Third one today," the doctor said as he moved to check Pascal's vitals and start a bag of IV fluids. "We'll get him good as new in no time. Remove his boots for me, please."

"He needs to be sent home to work at his local Dairy Queen if you ask me. These young recruits barely have a license to drive and yet here they are, sent into the wild to fight fires." Grizzly made a halfhearted attempt to unlace the boots.

The second crew member sat at the edge of a nearby cot, his head bowed. "It was brutal out there today—newbie or not. Go clean up and get some shut-eye, Chris. I'll stay with Pascal."

Pascal groaned and stutter-blinked as he came to. "Wh-what happened?"

Grizzly took full advantage of the vulnerable question. "Exactly what I told you would happen if—"

"Hang on a minute." Levi stepped forward, his hand out as if to block a coming blow. "Let's give the kid a chance to recover, okay?"

Grizzly shot Levi a murderous glare before swiping his helmet from Rayne's hands, much too roughly for Levi's liking.

Levi stared after him, his blood heating.

"Sorry about him," the other crew member said. "Just know Chris's short temper has nothing to do with this, or with either of you. His good friend and partner was medevaced to a hospital yesterday after a widowmaker trapped him near the fire line. Everyone's extratemperamental right now. He doesn't mean to be cross; he's just on edge."

Levi nodded and the man stuck out his hand.

"I'm Jason Albright. Thanks for your help, by the way. With Pascal."

"Not a problem."

Rayne joined their exchange, her clothes and arms streaked and soiled.

Jason glanced between the two of them. "Let me clean up and then I'd be happy to show you and your girlfriend around the camp."

Levi waited for Rayne to correct the man's observation.

She never did.

A fact that circled Levi's brain for the next hour.

CHAPTER SEVENTEEN

After a quick shower, Jason gave them a minitour of camp, tossing them each a turkey sandwich to eat as they walked. Rayne hung back, taking in all the sights and sounds she could. Everything here had a purpose. The tents covering the ground, the septic tank, and the trailer filled with generators in the center. All the pallets of extra hose, fire retardant, and equipment caused her imagination to unravel.

When another fire crew unloaded and stripped off their gear, Rayne studied them, their bone-deep fatigue notable even from several yards away. Their filthy bodies were covered in dust and debris from head to toe—except for their eyes, which shone like bright goggle-shaped cut-outs. But as she edged closer, she heard no complaints. Instead, she watched their selflessness toward one another on display. Their camaraderie. Their connectedness. One thing was clear above all: They'd chosen this life. To serve. To protect. To sacrifice for the good of others.

Rayne unloaded boxes of apples, pears, lettuce, tomatoes, and cucumbers alongside Jason and Levi. He'd asked her to take a break, to rest. But she couldn't. Not now, not with her adrenaline charged and firing on all cylinders. The opportunity to burn some of this nervous energy with physical exertion had become a necessity.

She stepped down the ramp, a box of pears wedged between her aching arms. Levi clamped his hands on either side of her cargo and relieved her.

"That's the last one," he said, setting the box on a stack with the other fruit.

She twisted toward the truck and pointed. "Actually there's still a few more at the back—"

He touched her shoulder. "I meant it's the last one for you. You look ready to drop."

"I'm fine."

"Rayne, please. Just . . . stop, okay? One misstep on that ramp and you'll end up like Pascal. You're exhausted." He raked a hand through his sweat-damp hair and then tugged on the back of his neck. "You've helped a lot today, done more than I would have asked if you were one of my employees. Which you're not."

"Then give me something else to do."

"Uh . . ." He exhaled and scrubbed at his jaw. "If you want to grab the clipboard under the driver's seat, you could verify what we've unloaded against the invoice. I'll need to get the delivery signed off before we leave, and I always like to check it myself first."

She crossed her shaky arms behind her back. "I can do it."

"Thank you."

Halfway through her count, Jason joined her inside the tent and downed a full bottle of Gatorade.

"So where you two from?" he asked.

She smiled at him. "Shelby Falls."

He nodded knowingly. "Beautiful area. I'm only a couple hours south. In Lewiston."

"Oh, okay, yes. I've driven through there several times on the way to Boise." She took note of her last box count and let the clipboard rest at her hip. "Have you been out here long, Jason?"

"At this camp—no. Just a few days so far. But there'll be about a hundred more joining us tomorrow."

A hundred more? She couldn't even imagine. Were the fires really that bad? "When do you think the fires will be contained?"

Jason's expression was distressed at best. "If I knew that . . ." He shook his head, picked up another ice-cold beverage, and downed half of it in a single swig. "Don't know what the media is reporting, but these winds have created a bit of a pressure inversion. If something doesn't shift soon, these fires will be headed straight over that ridge." He pointed toward a mountain she knew all too well.

"But there's a town on the other side of that ridge—Bear Canyon." As if saying the name would make the reality he painted any less true.

"I know," he said. "My grandmother lives in Bear Canyon."

So did many of Rayne's acquaintances. Bear Canyon sat just across the river from Shelby Falls.

He scratched the base of his buzzed scalp. "We're doing our best, but if you're the praying type, I'd advise you start praying for rain. Lots of it. Coming off of an unusually mild winter, the drought's killing us out here."

"I am, the praying type, I mean." Or at least she had been. She'd believed in God all her life, had attended private schools and church services, but lately she'd found herself wondering . . . "I'll pray." A promise she would keep. To pray for these men and women. And for rain. The very least she could do.

"God's firefighting is a heck of a lot better than what we can do out here any day of the week. With conditions this dry, we're really only one lightning strike away from disaster." He tossed his empty bottle into the recycle bin. "I gave your boyfriend my contact info. Don't hesitate to call if there's ever something I can do for either of you."

Her brain stumbled over his assumption and landed on a new trail of thought. It shouldn't be Jason offering to do something more for them—not when he and the rest of his crew were the ones sacrificing their time, their health, their very lives to protect people who hadn't a clue what their job, or service, entailed. Before today, she hadn't had a clue either. Not until she took the tour, saw the sooty faces, shouldered a sliver of their daily, burdensome gear.

Whatever problems she thought she had this morning in dealing with Celeste had long disintegrated. No longer would she see the smoke clouds hovering over the lodge as an annoying irritant or even as a loss of potential business clientele during the height of tourist season. Smoke was a symptom of a danger she'd chosen not to see.

Levi wiped his face and neck with a towel as he strode into the tent. He tossed her a water bottle. "You doing okay in here?"

"Jason was giving me an update on the fires."

"Pretty grim, isn't it?" The worry lines on his face confirmed what she'd been told.

"I need to catch some shut-eye before the burnout tonight. We're supporting the hotshot crew." Jason started toward the exit. "It's been good meeting you both."

He was only a few paces outside the tent when Rayne called out to him. She jogged back to the truck, retrieved her wallet, and circled back to hand him her business card. "If you're ever up north and in need of a place to stay, we'd welcome you. Free of charge."

He scrutinized the card before connecting the dots. "You're Rayne Shelby as in the Shelby Lodge?"

Sweat dampened her palms. "Yes, that's right."

"You have tea with my grandmother once a month. Vilma Albright."

A laugh bubbled up her throat. "No way! Vilma's your grandmother? I love her."

"I'm pretty partial to her too."

"Oh my goodness! You're Jason, her firefighter grandson. Wow. She's talked about you a lot—and all your siblings and your oldest sister's triplets."

He laughed. "Yes, the Albrights are quite a topic for conversation."

She hadn't heard him approach, but she didn't miss Levi's hand on the small of her back, or the way he'd leaned ever so slightly into her as Jason continued speaking. Her mind became a whirlwind of half-processed information.

"Idaho's a small world," she said in reply to Jason, hoping he hadn't asked a question in the last thirty seconds.

Jason lifted the card and dipped his chin to her and Levi before turning to leave. "You both take care now."

Levi's gaze heated her face, his hand still searing through the back of her cotton T-shirt.

"How's Celeste gonna feel about you giving away free night stays?"

Just hearing her cousin's name put a sour taste in her mouth. "Celeste might manage my schedule, but she'll never control my conscience." There were limits to how far Rayne would compromise.

Even for the lodge.

Levi inclined his head to his truck. "Come on, it's been a long day in the heat. Let's head out."

CHAPTER EIGHTEEN

Rayne's introspective quiet invited a quiet of his own as he steered through the maze of forest roads. When the tires finally met pavement, Levi's gaze flicked to the left automatically, the way it did every time he drove by the Sandy Shores trailer park off Highway 95. And like always, he tried to ignore the early eighties brown-and-tan Skyline parked kitty-corner to the dumpster. But trailer forty-seven, the one with the duct-taped kitchen window and the slashed screen door, could have doubled as the last home he had lived in with his deadbeat dad.

By the time he was ten, he'd inhabited a dozen round-the-clock pit stops for junkies and dealers. He'd been used to falling asleep to the sound of breaking glass and intoxicated voices. He'd been used to waking up to the smell of smoke and sweat and sin. What he hadn't been used to was all the attention he'd received after his father was carted off to prison.

No matter what his social worker told him, he hadn't wanted a forever family. There was too much liability in a permanent placement. Too much responsibility. Too much accountability.

By sixteen, he'd passed his GED, reading every college textbook he could get his hands on, determined to be better than his old man. But when he'd given the one-finger salute to his last group home, he hadn't planned on spending the next three months in a broken-down Buick.

But he also hadn't planned on Ford Winslow.

He slid another glance at Rayne. Her sleepy gaze remained transfixed on nothing he could easily identify. Perhaps a more selfless person would encourage her to use the last of their time together to rest, especially since her next shift started a mere nine hours from now. Only he couldn't imagine dropping her off at the lodge as if today hadn't meant something.

Because it had.

He just needed a bit more time to figure out what exactly.

"Feel up for a little detour?"

Her attention strayed to the road and then to him. "Sure."

After another couple of miles he pulled off the highway.

"The Falls," she said on a breath.

He parked to the side of the horseshoe turnabout that led to the trail at the base of the Falls. On a clear day, tourists stood behind the guardrailed precipice and tried to capture the panoramic view in a postcard snapshot. But some things couldn't be captured through a lens. Not the things worth living for anyway.

The community of Bear Canyon peeked above them, while a cascade of icy water snaked into the river below. Despite the smoky cloud cover and the low water level of summer, the Falls didn't fail to impress.

He rounded the front of the truck and opened her door.

"I could use a walk." His gaze tracked over her front. "Might also be a good place to wash the soot from your hands and arms. Afraid your shirt's beyond repair, though."

She pulled the fabric of her yellow cotton T-shirt away from her torso. "Oh, it's nothing I'm worried about." She shrugged. "I still look a heck of a lot cleaner than everybody at the fire camp."

True statement.

He led them to the boulder steps, the déjà vu of the moment tampering with his ability to form linear thoughts.

"I've always wondered how it would feel to have a waterfall named after my family." Or an entire town, for that matter.

Rayne navigated the sloped stretch of land, arms extended for balance. He remained only a half step behind her, at the ready to grip her arm, but she maneuvered over the shifting ground without misstep.

"Hmm. I guess I don't really think about it that way. I mean, sure, I've circled the Falls a thousand times on the maps we provide for our guests at the lodge, but . . ." She let her words trail off until she neared the bottom of the descending path. "I don't come out here enough to make that kind of connection, I suppose."

He said nothing as her statement clanged inside him.

His boots tromped over the mixed terrain, part river rocks, part ropey weeds. "Watch your step here."

"Got it." She lunged over a mossy tree stump.

They stood just a few feet out from the shore, the sound of the Falls around the bend beckoning them farther, but the slow-moving current seemed to stall their momentum, as if neither of them could keep going until they'd dealt with what they'd left behind.

Levi retrieved a flat stone near his boot, popped it into his palm, and then offered it to Rayne. The same way he'd done nine years ago. "Ladies first."

She took the chalky stone without argument, flexing her wrist side to side before twisting her hips. Her short flick and release skipped the stone three times on the water's surface.

"Not too shabby, Shelby."

"I'm pretty rusty. I haven't done this for . . . a while."

Levi gave her a sideways glance and picked up another stone for himself. "Three's better than a lot of people can do. What's your magic number?"

"Nine. But that was years ago." Rayne bent at the knees and scooped up a handful of stones, sorting them the way he picked through a handful of jelly beans. Tossing out the greens and whites and keeping the blacks, reds, and oranges.

Levi cocked his shoulder back and chucked the stone into the river. Seven skips.

"Whoa! You're really good!"

"I've had lots of practice."

"Guess I should have asked about your magic number?"

"Seventeen. Just once."

Her eyes widened. "Seventeen? And was anybody besides God a witness to such a phenomenon?"

Levi selected a rock from the pile in her hand. "Not a soul." The way he'd once preferred it. Up until recently anyway.

When they'd depleted her collection of stones, Rayne trailed to the river's edge. Balancing on her haunches, she dipped her arm into the water and washed the ashy streak marks away. Even as he watched her, he knew committing the sight to memory wouldn't be enough. Rayne's allure encompassed more than the beautiful line of her body or the effortless way she moved. Her appeal wasn't limited to the physical. There was so much more—the way she spoke, the way she listened, the way she cared for others without thought or complaint. In a matter of weeks, she'd recaptured his full attention and reclaimed something he'd left at the river nearly a decade ago. Hope.

She stretched her neck side to side and stood upright, tiny droplets of water dripping from the ends of her fingertips. As she moved toward him, a ribbon of hair slipped from behind her ear.

"I came back." The words escaped him without permission and her steps paused.

"I came back here. Every night. For weeks. Hoping you'd be here, like you promised you would."

She said nothing with her mouth, but her eyes couldn't be silenced.

"At first, I convinced myself I'd messed up, like maybe my own jacked-up view of reality had misinterpreted our interaction, made it into something more than it was. But then later, after I'd shed my new-kid status and learned the ways of this town, I had no choice but to accept the truth." He stepped toward her. "The reason you didn't show up wasn't because of who I was, it was because of who I worked for. Where I lived."

Her neck strained on a swallow.

"There's just one thing, though . . ." He was an arm's reach away.

"What?" A wavering question that sounded more uncertain than she looked.

"While you were a stranger to me that night—a nameless girl in a brand-new town—I couldn't have been a stranger to you." The Shelbys made it their business to know the happenings in their town, especially the happenings of their neighbor to the west. "You had to have known who I was that night, Rayne. And yet, you followed me anyway."

"Yes, I knew." Her eyes turned molten, a blaze of liquid fire that heated him through. "I just wanted to believe it didn't matter."

"It doesn't have to matter." He reached for her waist and tugged her against him. A sweet sigh grazed his lips and triggered the end of his patience.

Nine years had been long enough.

He captured her mouth in his.

Their kiss was fueled by instinct and impulse. By ragged breaths and erratic heartbeats. By nine years of forbidden curiosity and guarded freedom.

Desire urged him closer. His hands roved her back and inched up her spine to brace her head. Raven-colored hair spilled through his open fingers, and all at once, the tension in her neck and shoulders released. She was either giving in or giving up. He wasn't sure which, but he could taste the abandon in her kiss.

She explored the ridges of his back and then the planes of his chest as his lips dipped from her mouth to the base of her ear to her throat.

On the end of a soft whimper she tipped her chin back. "This is not what friends do."

"I know," he said between kisses. "But just so we're clear, *friends* was your idea, not mine."

"I know," she whispered. "But we need to—"

He kissed the words away, certain more words could wait another few minutes.

Unfortunately, Rayne wasn't as certain.

She pushed against his chest and he pulled back just enough to see her pink cheeks and wild hair—the exact opposite of what he needed to cool off.

And then he saw the worry on her face.

"We'll never see each other," she said.

"We're seeing each other now, aren't we?"

Amazingly, his astute logic didn't convince her.

"You know this can't work, Levi."

He bracketed her face between his palms. "And *you* know this thing between us is something. It's *been something* since the first time we met."

"Yes. I know."

At the sound of her throaty reply, he cupped a hand behind her neck and kissed her soundly, but again, she stopped him.

Rayne stepped back, her expression pained and panicked. "This is too risky."

"For who?"

"You. Me. Both of us."

"I'm not afraid of your family, Rayne."

Her eyes sharpened on his. "You should be."

Roughly, he swiped a hand down his face. His opinion wouldn't change, but he could accommodate hers. "Then we'll be careful."

"Because that worked out so well for Romeo and Juliet."

"I promise not to drink any secret potions if you don't." But the levity in Levi's tone seemed to go unheard as she rolled a piece of driftwood under her boot before kicking it into the current.

"You think I'm being a coward, but I'm not. I'm being realistic."

"No." He shook his head. "I think you've lived under the control of your family for so long you can't comprehend what freedom feels like."

She averted her gaze to the water, her voice flat and inflexible. "And what do you think Ford will say when you tell him you're sneaking around with a Shelby?"

The pang that struck his chest was not from guilt but from every blatant mistruth she must have been spoon-fed since childhood. He'd been the kid tossed around like yesterday's trash, group home to group home, and yet he felt a sympathy for Rayne he couldn't quantify in words. "Ford's not my warden."

"But he *is* your boss and—"

"And he doesn't dictate who I care about."

As Levi's words punched through the air, Rayne's expression morphed into bewilderment.

"It didn't take me three days to remember to call you, Rayne. It took me three days to figure out if I could do this—if I could be near you and not want to be with you."

"Levi—"

"The answer is no. I can't." He closed the distance between them again. "I want to understand you—this woman who shoots in high heels and dreams about community service projects. I want a chance to see where this goes, to explore what this is between us before you shut it down out of fear."

She faced the water, her shoulder brushing against his bicep. "I don't know how to be with you and be a Shelby."

"I'm not asking you to make that choice."

"Then what are you asking?" The fragility in her voice twisted his gut.

"For you to try, even if it means breaking some rules."

They stood in silence, yet just like the murmur of the water's current, the song of the finches overhead, and the whirl of wind through brittle pine needles, he guessed her mind was far from quiet.

And then, like an unspoken promise, he felt the whisper of her fingers sweep across the back of his hand.

"Okay," she said. "We can try."

He lifted their joined hands and kissed her soft skin. "We'll be careful."

CHAPTER NINETEEN

Being careful, it turned out, looked a lot like an extended version of summer camp. Their schedule was organized into risk-free zones, hours that minimized discovery—Levi slipping into the lodge before dawn, Rayne trekking to the farm after her shift. All in all, sneaking around had proved easier than she'd initially thought, especially since Ford left the premises to work on the land every morning around seven and didn't return until late afternoon, a schedule Levi claimed Ford hadn't changed since he'd come to the farm. And even though Cal returned to the lodge on weekends, his attention had been split between Celeste and the campaign for weeks.

For once, being the unnoticed Shelby had its perks.

She lifted her fist to knock on Levi's door and was met with a familiar set of hands gripping her waist. Levi spun her around, dug his fingers into the curve of her hips, and pressed her back firmly against the wall.

His welcome was as intense as his kiss.

He released her and cocked a wicked grin.

"Um . . . hello to you too," she rasped through a smile.

"Just trying to make up for lost time."

Reeling from the fire still ablaze on her lips, she said, "Um, you were the one who canceled on me this morning, remember?"

"Yes, I do." He raked a hand through shower-damp hair. "One of my packers called in sick late last night, and all three of my drivers are out on deliveries—which means, I still have fifty-two boxes to fill by eleven."

"So that kiss was a bribe?"

Levi wrapped an arm around her waist. "Or an early payment. Depends on how you see the glass."

"Half full, then." She laughed. "Remind me to fill out a W-4 later."

He hooked his hand through hers and led her through his kitchen to the back door.

"Wait." She pulled back. "You want me to help pack boxes in the warehouse?"

"In case you haven't noticed, my living room can barely fit the two of us, much less dozens of boxes. It's fine, Rayne. Nobody's here."

"But what if—"

"I wouldn't ask you to help if there were a risk to you." Something hard flashed in his eyes as he said the words. "You should know me better than that by now."

He was right, she *should* know him better than that by now. They'd shared hours upon hours of predawn conversation, yet the nagging fear of being caught, of losing what they had begun, of risking something too great to name, chipped away at her conscience every time they were together. The feeling had lessened a bit over the last few weeks, dulled only by her ever-present adrenaline. But any sudden change of plan, any uncharted territory, presented them both with a new threat level.

She followed him out the door, across the gravel divide between buildings, and into the warehouse. This wasn't like the barn she'd been in the night they'd shot Apple Adam with the BB gun. No, this place was the sanctuary for Levi's dream.

The smell of freshly harvested vegetables, herbs, and fruit tinged the air, and a giant rectangular sign was draped from the rafters at the back of the open room: "Second Harvest Distribution Center."

He pointed to the opposite wall. "We open those doors during the U-pick harvest in early September, and also for the farmers' market twice a month, and sometimes for the trucks, depending on the load."

His footsteps pattered through the warehouse and echoed back the beat of her palpitating heart.

Fragments of her grandfather's stories shoved into the cramped space of her overactive mind. Tales of a time when her family had owned this very property.

As the original Shelby homestead had expanded in acreage and increased in value, the land had remained under Shelby possession, passed down through multiple generations, sometimes through inheritance and at other times by share buying and community development. Her grandfather had purchased the estate and farmlands outright more than fifty years ago. During his last term as governor, he'd remodeled the lodge, planning to retire with her grandma Betty in Shelby Falls and live out the rest of his life by serving the people he loved most.

Of course, when he died eighteen years ago, Shelby Farm hadn't looked like this at all. There were only a few rows of apple trees back then, not a hundred-acre orchard. There was no Christmas-tree farm or pumpkin patch. No gift shop or holiday market tent. No big red barn bursting at the seams with farm equipment and harvest festival entertainment. And certainly no distribution warehouse.

Light punched through the dimly lit space, and she scrutinized the assembly line of tables. The organized packing stations of fresh produce and vendor commodities she'd smelled upon entry were placed next to the pallets of labeled, ready-to-use boxes. All was evidence of Levi's determination and grit. All contracts and partnerships he'd pursued.

He strode to the center of the concrete floor, an iPad in hand and pride in his eyes. The same pride that shone in every square inch of this building. Of this land.

A fresh realization sent tingles down her spine.

Levi loved his farm the way she loved her lodge.

"What's wrong?" he asked, scrutinizing her the way he did when he sensed her discomfort.

"Nothing." She tried to shake away her melancholy, to hide the burning guilt she'd felt for weeks, yet the feeling lingered.

"If you're worried someone is going to walk in and find you with me, then—"

"I'm not." Truth was, getting caught was only one slice of her worry pie.

He waited, but she couldn't quite reconcile her thoughts enough to speak them aloud. According to Cal's most recent lecture, her presence on this farm would be considered treason. She couldn't afford to add blasphemy to her running list of familial sins. And affirming the farm's efforts and its obvious success, while also encouraging Levi's aspirations for a broader reach and profit margin, was just that: blasphemy.

She brushed her fingers over the wooden produce sign next to a dozen dewy heads of lettuce and cabbage and repeated her internal motto. *Just don't think about it.*

"These signs are beautiful," she said. "Do you use them at the open markets?"

"Yes." His voice flatlined. She knew he hated her attempts at diversion, yet she hoped to prevent a trip on the Ferris wheel of family drama.

"Are they made here locally?"

"Can't get much more local."

He offered a half shrug at her questioning look. "Is that code for *you made them*? Have you been hiding a secret woodworking talent from me, Levi?"

His eyes softened and his lips twitched into a begrudging smile. "Ford may have taught me a few things over the slower winter seasons."

No matter how many times she practiced her face of indifference whenever Levi spoke the man's name, Shelby history prevented complete nonchalance. She couldn't pretend Ford wasn't the swindler who'd cheated her grandfather in the midst of his grief, or that the farm, her family's rightful inheritance, hadn't been jeopardized in the name of his greed. The mental line she'd drawn to separate Levi from his boss, to evade the darts of her guilty conscience, to justify her growing feelings for a man who saw her as more than a name, thinned.

The cool morning air nipped at her bare arms while she made her way to the end of the table, passing Levi, to reach the pile of empty boxes.

Levi had other plans.

He planted his hands on her upper back and pressed his thumbs deep into the hollow under her shoulder blades. Her body sagged against the comforting touch, but still, she pinched her lips together in preparation for his impending questions. Questions that would force her to be truthful. Questions that would put them at odds. Questions that would risk the balance they'd found in keeping their truce and their relationship intact.

"Whatever happened with Teddy the sci-fi writer? You said something about visiting him the other morning before I left."

Levi's purposeful change of subject was met with relief. "You mean Teddy the *mystery* writer. And I visited him yesterday actually."

At Levi's prompting, she lolled her neck forward, her voice coming out in muffled bursts. "I would have told you all about it this morning, but—"

"I bailed on you. Yeah, yeah. You don't have to keep rubbing it in," he teased. "It won't happen again. Scout's honor."

The tight coil in her throat prevented her laugh as his artful fingers carved into the space between her neck and shoulders. Because she knew it *would* happen again—maybe not by choice, but by circumstance. As soon as Cal decided to stick around for longer than a weekend, things between the two of them would slow. They couldn't keep this up forever.

She twisted to face him, taking in his light hair and his sea-glass eyes and his stern jaw. "Were you really a Boy Scout?"

"Sweetheart, I was much closer to earning my place in juvie than earning a Good Samaritan badge in the Boy Scouts. Trust me." He pressed his thumb to the dimple of her chin. "But since you've already dodged the honesty bullet once this morning . . ." He hiked an eyebrow.

"I'll tell you anything you want to know about Teddy. He's quite the character." And a perfect scapegoat. Better to fill their time with nonconfrontational topics than to voice her internal warfare. "But we can definitely talk while we pack. You only have"—she glanced at the clock on her phone—"an hour and fourteen minutes before cutoff. So tell me what to do, Boss."

"I could get used to that." He winked before giving her a rundown on the assembly-line-style system. His interactive spreadsheet kept the process easy and efficient.

She secured a well-fitted cardboard lid to a box stuffed full of vegetables and fresh herbs set to be delivered to a little Greek restaurant two valleys over. She'd eaten there with Gia several times over the last year.

Rayne packed seven boxes in the time it took her to tell Levi all about her visit with Teddy. How she'd checked in on him, brought him a few of Delia's special dishes, and left him with a standing job offer at her aunt Nina's restaurant.

When her monologue finished, the echoey room fell silent.

She swiveled her neck to the right and found him at the table marked "Personal Care." Handmade soaps, lotions, scrubs, and balms all around him.

"You got the man a job because Celeste fired him?"

"It was the right thing to do." She shrugged, but still she could feel his probing gaze. "He's older, and a little different, a writer type, ya know? He's worked at the lodge for so many years and was used to the quiet, the odd hours, the ability to let his mind free flow with story ideas as he managed his nightly tasks."

"You sound like you could write his résumé." Levi's tone was neither approving nor disapproving, so why did she feel the need to defend herself?

"I took his shift, Levi. I know how it feels to be booted out of something you've put years of your life into. Teddy was my grandfather's friend. He didn't deserve to be fired."

Levi hoisted the box to his chest. Tight lipped, he watched her for a few seconds more and then left to add the package to his truck. Hadn't she thought this topic a safe bet? So much for nonconfrontational.

When he entered the warehouse again, he stalked toward her. "I don't understand you."

"What do you mean?"

"I don't get this . . ." He waved a hand down the length of her. "This bleeding heart you have for everyone around you when you won't fight for what you want. You won't fight for yourself."

"I did too fight." She just hadn't won.

"No, you allowed Cal to hand your dream to a woman who sounds like his spitting image."

Rayne shoved a completed box at him, the second-to-last one on her assembly table. "Don't assume you know what happened in that meeting. You weren't there."

"No, I wasn't there," he said. "But I did read your proposal. And I know how many hours, days, months, you spent working on it. And for what?"

Levi had spotted the infamous blue folder tucked inside her laptop bag a few mornings ago. Refusing to take no for an answer, he'd read it straight through while waving away her attempts to minimize and distract. And when he'd finished, when he'd closed that folder, he'd strode to where she stood fidgeting at the desk and bracketed her face in his hands, kissing her so soundly she felt as if her heart might burst through her chest.

"You don't understand how things work in my family."

"No, I don't *care* how things work in your family, Rayne. Big difference. Because they're wrong." He shook his head. "You deserved that promotion. And your dream deserved to be given a chance."

"You sound like Gia." Only Gia knew the limits. Cousin Milton's fate had scared them both.

"If that's true, then I like her a whole lot more than I thought I did."

"You wouldn't say that if you knew how she feels about you."

"Yes, I would." He pointed to her breastbone. "Because out of your entire family, Gia's the only person who seems to care more about you than the Shelby image."

Heat rose to her cheeks as he continued that hard, unwavering stare.

When he spoke again, the edge in his voice had softened, but his eyes had not. "You really don't understand what an asset you are, do you? Rayne, your proposal is brilliant and creative and incredibly selfless. What you could do for this town, for this community . . ." Levi clamped his teeth together. "I wish I could afford to hire someone at Second Harvest with even *half* the heart and vision you have."

Rayne forced her gaze away. "Celeste won't stay in Shelby Falls forever. She's promoting her career, not the lodge. It's not over." *Yet.* "And given the circumstances, I chose the best option I could."

"Really? You think staying in that penitentiary is your *best* option?"

Their gazes collided again, and this time, she wouldn't be the first to look away. "Aren't you being just a tad hypocritical? Look around you, Levi! Would you ever walk away from the farm—for *any* reason?" Just watching the strain of his jaw made her own ache involuntarily. "Well?"

"I don't know." He stormed out of the warehouse carrying an armload of boxes. She followed him out to the back of his open delivery truck, the corded muscle in his forearms flexing.

"You don't know?" How could he not know? *She knew.* Everything about Levi, everything he said and did, declared the farm and all it contained *his* territory. His sweat. His heart. His purpose. They were the same in that regard, cut from the same devout cloth of loyalty. Just divided by a fence line.

She'd seen it for weeks now, yet she'd only just allowed herself to realize the depth of his dedication today.

"I don't know, Rayne." But there, in his words, she heard it again. The slightest inflection. A waver of doubt. A tell. The same one he'd pointed out in her so many times before.

"Why aren't you being honest with me?" It was an uncomfortable observation coming from the perpetually gullible, yet she knew she wasn't wrong. He'd trained her too well in detecting deception. His reading of people had been a major topic of discussion over the past weeks. He'd pointed out her tells time and time again, no matter what the lie. And now she'd done the same to him.

Levi set the next load down and braced his hips. He exhaled for several seconds, and when he lifted his head, the ferocity of his expression crippled her ability to speak.

"For the last nine years I've cared about nothing more than this farm and the man it's attached to. Until you."

She stared at the hollow of his throat, unable to meet his eyes, unable to accept his words.

But despite her shock, he continued. "Whatever I thought I wanted last year or even last month is not the future I've been thinking about lately."

The ring of her phone snapped them from their frozen stare down.

Missed call: `Cal Shelby`

And then an immediate text to follow: `Where are you? Celeste and I have already started the meeting. You're late.`

Two things hit her at once. One, Cal was back and it was only Wednesday. And two, Celeste had scheduled a meeting without bothering to inform Rayne.

Levi clambered down the metal ramp. "What's wrong?"

"I have to go." She tucked her phone into her pocket once more.

"Why?"

"He's back, Levi." There was no breaking it to him gently. Cal was home and their time together would suffer for it. "And I'm late to a meeting."

He wrapped a hand around her bicep before she could turn away. "It's not like he's roaming your lobby at four a.m. Cal being back doesn't have to change anything for us."

Only she believed differently. Cal being back *would* change things. It would change a lot of things.

"We'll see each other when we can, Levi." The best reply she could offer for now, yet one she knew he'd ultimately refute.

She freed herself from his hold and started for the exit.

Levi followed her out, matching her hurried stride up the driveway and into the trees beyond. "And when will that be?"

Hadn't she known he wouldn't accept her vague response? "I'm not sure yet. I need to figure some things out first."

"Fine. Then let's figure them out together. You're not in this alone."

Wasn't she, though? The question seemed to materialize out of nowhere, as if her doubt had been crouched in hiding, waiting for just the right moment to pounce. Yet the truth was . . . if the two of them were exposed, it would be *her* dreams at stake, *her* future at risk.

"Rayne."

At the sound of his voice, the spiraling disquiet in her mind morphed into the crunching of footsteps at her side. Levi was still trailing after her. Onto Shelby land. And by the look on his face, he was prepared to march straight into the lodge if she didn't stop him first.

With no time to spare, she spun toward him and pressed a quick kiss to the edge of his jaw. "I'll call you the second I can. I promise."

For now, it was the only promise she knew she could keep.

CHAPTER TWENTY

Levi replayed Rayne's hurried departure a hundred times over in the next few days, their interactions limited to phone calls and predawn text messaging. Cal's return and endless demands on Rayne had been met with ample frustration on his part—all of which could be summed up by a lack of face time with the only Shelby he cared about.

He kicked a pile of loose gravel and trudged up his front porch steps after a long day networking with his new vendors. His mind was everywhere but on the invoices and paperwork awaiting him inside.

A half step into his house, he stopped short.

Hauser's ears perked up, his eyes playing a game of tennis between Levi and his master.

The smack of the screen door against the frame elicited no reaction from either of the visitors in his home.

"Sit, Hauser. Stay." Ford laid a weathered hand on the shaggy dog's head, his bony shoulders bowed as if an invisible fifty-pound weight had been strapped to his back.

Levi tossed his wallet and phone on the coffee table. "Didn't you have a meeting in town with the Farmers Society this afternoon?"

"It ended early."

Those meetings never ended early. "How come?"

Ford shifted a shiny object in his hands, continuing on as if Levi hadn't asked the question at all. "Out of respect, I've tried not to notice the odd hours you've kept over the last week, your high spirits, your frequent phone calls. I've wanted to honor your privacy, refrain from asking too many questions."

"I've been seeing someone."

"I figured as much," Ford said, his tone flat.

"And I figured you'd be happier about it. Weren't you the one lecturing me last month about broadening my interests?"

Ford lifted his chin, steadied his no-nonsense gaze. "Les Jacobs told me he saw you with a woman a few days ago."

"Where?"

Ford crinkled his brow. "Shouldn't you be asking me *who*—*who* he claims to have seen you with?"

"No, I'm asking you where because we've been too careful to be seen within city limits together."

Ford winced and dropped his head. He blew out a weary breath. "Tell me it's not her, Levi. Tell me I didn't defend you to a room full of trusted friends—"

Levi shifted his stance and leveled his gaze. He would own this. He probably should have owned it sooner. "I'm seeing Rayne Shelby."

The air turned stale and the last of Ford's optimism drained from his face.

"Where did Jacobs see us?"

"On a delivery upriver. Said he saw her waiting in your truck in a parking lot."

Levi cursed under his breath. He'd taken her on a quick drop to one of Tom Hutchinson's franchises last week, two towns over.

"I care for her, Ford. A lot."

Ford's gaze sharpened. "And I care for you."

"Nothing is going to happen to me."

"Consequences aren't always physical. Not the ones that hurt the most anyway."

"You think she'll break my heart?"

"I think she's tied to a family who doesn't care nearly as much about heart as they do about image."

Ford's life was testament enough to such a truth.

"You don't know her."

"You're right." The break in Ford's voice startled the resting dog at his feet. "I was not given the chance to know her." He stopped toying with the shiny band in his palm and set it on the coffee table. William Shelby's ring. One of the few earthly possessions Ford treasured. William had given it to him just a few weeks before he died.

Levi cleared his throat. "I'm sorry, that's not what I meant."

"Is she as committed to you as you seem to be to her?"

Levi opened his mouth, but before he could speak, the memory of their last day together in the warehouse crammed into his thoughts. "She's trying to figure things out right now."

Ford settled into the sofa cushion while Hauser stretched, yawned, and wagged his tail side to side. "I've heard there's a lot of changes going on over there. Not only with her father's reelection announcement, but also with the management of the lodge staff."

"What are you getting at?"

"It's a lot of pressure for her, for anyone, but especially for a young woman who's been groomed to live up to the Shelby name. A moment of insurgence is a natural response to overbearing expectations."

"You think our relationship is an act of rebellion? She's twenty-six, not sixteen." But hadn't Levi questioned that himself a time or two? "It's not."

"Then why the need to keep your relationship a secret? Why the need to hide? To sneak around?"

Because she never would have agreed to see me if not.

Levi ground his back molars. He despised the idea of being anybody's dirty secret, yet there wasn't a bone in his body willing to consider the alternative. Not if it meant losing her. "We're taking it one day at a time."

"And then what? You think one day she'll wake up and be willing to let it all go because of you? Her family name, her reputation, her future inheritance?"

"It's possible."

"No it's not, Levi. Cal's hatred for me—for this farm—isn't something to be messed with. She knows that as well as I do." His apologetic tone ate at Levi's resolve. "You need to end things with her. Before he finds out."

"No." He respected Ford, loved him like the father he never had. But he wouldn't—couldn't—walk away from Rayne. He was in too deep to go back to how things were before. Too deep to be satisfied catching a glimpse of her through the tree line. "I won't let their lies take her from me the way they took her from you."

"Son"—a stabbing sadness crept into Ford's eyes—"their lies are the only thing she knows. The only security she trusts."

Levi fisted his hands at his side. "She trusts me."

"Not enough."

Levi ducked under the eaves of the warehouse and answered his phone on the first ring. He needed a break from the afternoon sun. "The old tyrant let you off on time today? I hope you're headed to get some sleep."

"Not exactly." Her words stretched on a yawn. "I was supposed to have lunch with Gia at the gallery today, but she's in one of her creative zones and asked to postpone so she could work in her studio. So now I'm here in an empty store."

He picked up on her subtle suggestion immediately. “I can be there in twenty.” No further prompting needed. He pushed off the wall and started for his house. A quick shower would do him good.

“Really? I wasn’t sure you’d be free.”

“If we left seeing each other in the hands of convenience, we’d never see each other at all.” Which wasn’t too far off from their current reality. “Shoot me a text with what you like on your sandwich and I’ll grab us some lunch. Unless you want to take a gamble and let me guess.”

“Your guesses are usually pretty accurate.”

The screen door slammed at his back and he pulled his sweat-drenched shirt over his head. “Tends to be the case when I’m invested in the subject.” He unlaced his boots and kicked them off. They thudded to the floor one at a time.

“I miss you.” Her quiet admission made his throat ache.

He turned the shower on and slumped against the bathroom cabinet. “I’ve offered to storm the Shelby castle a thousand times, slay the dragon master, and collect my prize. You just haven’t taken me up on it yet.” He wasn’t sure what bothered him more, Rayne’s mounting excuses, or the recycled conversation he’d had with Ford days ago.

“There are far too many dragons for you to slay.”

“You underestimate me.”

“Often.”

He smiled and reached past the shower curtain to adjust the water temperature. “Gotta run, princess. See ya in a few.”

CHAPTER TWENTY-ONE

The lodge wasn't the only place affected by the low-lying smoke. Gia's gallery hadn't tempted a single customer to push through the door since Rayne arrived two hours ago. An anomaly for a town like theirs. In the heart of the tourist district, the charming shop doors along Sherman Boulevard usually remained propped open during the summer months. Not so this year. The change in air quality had affected more than just sightseeing and tourism. Cotton-dry throats and red, itchy eyes had become the norm, so much so that Rayne had finally conceded to trade her contacts in for her glasses. Much to her chagrin.

The door swung open and the clay frog that doubled as a welcome committee croaked loudly.

"Nice frog," Levi offered.

"I hear they're all the rage."

"Then I must be in the wrong social circles." Levi's gaze slid from the ugly statue near his feet up to her eyes. The impact left her heart thumping wildly.

Her stomach dipped at the sight of him. Snug-fitting, olive-green T-shirt, dark-wash jeans, finger-combed hair. She wanted to rush him, loop her arms around his neck, kiss his mouth until oxygen became an afterthought. And if the way he was staring at her was any indication of what was going on behind his masked expression, she wasn't alone in her desire.

"You should have warned me," he said.

"About the frog?"

"About your glasses." A sloped grin, lazy and enigmatic, lifted the corner of his mouth.

She touched the frames.

"You like them?"

"That's not the word I'd use."

The backfire of a passing truck reminded her of where they stood. Next to the large storefront window, completely exposed to onlookers.

She hitched her thumb toward the storage-closet-office in the back. "We should probably—" His face shadowed and she edited her word choice. "We can eat back in the office. At the desk." Out of sight.

With the slightest dip of his chin, he acknowledged her request but said nothing as he zigzagged his way through the maze of art.

He set the paper lunch sack on Gia's cluttered desktop while Rayne secured the door, propping it open several inches. At least she could rely on the toady croak to alert her if a customer wandered inside.

She touched a hand to his back, the heat from his body seeping into her own. "Thanks for bringing lunch."

He unwrapped the butcher paper from the first sandwich and then twisted his head, a humorless laugh escaping him. "Guess there's a first time for everything."

She scrunched her face and scooted a chair out from the corner for him. "We had lunch at your house last week, remember? I brought Delia's Caesar salad over."

"I meant being shuffled into a back office like an employee who just got his hand caught in a till. *That's* a first."

"A tad dramatic, perhaps," she teased, pulling the phone from her back pocket and placing it on the desk. Just in case Gia called early.

He said nothing more and handed her the turkey, Swiss, and chutney on sourdough. Though her appetite had waned, she took a substantial bite, hoping the gesture might encourage him to do the same. Delia always said an empty belly was the root of all grumpiness.

"This is really good," she mumbled, wiping the crumbs from her lips. "See? I knew you could be trusted in sandwich pickings."

He lifted his own sandwich to take a bite, bacon sticking out from the folds of his bread. He eyed her as he chewed.

Fine. He could eat. She would talk. She excelled at warming frosty moods. Lord knew she'd been given plenty of experience appeasing disgruntled people—both in her chosen career and in her personal life. She knew how to turn on the sunshine. Pinching a piece of shredded lettuce between her fingers, she flicked it onto the crinkly wrap. "So, you know how I told you about the new campaign ads?"

He grunted a reply.

"Cal and Celeste are on this new kick to use the lodge for all the campaign promos, hoping the lodge's family-owned angle will appeal to a wider demographic. A producer sent over a list of 'family-friendly decor' to add to some of the rooms along with his lighting preferences. You wouldn't believe how many kinds of lamps I had to search through yesterday before Cal—"

"I really don't think I can discuss your uncle today. At least, not without punching my fist through a wall."

"Well, don't hold yourself back on my account."

"You have no clue how much I've held back."

Okay, then.

If bacon couldn't cure his funk, she doubted there was much hope left to salvage their impromptu lunch date. He tossed his sandwich down, scrubbed his napkin across his mouth, and then balled it into his fist. "I hate this."

Dread dropped like an anvil in her stomach. "You know I wish things could be different."

"Do I?" He kicked back from the desk and stood, yanking on his neck as if he could loosen the tension in the room like a pulled muscle. "*Do* I know that?"

"You should. I tell you all the time."

He let out a huffy laugh. "No, you tell me all the reasons why we can't work. Why we can't have a future. That's not exactly the same thing."

She swallowed the lump of bread lodged in her throat and discarded the second half of her sandwich. "I don't want to fight with you."

"And I don't want to be shoved into a closet like some soiled piece of laundry."

Guilt pooled in her chest. That was exactly what she'd done to him. "Levi, I'm sor—"

"No." An apology laced his voice and shone in his eyes. "I'm . . . I'm the one who's sorry." He reached for her face. "I'm not angry at you. I'm angry at this—at everything I can't control." He smoothed his thumb across her cheekbone. "I don't know how to fix this, but there's not a moment that goes by that I'm not trying to solve it. At least in my head."

Her heartbeat thudded as his gaze pleaded for something she couldn't give him. His jade-flecked eyes dipped to her mouth and her brain slowed. Everything slowed.

"I feel the same way," she said.

"I miss you, Rayne."

She didn't respond to him with words; instead, she drew him closer and brushed a kiss on his mouth, tasting the heat from the sprinkle of pepper attached to his bottom lip.

She'd missed him too. More than she'd allowed herself to realize.

The desk vibrated against her outer thigh. A phone was ringing. *Her* phone was ringing.

Levi looked from the caller ID and then to her. He spun the phone toward her, the screen bold and bright.

Jason Albright.

"Why's he calling?" she wondered out loud.

His eyes mirrored her question.

She picked it up, swiped a finger over the screen, and mouthed, *Don't leave yet.*

Levi wasn't going anywhere.

At the fire camp, Jason had seemed like a respectable enough guy, especially after he'd assumed Rayne and Levi were an item. And now, well, now Levi planned on sticking around to make sure his first impression of the fireman had been correct.

The healthy glow in Rayne's cheeks dimmed as her polite exchange gave way to short, tight-lipped replies. She cut a glance to the clock on Gia's unkempt desk and nodded. "Yes. Of course. However I can help. I'll stay in touch. Thank you for calling." She tapped the screen and faced him fully.

The fireman's call hadn't been social in nature—a fact that rivaled two opposite emotions. "What's going on, Rayne?"

"Bear Canyon is under a Level 2 evacuation. The fires are headed for the ridge." The strain behind her voice could have caused a stress fracture.

Levi's spine straightened. "They're evacuating the whole town?"

"Everyone north of the river has been put on standby, including Jason's grandmother. He doesn't want Vilma leaving in the middle of the night when they blow the official whistle. He said most people will probably leave voluntarily this afternoon."

"And Vilma is the lady you have tea with every month?"

"Yes. Her husband was a good friend of my grandfather's. The lodge can give her a safe place to stay until her home's been cleared. Her local family members all have children and pets to look after so—"

"He asked you to take her in."

"Yes."

"Okay," he said. "Let's do it."

"You want to help?"

He tried not to let the surprise in her voice irritate him, but did she honestly think he'd be content to pat her on the back and wish her well in her endeavor to rescue a grandma during a fire evacuation? He bit back a sarcastic reply and tempered his thoughts as best he could. "She'll likely have more stuff than your little sedan can hold. I'll follow you in the truck."

"But that means you'll be away from the farm most of the day."

He laced his fingers through hers. "It also means I'll be with you." An easy choice no matter what the circumstance.

CHAPTER TWENTY-TWO

Rayne marveled at Vilma Albright's ability to prioritize in a crisis. Not only had her suitcases been packed and ready to go when they'd arrived at her home, but so had her cat's belongings. Penelope's monogrammed cat carrier and matching satchel—both bedazzled with pink rhinestones—had been placed near the front door. She was, without a doubt, the most self-sufficient eighty-six-year-old woman Rayne had ever known.

Levi had lucked out. He'd won the job of hosting the white Persian cat and all her personalized gear in the cab of his truck while Rayne drove Vilma to the lodge.

Rayne obeyed the sequence of detour signs through Bear Canyon, flicking her turn signal in the direction of every blinking arrow. Meanwhile, her sweet passenger hadn't stopped talking. There was a tinny quality to Vilma's speech, a rushed cadence so different from their easy conversations over hot tea in china cups. Mrs. Albright seemed to be funneling her anxiety into ancient gossip and her jumpy nerves into deflective chatter that had little bearing on her present reality. But if it calmed her, if it took her mind off the circumstances around them, then Rayne would accommodate her friend. She would be a listening ear.

Rayne peeked in her rearview mirror, assured by the sight of Levi's truck trailing behind her car. Vilma must have seen the not-so-subtle glance.

"Are you positive that young man will be okay with my kitty?"

"More than positive. Penelope will be just fine. My friend"—whom she'd intentionally failed to name—"will keep her well cared for while I work out the kinks of our no-pets policy with Cal. It's better to have those kinds of conversations in person."

Vilma rubbed her palms down her polyester pant legs. "Callan's always been a bit too temperamental, if you ask me." She let out a soft chuckle. "Your grandfather once threatened to send him off to boarding school if he didn't simmer down."

"Oh?" It was hard for Rayne to picture Cal as anything but a refined entrepreneur. "I can't imagine Cal as a teenager."

Vilma turned in her seat, her attention fully engaged. "It wasn't just the teen years that put those two at odds. All children are born headstrong, but Cal's stubbornness never did lessen with age. Those two had more fallings-out than my daytime soaps."

Rayne wrestled with the image Vilma painted of Cal and her grandfather's relationship. She certainly hadn't sensed the tension as a child. Then again, the death of her grandfather had smudged some of her early memories—the same way the side of a hand can smear a charcoal drawing before it's finished. The overall impression might remain intact, but the details became hazy, dull, absorbed with the passage of time.

"What were their quarrels over?"

"What most quarrels are over, I suppose. Different views on life. William decided he wanted to pour his life into the lodge and community, and Cal wanted his father to continue in politics."

Rayne furrowed her brows. She'd known Cal once had a profitable business in Southern California before taking over the lodge and managing her father's political campaigns, but she'd always envisioned the three Shelby men—her grandfather, Cal, and her father—as a solid unit.

"Regret is a heavy burden to shoulder—even for people who appear to have skin made of steel."

Rayne pumped the brake hard. A steady stream of red taillights illuminated the bridge up ahead. Even a small town like Bear Canyon could produce a traffic jam when half its residents were given evacuation orders.

Vilma sighed wearily. "Jason said it could be days until we're allowed back, maybe longer, depending on the shifts in the wind."

Rayne reached over the center console and took Vilma's hand in her own. The woman's translucent skin was papery, her veins a map of marbled blue ridges. And cold. Too cold for a hot summer day. "We'll get you everything you need, Vilma."

She squeezed Rayne's hand in reply. "I just wish everybody had such a nice place to stay and wait this out. Jason said the Red Cross was setting up accommodations at Shelby High, and there's one chain hotel that's agreed to a subsidized rate, but even still, I doubt there's enough lodging to match the need. And in such a trying time too." Vilma pressed the pads of her fingertips to the window as they passed the exit for Bear Canyon. "The fire threat seems to elevate every summer, but this year . . . this year it's just hit so much closer to home. I think I'm still in a bit of shock."

"I'm sorry." Rayne glanced at Vilma, whose eyes shimmered with tears, and blinked back the emotion filling her own. "I know how much your home means to you."

"My Howie built it—right alongside your grandfather. And Ford Winslow."

"Ford?" Rayne nearly choked on the name.

"Yes. William was the one who referred Ford to Howie's construction crew—I guess that would have been forty some odd years ago now. Such a hard worker, that man. Howie was a bit miffed when William offered Ford a side job at the lodge, though." A faint smile touched her lips. "Ford never came back to work for Howie after that summer. He stayed at the lodge, working for your grandfather in some capacity or another up until the day William died. I expected Ford to step into the management position at the lodge, but, of course, Cal showed up instead. It's a pity to see what's happened since."

A pity was certainly one way to put it.

Rayne refrained from further comment. Vilma's version of the Shelby-Winslow tale had left out a few crucial plot points. The rumor mill in Shelby Falls had circulated many variations of the story over the years, but even still, the facts remained the facts: Ford had stolen from the hand that fed him.

That didn't make him devoted. It made him an opportunist.

Rayne's eyes flicked back to her rearview mirror once again.

Vilma continued to skip through conversation topics like rocks on placid water until Rayne settled her into a lower-level room at the lodge, complete with a gas fireplace, walk-in closet, garden tub, and complimentary glass of wine and cheese platter.

"This seems like too much." Her voice and hands shook as she glanced about the river-view suite. "There's just one of me—well, two, if Penelope gets clearance to stay."

Rayne wrapped her dear older friend in a hug. "I'll talk to my uncle about Penelope as soon as I can. I know you're worried, but we're standing with you and the entire town of Bear Canyon."

"Thank you, sweetie. Oh, and Rayne? Before you go, would you mind turning on the news for me? I can never figure out those fancy remotes, and Jason said there should be coverage on Rockvale and Bear Canyon."

"Certainly." Rayne clicked on the TV and punched in the numbers for their local news channel.

Tina Tucker, the evening anchor for Channel 9, stood near a tent of supplies, interviewing a fire marshal in front of a gas station in Bear Canyon.

"Good evening, I'm here with Fire Marshal Jack Harris in Bear Canyon, Idaho—which just a few hours ago was declared to be in a state of emergency by Governor Shelby. Marshal Harris, can you please tell us again how many residents could be affected if the wind doesn't let up?" Tina asked, swinging her microphone toward his mouth.

Annoyance edged his weathered features. The marshal either had zero interest in her canned questions or had little regard for news media in general. Perhaps both assessments were true. "About ninety homes up on the ridge and nearly twice that down on the prairie. Given what happened in Rockvale, we don't want to take any unnecessary risks."

Tina's eyes rounded into perfectly lined orbs—as if she hadn't heard all the fire statistics beforehand. "That's an estimated three hundred families who will be displaced because of this growing threat."

"We're doing everything we can, ma'am." He forced the words through tight lips and then glanced over his shoulder.

"And how many fires have been reported thus far? How many acres of national forest have burned at this point?"

"Fifteen fires of varying degrees and nearly a hundred thousand acres have burned. We're currently at twenty percent containment with four hundred and ninety-five firefighters working on the ground, but the high winds have compromised our fire lines."

Rayne slumped next to Vilma onto a tower of bed pillows, captivated by the red emergency banner scrolling along the bottom of the screen.

Vilma covered her mouth with a shaky hand. "Oh my."

Rayne could only stare as the marshal detailed evacuation procedures and rattled off the 800 numbers for local Red Cross shelters. The live camera cut away from the interview and rolled footage of the raging fire that had swept through Rockvale the day before. She watched the destructive monster of heat and flames devour everything in its path. Charred remnants of homes and properties just north of Bear Canyon flickered across the screen like casualties of war.

Vilma jerked forward on the mattress and jabbed her finger at the TV. "That's Roy and Marsha Benton's ranch! Oh sweet Lord, no."

Through a sequence of time-lapsed images, the footage revealed that fires had reduced the once-picturesque equestrian property to nothing more than a pile of blackened lumber and ashy remains.

"I was just there a month ago, watching my great-granddaughter ride her horse." Vilma's tears streamed in earnest.

Rayne clutched at the base of her throat, wishing there were something more she could do besides sit and watch the devastation unfold. If there was a worse feeling in the world than helplessness, she didn't know it. The Bentons were simply one family of many who were facing this horrible reality of loss.

She touched Vilma's back in hopes her presence brought more comfort than her silence and kept her eyes on the television. After the footage recycled for the third time, Rayne finally stood, her sleep-deprived body feeling overwrought with several emotions all at once, none she could define with words.

"I should go ask about Penelope for you."

"Thank you," Vilma rasped, her eyes still plastered to the news. "I need to make some phone calls."

Rayne pulled the door so it latched behind her and started down the long, empty hallway. The time read a quarter after five, but knowing Cal, he would still be in his study.

With each step, the graphic news images from moments before flooded her mind. What would tomorrow bring—or the day after that? What happened when fires broke through fire lines? How many more people were about to watch their homes and dreams burn?

As she rounded the corner into the lobby, her gaze sideswiped the wall of photographs that had documented more just than her family's history, but their legacy as well. The same legacy that had inspired her to stay in this town when the majority of her family had stretched their influential wings and flown from the nest.

She'd memorized the pictures and stories of her ancestors by her tenth birthday, but tonight, one picture stood out from the rest.

Her footsteps halted.

An invisible weight rammed the center of her chest as her focus narrowed on her great-great-grandmother's weathered portrait. Rayne had always felt a special connection to Nettie Shelby through her grandfather's stories. But there was something else tonight, something urgent that tugged at Rayne's heart. Something that pleaded for her to understand.

The promise. Nettie's promise to her community after she'd lost so much, her drive and dedication to serve others, her open-door commitment to help those in need . . . all of it came rushing back.

The helplessness Rayne had felt moments ago in Vilma's room was replaced by an idea that captured her mind with overwhelming possibility and purpose: *What if Shelby Lodge became an evacuation shelter for their community?*

Rayne had waited her entire life for her passion to align with her position . . . and tonight it finally had.

She bypassed Cal's study and headed for her laptop. She'd spend her shift researching so that, come tomorrow morning, she'd be ready to face the firing squad.

—

On a surge of adrenaline and courage, she rapped on Cal's study door, her research in hand. Unfortunately, when she entered, Cal wasn't alone. But not even Celeste's presence could dim her elated spirit.

"Rayne? I thought you'd gone home. Your shift ended"—Cal consulted his designer watch—"thirty-five minutes ago."

Celeste slid her gaze from her digital spreadsheet to Rayne, taking in her outfit the way one sorted through a recycling bin. "Maybe she's here to submit her notice."

Wouldn't she be so lucky.

"No, I'm here to show you this." Rayne pulled Channel 9's website up on her phone and turned the screen to face Cal. "As of this morning, over three hundred homes in Bear Canyon have been placed under evacuation orders with more expected to evacuate in the next few hours. The crews have been working through the night, but conditions aren't improving. I brought Vilma Albright to the lodge yesterday afternoon so she'd have a safe place to stay until her home's been cleared."

Cal's reading glasses balanced on the tip of his nose as he studied her phone screen. "I take it you didn't come to ask for my permission?"

"No."

Cal frowned with his entire being, and Rayne shifted on antsy feet. "There are hundreds of people displaced from their homes right across the river from us, preparing for what could be the most devastating loss they've ever faced and—"

"And you're gonna join the fire crews?" Her cousin's snotty response missed her intended target by miles.

"I think Shelby Lodge should become an evacuation shelter."

Silence reverberated off the walls as her uncle and cousin gaped at her like she was some sort of circus-sideshow act. When they finally spoke, their replies toppled over one other.

"Absolutely not," Celeste said.

"Not possible," Cal added.

But it *was* possible, and she'd prove it.

She held up the printed documents clutched in her hand. "According to FEMA's disaster relief policy, it's not only possible, but running a shelter out of our lodge would be subsidized by the government. The lodge would be reimbursed not only for basic overhead costs like utilities and overtime wages for our employees but also for whatever supplies we purchase for the evacuees."

She laid the stapled packet in front of him. "Cots, food, linens, personal-care kits, extra towels, all of it would be covered."

"This is insane," Celeste interjected. "If you haven't noticed, we've been trying to cut back on the budget this summer, not add to it by housing freeloaders."

Rayne flipped to the third page of her research packet and pointed out a highlighted clause. "FEMA will reimburse the fair market value of any room used for the purpose of disaster relief. Our lodge is sitting at thirty percent occupancy as of right now, which means that seventy percent of our rooms are vacant and available for families who desperately need a safe place to wait out the fires."

Cal leaned back in his chair and rubbed his chin. "And what about the extra hassle for our staff or the wear and tear on our property? I doubt FEMA has a clause that covers that."

"If you'll allow me to work the day shift again, I will personally oversee everything having to do with the shelter."

Cal's face remained firm, a solid rejection lurking in his eyes. "It's not worth the effort."

The smirk on Celeste's face ignited Rayne's blood like a match thrown on a lake of gasoline. But thankfully, she'd come prepared for every possible outcome, including Cal's first instincts. Celeste might know good business tactics, but Rayne knew her uncle. His hard-edged ways. His bottom-line mentality.

"We could film my father's campaign ads while operating as a shelter. It's the perfect opportunity for him to interact with our local community. He'll be seen as a philanthropist and a humanitarian."

As if he'd stumbled upon a pot of gold, a grin stretched wide across Cal's mouth and didn't stop until it reached his eyes. "Now, *that* is thinking like a Shelby. Well done, Rayne."

She ignored the sickening clench in her gut that betrayed her true motives, but she couldn't ignore a compliment from her uncle. Positive reinforcement in her family was rare.

Whatever it took to serve the families in crisis and bring the lodge back to its roots—its core values of faith, family, and community—she'd do it.

Cal focused on each of the women before he spoke. "Celeste, you will continue to supervise the daily operations of the lodge while Rayne supervises the activities of the shelter."

As if stunned into momentary silence, Celeste waited several beats before forcing a tight smile and gritting out the words, "I will expect a full work-up of the projected costs and reimbursement plan from FEMA on my desk by late afternoon, Rayne."

Her cousin didn't glance back as she exited the study, leaving Rayne alone with her uncle.

Cal studied Rayne for so long she wondered if she'd missed his dismissal cue.

"Call Teddy. You can offer him the night shift back," he said. "We'll need all hands on deck to make this work."

Another victory.

"I will, thank you." A question she'd forgotten to ask her uncle last night popped into her head. "What about pets? Small ones. Like harmless little cats."

He crossed his arms. "I hate pets."

"Yes, but think of the cameras, the coverage . . ." A stretch for sure.

He sighed and flicked at a piece of lint on his black suit coat. "Fine. Small ones *only*. And they must be in their cages."

Crates, but okay. "Got it."

"And Rayne?"

"Yes?"

"Don't let me down. I don't offer second chances often."

The magical high she'd felt seconds before swooped in for a crash landing.

"I won't."

CHAPTER TWENTY-THREE

Rayne snapped her head upright at the sound of the text chime and searched haphazardly for her phone. She squinted at the too-bright screen and fumbled for her glasses.

10:34 a.m.

Levi: `So I offer to help drive an old lady away from potential harm and then get stuck playing cat sitter all night? You play dirty, Rayne Shelby.`

She'd gone back to her cabin to start the necessary phone calls and procedures, but somewhere in the last two hours, she'd fallen asleep facedown on her sofa.

Despite her delirious fog, she typed on the tiny phone screen.

Rayne: `Sorry, I'll come pick her up ASAP.`

Levi: `You still at the lodge?`

She shielded her eyes from the beacon of digital light and attempted four separate replies to explain what the last twelve hours had entailed.

Finally, she gave up and decided she was better off explaining it to him in person.

Rayne: `Is Ford gone?`

Levi: `Out in the backwoods on the backhoe.`

Rayne: `I'll be over in ten.`

Levi: `Good. That will give me plenty of time to get Miss P out of the garden shed.`

Rayne: `Not funny.`

Levi: `Not a joke.`

Rayne swept her hair into a high ponytail, brushed her teeth, and stepped into her only pair of flip-flops. The morning felt unusually warm, even for mid-July, but even more unusual was the layer of orangey fog that masked her view of the property line. More smoke had settled overnight while she'd been researching away on her laptop.

Her stride was quick until she reached the fence and slid between the open slats like a professional outlaw.

Levi held the fluffy cat out his open doorway. "Not a moment too soon."

Rayne cradled Penelope to her chest. "That isn't very nice. Her owner's been through a lot." She stroked the feline's silky fur and met Levi's probing stare.

"You look like you haven't slept in weeks."

Not weeks, just days. "I'm great."

Concern crimped his brow. "Did you not sleep before your shift last night?"

"I didn't really work last night—well, technically, I worked all night, just not my usual night-shift duties."

His concern morphed into confusion. "You're making so much sense right now." He pointed to his couch. "Sit. I'll make you some coffee."

"I actually can't stay, Levi. I need to compare notes with Celeste and make a game plan for—"

Levi stopped short of the kitchen and retreated his steps. "You either need to start from the beginning or start from the beginning. I'm not following you today, sweets."

"Okay." She took a deep breath and tried to organize her scattered thoughts. "We're turning the lodge into a shelter."

If she hadn't witnessed that same expression earlier this morning, she would have repeated herself. But Levi wasn't hard of hearing; he was simply sifting through the validity of her statement.

"You're turning the lodge into a fire shelter. For evacuees."

With all the enthusiasm she could muster on two hours of sleep, she nodded. The lilt in her laugh seemed to have Levi drawing closer as if to examine her sanity level.

"And your uncle approved this act of community benevolence, *why*?"

"Because it's the right thing to do. The community needs us right now, Levi. Hundreds of families have been displaced. We have the room and the staff and the—"

"Rayne." He shook his head. "That doesn't answer my question. What's his angle for doing this?"

Penelope climbed up her shirt and propped her plump self on the back of the sofa, swatting Rayne's hair. "Ouch."

Levi bowed. "Welcome to my personal cat hell."

Despite his deadpan tone, she snickered at the mental image of Levi batting away cat paws all night long.

"You'll think it's funny until the thing tries to gouge out your eyeballs," he said.

"Awww . . . is someone afraid of a sweet little kitty cat?" Rayne gathered the animal in her arms and kissed her between the ears.

"Well, right now I'm not nearly as afraid as I am jealous."

Rayne scooted to the edge of the sofa, needing an extra dose of support to push herself into a standing position. "How about I'll call you after I get through my checklist."

"You really won't stay and have a cup of coffee with me?"

Those darn puppy-dog eyes pleaded with her. "Technically my shift has already started."

"Your shift? You moved back to days?"

She struggled to her feet, Penelope's tail curling around her arm like a serpent. "Oh yes, I guess in all the excitement I forgot to mention that part. Teddy is going to start back up tonight. I'm so relieved."

"That's great." But nothing about his body language seemed to agree with his statement. Levi stepped into the kitchen, saying nothing more as he removed two ceramic mugs. A soothingly familiar aroma tinged the air a moment later as coffee brewed into the old-style pot.

"Are you trying to tempt me into staying longer than I should?" she asked with a hint of humor.

He pressed his palms to the counter's edge and hunched his back. "I don't know what I'm trying to do anymore."

"Levi." She pinched her eyebrows together, trying to force her brain to cooperate. "We'll still see each other."

"You keep saying that, and yet here we are again, counting down the minutes before our relationship goes into yet another underground tunnel."

She set the cat onto his couch and moved toward him, the ache in her chest palpable. Wrapping her arms around his middle, she pressed her cheek to his taut back. "I don't want to stop seeing you."

He rotated and pressed his lips to the crown of her head. "I don't want to stop seeing you either."

There was a *but* coming. She could feel it, even through her exhaustion. She tilted her chin upward and nearly buckled under the sincerity of his gaze.

"Let me help you with the shelter."

She pushed back, but he refused her efforts. "That's impossible."

"Why?" He repositioned his grip on her waist. "What if there's an opportunity for us in all of this—in the fires and the evacuations? We can join forces, become a united front. Cal couldn't deny us in such a public position."

"Levi, be serious—"

"I am. When that lodge transforms into a shelter, the doors are going to be open to everybody, not just the elite and the affluent. Your guests will be modest families, neighborhood merchants, local farmers. Regular folks. My kind of people."

"Please tell me your plan doesn't involve disguising yourself as a Bear Canyon evacuee."

He laughed. "No, but Second Harvest has plenty of produce and supplies to donate for such a worthy cause, especially with a FEMA tax write-off. Ford might not be our biggest fan, but he's—"

"What?" She broke away. "You told him about us? Why would you do that?"

"Are you really so bound to the judgments of your family that you won't give him a chance? Even for me?"

"That man screwed my family." A fact she'd stuffed into a back pocket of denial for too long.

He reached for her hips and pulled her close again. "Meet him, Rayne. Talk to him, just once. You'll see that he's not what you—"

"No." She'd crossed a lot of lines for Levi. But she couldn't cross that one. "You may think I'm different from the rest of the people who share my name, but that doesn't change what's written on my birth certificate. He deceived my family. Meeting him won't change the past."

"But what if *we* could change the future of the lodge and farm?"

"We can't." She thought about Cousin Milton, the mistakes that led him down a path of permanent ostracism. Couldn't he see what she'd risked for him already? Why couldn't that be enough?

"How did you get Cal to agree to the shelter?"

She looked away.

"Rayne."

He brushed the pad of his thumb over the dimple on her chin. "How?"

She'd played to her uncle's weakness. Stroked his greed. Built his ego. "I baited him by suggesting we use the shelter for my father's campaign ads."

For an instant, she couldn't read the mixed expression that crept into Levi's face. "It's just, I knew it was the only way to—"

Levi shut her up with a kiss that awoke all her senses. He cupped the back of her head and pushed his fingers into her hair, his lips tender and firm and everything Rayne couldn't bring herself to walk away from.

"You seized an opportunity," he said, pulling back enough to finish the sentence she'd long forgotten. "Which is exactly what we need to do too. Together."

Bewildered, she blinked up at him. "Don't push this on me, Levi. I'm not ready." A nagging voice told her she'd never be ready. She would no sooner parade Levi around the lodge than she'd agree to a social outing with Ford. Both options spelled ruin.

"Two days ago you wouldn't have thought you'd be ready to open a shelter either. This is our opportunity, Rayne."

No, it was a plank walk to certain death. Death of her dream. Death of her career. Death of her future.

At the sound of claws shredding fabric, they turned their heads toward the living room.

"Here." Levi poured the coffee and practically shoved the mug into her hands. "Drink this and then please get that thing out of my house."

She kissed his cheek, downed her coffee, and then delivered Penelope to her rightful owner.

All before her first showdown with Celeste.

They received the final stamp of approval from FEMA by noon: Shelby Lodge had officially become an evacuation shelter for families threatened by the Bear Canyon wildfires. And Rayne and her team had only hours to set up before the first evacuees arrived.

Using a dolly, Rayne rolled a stack of extra chairs into the Great Room. Sweat stuck to the underside of her bra straps and at the waistband of her jeans. She rocked her hip into a nearby table to catch her breath and pointed to the back wall near the window bay.

"I was thinking we could set up several buffet-style tables over there to allow lines to form on either side."

"No," Celeste said, hands anchored on her hips. "We aren't going to lower our standards to hillbilly class. This isn't some Podunk cafeteria."

Rayne bit the insides of her cheeks and exhaled through her nose before responding to yet another objection from her second cousin. "Celeste, we agreed to work together on this. If we fill ourselves to capacity by tonight, we'll need a better way to organize the meal chaos."

"The lodge has had a waiting list nearly every summer. We can keep our traditional approach, even at capacity," Celeste retorted.

"We've never been full of families." Not by a long shot. The lodge catered to wealthy retired couples and upper-business-class singles. "*Families* will mean lots of young children. Our traditional dining style won't work. Not for this. Delia's already working on food orders for continental breakfasts, boxed lunches, and simple dinners."

Not a second too soon, Gia sauntered through the open double-door entrance wearing her typical artist smock and Converse high-tops. "How goes it, ladies? Where do I sign up to be a camp counselor?"

Celeste groaned and shoved a round table toward the far wall. "Awesome, now I get to work with two country bumpkins."

"Better that than an urban—"

Rayne shot Gia her best don't-you-dare-stoop-to-her-level glare and simply stated, "We don't have time for bickering. Our doors open to the public in less than two hours, and we still have a ton of work left to do in here. Gia, can you please grab the last stack of chairs from the hall closet?"

"Sure thing," Gia replied with a casual salute.

"And, Celeste, why don't you—"

"No." Celeste stared her down. "You don't get to boss me around. I'm *your* supervisor, not the other way around."

"We're equals in this."

"That's not the way I understood it."

Three hours of broken sleep over the last thirty-six meant that every rebuttal in Rayne's mental arsenal consisted of words she hadn't spoken since Gia had made her "practice cuss" in the seventh grade. With the limited willpower she had left, she clamped down on the underused insults threatening to spew from her mouth and merely exhaled.

"Please, let's try to get along. For the sake of our future guests."

"You sound like one of those cliché pageant queens." Celeste flashed a peace sign. "Peace. Love. Harmony. No wonder Cal called me when he did."

She whirled out of the room.

"Whoa," Gia said a moment later, studying Rayne's sharpened face. "You should have called for backup sooner."

"Can you do me a favor?" Rayne asked.

"I'm pretty sure I'm already doing you one, but shoot."

"Find a Celeste-size tranquilizer, preferably before our guests arrive."

Gia choked out a laugh. "Ya know, if I didn't have to worry about bail money after the family cut me off, I'd seriously take you up on that."

By the time the line formed outside Shelby Lodge, Rayne's focus had splintered into a million different directions. Even with their streamlined check-in process—Gia assisting the volunteer crisis workers—chaos was unavoidable.

Every available common area in the lodge was crammed to capacity. Grandparents to babies to small, housebroken animals. And despite the extra workload, stress, and lack of sleep, Rayne had never felt so fulfilled in all her life.

Her dream was no longer confined to her heart.

CHAPTER TWENTY-FOUR

Bucking hay in the middle of fire season could easily make a top five list for Worst Jobs in the World. Even still, Levi would gladly choose the backbreaking labor over watching another round of news crews enter and exit Shelby Lodge. He only had so much patience.

Rayne had asked him to wait. She'd asked him for time—more time for her to adjust to the idea of them working side by side at the shelter. Together. Only, every day that ticked by was another day of opportunity wasted.

Levi stabbed the prongs of his hay hooks through another bale of premium timothy hay and chucked it from the field into the flatbed. The driver of the truck—the fifteen-year-old son of Travis's employer—inched along the field slowly enough for Travis and Levi to buck and stack the bales. With more reports of wildfires spreading to neighboring communities, every hay farmer in the area seemed to be of the same mindset. *Harvest now.* To wait any longer would put too many livelihoods at risk.

Under the heat of a merciless sun, the once muted gray of Levi's cotton shirt had darkened to a sweat-soaked shade of granite. The damp fabric clung to his chest and back, yet even while his gloved hands cramped around the hook handles, and his jeans felt both suffocating and constrictive, Levi remained grateful for the distraction. He would have been content to work the day away in shared silence, allow the burn in his muscles to clear his head of the drama surrounding them, but, like usual, his friend had other ideas.

Travis stretched his arms before puncturing another bale. "You hear about Benton's ranch?"

"Yeah. Awful." The charcoaled images of the equestrian center were burned into his mind's eye. He'd met Roy Benton for the first time only a few months ago—a stand-up man looking to partner with Levi's efforts at the farm. Enrich the local economy. Help spread the word about Second Harvest deliveries.

Levi shook his head and jogged along the trailer toward the last couple rows of baled hay. It'd be years before the Bentons could rebuild. Years before their facility would be up and running again. And while Levi felt certain the insurance claims would pay out, he also knew the charred remains that Roy would face day after day would be nothing short of demoralizing.

Structures could be rebuilt, but dreams . . . those were much harder to salvage after a tragedy.

"It's nice to see so many people chipping in their time and money to help, though." Travis wiped the sweat from his eyes with the back of his arm as they reached the next area of baled hay. "Like your neighbors."

Levi climbed into the back of the flatbed without comment, unwilling to engage Travis in a conversation about the Shelbys. Especially today. With his jaw firmly set and his back a plank of rigid muscle, he stacked each new bale into a wall.

"Kind of ironic that the first time I saw the inside of that lodge was on the local news. Regular folk running in and out. Tons of kids and—"

"How many more bales do you think we can load on here this afternoon?"

Travis stopped to count, shot out a number, and then ran his mouth some more. "Some blond chick was talking from there this morning, but it only got interesting when the reporter interviewed Rayne . . ." He grinned, then spit. "Now that woman can turn some heads. All sweet and innocent looking while she made that plea for a food drive—"

Levi stiffened, certain he'd heard wrong. "A food drive?"

"I think that's what she was saying, although I had a hard time focusing on her words. Girl has some distractingly beautiful—"

"What *exactly* did she ask for?" Levi tossed his medieval weaponry aside, shutting Travis down before he could take that sentence a breath farther.

His friend's expression remained irritatingly passive. "Like I said, I can't be sure. But I think she was after food donations for the shelter. Aren't you watching the news?"

"No." Not if he could help it, although Ford rarely missed a night.

Levi ripped his hand from his glove and scrubbed at his sweat-slicked face. Hadn't he offered to donate food to the shelter? Hadn't he asked her to let him help?

"Man, you're moody."

"Am not."

"You are. And you've been this way since the night at BlackTail when you left your jackpot on the poker table."

Levi anchored his shoulder on a freshly stacked wall of hay. "Must have been rough—keeping all that cold cash to yourself."

"We split it."

"Sure you did."

Travis laughed and then whistled to the driver to stop. He grabbed two cold Gatorades from the cab of the truck and tossed one up to Levi. "So what, then, you done with us? No more blue-collar games for such a sophisticated entrepreneur like yourself?"

Levi crinkled his brows at the title and hopped off the back of the truck onto the brittle ground. "Sophisticated entrepreneur? Where'd you hear that?"

"I've heard lots lately."

"Like?"

"Like how you've been sniffing around the Shelbys, collecting their business contacts the way we used to pick pockets."

"I'm not sniffing anywhere. And any client I've acquired has been aboveboard." *Almost.*

"So what's happening between you and Rayne is aboveboard too, then?"

A storm brewed in his chest. "You were baiting me."

"Levi Harding would never leave a jackpot on the table during a high-stakes poker game unless he had a better incentive. I saw you go after her that night, remember? And the next thing I knew, your truck was gone and so was she."

Travis's accusation had substance, he'd give him that much. But out of respect for Rayne, he wouldn't admit to anything more. Not even to his oldest friend. Telling Ford was one thing. But telling Travis? Might as well take out an ad in the town's gossip column. "That's a stretch. Even for you."

Travis lounged against the trailer tire and crossed his ankles, as if the blazing heat made for comfortable conversation. "I've drunk the water, Harding. Tasted the Shelby allure firsthand, and I'm telling you, it's not worth it."

"And there it is. I knew you'd find a way to wiggle her into this conversation. I swear, the drama between you and Gia has more lives than an accident-prone cat. Let it die, Trav."

"Maybe you should take your own advice."

Levi guffawed at the absurdity of this discussion. In no way was his relationship with Rayne even close to the same situation. "Gia's the sheriff's daughter, although I shouldn't have to remind you of that since he was also your *arresting officer*."

"Oh, and your past mistakes are so much prettier than mine."

"Never said that." He'd been an idiot plenty of times in his youth; he just hadn't been dumb enough to get caught sneaking into the sheriff's house to visit a certain fiery female after curfew. It was shortly after his friend's run-in with the law that Ford had asked Levi to start accounting for his hours spent off the farm, a stipulation he'd created for free housing in addition to his monthly paycheck, a stipulation that managed to keep Levi—and Travis, by default—from many nights of stupid.

"You'll have a bounty on your head the size of Texas if you get caught with Rayne—arrest record or not. Guilty or not. All those scriptures Ford quotes about grace and forgiveness and loving your enemies . . . well, the Shelbys don't subscribe to his same stance on God or faith. Believe me."

"There's nothing going on with me and Rayne." The lie wasn't seamless. His voice was off, his words too sharp, but he didn't need his friend to believe him. He just needed the subject buried.

Travis eyed him for several seconds before he turned his attention back to the field, a smile on his face. "Well, that's good to hear. You know me, I hate saying *I told you so*."

About as much as he hated a royal flush.

Levi downed the rest of his drink and tossed the empty bottle into the flatbed. "Come on, let's finish this thing up."

Travis waved him off. "Nah, there's not much left to do. I got the rest. You should head home and take a shower. You stink."

"You don't smell any better. Trust me. You sure?"

"I'm sure." Travis laughed. "I asked for a couple hours of help, and you've been out here all day. Get going already."

"If you need something else, call me." Levi stripped his cotton T-shirt over his head, his damp skin instantly relieved.

"Will do. See ya."

As Travis trotted into the field, gesturing for the young driver to roll ahead, Levi pulled his phone from the back pocket of his jeans. On the way back to his truck, he scrolled through his missed messages and notifications. He stopped on a single text delivered just fifteen minutes ago.

His pulse kicked into high gear at the mere sight of her name.

Rayne: `You home? I'm free for a bit.`

Levi stood in his open doorway and committed the sight of her to memory.

"Hi." Her shy greeting shot a bullet through his earlier resolve and crippled whatever confrontation he'd prepared to have with her about media pleas and food donations.

Rayne was here. In his house. Wearing her glasses.

And the girl took sexy to another stratosphere in those glasses.

She lifted a plate off the counter and moved toward him, her eyes flickering briefly to his bare chest. Her boldness—sneaking over this late in the afternoon, waiting inside his empty house, bringing him something to eat after a day of laboring in the sun—awakened every physical desire he'd suppressed for weeks. Rayne's cropped white pants and satiny turquoise blouse swished in time with her hips, tempting him beyond the smell of the baked goods lingering in the air. Every inch of his skin seemed to buzz at her nearness.

"I brought you cookies," she said, the slightest hitch of hesitation in her voice. "Only I wasn't sure which kind was your favorite, so I just chose an assortment of Delia's best."

"Oatmeal." The hoarse word scraped over his dry tongue and he cleared his throat, suddenly desperate for water. Preferably ice-cold water. "I like oatmeal." But who was he kidding? He'd eat tree bark if she'd brought it for him.

"Good to know." She smiled then, her gaze lingering in a way that made his every muscle ignite.

"You have hay in your hair." When she reached her hand out, he practically leapt backward. Six hours of blazing heat and cramped hands had stripped his mental inhibitions bare. If he allowed her to touch him now . . .

He tugged at the back of his neck and then raked a hand through his hair. "How 'bout I take a quick shower and then we can . . . we can . . ." His brain tracked through the limited list of options at snail speed. "Talk."

"Okay." She nodded. "Go take a shower and I'll pour you a glass of cold milk. I have a little over an hour before I need to head back for dinner."

He was down the hallway with the door closed behind him before his mind could register she'd even spoken.

Ten minutes. He hadn't taken longer than ten minutes to rinse, towel off, and dress, but Rayne's propped elbow and heavy eyelids told a different story. How poorly had she been sleeping? He knew her workload at the shelter kept her days full, but the purplish tint under her eyes and the tired sag of her shoulders made him wonder about the schedule she was keeping at night. Why was she pushing herself so hard? What more was she trying to prove?

A tall glass of milk and a plate of cookies sat atop the stacked pallets doubling as a coffee table. He sank into the cushion beside her, placing his one and only throw pillow onto his lap before sliding her glasses off. On a yawn, she accepted his invitation and repositioned her body, her head resting atop the pillow.

She inhaled deeply. "You smell nice."

He smiled at the tired slur of her words. "Not nearly as nice as you."

"It's the cookies."

"No." He kicked out his legs and relaxed against the back of the sofa. "It's you."

She tipped her face to him and chuckled softly. "What do I smell like?"

"Summertime."

She curled her legs onto the cushion beside her and yawned again. "With all the smoke, I can't even remember what summer smells like anymore."

He stroked the silky strands of her hair, mesmerized by the feel and the shine. "Like every flower's in bloom all at once."

Her lips curved and his hand stilled. Travis hadn't been wrong about her—Rayne's smile could drop a man to his knees. And unlike many of the women he'd known, she hadn't a clue how alluring she was. Her hair. Her eyes. Her smile. That dimple in her chin.

All of it. All of her.

But just beneath the surface of this perfectly packaged Shelby lived a quality, a passion, a selfless kind of beauty that could only be uncovered with time. He smoothed a lock of her hair off her cheek and studied the slender curve of her neck, the shapely ridge of her collarbones. With the lightest of touches, he grazed the tender skin behind her ear, trailing his finger to the arch of her eyebrow. He'd known of her most of his adult life. But he'd only *known* her—the heart behind the name—for a month. A single month. And yet, in much the same way Ford's faith and generosity had impacted his life nine years ago, the sweetness of Rayne's spirit was already reshaping him. Changing his wants, his dreams, his desires to something he hadn't known existed until now.

Who would he be in a year with Rayne in his life? In two? In twenty?

"You're gonna make me fall asleep for real." She tried to push up to her elbow, but he denied her efforts.

"Good."

"No, not good. I have too much to do. I can't stay."

"Yes, you can."

"I need to manage the dinner lines. They can get crazy. It's easier when I'm there to hold the children's plates for their parents. I should—"

"Let me take care of you." He touched her forehead, pressing out the worry lines with his thumb. "You're always so busy taking care of everybody else, managing everybody else. For once, let somebody take care of you. Let me take care of you."

He'd expected her to put up more of a fight, a detailed argument outlining all the reasons why she couldn't leave the shelter unattended for a few more hours. But instead, her shoulders relaxed. Within minutes, her breathing deepened, her body yielding to the persuasion of sleep.

There'd been so little resistance to her surrender.

The same could be said of him.

As he studied her tranquil face, he curled a strand of her hair around his finger and said a prayer he hoped God would answer soon. Whoever had caused this sleeping beauty to believe she needed to be anything more than who she was right now deserved to be throttled.

Because Rayne Shelby was more than enough.

CHAPTER TWENTY-FIVE

A cocoon of blissful sleep enveloped her mind and body. Levi's touch had lulled her into a dreamless place where peace smelled like dusty work boots and minty soap.

She uncurled her legs and pointed her toes to stretch her calves, her eyes opened only a crack. Just enough to watch the shadows of dusk play across the empty cookie plate and milk glass. Nightfall. He should have woken her. Yet the moment she thought it, she could hear the plea of his words again, could feel the dip in her stomach. *Let me take care of you.*

She slung an arm over her eyes, her cloudy mind emerging slowly from slumber. She patted the cushion with her free hand. Levi's legs were no longer beneath her. She couldn't blame him for repositioning. She'd comforted a sleeping toddler a few nights ago, and within thirty minutes her arms had morphed into dead-weight appendages.

Thankfully, Levi hadn't gone far. Even if she hadn't seen the toes of his work boots peeking from between the slats of the coffee table, she could sense his presence. A presence she would thank momentarily. And not with a plate of cookies this time. With a kiss.

"Perhaps I should hire you to help me fall asleep every night." She yawned and reached for her glasses on the sofa arm. "What time is it?"

"Just after eight."

Every cell in her body tensed, her mind suddenly wide awake.

That voice did not belong to Levi.

Her leap from the sofa and guarded about-face took only a second, yet her recognition of a man she hadn't seen up close for over a decade was instantaneous.

Ford Winslow.

"Hello, Rayne." The crackle in his voice shook her—everywhere. He remained seated yet lifted a hand that matched his worn appearance. "I'm sorry to startle you. That wasn't my intention."

"Where's Levi?" Her eyes darted around the room in a manic frenzy.

"He's not here."

Where was he? Why would he do this? Why would he leave her alone with this man? She couldn't stop the twitching in her arms or the pounding in her chest. Her gaze fixated on the exit beyond Ford's chair. The front door beckoned to her. Would he try to block her if she ran past him?

"I'd invite you to have a glass of iced tea with me, but I'm guessing you're about five seconds from darting past my chair and out that door."

She said nothing, her jaw as frozen as her stare. Had he expected this invasion to be anything less than disorienting?

On a sigh, he clasped his hands together and leaned forward. "I realize you don't know me anymore, but—"

"Yes, I do. I know you." Her fear transformed into something solid. Something indignant. Something she'd never been given the freedom to voice aloud. Before now. "You stole this farm from my grandfather. Eighteen years ago."

His gaze held steady, unblinking. "I loved your grandfather."

Disgust filled her every sense, becoming a taste, a smell, a sound pulsing in her ears. "You don't cheat the people you love or the people they love." The accusations and allegations of her father, her aunt, her uncle stacked up inside her like a tower of building blocks. Years of hateful word darts she'd had nowhere to aim. "You robbed a wonderful man. A man who trusted you, a man who gave you his time and money and heart. And you repaid him by robbing his family? That is the opposite of love."

Again, he didn't react to the bitter assault of her statements. No flinch, no wince, no cringe. Was the man so used to being hated? Had he so willingly accepted his fate as a soulless monster?

"He used to call you his Little Blue Jay. Your hair was so dark when you were born it had this brilliant blue hue around it. Almost like a halo."

"Who told you that?"

"He used to carry you on his shoulders through the back pasture so you could reach the tree house door. Your cousin Joshua used to lock you out because he said you weren't tall enough to join his secret clubhouse. But William made you tall enough."

Her mind stumbled over memory boxes she hadn't opened in years. "Stop it."

"You always begged to go huckleberry picking in the summertime and you loved making jam with Delia in the kitchen. You two would sing and carry on." He chuckled. "It made everybody laugh. You'd tie a red ribbon around the lids and press a Shelby Lodge seal to the glass, and then William would take you on a ride into town. To give the jars away to families who served our country."

She reached for the wall behind her. She needed to steady herself. Steady her thoughts.

"He loved all his grandchildren, but you were special to him, Rayne. Your bond was unique. When you lost your mother at such a young age, William moved heaven and earth to convince your father to come live at the lodge. He wanted to be a part of your life. He hoped he could right some of his past mistakes with his own children by pouring his life, his wisdom, his renewed faith into the next generation. Into you."

No, this wasn't real. This man didn't know her. He didn't care for her grandfather. He was a manipulator.

Though her mind screamed the command, her feet wouldn't move.

"You've always been able to see people with your heart, Rayne." Ford swallowed and she felt her own throat thicken. "It was the way William saw people too. Even when you were seven years old, he recognized your gift, your way with the patrons. And what you've done with the lodge this week, with the shelter, William would have made the same decision. He'd be proud of you."

Emotions swarmed inside her, blurring her vision and bucking against her instincts. How she'd longed to hear those words from her grandfather. To share her dreams with him, to seek his counsel, to feel his acceptance.

"I know my boy cares for you—deeply," Ford continued.

Her attention snapped back to reality. To the present.

So that's why he'd come. "You're here to tell me to stay away from Levi?"

He tipped his blunt chin toward the floor and dragged the sole of his boot against the carpet threads, as if pondering something she hadn't asked. She studied his face, his angled features, his woolly, wiry mustache, his parched skin, mapped by years of sun exposure. She wondered at his age. Despite his weathered appearance, he was younger than she'd imagined—perhaps not much older than her uncle Cal.

He lifted his gaze. "You saw me once, at the grocery store, just a year or so after your grandfather passed away. You had a green sucker in your hand and you were supposed to be trading it out for a different color—orange, I think—while your cousin and aunt waited for you in the checkout line. But you forgot about the candy when you saw me. Do you remember what you asked?"

She'd asked him a question? It took her the better part of a minute to access the memory, but it was too out of focus. Too cloudy. Too covered in the dust of an emotion she couldn't understand. "I don't remember."

He waited, his stoic gaze probing through her as if time could erase his transgressions.

She needed to get away from him, escape whatever kind of manipulation game he was playing. She scooted along the wall toward the door.

"Secrets don't keep forever."

Panic stitched the length of her spine. Was he talking about Levi? Was Ford planning on exposing them? She pinched her eyes closed and fought against the pain jabbing between the slats of her ribs.

She yanked open the door and fled down the porch steps, slicing through two beams of moving light. A truck door slammed at her back and a familiar voice called out her name.

No, she wouldn't stop, not for the man who'd just trapped her in a house with Ford against her wishes.

Despite the quickening thud of Levi's footsteps, she continued to propel herself toward the safety of the fence.

"Rayne, will you please stop!"

She kicked each of her legs through the narrow fence boards. In her haste, her blouse snagged on a raised nail, shredding the fabric at her side and exposing the flesh from her rib cage to her hip bone.

But unlike a blouse, repairing trust wasn't an easy mend.

The instant both of her feet were planted on Shelby soil, Levi hurled himself over the barrier, avoiding the bob and weave altogether. Chest heaving, he gripped her shoulders and blocked her path.

"Mind telling me why we just competed in an after-dark obstacle course?"

She jerked away from his hold. "How could you! How could leave me with him?"

Through narrowed eyes, he swiveled his gaze between his cabin and her. "What happ—"

"You left me asleep. In your house. *With Ford!*" Despite the warm pocket of smoky air surrounding them, chills broke out over her arms and legs.

"Ford talked to you?"

"Oh, don't act like you didn't know. Don't act like you didn't set this up tonight. You told him—about my grandfather, about things I've shared with you in confidence." The tears in her voice leapt out in a hoarse, angry cry. "How could you?"

"Think, Rayne." When he reached for her again she stumbled back. "Why would I plan that? What could I possibly gain by cornering you with Ford before you were ready?"

"That's just it!" She thrust a finger in the air toward his chest. "I'm never going to be ready, and yet, you've wanted to change my mind about him from the beginning."

"Of course I have, but not by ambushing you. Give me a little more credit than that, please." He trapped her wrist, pressed her hand to his heart. "I was only gone for fifteen minutes. Seven minutes down the road to deliver a receipt and then back. I'm sorry if Ford startled you, but I won't apologize for him. He belongs in my life, Rayne, just like you."

She shook her head, backed away, broke contact. "Just because he means something to you doesn't mean I can forget everything I know about him—how he's hurt my family, how he used my grandfather! How can you overlook everything he's done? How can you be okay with the way he acquired the farm? You're building your future on a stolen inheritance!"

He seemed to process every word out of her mouth, every accusation she threw at him, and yet, he skipped over her questions to ask one of his own in a tone much too quiet, much too calm. "What did he tell you, Rayne?"

She pressed her fingers to her temples as if to prevent Ford's words from leaking out. The memories. The nicknames. The sadness. "It doesn't matter."

"Ford doesn't waste words. It matters."

"Secrets don't keep," she snapped. "That's what he said. He's planning to go to Cal. He's planning to expose us both."

Levi's eyes shimmered in the moonlight, his tone only a few clicks away from patronizing. "Sweetheart, Ford confronting Cal would be about as out of character for him as this display of irrationality is from you. Believe me, Ford has his reasons for keeping a low profile around your uncle."

Levi's lack of alarm was maddening. How could he be so calm when he'd put them at risk? All of their careful planning, their sneaking around, their playing it safe . . . all of it had been in vain.

"You think I'm being irrational? That all our time staying under the radar has been some kind of joke? If my uncle finds out about us he'll . . ." Squash her dreams. Cut her off. Take the lodge away from her forever.

His expression hardened. "I don't know how many ways I can tell you this, but I will not fear that man. I will not cower under him like everyone else in this town. And frankly, I've grown tired of being your closet boyfriend. I'm done with all the hiding, Rayne. I've been done for weeks now."

Done. A plunge in the icy river couldn't have shocked her system more—then again, maybe she was still in shock. Maybe waking up to Ford Winslow had not only stripped her inhibitions and shattered her excuses, but maybe it had also given her something else . . . the strength to say what she must.

"So let's stop, then." Her gaze shifted to the glow of the lodge in the distance, to the shelter, to the community she longed to serve. The pull was as strong and steady as a heartbeat, a constant companion she'd felt even as a young girl working alongside her grandfather. Her dreams were only just beginning, only just being realized. *The lodge* was her passion. *The lodge* was her future. "We always knew this would be temporary."

"Don't twist my words. You know that's not what I meant—not what I want. I said I'm done with all the hiding, not with you. Not with us."

Her heart pounded in her throat, in her ears. "I tried—I promised you I'd try, but—"

"But what? You're only willing to feel something for me when we're alone? When there's no chance we'll be caught? That's not trying. That's convenience."

She shook her head. He was missing the point. "This is bigger than your pride, Levi."

"My pride? You think this is about my pride?" He strode toward her. "If this were about my pride, I'd have thrown out the rules the first day we met. If this were about my pride, I wouldn't have bent my life to fit around your ever-changing schedule." He stared her down. "*None* of this has been about my pride, Rayne. It's been about you. About us. About this moment right now."

Her body short-circuited the instant his fingertips grazed her skin. He skimmed the top of her shoulders and then the length of her arms. He wasn't confining her, wasn't holding her captive, yet she couldn't move away. Couldn't fight the ache in her throat. Couldn't beg him not to speak the confession she read in his eyes.

"It's about how I fell in love with you." His breath caressed her lips, each syllable stretching out for an eternity until another crashed into it. "So let me." He traced the curve of her spine until her legs felt as unsteady as her ability to reason. When the warm breeze blew her torn blouse like a white flag of surrender, he moved his hands to the bare skin at her waist, and a feverish heat climbed her torso. "Let me love you, Rayne."

Tender. So unbelievably tender. His eyes, his mouth, his voice, his touch. She fused her lips together, hoping her refusal to speak would make the truth less true. Would make her heart less pained. He brushed his lips across her cheek to the base of her ear, breaking her down kiss by kiss, touch by touch.

Only, if *she* broke down, so would her dreams.

So would her future.

Their extended curiosity had landed them in an inevitable quicksand, and the only way to climb out was to let go of each other.

She'd allowed this to go on too long.

A rasped reply squeezed from her throat. "I can't."

"Can't what?" he murmured through lips pressed to her neck.

Hot tears gathered on her lashes as she pressed her palm flat against his chest. She pushed, gently at first, and then not so gently. "I can't do this anymore."

As if waking from a deep sleep, Levi lifted his head, his expression changing from confusion to clarity in a single blink. "You're scared."

More than he realized. Did he not understand the position she was in? The choice he wanted her to make? The plans he wanted her to deny? "You're asking me to choose—between you and my dream. Between you and my family."

"No, I'm asking you to open your eyes, to see Cal for who he really is—"

Her shoulders tensed. "That's just it, Levi. To you, Shelby Lodge will always be about the man who signs my paychecks. But to me . . ." She gestured to the building behind her. "To me that lodge represents everything I've loved since I was a child—every hope I've ever clung to despite my shortcomings as Governor Shelby's daughter. You were right when you said I don't fit in with my family. I never have. But I fit there. I *belong* there. That lodge isn't just my grandfather's legacy—it's mine too. I won't leave it."

He scrubbed a hand down his face and blew out a sharp breath. "You actually believe this fire shelter will change him, don't you?"

"Things *are* changing."

"Come on, Rayne. The only reason Cal agreed to open those doors to the community was to suit his own agenda—you *know* that."

Her temper ticked higher. "It doesn't matter how it happened, the lodge is open, and people are being helped because of it. It's a whole new beginning there—I can feel it."

On a half rotation, he shoved his hands through his hair, the labored sound of his breathing as unsettling as the look on his face when his eyes found hers again.

"There are things you don't understand about the past, things I'm not at liberty to share—"

"Not at liberty? Who is stopping you? Ford?"

His hesitation was answer enough.

Unbelievable. "You have no problem accusing me of taking sides with Cal, and yet you're doing the same thing with a man who isn't even your blood."

He flung his arms out wide. "You want to know about my blood, Rayne? Fine, I'll tell you. My mom overdosed in a pay-by-the-hour motel south of Tacoma before my fourth birthday. My dad was a low-level dealer who scored most of his sales by hanging out in high school parking lots. I grew up on borrowed couches and expired groceries and thought father-son time meant sorting out his dirty wads of cash—that is, before he ended up in prison and I ended up in the system. So, no, Ford isn't my blood, but he *is* the best thing that could have happened to me as an eighteen-year-old kid hell-bent on screwing up my future."

Sickness sloshed in her belly at his confession, at the pain in his words, at the prick in her conscience. "I'm sorry."

"I don't want your pity. I want you to trust me." He thumped his chest with the flat of his hand. "Trust me when I tell you your dream will never be a priority to Cal. He doesn't see you, Rayne. He doesn't understand your heart. He doesn't care about your ambitions. Your uncle is no better than my father. No matter how hard you slave, or how much you sacrifice, he will never choose you."

Hurt gnawed through her back and clawed into her chest as an unspoken truth seeped through the cracks of her stubborn heart: *Levi would never choose her either . . .*

She could fall on her sword for him, expose her disloyalty to Cal, reject her dream, and hand Levi her heart, but he would never do the same for her.

Levi would always choose Ford.

She'd compartmentalized the truth for weeks, placed Levi on a mental pedestal detached from his employer. Time and time again she'd ignored her better judgment and pacified her guilty conscience by embracing a desire as futile as her justification.

But everything was clear now.

Ford and Levi were joined, welded together. Not only by a farm but by a bond he treated as family.

He would never cut ties with the man who'd cheated her grandfather.

The same way she would never cut ties with the home her grandfather had cherished.

All at once, the double lives she'd lived for months merged into a single, focused resolve.

She didn't need to be chosen. She needed to be the one to choose.

"I'll never walk away from the lodge," she said with a strength not quite her own.

His expression sobered. "But you're willing to walk away from me?"

She distanced herself from the shadows that danced between them.

"Don't do this, Rayne. Don't shut me out again." His voice caught and she swallowed against the pressure building in her throat, against the pain blazing in her chest.

"From our first night together at the Falls to this moment right now—nothing has changed. We are still two people torn between our loyalties, and we always will be." She formed the words in her head, careful to avoid a collision with her heart, and forced them out on a single breath. "You were wrong—what you said before. We haven't been done for weeks, we were done before we ever began."

Like a coward, she retreated, unwilling to watch the repercussions of her decision unfold, unwilling to feel the pain she'd just inflicted.

Unwilling to change her mind for a man who would never change his.

She couldn't escape the stale night air or the burn in her lungs, and neither could she escape the rejection that pulsed in her wake with each lonely stride back to the lodge.

And unlike every other time she'd walked away from him in the past, this time, Levi didn't follow.

CHAPTER TWENTY-SIX

Rayne had hoped to sneak through the back kitchen door unnoticed, but Gia had other plans. Her cousin eyed her from the counter.

"You totally owe me for skipping dinner. I had to play crossing guard with all the children—and you know how much I love sticky fingers pawing all over me."

Rayne cleared her throat and angled her shoulders to hide her puffy eyes behind a wall of windblown hair. Unfortunately, she hadn't remembered to hide the tear in her blouse.

"Uh, excuse me, were you attacked by a wolverine since I saw you last? What's with the wardrobe malfunction?"

"It's nothing. Thanks for helping with dinner." Rayne's robotic voice matched her robotic movements. Out of habit, she pulled the drapes over the back door closed and flicked off the porch light before sneaking a glance at the clock above the stove. Had it really only been three hours since she'd stood in this kitchen making a plate of cookies for Levi? The thought made the tip of her nose tingle.

"Hello? Earth to Rayne. Why does your shirt look like it could have been worn on an eighties rock band album cover?"

Rayne said nothing as she moved across the kitchen, keeping her shield in place, her emotions in check.

"Come on, that was funny."

Rayne shuffled to a stop before she reached the end of the counter. "I'm not in the mood for funny tonight. And I'm not in the mood for a game of twenty thousand Gia questions either. So please . . . not tonight."

Geesh, how many more people could she tell off in a single evening? First Ford, then Levi, now her best friend. Had her entire personality changed over the course of just three hours?

"Sorry," Rayne murmured. "That was rude."

"Hey, I'm rude to people every day. Of course, I've got the whole fifty-percent-Italian thing going on. But still, I couldn't imagine having to be sweet day in and day out. You're pardoned."

"Thanks." Rayne almost smiled, but the weight bearing against her chest wouldn't allow it. She plodded toward the service door to check in with Cal and Celeste before—

"I saved you a piece of Delia's coconut cream pie." The only sentence that could give Rayne pause. A customized dangling carrot.

She slowed. "No questions?"

"Scout's honor."

"You weren't a Girl Scout."

"Yeah, but I sold their cookies."

"No, you pushed their red wagon down the hill into the Pattersons' pond, and then Cal had to give a large donation to the troop leader to cover the cost." And to clear the family name.

"Well," Gia huffed. "For being in such a sour mood, someone has an excellent memory."

Rayne pivoted at half speed, exposing her face to her cousin's full examination, as if each one of the dried tears on her cheeks were a map of tonight's events.

She could almost hear Gia's drama detector dinging. She was likely regretting her fake Girl Scout pledge as much as the time she bleached her hair in eighth grade.

Rayne slumped onto a barstool and staked both elbows on the cold granite.

"Please note that I'm happy to converse with you about that which shall not be asked, if you change your mind."

"Noted."

Gia opened the refrigerator, took out a red plate with a single slice of coconut pie ready to be devoured, and then slid it down the counter.

Rayne dipped the prongs of her fork into the peak of the triangle, the way she had a dozen times in her life, but before she could bring it to her mouth, the fork slipped from her fingers and clinked against the porcelain. Unbidden, her tears came again—only this time, they couldn't be coaxed away.

"Okay, screw this Girl Scout crap. What the heck is wrong with you? Why are you crying on your favorite pie?"

"It was never supposed to get this far. I was never supposed to feel like this about him." Her shoulders shook in unison with her muffled vibrato.

Gia shuffled around the counter. "Uh, okay . . . just stay there. I'm gonna close the door."

The swinging door whooshed closed.

"So there's a guy?" Gia asked.

"*Was* a guy. It's over now." The words knifed through her insides.

"Who?"

Gia handed her a paper towel, and Rayne blotted her cheeks and then blew her nose. She met her cousin's eyes with purposeful silence, saying everything she refused to speak aloud.

"No." Disbelief masked every line and curve of Gia's face. "No way. You've been seeing him? In secret?"

"Shhh." Before another gush of tears, a hushed reprimand squeezed from Rayne's throat.

Gia hunched down farther, her palms flat against the granite, her pupils large and focused. "How long has this . . . this whatever it is been going on?"

"A month. And like I said, it's not going on anymore."

"A *month*?" Her cousin straightened, her springy curls framing her face like a glossy beauty-salon poster. "I don't even know what to say."

Rayne swallowed another batch of rising guilt. She'd turned into a deceiver—the worst kind of secret keeper—and she'd lied to the girl who'd taught her how to tie her shoes and script her name in cursive. "I know, I'm sorry." She exhaled, hunkering down for a storm she'd brewed all on her own. Whatever lecture Gia planned to spew, Rayne deserved.

Only, Gia's emotional pendulum didn't swing toward outrage. "It's not that I can't see the appeal—I dated He-Who-Must-Not-Be-Named, after all. You probably saw Levi as something new and exciting, something different than all the pretentious jerks who check in for weeklong business trips and flaunt their connections like designer watches."

True, but Levi was more than that. So much more. "Yes."

"And I'm sure he made you feel unique, special, even?"

Again, Rayne nodded. She'd been a small child the last time she'd felt so cared for, so cherished.

"Well, then be grateful you were smart enough to end it when you did. The whole forbidden-romance thing . . . it's a myth. No woman ever marries the man they have to hide. The adventure, the adrenaline, those things are fun while they last. But that kind of commitment is as temporary as the heartache you feel now."

Levi's haunted expression appeared like a mirage. "I hurt him, Gia."

Her cousin pushed off from the counter and leaned against the oven. "Better him than you, unless you were hoping to end up like Cousin Milton."

Cousin Milton's fate took precedence in her mind—the man's permanent removal from the Shelby history wall. From their family.

Gia pinched the edge of the pie plate and pushed it closer. "Maybe you'll change your mind about this piece of pie after you hear what happened between Cal and Celeste at dinner."

Gia could shift a conversation as fast as a NASCAR driver could shift gears.

"Tonight's dinner?"

"Let's just say, this shelter idea of yours could be the ticket to getting Celeste on a plane home. And soon."

"Why?"

"She's horrible with people. Snapped at a family of four checking in right in front of Cal. Celeste may know business on paper, but she doesn't understand the art of common courtesy."

Despite her churning stomach, Rayne ran her pinky along the crumbly edge of the piecrust.

"Cal scolded her in the hallway like she was an unruly teenager."

After being on the receiving end of so many of Celeste's finger-pointing sessions, Rayne felt the tiniest tickle of glee at Gia's report. Right or wrong, it was impossible not to. Slowly, she lifted her fork and trapped a fallen chunk of coconut between the tines. And then, she brought the bite to her lips.

"You belong here, Rayne, because when you're not, everything falls apart."

CHAPTER TWENTY-SEVEN

He ignored the fatigue in his arms and tightened his grip on the ax handle, driving the blade straight through the center of another green pine round. The stiff recoil shot through his forearms and into his shoulders. A satisfying mask for his pain. He assessed the damage. The splintered kindling lay at his feet like matchsticks.

It hadn't been the first time he'd been left with a bullet wound of rejection. But unlike the hole his father had left, Rayne's rejection felt closer to a grenade blast. A grenade he'd handed her.

He shifted his stance, crunching foliage and sun-warped vegetation underfoot, his mind plagued by her words, her body language, her perfectly pitched voice. He sailed a curse through the air and struck the hard block again.

With fires raging east and west, the air reeked of ash and irony. The burn ban for residential properties tacked a hefty fine, but Levi didn't need the wood for burning. He needed it to keep him sane. Keep his uncivil and unlawful thoughts in check.

He'd split and stacked another five rounds when Ford appeared in his peripheral vision. He swung again, not yet ready to chop the mound of fury building inside him into coherent words.

"Enough, son."

"You don't want to do this right now."

"I know you're angry with me."

Levi squeezed the hickory handle, his calluses splitting under the strain. "You had a golden opportunity, Ford. She was right there, right in front of you, and you let her run. Without the truth! Without the real story of what happened between you and William's sons!"

"You didn't tell her?" Ford's calm question only fueled Levi's frustration.

"I gave you my word." And Levi wouldn't break it. Not even for the only woman he'd ever loved. Not when the consequences weren't his alone to bear.

"I appreciate that, Levi. More than you know."

Too bad Levi was in no mood to be appreciated. "You should have told her, Ford."

"She isn't ready."

Levi embedded the blade into the center of the wood round and kicked his stack of freshly cut pine. "Seriously? Eighteen years isn't long enough?"

"Lies are easier for people to accept. Especially the ones with roots."

"That's your answer? You freak her out and then decide she's better off believing Cal's brainwashing?"

"I shared as much as I could. My words will mean nothing to her if she doesn't trust the man who speaks them. To her, I'm a stranger."

Levi slashed a finger through the smoky air. "You are her *family*, Ford! Her *blood*! She deserves to know you and you deserve to be known!" His heated words echoed through the darkness.

"I understood the cost the day I signed my rights away."

A martyr's explanation if ever Levi heard one. "Doesn't matter. Cal manipulated you. His ultimatum was a lose-lose."

"I don't disagree, but the what-if game will only take you so far. If I hadn't signed those papers, Winslow Farm wouldn't exist. Second Harvest wouldn't exist. And neither would your future inheritance. This land—this property—was the avenue God chose to bring you to me. A provision, not a punishment. Never forget that." Ford shuffled closer, the dry brush underfoot snapping and popping. "I've planted the seed, son. If Rayne wants to find the truth, she'll have to ask."

"She's made her choice; she chose her family, the lodge. You were right."

"I take no joy in being right. I'm sorry you're hurting."

"And I'm sorry she's too afraid to stand up to her family."

"A lesson we've both learned the hard way."

Levi scrubbed a hand up the back of his neck and expelled a weighted sigh. He'd acted out of fear plenty of times in his youth, believed physical pain was the only remedy for the pain within. Before Ford had taught him to think with his mind. To use his God-given gifts for something better. For something bigger than himself. His gaze dropped to the ax he held. But this time, before Levi could lift it, Ford gripped the end of the handle.

"Enough."

At the sound of Ford's hushed command, Levi's hold relaxed. He pictured Rayne again, the way she'd kissed him, the way she'd fit in his arms . . . the way she'd shut him out and left him standing in the dark. Alone.

Enough, he repeated to the urge within. *Enough.*

CHAPTER TWENTY-EIGHT

Her shriek could have shattered Plexiglas. Cold water trailed over her scalp and dripped down the back of her neck onto her pale-green shirt. A gaggle of giggles issued from behind her favorite old climbing tree out back. Incredibly, the oak's drought-resistant leaves still held their waxy shine—a sight she took comfort in, despite the ever-changing climate.

"We're sorry, Miss Rayne! It was kind of hazy over there. We weren't sure that was you," came the playful voice of a boy peeking around the tree trunk. Brian Miller.

Rayne whisked her damp hair off her shoulder and wrung it out, holding back a smile and a giggle of her own. "Sure, sure, try and blame the smoke. Too bad I can see you just fine." She reached into their bulging bucket of water balloons and selected the plumpest one she could find. "Brian Miller, this one has your name written all over it." She flung it toward the tree, missing her target by several feet. Apparently her sure-shot aim with a pistol didn't translate into water play.

Another eruption of laughter echoed through the property as the children chased each other, smashing swollen balloons and squealing as if they were at summer camp and not a fire shelter. Regardless, the sound instantly lifted Rayne's divided spirit, providing a momentary pause from the drama in and out of the lodge.

Despite the latest fire updates and neighborhood clearances in Bear Canyon, every available room at the lodge remained occupied. The fire evacuations were far from over. Several more bordering towns had been alerted to the emergency-protocol procedures over the last few days. The total number of firefighter recruits had increased to over eight hundred in the last week, but due to the thirsty topography, the containment level still remained just under 30 percent, and current statistics showed these fires were not only the worst in Idaho's history but the worst in the nation.

Rayne passed a young couple—Dan and Michelle Braiker—who'd checked in last night. They sat on the porch swing out back, cuddling their baby boy and whispering sweet assurances to one another. Unlike the Bear Canyon residents, they'd only been given a five-minute evacuation warning. Five minutes to lock up their home and flee to safety. Rayne wasn't about to turn them away. Luckily, one of her father's assistants hadn't arrived with his entourage yesterday afternoon, so she'd been able to give them a suite on the top floor.

She strolled around the corner to the dead garden and plucked several crispy weeds from the soil. The Pinskey family waved from the picnic table nearby, a game of Monopoly in play.

"Ha! I got Park Place! I'm *so* going to win this thing," their middle son boasted, waving the miniature deed in the air like a winning lottery ticket. Rhonda Pinskey chuckled and nodded at Rayne's soaked shirt. "Please tell me you retaliated."

Rayne tucked her damp hair behind her ear and shrugged. "Tried but failed."

The woman winked. "That's exactly why I stick to board games."

"Smart woman."

Rayne climbed the side steps onto the back porch and peered into the Great Room from the outside window. Several parents had adopted the mind-set of the Pinskeys during their wait, keeping their children entertained and their anxiety in check. The common areas brimmed with activity. Families and friends gathered in every pocket of the lodge. And the sight of such camaraderie warmed the uncertainties of Rayne's heart. *This* was what she loved. *This* was why she'd stayed. *This* was why she'd chosen the lodge. She'd been a young girl the last time she'd seen such a beautiful display of community inside her grandfather's lodge, not to mention the last time their open-door policy had applied to more than just the affluent.

She scanned the yellowing lawn and spied a trio of teenage girls, water balloons behind their backs, creeping up on a group of unsuspecting boys. She laughed as their sneak attack was met with hoots and hollers. Could Levi hear them from the farm? Was he even home? Did he hate her?

The dip in her stomach and the hum of her meandering thoughts were almost enough to derail her efforts to forget her heartache, but then she focused her attention on the yard in front of her, forcing herself to remember the Shelby Falls Easter-egg hunts that her grandfather had hosted right here. And then, how on Sunday afternoons in the summer, their barbecue chicken and watermelon feeds would draw families from several communities over. Kids would splash in the stream at the edge of the property while adults chitchatted in the sunshine.

Much had changed since then, and yet, the shelter had brought it all back. The purpose. The meaning. The legacy. She couldn't be the only one who felt it. The people of Shelby Falls were as much a part of Shelby history as her own blood.

"Rayne—" Her father jerked to a stop while straightening his suit coat. "What happened to you?"

She shrugged. "Water balloons."

If there was ever a time she saw the resemblance between her father and Cal, it was in their shared scowl of annoyance.

"Well, you'll need to get presentable quickly. You're giving a tour of the shelter tonight."

"To who?"

"Celeste didn't tell you?"

"She tends to have her own communication style." As in cold-shoulder communication. Although Celeste had wasted no time fawning over the governor by asking him all sorts of who-do-you-know questions. Her father's favorite kind.

"I'm sure she was just busy."

She caught herself before she could ask, *Busy with what, exactly?*

Celeste had done nothing but complain about excess clutter. Cal hadn't been much better. This morning at breakfast, Rayne had overheard him recounting a near-death incident involving an abandoned Matchbox car and the bottom of his shoe.

But truth be told, the lodge was holding up amazingly well, considering . . . well, everything.

"I thought the producer for your ad campaign was delayed until tomorrow," Rayne said.

"He is, but Tina Tucker from Channel 9 will be here in an hour. They're doing a live on-location shot from the Great Room for the six o'clock news—which reminds me, I need you to round up a few families to sit in the background. Preferably the ones with the most compelling evacuation stories."

"Round them up?" Were they cattle or people? "To do what?"

A cloud of disapproval passed over his features. Randall enjoyed being questioned about as much as Cal did. "To share how Shelby Lodge stepped in during their time of need—if the opportunity arises."

Her stomach seemed to digest his words at the same rate as her mind. "You want me to ask them to cheerlead for us while they're waiting to find out if they still have a home tomorrow?"

"Just position them, Rayne." Position them. The way he'd tried to position her before finally throwing in the towel on the whole *politics is in our blood* speech. The Shelby comparison game had started soon after.

He patted her on the shoulder before striding back inside. Conversation over.

She swallowed, looking from the Pinskeys to the Braikers to young, freckle-faced Brian Miller. They were all supposed to be guests of the Shelbys, not spokespeople.

—

Rayne was no stranger to the media. She and Gia had been on a couple of commercials with their grandfather back in the day, one for a lodge advertisement and the other for a voting measure demanding safer school playgrounds. But the starry-eyed little girl who'd loved climbing into Grandpa's lap and waiting for prompts to smile and nod like a glorified puppet would trade places with a root canal patient right about now.

Tina Tucker's perfectly sprayed-in-place hairdo would be entertaining if she weren't so utterly enthusiastic about everything Governor Randall Shelby said. Sure, her father was handsome, even Rayne could see that, but this was live TV. And the man was a governor. A married governor. *Keep it in check, lady.*

"It's an honor to have you with us in Shelby Falls, Governor. Have you been surprised by the quick turn of events in this year's fire season?" Tina asked with Miss America flair.

His smile was as shiny as his gold cufflinks. "My team has been keeping me up to date since the first fire broke out near Wenatchee. With the dry climate and lack of winter snowfall, we were prepared for a bad season, so we had very specific protocols in place to declare a county—or several counties, in this instance—in a state of emergency. Swift reaction time is the first key to providing help in a crisis."

"And what about deeming your family's lodge—Shelby Lodge—a temporary shelter? How was that decision made?"

"Some decisions are simply the right ones to make. As my late father, Governor William Shelby, used to say, 'Don't expect anyone to follow what you don't live.' If we aren't willing to open our door to help families in crisis, how can we expect anyone else to? God, family, and community. That's always been our family's position."

Wait—had her father just insinuated the decision to open the shelter had been his idea? She blinked hard, only to be caught in Cal's calculated glower from a few steps behind Tina. She could practically hear his thoughts pummeling into her head. *Smile. Nod. Support your father. Be a Shelby, Rayne.*

"And Rayne." Tina swooped her unmovable hair in Rayne's direction. "I'm told you've grown up in the lodge, worked here since you were of legal age. Can you describe what the mood's been like in the shelter for the past few days? I'm sure you've seen many tears."

"Yes, we've seen tears, but we've seen just as many smiles," Rayne answered honestly. "The atmosphere around the lodge has been incredibly inspiring. To hear the stories of Bear Canyon, even from those who've lost their homes—there's an undercurrent of hope that never seems to fade. I've witnessed neighbors helping each other, crying with each other, and encouraging one another time and time again. It's given me hope for our community."

Her father pressed a firm hand to her upper back. "We'll get through this together. As a community. Northern Idaho needs all the resources we can get—to rebuild and reestablish, which is why I've petitioned for help from the federal government."

Tina urged with a nod. "Yes, and as your daughter pointed out earlier in our interviews with the families, our community couldn't be any more grateful."

Her father turned toward the camera. "Again, I'm committed to seeing Idaho thrive—in whatever season we find ourselves."

Her father, the hero, the knight in shining armor of Idaho. Suddenly, she was the one who wanted to cry. Had he heard their guests' stories? Had he seen their faces? Their need? Their heartache? Their courage? Or had he only seen the potential for favorable publicity and future votes?

CHAPTER TWENTY-NINE

Mindlessly, Levi riffled through his stack of poker chips. He hadn't blinked in close to a minute. Hadn't reached for his drink. Hadn't celebrated his winning hand. No, his mind was far from the four kings and a jack slapped faceup on the table in front of him. He'd been transported 9.2 miles away. Inside the Great Room of Shelby Lodge.

Ranger Hat Guy had flipped on the local news ten minutes ago, cranking the volume above the twangy country chick blaring through the overhead speakers.

And now Rayne, *his Rayne*, stood next to the governor. Only she wasn't his Rayne. She wasn't the work-boot-wearing, get-her-hands-dirty Rayne. *This* Rayne was a politician's daughter. Proper, poised, and perfectly untouchable.

His fingers stilled the chips as he listened to her father's phony speech about *family taking care of family*. The man didn't have the first clue about what it meant to take care of his family.

If Ranger Hat Guy didn't turn the channel soon he'd—

Her voice broke through his agitation and everything inside him seized up at once. He leaned forward, as if his proximity to the television might cause her to notice him. But unlike her father, sincerity flowed from her lips in a smooth, confident cadence. Her gold-flecked eyes were alight as she spoke of the shelter, the stories she'd heard, the hope she'd experienced. Adoration for the community radiated off every inch of her face, and a missile of jealousy fired straight from his core and leveled his inhibitions. She'd stared at him the same way not even three days ago.

He knew then he'd been wrong. It wasn't enough to let her go. He had to make it right, do what he should have done weeks ago.

"I know that look." A rough baritone cut through his plotting. "You're about to do something really, really stupid, aren't you?"

"Maybe." Levi pushed out from the table and stood. "I'd invite you along but . . ."

Travis eased back in his chair and gave Levi a see-ya-later salute. "If you're going where I think you're going, then I best stay put."

"Exactly."

There was no lack of activity surrounding the lodge. The cramped parking lot overflowed with cars, trucks, and small trailers. Orange safety cones lined the end of Levi's driveway and spotted the country highway for a quarter mile.

Levi pulled into the lot as a black Escalade with tinted windows was pulling out. Governor Shelby's entourage, he was sure of it. If the man was headed back to Boise, then he'd lasted longer than Levi had expected. Long enough to pat some backs, shake some hands, and smile for the camera. *A saint of a man, really.*

Levi flicked his hazards on and parked in the loading zone at the side of the kitchen. He gripped the steering wheel, said a silent prayer, and then carried his first box up the steps to the lion's den.

Like the front door, the side entrance remained unlocked. It popped open at the slightest push of the handle. The clattering of pans pinged against his eardrums as the smell of sugary pastries laced the air. Stepping inside, he off-loaded his cargo onto a granite countertop.

He cleared his throat to alert the woman at the sink of his presence.

She rinsed away the suds on a shiny baking sheet. "Oh, sorry. Didn't hear you come in." She dried her hands on her apron front and turned to face him. "You must be from the Red Cr—" Her words vanished along with her smile.

So this was Delia. The lodge's longtime cook. The same woman who'd made the cookies Rayne had gifted him with. The same woman whose timeless smile was framed on Ford's bookcase. Though Levi had never seen her up close, never spoken to her, he hoped whatever affection she'd shared with Ford hadn't faded as quickly as their relationship.

Levi patted the cardboard lid. "I have a delivery for the shelter, a donation of perishable foods and other supplies. There's a few more in my truck out back too, along with a list of vendors who'd like to help."

As if trying to orient herself, her gaze dropped to the label on the box. "You're Ford's boy?"

"Yes, ma'am. I'm Levi Harding." He gave her his best boy-next-door grin. "It's nice to meet you, Delia."

She glanced at the service door with the same anxious gaze he'd seen on Rayne a thousand times. Voices echoed and chair legs screeched in the next room. Delia's stance grew antsy. "That's awfully kind of you, but I'm just about to serve dessert, so this really isn't the best time for—"

A blonde pushed into the kitchen, a snarl on her lips and a manicured hand at her waist. "The natives are growing restless out there. Can we get the kids their cookies already?"

Levi clamped his mouth shut before a laugh could escape. Celeste was everything Rayne had said and more. Emphasis on the *more*.

"Oh?" Celeste waltzed his direction. He didn't miss the flick of her gaze to his left hand. "I didn't realize you had company, Delia."

He wasn't an expert in women's fashion, not hardly. But he was fairly certain he'd seen her footwear in one of Ford's World War II books, as a torture device.

Delia touched Levi's shoulder, and he couldn't help but note she smelled like cinnamon-sugar toast. "He was just leaving," she said. "I was about to walk him out."

"Actually," Levi countered, "I need to get a signature from Rayne before I can go."

"From Rayne?" the women asked in unison.

Levi nodded and hitched his thumb toward the noise in the Great Room. "I'm fine to find her on my own."

"Or perhaps I can sign whatever it is you need." Celeste's tone suggested her signature offered more than pen and paper.

"Sorry." Levi shook his head. "Has to be Rayne. Boss's orders." Self-employment had its perks.

"I'll get her," Delia said, her eyes flicking to the tray of warm cookies set near the stovetop. "Celeste, take these cookies into the Great Room and make sure you limit the little ones to two each."

Celeste's rumpled brow made her seem much older than a woman approaching thirty. "I could just take him out there, she's right around the—"

"No. I'll do it. Just take care of the cookies." Delia pushed through the swinging door and shot a silent warning over her shoulder.

"Humph." The blonde reached for the cookie platter, giving him a last once-over before exiting.

Less than a minute later, Rayne breezed into the kitchen, her heels skidding to a stop, her lips framing his name in a soundless whisper.

Obviously, Delia hadn't mentioned who was waiting for her behind door number one.

Rayne wore the same pink politician's-daughter getup she'd worn on camera, her obsidian hair hidden in a tight knot behind her head. White pearls stabbed through her earlobes, and a matching string of beads choked her neck, peeking through the window of her open collar. But even still, *even still*, the sight of her up close wrecked him. A confirmation he needed. This was his chance to make things right—for her.

She deserved the truth.

Delia latched the kitchen door, her gaze sliding from one to the other. "Say whatever needs to be said, but you both better make it quick. I'll be in the pantry." She pointed to the lighted doorway a few steps away. Thankfully, he didn't need privacy for this conversation.

He expected his first line to be smoother, but her nearness seemed to strangle the words in his throat. "You gave a good interview."

Rayne shook her head as if to skip over any explanation he could possibly offer for why he'd shown up unannounced. "You can't be here, Levi."

"As a concerned citizen of Shelby Falls, I thought it best not to ignore the governor's request for supplies and fresh produce."

"Why are you doing this—to hurt me?" She cut her voice to a fraction above a whisper. "You asked me to choose. I chose."

If she only knew how many times he'd replayed her choice.

"I love you, Rayne Shelby. I need you to hear that."

Delia mumbled something from inside the pantry in a language he didn't recognize.

Rayne's bottom lip quivered. "You're the one not hearing me. You can't be here."

"I love you."

"Stop." It was a cry more than a command.

His fingers burned to touch her, to pull her close. What he wouldn't give to breathe her in one last time before he struck the match that would set her world on fire. "Why? Would my feelings for you be any less real if I didn't speak them? You know they wouldn't." He knew Rayne was familiar with the art of omission; she'd used it on him the other night. She hadn't denied her feelings; she'd simply excluded them. A genius move on her part. One that had taken him the better part of two days to unravel.

"You're making this so much worse. For both of us." The slip in her voice sharpened his senses.

"Worse?" He shook his head. "No, *worse* is watching you on a flat screen and wondering if that's the only version I'll ever get to see of you again."

She pressed the tremble from her lips and peered at the floor through dark lashes.

He inched closer, his voice pinched and hoarse. "For what it's worth, you were right when you said this is bigger than us. It's always been bigger than us."

Rayne angled toward the back door, as if to encourage him to leave, but instead he succumbed to temptation. He captured her wrist and brushed his lips across the back of her hand.

When her glassy eyes met his, he said the only thing he could. "I'm sorry, Rayne, but this is the only way."

There were only two people on the planet who could unravel the web of deceit Rayne Shelby lived in: one she called a cheat and the other she called an uncle.

He released her hand and headed in the opposite direction of the exit.

In four long strides, he reached the kitchen's service door and entered the Great Room.

It was time to set the lies on fire.

CHAPTER THIRTY

Like in the worst of her nightmares, she couldn't force her muscles and bones to synchronize. Her legs felt like they were wading through a sea of wet concrete, every part of her moving in slow motion until she gripped the door Levi had disappeared behind.

Perspiration gathered underneath her arms and at the back of her neck. Her belly churned with the kind of dread that could make her retch into the nearest trash can. He'd tricked her, pulled a bait and switch on her heart, and for what?

Her vision clouded as she wove through the maze of tables in the Great Room. The urge to call after him pressed against her vocal cords. But he'd already been swallowed up in the crowd. He patted several men on the back, greeting them by name and asking for updates on their homes, their families, their properties, all while continuing to push toward the front of the room.

He knew their community well, likely better than she did. He'd worked with these people, sold goods to these people, shared his life with these people.

She picked up her pace. He stood only two table lengths away now. When she bumped the back of a chair, a tiny hand stretched out and tugged on the sleeve of her suit coat.

"Miss Rayne, will you play Go Fish with us?"

The mental downshift was painful, but somehow, she formulated a polite decline before spotting Levi near the picture windows. In less than two minutes, he'd managed to capture the attention of every adult in the room.

Including Cal's.

Bricks of fear stacked up inside her as her uncle stalked toward him, his glower honed and sharp.

Now one table away, her legs finally caught up to her mind. Cal wrapped a hand around Levi's arm, bearing a tepid grin, the kind that masked murder. He pushed in close, his mouth less than an inch from Levi's ear. She studied the snarl of his lips as they spoke in a hushed staccato. To the casual eye, the exchange could look cordial, but she knew differently. Her uncle's words were a calculated death sentence.

When she closed the distance, Levi didn't reach for her. He simply shifted his gaze to a look that made every bone in her body liquefy.

"Tell Rayne the truth about the farm."

Cal angled his back to the curious onlookers and spoke through gritted teeth. "You have ten seconds to vacate my premises or—"

"Tell her you've lied to her for the last eighteen years or I'll start telling a bedtime story to this room full of people. It's your kind of tale, Cal. Full of villains and deceit and family betrayal." Levi stared him straight in the eye. "You may own half of Shelby Falls, but you will never own me. And your lies won't own her for another minute."

Cal's grip tightened on Levi's arm. *"Shut your mouth."*

"Then start talking."

Rayne's lungs burned as she waited for her uncle to dismiss Levi's claim, to cling to the only story she'd been told since Grandpa Shelby's funeral.

Cal shifted his stance. "We'll discuss this in my office."

"No." Levi's jaw pulsed on the word. "We'll discuss it *right here*. Look your niece in the eye and tell her she's believed your lies for the past eighteen years. Tell her Ford didn't manipulate that land from your father. Tell her you offered Ford the farm in exchange for his signature and his silence."

Nostrils flaring, Cal's scowl turned lethal. "You will pay severely for this stunt."

Unfazed by Cal's threat, Levi continued, "Story time begins in three seconds. Three, two—"

Cal turned his hate-filled eyes on her. "I lied about the farm." Her uncle's overly pronounced words stabbed into her eardrums, a pain that reverberated throughout her skull and knocked the breath from her lungs.

Teeth bared, Cal jerked Levi closer. "Now get off my property before I have you arrested for trespassing."

Levi broke away from Cal's hold and started for the exit as if to leave her behind with a million unanswered questions.

On impulse, she reached for him—*"Wait."*

Every hushed murmur in the room paused as her plea echoed throughout the hall. In the span of a few lost heartbeats, Levi's gaze trailed from her face to the hand on his forearm.

There was a look—something like an apology in his eyes, yet no words followed from his mouth. He slipped out of her grasp and didn't turn back.

Gone.

"My office. *Now.*"

Ice licked the length of her spine, crystalizing every organ in her torso.

After a stiff yank on the lapels of his coat, Cal trailed through the chairs and tables, his pace eerily understated for the drama that had just occurred. Rayne stayed close on his heels, catching sight of Delia as they rounded into the lobby. Had Delia witnessed what had happened? Did she understand it?

Cal's footsteps paused when he addressed the cook. "Make sure he leaves the premises *immediately*."

"Yes, sir." Delia met Rayne's eyes again, pity replacing her earlier bewilderment before she turned away.

Cal tapped a bony finger to his study door, and it creaked open as if on its own. He waited in the doorway for her to pass, the narrow gap a tight fit, even for her small frame. Heart pounding, head swimming, Rayne jetted past him into the familiar den. Clove and tobacco seasoned the air and her eyes drifted to the sealed cigar box on his right.

"Sit," he ordered.

Her adrenaline would never allow her to sit. "I want to stand."

"I didn't ask what you wanted. Sit down."

She perched on the edge of a seat closest to the door, her knees bouncing to the second hand of the clock. The tick, tick, tick of a bomb that had already been thrown. She waited for him to speak, to explain, to fill in the hidden holes of her history, but he said nothing as he lowered his rigid frame into the leather chair.

"Tell me about the will—about what really happened with the farm," she said.

"Are you really going to question *me*?"

Rayne flinched, but no matter how glacial his stare, she wouldn't be deterred. "What happened with the farm, with Ford Winslow?"

Cal pressed back in his chair and drummed his fingers on his desk in slow repetition. "Do you know what I find so interesting? Why, after all these years, Ford's little charity case would turn up inside my lodge and demand answers . . . for *you*."

She coached herself to remain calm. He wanted nothing more than to mask the scent of his own sin by a curtain of accusations. She wouldn't let him. She wouldn't leave without answers.

"What did Ford sign? What did he have to stay quiet about?"

Cal angled his head as if to retrieve a piece of information he'd filed away in the back of his mind. "You've always been so naive, Rayne. A trait I've tolerated out of respect for your father. But the problem with naive people"—he leaned forward and steepled his fingers—"is that they trust too easily. Get taken advantage of too often. And worse, they become pawns in a game they were never meant to play."

"Don't be a politician with me. I'm your niece; I deserve to know the truth about my grandfather's will—that does not make me a pawn."

"No?" The weak overhead light and dark-mahogany walls carved shadows above his eye sockets, in the hollows of his cheeks, and in the family divot at the base of his chin. "What do you know about that boy? Please tell me you don't actually believe his hero ploy." Cal inched closer. "The son of a convicted cop killer is hardly a hero."

Blood drained from her head and sloshed in her belly. Cal's mouth twisted into a venomous smile. "Oh, he failed to mention that tidbit of information? It's true. A life sentence for shooting a state trooper in the head during a drug run."

She squeezed her eyes closed and replayed Levi's words again—hearing the pain laced in his voice, the hurt etched into his face.

"Trust me when I say, you're the easiest mark he's ever had," Cal continued, flicking the brass closure on the cigar box open and then lifting the lid. "He doesn't want you. He wants the same as everybody else—connection, power, money, a slice of your inheritance. Sound familiar? It should."

"No." She shook her head. "Stop trying to make this about Levi." She wished she could cut the fear from her voice. "*This* is about what happened eighteen years ago. What you did."

Cal slammed the lid and her body jerked upright. "What I did eighteen years ago saved this family!"

She gripped the arms of her chair. "From what?"

"From the same spineless betrayal you're exhibiting right now. I saw the way you reached for him, the way you looked at him—I *hear* the way you're protecting him even now. Do you think that because your daddy is governor you don't have to abide by our rules? That you can behave however you please, sneak around with whomever you want, share a bed with whomever—"

"How dare you assume—"

"You live as if consequence doesn't exist!"

She pushed forward. "No, I live as if consequence is the *only* thing that exists! Every decision I make is weighed and measured against my last name." A sob caught in her throat. "You've known me my entire life. You gave me my first job, wrote my letter of recommendation to Gonzaga University. You groomed me to be your successor and yet you still won't trust me enough to tell me the truth about our family."

"You haven't *earned* my trust. I told you to stay away from that farm. You ignored my warning. Twice." He tipped his head to the side, his chest heaving in uneven pumps. "It's time you figured out how to live without the Shelby safety net. You have two hours to vacate my property."

Her grip on the chair slackened.

"You're fired."

CHAPTER THIRTY-ONE

Icy water lapped over her naked toes, numbing her feet the way she wished to numb her heart. A vastly different reality from the last time she had stood here. With Levi. Possibility had seemed as deep as the attraction they'd felt. As the kisses they'd shared. As the promises they'd spoken.

The sun's dying light, suspended in a smoke cloud, stretched across the water, the hues dull and lifeless like the vegetation all around her. Limp weeds dragged behind the pull of a slow-moving current, while brittle pine needles spiraled to the ground below. No birds chirped nearby, and the only scents tainting the air now were of soot and decay and the ashes of dreams set aflame.

The most sought-after view in Shelby Falls had become nothing more than a grainy blur, much like the last three hours of her life.

Cradling a rock in her palm, she peered into the haze across the narrow shoreline. How many times had she held a stone in her hand just like this one—hoping her practice paid off, hoping her efforts would be seen, hoping her best would be enough.

Hoping she would be enough.

She plopped the dead weight into the water and watched it sink to the bottom.

How foolish she'd been to hope.

"There you are." Gia meandered across the rocky terrain. "I was beginning to think you'd sent me on some kind of smoky goose chase." She coughed in the crook of her elbow. "I was finishing up a glaze when I got your text and . . ." Gia's words died out. "Rayne, what's going on?"

"What do you know about Granddaddy's will?" The question seemed as haunted as her voice.

"His *will*? Why? What's this about? And where are your shoes? That water has to be freezing."

She'd abandoned her shoes and overcoat somewhere along the trail, not bothering to note where. She didn't budge. All feeling below her ankles had died before she'd even had time to care about the pain. "Did Aunt Nina ever mention how the land was divided or how the inheritance was split?"

"I don't think so, although I make it a point not to dwell on anything prior to nineteen ninety-nine. Messes with my creativity. Again, *why* is this important?"

"Cal lied."

"Cal makes a living off his lies. He works for your father, remember?"

"This is different. This isn't about politics; it's about us. Our family. Something happened eighteen years ago. Something big."

Gia twisted her hips, her face a mask of confusion. "Like what?"

Rayne wished she knew. "Levi came to the lodge tonight."

"Like . . . *inside* the lodge? You told me your fling was over." Gia's irritation sparked through the humid air.

"He confronted Cal, Gia. He threatened to expose him in front of the entire shelter if Cal didn't admit to lying about the will—about how Ford Winslow really acquired the farm."

For a girl who never missed an opportunity for a snarky comeback, Gia's silence said she didn't know what to make of it either.

"I've never seen Cal look so"—a shiver feathered over Rayne's skin—"terrifying."

"I don't understand what you're telling me."

How could she possibly help her cousin understand what she couldn't even put into words? "I don't have the answers, Gia. I just know what I saw—what I heard."

Unbidden, the memory of Levi's apology whispered from the hollows of her heart. *I'm sorry, Rayne, but this is the only way.* And for the thousandth time since packing up her cabin, she pushed his voice away.

Pushed him away.

The feelings inside her were too strong—too confusing—too tangled for her to sort.

"Why wait—I mean, if Levi knew a secret about our family, why wouldn't he tell you sooner?"

Rayne had asked herself that same question. Over and over again. "I don't know. At first I worried he showed up to expose us, to hurt me for hurting him." Her throat tightened around her impending vulnerability. "But now I wonder if he was trying to warn me." Rayne focused on the obscured mountain peaks and exhaled. "Do you remember him, Gia?"

"Who?"

"Ford."

Gia's top lip curled. "Not much, and that's how I prefer it."

"I saw him. The night I ended things with Levi. I saw Ford, talked to him."

Her mind drifted back to that night, to Ford's tranquil demeanor, to the steady cadence of his voice, to the question that haunted her for days. *What had she asked him in the grocery store?*

"I may not remember much about him, but I definitely remember the lectures from my parents after the funeral," Gia admitted. "To never wander over to the farm and to stay away from Ford and his employees."

Rayne remembered the same, only there was something more, something scratching at the corner of her mind, a memory she couldn't quite retrieve, a dog-eared page too faded to decode.

They fell into a pensive quiet, each lost to some piece of the past.

"Handcuffs," Gia said absently.

Rayne turned. "Handcuffs?"

"Yeah, I remember my dad used them the day of Grandpa's funeral. I asked him about it when he tucked me into bed that night and he told me not to worry, to go to sleep, but I snuck onto the stairs and overheard my parents recounting the story. My dad cuffed Ford. For trespassing."

"Trespassing?" Her disbelief tangled with surprise.

"Don't look so shocked, Pollyanna. You know what kind of person he is—"

"No, I'm not sure I do." The thought slipped out of her mouth unfiltered.

"Listen, Rayne, I know this may be hard for you to believe, but scorned lovers do a lot of crazy, stupid things after they've been rejected. You're giving Levi too much credit. Maybe you're overthinking this whole thing."

But Levi's face hadn't been crazed or wild. He'd been intent, focused, determined . . . so why had he put her at risk? Why had he gone to her uncle? Why, if he loved her, hadn't he told her the secret? Unless Gia was right and there was no secret. "Maybe so."

"Cal's a power-hungry rat for sure, but even he has his limits. If there were some big discrepancy in Granddaddy's will, he wouldn't have been able to hide it this long. Not in this town. Whatever happened tonight between Levi and Cal isn't enough to lose sleep over."

The irony of Gia's statement penetrated the last of her emotional armor. "I lost my job."

Gia's curls whipped behind her back. *"What?"*

"Cal fired me. After Levi left, I questioned him too, begged him to tell me the truth. And he fired me."

The shock on Gia's face reflected the shock protecting Rayne's mind from processing the implications of her statement. Only now that it was out, now that she'd spoken the words with her own mouth and heard them with her own ears, a suffocating panic tore at her chest from the inside.

She'd lost the lodge.

Her cousin's olive complexion paled under the strain of silence. "Oh, Rayne. What have you done?"

CHAPTER THIRTY-TWO

Levi pressed his free hand to his ear to block the sound blaring from Ford's living room. His phone had been permanently affixed to his head since midmorning. "Tom, listen, I can assure you that Second Harvest's numbers look great for next year. Our vendors are producing double their—"

"I'm sorry, kid. It's just business."

But Levi had the distinct feeling that it wasn't. It wasn't *just business* that had caused nearly every one of his handpicked investors to pull out of the expansion launch in the last thirty-six hours. It was personal. Very, very personal.

He slammed his phone onto the desktop and vented with a few choice words.

The volume on Ford's television ratcheted higher. Tina Tucker's mousy voice seeped through the walls. More fire updates. More recruits coming. More aid en route.

Levi stalked down the hallway to deliver some news of his own. "We're in trouble."

Ford didn't shift his eyes from the talking head on screen. "Whole state's in trouble, son."

"I'm not talking about the fires. I'm talking about the farm."

"Good, 'cause I hoped you weren't in my office praying to God with that language. Although, even if you were, He'd still hear you."

Levi exhaled through his nose. "I wasn't talking to God. I was talking to Tom Hutchinson. He's out, Ford. Just like John Matters and Sam Potter and Bobby Rothschild. We have two left standing. *Two.*"

He should be used to Ford's delayed reaction time, used to the way he processed information like he was eating a fine steak dinner. The man savored every bite, dissected every flavor, and then chewed and swallowed with care. In their nine years together, Levi had appreciated the man's patient personality more times than he could count.

Today was not one of them.

"If we don't have investors, I'll have to cancel all the orders I've collected over the spring, tell our biggest clients to find another distributor. We don't have enough margin to cover the costs of the expansion on our own. Not long term." Levi spliced his fingers through his hair. "What should I do? Do I scout for new investors? Do I inform our vendors? Do I push the launch date back a few months?" Levi rattled off the questions while Ford remained in the same relaxed position on the sofa. "*Ford*, this is important. Tell me what to do."

"Pray. We need to pray for rain."

The statement ripped through him. He was certain Ford hadn't meant Rayne Shelby, but she was the only Rayne on his mind. Had been for three deafeningly silent days. Not that he'd expected anything less. The minute he'd charged into the Great Room, he knew she'd begin to question everything—his integrity, his motives, his heart. But she'd also question Cal, fight for the answers Levi couldn't provide. And he'd do it all over again if it meant Rayne hearing the truth from a source she trusted, even if Levi believed Cal Shelby to be the least trustworthy man on the planet. At least she would know.

What happened next would be her choice.

Ford eyed him. "Without rain, these fires—this drought—will kill everything you've banked your future on."

Levi gripped the back of the sofa chair, his fingers digging into the worn fabric. "We need to make a plan."

"Prayer *is* the plan."

Levi opened his mouth, but his words stalled. The voice charging from the speakers could make his blood curdle in under ten seconds.

". . . in the best interest of our community to close the shelter at the lodge and divert all remaining and future evacuees into the shelters in town. Unfortunately, our remote location puts our guests at too great a risk, so as of tomorrow morning, our doors will be closed to the public. We apologize for the inconvenience but must comply with safety protocols . . ."

The left side of Cal Shelby's cheek ticked as he spoke, his eyes skating to the upper right before blinking.

"He's lying."

"Yes," Ford concurred with brows drawn. "He is."

"Why would he close the doors?" Levi muttered more to himself than to Ford. "Rayne's put everything she has into that shelter. He doesn't do a darn thing to help her run it, so why would . . ." A cold, clawlike grip latched onto his gut. *No.*

No, no, no! He tore down the hallway toward the office again, bumping into the doorjamb, and then scrambling for where he'd so carelessly tossed his phone. He fumbled through his recent call list and tapped Travis's name. If there was information to be collected, his friend would know it.

Travis answered on the second ring. "Hey, what's—"

"What have you heard about the shelter closing at the lodge?"

"You mean how they're kicking everybody out tonight? They're making them stay in the high school gymnasium or in the basement of the Baptist church downtown."

"And Rayne?" It hurt to say her name, to ask such an exposing question, but what choice did he have? "Have you heard anything about her? Anything at all?"

A pause.

"Travis, tell me what you know."

"She's not there."

"Not *where*—at the lodge?"

"Their night-shift guy, Teddy, he's good friends with my boss. I overheard them talking this morning. She hasn't been around in days."

Days. A blinding pain radiated from the back of Levi's eye sockets and stabbed into his temples. Travis's voice faded out as the phone slipped away from his ear, his spine as rigid as Ford's bookcases.

Suddenly, Levi could think of every reason in the world to petition God.

He freed his keys from his jeans pocket and started for the driveway, one question wreaking havoc on his mind.

What have I done?

CHAPTER THIRTY-THREE

On Levi's third knock, Gia jerked the gallery door open, her face shadowed by the "Sorry, We're Closed" sign.

"Do you realize that in the state of Idaho I could shoot you on my doorstep for trespassing and walk away with clean hands?"

Okay, he deserved that. "Gia, *please*. I need to see her."

Her laugh was a mix of intrigue and outrage. "For what? To fill her head with your hogwash? To crush her dreams? Or maybe you just want to expose her sins and then run like a coward. Wait—you've already accomplished all of those."

He splayed his fingers wide. "Five minutes. That's all I'm asking for."

She flattened her hand to the doorjamb. "You have exactly one try to convince me why I should even give you another five seconds." She stopped him with her palm. "But here's a disclaimer: I'm immune to romance. So any gag-worthy line about being star-crossed lovers will result in a swift kick to the groin."

In record time he sorted through his entangled regrets, searching for an answer that wouldn't leave him limping. "I only wanted Cal to be honest with her. I never thought he'd—"

"*Buzz.* Wrong answer." She slapped the back of the door, but he caught it an inch before it latched.

"I never told Travis what I saw the night your dad found you together. I never told a soul."

She rocked back on her heels, her eyes widening before her man-hating scowl returned. "So what? If I don't let you in, you'll—"

"No." He shook his head. "I'm saying I know the difference between exposing a secret for the purpose of shock value and exposing one for the purpose of truth." He glanced over Gia's shoulder inside the dark gallery. "Please."

"Five minutes."

He nodded, his chest sagging under the relief of her compromise. "Five minutes."

The unfriendly toad at the base of the door croaked Levi's entrance as he followed Gia past several mediums of art before taking the narrow staircase to her apartment. His heartbeat thudded in time with his footsteps. Clearing the guard at the gate was only the first blockade.

Gia pushed through the doorway. "You have a visitor, but don't worry, I've already given him the third degree."

And the fourth and the fifth.

Levi rounded the corner, and Rayne pushed up from the sofa. A littering of yellowed paper and curled photographs lay in piles all around her, yet it was the medley of expressions that crossed her face that transfixed him. Shock. Hurt. Anger. And then the one that cut him deepest: uncertainty. The emotions of self-preservation were often quick lived, but losing someone's trust? There was no quick fix for that. The feelings of betrayal couldn't be outtalked.

Need pushed him toward her. "What did Cal do to you?"

Gia caught his sleeve and yanked him back. "Hold on there, bucko. I didn't give you an invitation to roam. You can talk from here." She folded her arms and eyed him as if she were six foot four and not five foot jack.

Stray pieces of hair framed Rayne's makeup-free face. "Nothing you can change by being here."

"What did he *do*, Rayne?" he asked again.

Gia threw her arms up. "What do you think he did? He cut her off—fired her. Thanks to you."

Every self-justifying explanation he'd concocted on the drive over shriveled away like a diseased houseplant. The revelation hammered against his chest. She'd been fired from the lodge, fired from her dream. All because he'd unlocked Pandora's box and left her to open it alone.

He should have known a coward like Cal would never be the one to lead her into the light.

"I'm sorry." Two words perched atop an iceberg of unknowns.

"For which part?" Rayne's voice was pitched low. "Exposing us to Cal or for using the *naive* Shelby to take a shot at my family?"

"You can't actually believe that," he said.

"Why shouldn't I? Weren't you the one who said, 'Opportunity is either sweat or sacrifice'? Which one was I?"

"Neither," he bit out.

"Then tell me the truth—*all of it.* Tell me I didn't lose the lodge over your brainwash—"

"I'm not the one who's been brainwashed!"

"Clock's ticking," Gia blurted. "You have ninety seconds."

He quieted the fury inside him. "You heard it from his own mouth. Cal's been lying to you for eighteen years, and he's *still* lying."

"A common theme, it appears," Gia said.

He shot Gia a look. "I am *nothing* like that man."

"Then tell me." The crack in Rayne's voice tore through him as she reached for a handful of pictures and held them out. "Tell me what you know about my grandfather's will. About the farm."

A cold dread washed over him. "I can't."

"Why not?"

"Because I can't be responsible for devastating another person I love—and telling you like this, in this way, it would ruin Ford. Your uncle made certain of that the day William died. I've already said more, done more, than I should have—"

"So this is about protecting Ford, then." She pursed her lips, glanced at the ceiling.

"Rayne." He scrubbed his hands over his face. "If the consequences were only mine to accept, this conversation wouldn't even be happening right now. But they aren't. If I break Ford's confidence, if I break my promise to him, he could lose everything . . . and he's already lost so much."

"And I haven't?" Tears gleamed in her eyes and the ache in his chest intensified.

"I know you may hate me for keeping my word, but not more than I'd hate myself for breaking it." He stretched his hand out to her. "Please, come with me. Let me take you to him."

How many more times could Rayne clutch the hand of a dishonest man?

She stared at the olive branch Levi extended, his eyes pleading with her to make a move, to take his hand, to trust him in all the ways her heart desired.

But her heart was a fool. "No."

Gia belted out a ten-second countdown.

"You'll never find what you're looking for in that box of old photographs. There aren't any bread crumbs."

"Truth always leaves a trail." A saying her grandfather had used when any of her cousins were caught in a fib or sneaking an extra cookie from Delia's special stash. If there was a secret to be found, there would be a trail.

"Time's up," Gia announced, slapping a hand to his back. "Hope that was as productive for you as it was for me." She pointed to the darkened stairway.

When he didn't flinch at the curt dismissal, Rayne averted her eyes, silencing the part of herself that yearned to be held more than she yearned to be right.

She locked her arms around her middle and denied herself another chance to fall prey to poor instinct.

"Let's go." Gia nudged his shoulder. "I have Chinese takeout to pick up."

He turned to exit but stopped just shy of the doorway.

The determination in his gaze made Rayne's heart shiver.

"Whenever you're ready, you know where to find me," he said before Gia ushered him out of sight.

Ready? The word mocked her. No part of her had felt ready since the day they'd struck a deal over a hundred and thirty-six jars of honey all those weeks ago. She had been too enraptured, too enamored, too completely enchanted by a man she couldn't love, but did anyway.

Tears she refused to cry burned at the base of her throat. But this wasn't the time to weep over her losses, or return the phone calls from her father, or answer another round of go-nowhere questions from Gia. She fingered the photograph she'd discovered just seconds before Levi had entered and then tucked it into the back pocket of her jeans.

She'd find the truth on her own.

CHAPTER THIRTY-FOUR

"I wondered when you'd come." Delia's plump cheeks and cinnamon-swirl hair were easy to spot, even in the expiring daylight. She sat on her porch swing, looking out over her wilted garden. "Not even an extra watering a day can take the place of a good rainstorm."

Rayne lifted the toes of her sandals, unveiling a patch of crusty foliage, as Delia rose and waved her closer. "Let's go inside. I have some lemonade and biscuits cooling."

With a nod, Rayne trailed after her, taking note of the tiny terra-cotta pots that lined the inside of every windowsill visible to the outside. It'd been years since Rayne had visited the rusty red bungalow. Years since she'd seen the seat-less antique bicycle perched against the siding, opposite the porch swing.

She stepped inside the entryway, the smell of rosemary and thyme filling the air. Something succulent was cooking in the oven. "Looks the same in here. Smells the same too." Rayne dragged her fingers along a ruffled throw pillow on the gingham sofa chair.

"You know I don't care much for change."

Rayne smiled at that. She did know. Delia's no-nonsense personality and candor hadn't lessened over time. She wheeled back the rolling dining-room chair and sat, the contents in her back pocket burning a hole in her conscience. "I found something."

"A pot of gold?" Delia carried two glasses filled to the brim with lemonade and placed them on a small oak table between them. Next came the warm biscuits.

"Sorry. I'm still looking for that." This was their way. Their casual avoidance of deeper issues with the distraction of food and drink. Working in a lodge full of prestigious world travelers and uptight political acquaintances had taught them the art of speaking in code, of saying much with very little.

Delia lifted the glass to her mouth and drank deeply, a sheen of perspiration on her forehead. The glass clinked against the wood. "I should have stopped him."

Rayne swiped at the droplets of rolling moisture on the bottom of her glass. "Levi's a grown man. He made up his mind before he ever stepped foot into your kitchen."

"That's not who I should have stopped."

Rayne washed the rising swell in her throat with another sip of the cool beverage and then set it back in the sweat ring. "There's no stopping Cal."

With a slight jostle of her hand, Delia clacked the ice cubes in her lemonade together. "True, but no part of me believes you quit."

Quit? "That's what he told you?"

"It's what he's told everybody."

Rayne slumped against the back of the cushioned dining chair. "I was fired."

"I know it. Teddy knows it. Any of us who have half a brain know it. The day you'd quit your granddaddy's lodge is the day apple pie can be harvested straight from an orchard."

Interesting choice of metaphor, since there was only one apple orchard in Shelby Falls.

Rayne reached into her back pocket and slid the photograph across the table. Two people dancing clung to each other in an embrace that spoke as plainly as the tenderness in their expressions. The female's face in the picture was smoother, her waistline narrower, her hair longer, but there was no mistaking the woman in the photograph.

There was no mistaking the man either.

"Where's it from?" Rayne asked.

"*When's it from* is a better question. And the answer to that is a very, very long time ago."

"Why are you dancing with Ford?"

It was Delia's turn to slump against her chair and pick at her biscuit. "Stirring this up won't help you."

"At this point, there's not much more I can lose."

Delia's mouth soured into a frown. "There's always more to lose where your uncle's involved."

"Delia. Please. I need to understand what happened between Ford and my family. Was something going on between the two of you?"

"We had a . . ." She stared off into the distance, as if she could travel through time with a single blink. "Connection."

"Did you love him?" The thought hardly felt plausible.

The fog cleared from Delia's gaze. "I never expected to win the affections of any man after I lost Phillip, especially since I couldn't have children. People just aren't that lucky twice in a lifetime. Only I was. Ford doted on me. He brought me gifts every time he came in from working William's land or running an errand for him. Most the time he gave me flowers, but other times he'd bring me artifacts he'd dug up from the old logging road behind the property." She pointed to a rusted coil nailed into a warped board on her coffee table. A glass tube had been placed in the center, the stems of flowers stuffed inside it as petals spilled over the rim. "He found that old bed spring there—probably dates back to the first Shelby homestead. He knew how much I loved my antiques." She sighed and shook her head. "You don't remember much about him, do you?" The trace of sadness in her voice rubbed at Rayne's conscience.

"I was young." A cover for the memories she'd been forced to forget.

"You used to think he hung the moon."

Rayne dismissed Delia's sentiment immediately. "The only man I've ever thought that about was my grandfather."

Delia's stubby fingernails pinged against her empty glass. "Yes, you two had a special relationship. He loved you dearly." Delia gave a soft chuckle. "I witnessed many moments at the lodge after you moved in, and my favorite were the celebrations. I remember one quite well. Your seventh birthday. Do you remember it?"

"Yes, I remember." And where her own memory had faltered, her family had been sure to fill in the missing holes. This was one legendary tale she could recite by heart.

"So you remember what he gave you?"

"An apple tree. Grandpa helped me plant it on my birthday in the orchard." They'd spent an entire afternoon together, planting and then painting a garden stone to lay beside it, the words *Rayne's Tree* brushed in bright-purple paint.

Pity overtook Delia's face. "He did buy you the apple tree, but William couldn't be at your party that day. He was with your grandma Betty. She'd fallen again, and he didn't leave her hospital bedside for nearly a week."

"But how could that be? I remember him there. With me." Rayne shook her head as the memory unfolded. "He was with me in the orchard. He gave me a pair of work gloves, and I told him I wanted to use my hands. I told him I didn't care about dirt in my nails. And . . . and I told him that purple was my favorite color. We painted the garden stone and he complimented my sad attempt at cursive."

"No, child," Delia said with a surrendered tone. "William wasn't there."

Rayne's mind trailed down a familiar rabbit hole until she slammed to a stop. Her discovery reared back.

No. No. Delia had to be wrong.

Rayne had pictured those strong hands around hers a thousand times. She'd heard his deep laugh and his careful guidance. She saw his eyes, their kind and thoughtful gaze—

She gasped.

Ford's eyes.

"No, but how could . . . no, *why* would Ford be in the orchard with me? He was just an employee."

"William took fondly to him after he hired him to work on the remodel, when Ford was in his early twenties. They were like-souls, the same way you and your granddaddy were." Her eyes shaded. "Unfortunately, jealousy's an ugly thing between men."

"Cal." It wasn't a question but a certainty.

"Cal and William never got on too well, and Ford's presence muddied the waters for sure. Cal wanted your grandfather's influence to grow, to take the family further into politics. But with your grandmother's mental faculties failing her, William was content to remain in our small town, make a permanent life for him and Betty in Shelby Falls, and watch his grandchildren grow up in the lodge of his ancestors." She tapped her tongue against her teeth. "After William stepped down as governor, Cal blamed Ford's influence for stunting the family's political trajectory, even though William argued otherwise." Delia sighed. "Cal moved to Southern California after their last blowup and didn't come back again until your grandmother Betty passed away. Little did we know then that your grandfather would die shortly after."

Rayne pinched her brows together. "Cal was estranged from Granddaddy all that time? Living in California?"

"Cal made a fortune in real estate. He backed your father financially, of course, perhaps because he felt Randall could do what William had failed to do for the Shelby name."

"But if Cal was so hung up on politics, then why didn't *he* run for an election?"

The crooked twist of Delia's mouth made Rayne lean in. "Guess he was smart enough to realize that he had the backbone but not the charm."

"And what did Cal do after Granddaddy's heart attack?"

Rayne inched forward, and Delia braced the glass between her palms. "There was a meeting."

"I think I remember that. Gia and I were peeking down from our hiding spot at the top of the stairs while the adults met in the Great Room and Cal talked about Granddaddy's estate."

"No, that was the family luncheon." Delia exhaled through her nose. "The meeting I'm talking about happened the morning before, predawn. I was in the kitchen prepping food, when I saw them come in. Just Cal, your father, and Ford. They were in that study for hours."

The air felt too thin to breathe. "My father was there too?"

A hard nod.

"What happened in that meeting, Delia?"

"Child, as far as anybody else is concerned, that meeting never happened. But after that morning, Ford Winslow was never allowed to step foot onto Shelby land again. When he showed up for the luncheon the next day, Tony cuffed him and led him away." Delia clucked her tongue. "A disgraceful sight."

"Somebody has to know what was said in that office."

"Three somebodies know, but I'd bet my best cooking pans that nobody will ever speak of it. As far as the Shelbys are concerned, Ford Winslow is a crook."

Rayne pushed the question out her throat, her stomach churning. "You don't believe that?"

"I never have, not for a second, only, I was too much of a coward then to do what I finally had the courage to do today."

"What are you talking about? What did you do?"

"I quit."

The sky split open. Bright veins of light pulsed in the distance beyond and thunder boomed, echoing throughout the valley. The rumble vibrated Rayne's rib cage, but even still, the windshield and the gravel turnabout she'd parked in remained bone dry.

She tapped the highlighted contact on her phone screen and exhaled.

"Nice of you to return my call." Her father's greeting tugged at her insides, but for the first time in years, she hadn't returned his phone call out of obligation or obedience; she'd made the call out of her own necessity.

"It's been a busy week," she said. There was no pretending Cal hadn't already filled him in on her every transgression. Fraternization with the dark side would not be easily overlooked.

"So I've heard. I assume you've been staying with Gia?"

Had he really left all those voicemails to ask her where she was staying? "For now, yes." Though she hadn't a clue what later held.

She opened her mouth to—

"I've been concerned about you, Rayne. Actually, Cal and I are both concerned." Cal's concern had kicked her to the curb with a two-hour notice. She dug her fingernails into the rubber grip of her steering wheel as he continued. "Despite your most recent lapse in judgment, I've spent the better part of two days securing an opportunity for you."

She blinked twice, tiny black dots obstructing her vision as lightning flashed for a second time. "What kind of opportunity?"

"Your dedication to public service while I visited the shelter last week was commendable." His approving tone awakened a childish hope long ago buried. "Which is why I'd like for you to join me here in Boise. I've recently partnered with an advocacy group for underprivileged children. I'm offering you a position on the committee."

Not even in the furthest reaches of her imagination could she have concocted such an offer from her father. Move to Boise? Work alongside him? Partner with a children's welfare group?

"The position comes with a reasonable salary, but more than that, you could finally put that degree of yours in public relations to good use."

How many years had she longed for her father's approval, for his eyes to see her, for his heart to understand her? She'd ached for his acceptance, support, and love, yet foreboding and dread swirled in the pit of her belly.

"Wow . . . I'm definitely surprised," was the only response she could muster.

"It's been a long time since you've had a break from the lodge."

As quickly as her lungs had filled, they deflated. "I'm not on a break. I was fired."

"I'm well aware of the circumstances of your dismissal, Rayne. Were you hoping to rehash your mistakes with me or look ahead to your future?"

Once again, Cal had taken on the role of disciplinarian while her father managed the cleanup crew.

She pinched her eyes closed and forced out the only question on her mind. "Who planted the apple tree with me on my seventh birthday, Dad?"

Silence and then he said, "You know that story frontward and backward."

"*Who*, Dad?" The punch of her voice rivaled the clap of thunder above.

"Your grandfather."

Another lie. She bit the inside of her cheeks as if the effort alone could close the valve to her pain.

"I'll arrange for Sharon to call you first thing tomorrow morning so we can get you set up in an apartment near the office—"

"No."

Her father wasn't inviting her into his sacred political circle because of any talent she possessed. He simply wanted to remove her from Shelby Falls.

From the farm.

From Levi.

From Ford.

"Excuse me? I've pulled a lot of strings for you, young lady—"

"Then, please . . ." Her voice swelled with a strength that rose from somewhere deep within. "Cut me loose."

With the stab of her finger, she ended the call, and she rejected the next two that came after it. She studied the two properties from the same gravel turnabout she'd parked in just six weeks before. Rayne veered her gaze from the lodge that held her dreams, to the farm that held her heart.

This time, her decision was easy.

CHAPTER THIRTY-FIVE

Levi braced his hands on his hips and stared at the cyclone of dust swirling in the empty space beside the barn. Either Bess the Backhoe had been stolen, or Ford had taken it off the property. Again.

When the third sharp crack shook the night sky, he glanced at the clock on his phone. If the old man wasn't back in the next twenty minutes, he'd go after him. Hauser scurried up the breezeway, his fuzzy golden ears alert to every sound, near and far.

"It's just a storm. He'll be home soon." He scratched the dog's head and then turned off the lights in the warehouse, sparing one last glance toward the property to the west.

In the same way Ford's companion wouldn't stray far from the property, Levi's mind hadn't strayed from his last interaction with Rayne. If he hadn't heard the dedication in her voice or seen the determination in her eyes, he'd be going out of his mind. But for reasons he couldn't understand, a part of him loved her even more for turning his invitation down.

The crunch of tires on the gravel drive provoked a barking fit from Hauser. "*Easy*, boy. He'll be just as excited to see you." Only the headlights were all wrong. So was the shape of the vehicle. So was the face of the driver.

Ford wasn't back.

Rayne was.

The impulse to run toward her and crush her to his chest was as painful and palpable as it was achingly familiar. Yet somehow, he resisted. Her door swept open and shut in the time it took him to cross the lot. The sky sizzled again, swallowing her in a blaze of firelight.

Levi's stride slowed, allowing his mind to lope ahead. *Rayne is here.* Unlike that early June afternoon when she'd come to strike a bargain in secret, he saw nothing skittish or frail about her now. Whatever tears she'd shed had dried, and whatever fear she'd battled had lost.

"You were wrong," she said. "There was a trail."

"And it led you here."

She nodded. "Yes, it led me here."

"Then I'll be wrong anytime."

A slight dip of her chin. "Where is he?"

"Somewhere in the backwoods."

"In a lightning storm?"

"He'll be back soon." And if he wasn't, Levi would bring him back. Ford had been waiting eighteen years for this moment. There was no way Levi would let him miss it.

She said nothing more as he led her up the steps into Ford's cluttered bachelor pad. Hauser followed behind them with an anxious pant. The screen door creaked open, a rival sound to the echo of distant thunder.

Ford's leather-bound Bible lay open on his coffee table, surrounded by mechanical trinkets and scribbled blueprints. Levi watched the way she took everything in, watched the way her fingers ticked at her sides and scrunched the bottom of her cotton shirt.

"He'll be glad you're here."

A glassy vulnerability shone in her eyes. "I wish I felt the same way."

He wouldn't fill the silence with empty reassurances. There was no predicting how this conversation would go, and yet, everything in him wanted to shelter her, to carry the burden she shouldered. "Rayne, I—"

Hauser shot to his feet. Only this time it wasn't a thunderclap that set him on alert, it was the low, rumbly hum of his master's backhoe.

Another eighteen years seemed to pass in the time it took Ford to walk through his front door.

Rayne's spine lengthened to the kind of ruler-straight posture her fifth-grade teacher, Sister Meredith, had insisted upon. With a half turn, she faced the doorway, her hands clutched in tight fists.

Levi strode past her, but Ford beat him to the punch, his heavy work boots vibrating the floorboards upon entry. He slid his worn leather hat from his head. "I prayed you'd come."

The room pulsed with a static current that seemed to awaken every nerve ending in her body.

"I remember—what I asked you in the grocery store." Her words sounded submerged in half-developed memories. She hadn't budged an inch since the dog had leapt from the corner of the room to circle the man's calves, his tail thump, thump, thumping against the back of a recliner on every revolution.

"Please, have a seat." Ford eased closer, his footsteps like those of a skilled huntsman, silent but intentional. "Levi, will you bring our guest something to drink?"

Levi ducked into the kitchen while Rayne perched on the edge of the sofa. There was no cushion in the world soft enough to make this exchange comfortable.

Ford sat in the recliner opposite her, clasping his hands into a loose fold. "I've thought about that day many times."

While she'd done just the opposite. She'd blocked it out, stuffed it into a box labeled "Do Not Touch, Do Not Ask, Do Not Open." What else had she repressed for fear of repercussions? What else had Cal and her father kept from her?

Levi placed a steaming mug into her hands, his thumb brushing an arc along the delicate skin of her wrist. Somehow he'd known her fingers were frozen despite the sticky, hot air outside. He retreated to the edge of her vision, propping himself against the wall and studying her with an expression she could feel in her bones.

The faint aroma of lemon and chamomile filled her next breath, strengthening her courage. "I asked you about the apple tree. The one we planted on my seventh birthday."

"Yes, you did." An encouraging nod. "You were concerned it wouldn't produce fruit since you weren't able to come to the orchard and tend to it."

She set the mug on the coffee table, remembering the way he'd crouched before her in the aisle. "You told me not to worry. You told me that God takes care of his creation . . . that his timing is always perfect."

Kind eyes brimming with patience waited for her to continue, for her memories to lead her to a place with far more questions than answers. "But what I couldn't understand was *your* timing. Why would you leave us after Grandpa Shelby died?"

The single flare inside her abdomen sparked a fire through her veins. And this time, it couldn't—*wouldn't*—be stomped out. Not by the tactless deflection of her uncle or the saccharine-coated words of her father. Lies and deceit had dripped from the tongues of every man she'd been taught to trust. And here she was, placing her hope in the only man she'd been trained to despise.

"William's death was the hardest day of my life." His gaze held steady on her mug. "Until the day I walked away from the lodge."

"What happened in the meeting between you and Cal and my father?" Her voice snagged on the persistent lump in her throat.

Ford regarded her as if the question popped the lock on a memory box of his own. "You know about the meeting?"

"Yes." Only that was about all she knew.

The lines etched around his mouth sagged. "Cal wished to discuss your grandfather's requests in private."

Snippets of old conversations—rumors she'd treated like certainty, hearsay she'd treated like God-breathed truth—clawed at her subconscious. "What requests? Were you or were you not named in his will?"

His exhale was weighted. "Yes, he named me in his will. But he did so of his own accord."

"You're telling me that you didn't coerce him in any way to gain ownership of Shelby Farm?"

"No, Rayne. I did not coerce William."

Her intuition kicked against the accusations fed to her since childhood. This man sitting before her, the man with the soothing timbre and the serene gaze, was not the hateful monster who'd starred in her nightmares. Her uncle was far more cunning and ruthless, her father far more strategic and arrogant.

She wet her thirsty tongue with a sip of tea and let it cool in the hollow of her belly before she spoke. "If you didn't blackmail my grandfather, why would he leave you the farm? Why would he give you a piece of our inheritance—the land we've kept in our family for generations?"

Crestfallen, he met her eyes again. "In that early-morning meeting I was asked to sign a nondisclosure agreement, a legal contract that bound me to keep the specifics of the will and our negotiations confidential."

"Wait." Confused, she looked from Ford to Levi. "If you're legally bound to silence, then how does Levi know the details?"

"Ford didn't tell me," Levi offered. "Cal showed up here the day after you and I met at the Falls. He threatened Ford, told him to keep me on his side of the property line or he'd find a reason to take him to court for breach of contract. I overheard more of their conversation than Cal ever intended me to."

The knocking in her chest climbed into her temples, her gaze locking on Ford. "But why breach of contract? What did you agree to?"

"To cut all ties with the lodge and your family." The sadness in his voice stirred something forgotten inside her. "It's why I never attended your birthday parties or your graduation ceremonies, why I couldn't tell you everything I wished I could have in the grocery store that day."

Like the release of a dam, his regrets rushed into every abandoned cavern of her soul, flooding her with a sorrow she'd only ever felt when her grandfather had passed. She hadn't only lost her grandfather that day . . . she'd lost Ford too. Had she loved this man? Had she cried over his absence? And if so, how many lies had she swallowed before her grief had turned to hatred?

Her vision blurred. "What secret could possibly be worth all this?"

Levi pushed away from the wall. "Ford, can't you just—"

Ford raised his palm and dropped his chin. "I'm still bound to it, Rayne. And Levi made a promise to me that I've held him to for his own good—despite himself."

Levi's jaw clenched and her heart nearly punched through her chest. She stared at him, her breath shallow and uneven. "What could you lose—if you broke the agreement?"

Levi averted his gaze as Ford answered for him. "Everything. The lawsuit would wipe out the farm and Second Harvest."

The fog of confusion cleared from her mind for the first time in days. She'd been so focused on the loss of her childhood dream that she hadn't considered the ripple effect of repercussions to follow. Not only had Levi risked his business aspirations the night he'd confronted

Cal, he'd risked the trust of every vendor who'd partnered with him. Every vendor who'd shared his vision for expanding Second Harvest and linking their community together in all the ways the lodge had failed.

And Levi had jeopardized it all. For her.

She steered her focus back to Ford, desperation snaking around her heart. "How do I uncover the truth if nobody in that meeting will tell me what was said?"

"Words are not nearly as important as motives."

She closed her eyes against the throb in her temples. In many ways, the men in her family were as alien to her as her estranged neighbor. But their motives were not. She'd witnessed many manipulative takedowns for the sake of power—business deals, political agendas, media posturing. So why did Cal see Ford as a threat to their family name? And why would Ford choose to stay at the farm instead of taking a bundle of Cal's cash and living free from hostility? What kind of secret would require a nondisclosure agreement?

She pushed up from the couch. "I need some air."

Ford gave her a sympathetic nod and gestured to Levi. She didn't have to turn around to sense he was behind her. She knew. The same way her heart whispered words her mind would not fully accept.

She was down the steps and pacing the gravel when Levi planted his feet in her path.

"Breathe," he said.

"I am."

"No." He set his hands on her shoulders, calming the static inside her. "You're not."

She licked the dryness from her lips. "This is just so much to—"

The two-second blare of a police siren rattled her teeth and sliced through the smoky night sky. Levi spun, pushing her behind him, as if to shield her from the sheriff's cruiser rolling down Ramsey Highway in first gear. But concerns of her uncle Tony discovering her on the

Winslow property vanished the instant the intercom crackled a warning. "Evacuate now. This is your five-minute warning. Evacuate now . . ."

Ford stepped onto the front porch, his steady-as-a-rock appearance contradicting her own.

"Wait here," Levi called out as he jogged toward the police car.

But there was no time for waiting.

She darted to her car.

If the farm was being evacuated, the lodge would be next.

CHAPTER THIRTY-SIX

Locked? She rattled the knob and banged on the door glass with the flat of her hand until she heard the thud of heavy footsteps. The instant the dead bolt turned, she pushed into the lobby.

"Teddy, how many rooms are occupied?"

"Uh . . ." He crinkled disorderly eyebrows. "Maybe four?"

She surged toward the laptop on the front desk. "Four not including Celeste?"

"Yeah. I think so. What's—"

"We're under a five-minute evacuation. I need your help." She logged in and clicked into the reservations screen, relief flooding her at the sight of the vacant rooms. "I'm gonna pull the fire alarm, but I need you to go to rooms eleven and seventeen. Tell our guests not to panic and to grab whatever they can and drive to the high school. I'll alert the guests on the third floor, and Celeste." She started for the stairs and whirled back. "Cal's not here, right?"

"Right." He shook his head, his basset-hound eyes round and alert. "He was gone before I clocked in tonight."

"Good, okay, go! Sheriff's just down the road; he'll be here next."

Adrenaline pulsed into her fingers as she yanked the red handle near the bottom of the staircase. A staccato shriek pierced through the sleepy hallways. Covering her ears, she hurtled up the staircase, reaching the third floor in time to see the retired couple from room thirty-one stumble into the hallway. The woman wore an ankle-length nightgown while the balding man at her side fumbled with the white lodge-issue bathrobe at his waist. A heartbeat later, the door to room thirty-four opened to reveal a midthirties man clad in nothing but boxer briefs.

"Is there a fire close by?" Boxer Man asked, shielding his ears.

"Yes, we're under evacuation," Rayne yelled over the screeching alarm.

"From the lightning storm?" he asked.

Rayne couldn't be sure, but it was her best guess. She nodded. "We need to evacuate immediately."

"But what about our luggage?" the woman cried, cupping age-spotted hands to her ears.

Rayne held up three fingers. "Grab what you can, and I'll meet you in the lobby in three minutes. *Please hurry.*"

The guests scurried back to their rooms while she ran to the top floor. Celeste met her at the staircase, her scowl as unmovable as her stance. "Did you pull the fire alarm? Turn it off."

"We're under evacuation." Rayne reached for her cousin's arm—she'd need a few things from her room. Like a shirt that reached past her rib cage for starters. "You need to get dressed. We have to go."

Celeste shrugged her off. "I'm not going anywhere. The fire can't jump the river."

Was she serious? "This isn't New York, Celeste. Lightning can strike anywhere, and with the drought, these trees are unlit matches. Uncle Tony's outside right now evacuating everybody along Ramsey Highway."

Her cousin didn't budge, so Rayne charged into the suite without her. If Celeste wanted to argue, she could do it after Rayne collected her things.

"Don't go through my stuff."

"Then don't stand there like I'm not speaking to you." Rayne yanked a navy blouse off a hanger in the closet and tossed the garment at Celeste's chest. "Get dressed and get downstairs. This isn't some power play. It's your life."

Rayne kicked a pair of red flats over from the corner while Celeste slid the shirt over her head. "Here, put your shoes on." She swiped the Louis Vuitton purse off the nightstand. "Are your car keys inside?"

A curt nod from Celeste. "Yes."

"Good, now let's go."

Rayne cupped her elbow, and much to her surprise, Celeste didn't jerk away. As they reached the bottom of the staircase, the deafening alarm fell silent, and the sudden quiet felt nearly as disorienting as the initial blast of sound.

"How—how did it stop?" Celeste asked, removing her hands from her ears.

"Teddy must have switched it off from the control panel."

After Rayne led Celeste and the third-floor residents into the paved lot at the front of the lodge, Teddy met them outside, where the lights from Uncle Tony's cruiser flashed a sequence of red and blue. He rolled closer and Teddy jogged toward him.

"All the guests have been accounted for, sir," Teddy confirmed loudly. "Rayne swept the top two floors and I took the first floor. The second has been closed for cleaning since the shelter guests vacated."

Smoke permeated the air and caught in the back of Rayne's throat. She coughed into the crook of her elbow, escorting the retired couple to their gold Mercedes. She heaved the woman's suitcase into the open trunk.

"Thanks for your cooperation, folks," her uncle Tony's voice boomed through the PA system. "Please head to the high school, and we'll keep you updated through the evening."

Celeste pulled her shirt over her nose, genuine panic in her voice. "Where is the high school?"

"Follow Teddy." Rayne called out to Teddy, asking him to hold up. "He'll lead you, and I'll be right behind you."

Celeste hurried after the man she'd fired her first day at Shelby Lodge.

"Rayne," Tony called, "I need to head up the road to the Gourleys' place. They're my last stop on Ramsey. You did well, kiddo." Tony's thick mustache twitched, exposing a toothy grin. "Now get to your car and take off, will ya? Gia will be waiting for you."

"Yes, sir."

The last two cars vacated the lot, and Tony whipped a U-turn, heading in the direction of the Gourleys'. Halfway to her car, Rayne felt a sickening knot form in the base of her belly. What she was running away from nearly dropped her to her knees.

The lodge.

Her granddaddy's lodge.

An invisible pulley cinched her waist, tugging her back a step, and then another, until the only thing in front of her was a past she couldn't bear to leave behind.

Just a minute. I only need a minute.

She shot through the lobby again and into the kitchen, pulling down the empty boxes Delia stored in the pantry. Sweat dampened her palms and the back of her neck as she tossed them to the ground and unhooked her family's heritage from the wall of Shelby history. The tattered maps, the first sketch of Shelby Falls, her great-great-grandmother Nettie's portrait, the award-winning plaques, and—

"Rayne!" The urgency in Levi's voice constricted every muscle in her body, but still she couldn't stop. Not until she was done. Not until she'd made it to Cal's study to collect the albums and the journals.

"I just need another minute to—"

"We don't have another minute!" His boots thumped behind her. "We need to leave, *now*."

"There's too much here, I can't leave it all behind."

"The fire's close. Just on the other side of the old logging road." He touched her back. "I had to walk away from the farm, and you have to walk away from the lodge. There are more important things than—"

She yanked the last frame from the wall, her throat choked with tears as her grandfather's face stared back at her. "None of this can be replaced."

Levi tore the picture from her grasp. "Neither can you."

"He's right." Ford materialized in the doorway. "Your grandfather's legacy isn't attached to this building."

Her gaze flitted between the old farmer and her memorialized hero, a man whose picture she'd passed a dozen times a day in this lobby, a man who'd kept her secrets and heard her sorrows, a man who'd planted a dream in her heart and died before he could watch it bloom.

A man with the same kind eyes and the same cleft chin and the same humble spirit as Ford Winslow.

Air squeezed from her lungs, leaving her chest hollow and heartsick. "You look like him."

"Yes." A single word that flattened her world.

A thousand questions leapt to her lips, yet only three words could slip past the sob building in her throat. "You're his son."

"Yes, Rayne."

Light and sound seemed to fade out intermittently while her mind and heart stuttered to a stop.

Ford Winslow was her family.

Her blood family.

Her uncle.

"All these years . . . all these years you've lived next door, and I never knew." She swallowed down the rising regret.

"Cal made it so you couldn't know," Levi interjected.

Ford held her gaze. "Yet I prayed that someday you would."

"Truth always leaves a trail," she whispered.

Somewhere deep inside her, somewhere buried under decades of deceit, she'd known her curiosity had been more than childish wonder. She'd felt a draw to the farm on that very first day with Levi, and she felt it still.

Levi dropped the frame inside the box and tucked her into his side. "Sweetheart, I promise there are answers for all your questions, but we need to leave. Now." Levi planted a firm hand to her hip and led her toward the open doorway.

The farmer slipped past her and lifted the box she'd packed full of Shelby history. He carried it to his truck. Only now, the relics of her past seemed far less important than the reality of her future.

Before Levi closed her inside her car, he pressed his lips to her forehead, instructing her to follow them to the shelter.

She pulled out of the lot and glanced in the review mirror one last time. Dense plumes of orange-tinged smoke rose up from behind the lodge. Grief choked her heart and streamed from her eyes, not only for the lodge she stood to lose but for time she'd never get back.

For the family she'd lost to eighteen years' worth of lies.

The sky's fiery tantrum had calmed by the time Levi arrived at the high school, Rayne never more than a car length behind. There were no more flashes of lightning or peals of thunder, yet even still, chaos abounded. People lingered all around, some volunteers, some evacuees, and some who simply sipped on crisis like a round of cheap beer.

Hands shoved deep into his pockets, Levi balanced on a cement barrier, waiting for Rayne to process eighteen years of falsities from the driver's seat of her car. A pale light from the high school's foyer spilled over the blacktop and onto her hood, illuminating her face—Levi's only focal point for the last ten minutes. He promised himself he wouldn't rush her, wouldn't force her to make another choice on his timeline.

Like the people who waited in the shelter and those who'd been displaced all around Shelby Falls, Levi had also resolved himself to wait.

Not only on the fire reports to come.

But for Rayne.

Her mind had to be a mess, her emotions scattered and charred like the ash in the wind, but whatever she needed, be it time or space or heart-sucking details, he'd be here. She'd spoken the words, solved the mystery, unlocked a secret he'd been bound to keep. And as soon as she was ready, he'd be the one to fill in the gaps.

There were so few outcomes he could control tonight, but only one consumed him. The second she opened her car door, his lungs constricted.

Basked in hazy moonlight, she stepped toward him, the gesture a mile marker in the marathon of uncertainties to come.

She lifted her chin and their gazes locked.

"I've been so wrong." Her humility tore through him. "I've hated a man I should have loved, and I'm in love with a man who should hate me."

His gaze trailed to her tear-stained cheeks. "Hating you is the furthest thing from my mind, Rayne Shelby."

"But I've thought so many awful things about him. Said so many awful things—been so naive—"

"No. Stop." Though Ford had drilled the importance of grace into Levi's brain a thousand times, it had never felt so relevant than in this moment. He reached for her, brushing her hair away from her face and anchoring his hands on his shoulders. "You're the one who found this truth, Rayne. You're not naive. You don't get to blame yourself for what you couldn't know. This didn't happen—*we didn't happen*—so that you could focus on eighteen years of regret. This is about what you do with the next eighteen years. And the next after that."

"You're right." She emptied her lungs with a sigh. "My grandfather, he had an affair, didn't he?"

"Yes. William had an affair."

With a resolute nod, she searched his eyes. "It's the only story I could come up with that matched what I know about the secret meeting and Cal's paranoia over the family image—" She shook her head. "I'm trying to make sense of it all."

He chose his next words carefully. "There's a lot to make sense of, but I'll answer whatever I can. You've already figured out the biggest piece of the puzzle." The piece that freed him from his promise, and Ford from his prison of silence. "From what I know, the affair was short-lived, and when it was over, your grandfather's lawyer paid the woman off. She left the state and moved to Nevada."

"Did he know she was pregnant?"

"I don't know the answer to that; I'm not even sure Ford knows. The lawyer handled everything, and the Shelby family—and the public—was none the wiser."

"Then how did Ford meet my grandfather?"

"His mother battled cancer through most of his teenage years, and even though she'd put a savings account aside for him, she knew he would need more than just financial support. She wrote William a letter during her treatments, asking him to watch over their son in the case of her death. Ford was nineteen when she died."

Two wailing ambulances shot down the main drag, and their conversation was muted by the sounds of disaster all around them.

"When William reached out to Ford, he did so as a friend of Ford's late mother, not as a father figure. William secured a construction job for him with one of his close friends in town, and then eventually, he hired him to work the grounds at the lodge. Your grandfather was still governor and living in Boise, so he was only at the lodge every few months to check in. It wasn't until your grandmother Betty became too unstable that your grandfather stepped down from politics and made the lodge his permanent home."

Rayne squinted her eyes and bobbed her head as if trying to connect the timeline. "That was a few years before I was born."

"Ford worked with William at the lodge and on Shelby land for nearly twenty-five years. They were close."

The acrid scent of smoke thickened and she coughed into her elbow. "But wait—did Ford know he was my grandfather's son all that time?"

"No," Levi said, working to detach his feelings on William's cowardice from his answer. "Your grandfather kept that secret from Ford until after your grandmother passed away."

She gaped, blinked, and then shook her head. "But that was only a few months before his heart attack."

"I know." Levi paused as a car passed them in the parking lot. "William asked for Ford's forgiveness for keeping the truth from him so long, and he vowed to make it right. He told Ford he'd met with his lawyer and had added him to the will, made him a co-heir along with his three other children. He'd divided the assets of his estate into equal quarter shares. William asked Ford to give him time to connect with each of his children privately before it went public."

"But there was never an announcement made," she said.

"No. William met with Cal soon after, told him the truth along with the changes he was making to his estate and will. You can imagine how well that went over."

"It had to be a horrible shock but—" Rayne touched her fingers to her lips. "Wait, how long after that meeting did . . ."

"Your grandfather's heart attack happened the following week. Ford was working with him in the orchard when he collapsed. There was nothing he could do."

She squeezed her eyes closed.

"I'm sorry." He pressed a kiss to the arch of her brow. "I don't want to hurt you."

"I want—I need to know. The meeting . . . Cal must have told my father the truth since he was there."

"Yes. Cal was the executor of the will, but he needed a majority. He made Ford an offer of double the price of Ford's share if he agreed to leave town. But Ford didn't want Cal's money. He'd barely wrapped his head around the idea that his closest mentor and friend had actually been his father, much less the shock of his sudden death. He had no desire to leave the land they'd worked on together for so many years. But Cal assured him that no matter what kind of deal they struck, Ford would never be welcomed by their family. He called him a blemish on the Shelby name, and on William's legacy." Levi tempered his anger. "After hours of Cal's badgering, Ford relented and accepted Cal's final offer."

"The farm for a nondisclosure agreement," Rayne supplied.

"Ford would never force himself on your family, but I think a part of him always believed that someday Cal and Randall would have a change of heart."

"So all these years, *all these years*, Cal made Ford out to be the scam artist who played on my grandfather's grief-stricken heart and stole from the next generation of Shelbys, when Ford *is* a Shelby, a rightful heir. Oh, Levi . . ." She rested a hand to his chest, the heat of her palm searing through the thin fabric of his shirt.

"Ford refused to bring dissention to William's family, even if that meant he would never be known by them. By you."

Rayne turned her face, her gaze drifting to the movement at their right where several Red Cross workers unloaded water bottles off a nearby truck. When she spoke again, her voice was far away, as if buried under layers of thought and debris.

"I loved my grandfather, the way a little girl loves a knight in shining armor, but that's all I ever saw of him, the shiny parts. I think I've fictionalized William Shelby for so long that I never quite saw him as a real person, with real flaws and real struggle and real regret." Another strong, smoky breeze whipped through the parking lot, and Rayne cleared her throat. "But still, I have to believe that all his talk about truth having a trail was because of Ford. *He* was the trail." She paused as a group of teens passed them and entered the high school. "I can't force my family to see Ford the way you do, Levi, but I can change the way I see him."

Levi folded her into his arms and cradled the back of her head, her cheek pressed to his chest.

Love always protects. The scripture came to him unbidden. Something he'd never been shown in his younger years, but it stabbed him through the chest with clarity now. This precious gift in his arms, this woman he loved with a ferocity he couldn't explain . . . he wanted to protect her. Always. Her trust. Her heart. Her life.

He slackened his hold just enough to glimpse her face. "Whatever tomorrow brings, I have everything I need. Right here. With you."

Her eyes shone bright in the darkness. "I love you, Levi."

She stretched on her tiptoes, her hands curled around his biceps, his arms wrapped around the curve of her waist. He captured her mouth with his, her lips warm and expectant, as if they'd been waiting for his return. As if they'd known he would return.

She threaded her fingers through his and sighed. "We should probably go inside."

He stared at their joined hands. "Lead the way."

CHAPTER THIRTY-SEVEN

Hand in hand they entered the shelter as a united front, a scenario Rayne never could have imagined. The double takes and behind-the-back whispers followed them inside the building the way smoke clung to their clothing, hair, and skin. But the scrutiny didn't rattle her. Whatever happened tonight, whatever outcome befell them, she wasn't going to let him go. Not again.

Despite the midnight hour, fluorescent lights hummed overhead, their glow not quite strong enough to chase away the shadows of apprehension etched into every face. Levi tugged her toward the huddle gathered around a black roll-away TV cart near the admin offices. She searched the crowd, taking a mental inventory of the residents she knew by name. When she lifted onto the balls of her feet to catch sight of the screen, Ford caught her eye. What must he think of her?

Levi released her hand and instead wrapped a protective arm around her shoulders. His fingertips stroked a rhythmic path from her bicep to her elbow, his gaze glued to the scrolling updates along the bottom of the emergency channel.

"What does it say?" Her view was blocked by the couple in front of them.

"There were four fires started from lightning tonight." The dread in his words sank to the bottom of her stomach. "It's too dry, the woods are too brittle. Perfect fire fuel. They closed Ramsey Highway."

Their road. The only road that spanned between the farm and the lodge. The tight bob of his throat told her there was more. Something else. Something worse.

"What?" she whispered.

"Fire crews have pulled out of the Ramsey Creek area due to dangerous conditions."

"They've evacuated? But what does that mean?"

"They're relying solely on the night helicopters to drop the fire retardant." The undefined tension in his face held. "They've lost four structures in the area already."

All the condolences she'd offered over the last couple weeks, the families she'd assisted, and the stories she'd heard reverberated throughout her mind. Her intentions had been well meaning, her words genuine, yet not even the sincerest of hearts could bridge the gap between sympathy and empathy. The difference was clear now. One watched the fire from a safe distance, while the other stood amid the flames, dreams and futures burning all around them.

She pressed into his side, as much to hold him up as to keep herself upright. She studied his profile, wishing she could do more, wishing she could fast-forward the agony of their wait ahead. No matter what Levi said, or how strong he appeared, losing the farm would devastate him and Ford. The screen flashed a solid blue before returning to the channel's regular programming.

A chilling hush fell over the room. Dazed expressions mixed with anxious fidgeting—twirling of hair, rubbing of arms, tugging of necks. A sign with a painted red arrow pointed down the hallway to her left to the sleeping area, yet nobody made a move for it. Who could sleep at a time like this?

"I'd like to say a prayer for Shelby Falls." The deep voice swung her gaze to the far side of the foyer. Ford's hat was in his hands. The worn leather curled over his fingers like an orange peel. "God hears all prayers, but scripture encourages us to join together in agreement. If anybody would like to join me, seems now would be a good time."

The swell in her chest propelled her feet toward the circle forming around Ford's outstretched hands. The sight both humbled and strengthened her as she settled into place across from him. Several Red Cross volunteers joined in, along with a few residents who'd lingered outside the doors.

With her hand tucked in Levi's, she bowed her head. Ford opened the prayer by thanking God for everything imaginable. Through squinty eyes, she peeked at him. All her life she'd lived under the influence of power-hungry men. Men driven by success, wealth, position, and fame. Ford was none of those things. He was a humble farmer, yet the unshakable confidence in his voice and the assuredness of his faith held a type of authority she'd never witnessed.

She wanted to hold on to this moment long after night turned to morning, long after the unknowns had faded from present to past.

The shift in Ford's prayer, from praise to petition, was as seamless as a tide rolling onto the shore. He prayed for the safety of every crew at work, those on the ground and those in the air. And for every evacuee affected by the fires.

And then, he prayed for rain.

The echoed "amen" around the room blanketed her in a soul-deep warmth. At the encouragement of the aid workers, the crowd dissipated along the hallway and through the auditorium doors, each evacuee collecting a small Baggie of personal items: a toothbrush and toothpaste, face and body soap, deodorant, and mouthwash.

A flash of blond in her peripheral vision pulled Rayne's focus to her second cousin. Celeste pressed a phone to her ear and paced the hallway adjacent to the gymnasium.

Rayne touched Levi's upper back. "Hey, I need to chat with Celeste for a minute."

He nodded. "Yeah, I should probably discuss a few things with Ford too."

He pressed a kiss to the crown of her head. "I'll find you in a minute."

A promise she tucked into the pocket of her heart.

Celeste pivoted near the locker bay, next to a darkened science lab, her steps halting midstride as her gaze snapped to Rayne's. She muttered a few quick phrases into her phone's receiver and tapped the screen. Her arms went stiff at her sides.

Rayne approached with caution. "How are you?"

A slight lift of her chin. "It's not every day I'm pulled from my bed because of a forest fire. We don't have many middle-of-the-night evacuations in the city."

"No, I wouldn't think so."

Celeste scrunched her lips to the side of her mouth. "But the good news for you is . . . I'm leaving."

Rayne glanced down the hallway. "Leaving where?"

"Shelby Falls. The lodge. I'm not cut out for this kind of life." She flicked her wrist. "Sleepy towns, cowboy-farmer types, fire season. All of it."

Just a month ago Rayne had banked on Celeste speaking those exact words. She'd been willing to wait her out. To celebrate her departure.

Strange how she didn't feel celebratory at all now.

"Well, for what it's worth, I've lived here my entire life and this is my first fire evacuation. Although the cowboy-farmer types aren't all bad." Rayne's lips quirked into a shy smile.

"Still." Celeste slid the toe of her red sandal in an arch against the tan linoleum. "Earlier tonight, when you were trying to help me,

I should have taken you more seriously." She gestured to the shelter signs in the hallway. "I didn't give any of this too much thought. Until it was happening to me. Suppose that makes me sound even more self-centered than you already think I am."

"No, I actually thought something similar myself only a few minutes ago. Perspective has a way of changing things."

Celeste worried her bottom lip. "Also . . ." The word dragged on, and for a second, Rayne doubted Celeste would finish her thought. "I'm sorry. For how I've treated you, for how I've always treated you. I guess I've felt . . . threatened by you."

"By me?" Rayne's question was strangled by shock.

Though Celeste avoided eye contact, a torrent of unfiltered emotions flooded her face. "It may be hard for you to believe, but coming to the lodge wasn't about boosting my ego. Sure, I wanted to show off my strengths in business, my résumé, but . . . I don't know, I wanted to be a part of something that mattered. Something connected to my roots. But just like when we were young, when I arrived here, you were still the little sweetheart of Shelby Lodge. I was glad Cal fired you. I figured everything would finally fall into place for me with you gone."

Rayne guessed at the words she hadn't spoken. "So when you saw me tonight, you must have assumed I'd come back to claim my place."

"It's what I would have done." Celeste sucked in her cheeks and then blew out a hard breath. "But it's not what you did. You weren't there as a ploy. You were there to help. Because that's who you are, a martyr."

Rayne laughed. "I'm hardly a martyr, Celeste. Believe me. And I'd be lying if I said I haven't felt threatened by you since you arrived. I suppose this summer didn't turn out the way either of us planned."

The pause that settled between them prodded Rayne to speak again. "So when are you headed back to New York?"

"I haven't booked a flight yet." Celeste pursed her lips, but Rayne could tell a private debate was taking place inside her cousin's overactive mind. "I, um . . . I actually turned in my notice to Cal this morning."

"This morning?" Rayne asked, confused. "But you just said—"

"I lied." Celeste's cheeks flushed. "I'm not leaving because of the town or even because of the wildfires." She hesitated as if searching for the right words. "After Cal fired you, things were . . . tense around the lodge. When he decided to close the shelter doors, I disagreed with his approach to handling the media. And he made it clear my opinion wasn't wanted. He may have said he was looking for a family-oriented replacement, and sometimes it did feel like he cared about my insights." She shook her head. "But other times I got the impression he was really only looking for a puppet. Someone who would simply follow his orders blindly. And I didn't work so hard in school all those years to be micromanaged by a man with a God complex."

"I'm sorry, Celeste." And surprisingly, Rayne was sorry. A puppet was exactly the kind of employee Cal desired. He'd nearly succeeded at making one out of her, the same way he'd made one out of her father.

"Don't be. I have a lot of opportunities at my disposal," Celeste said before clearing her throat. "Also, about your proposal. It wasn't all bad."

A validation Rayne no longer needed but appreciated just the same. "Thank you."

Celeste's phone lit up in her palm. "I should probably grab this."

Before her cousin could turn away, Rayne felt that familiar prodding once again.

"Wait, Celeste?"

"Yeah?"

"I was thinking that maybe you could stick around for a few days."

Celeste's brows rose, though her voice held none of its usual sass or sarcasm. "Why would I do that?"

"Because if you leave now, we might never get a chance to get to know each other." And hadn't she missed out on enough time with family due to biased judgment?

Her cousin's lips parted, but no verbal response followed.

Rayne continued, "There's a couple new hiking trails and restaurants that have opened up farther south. And remember that old ice-cream shop with the carousel we loved as kids? It's a sub shop now. Best sandwich you'll ever eat. And that little pond we used to fish at with Gia and Joshua, it nearly dried up about six years ago and someone turned it into the most gorgeous Japanese garden. There's a lot you haven't seen outside the lodge. I could give you an unofficial tour. And maybe you could even add a few new contacts to your fancy spreadsheets."

A bewildered look crossed over her cousin's face. "Okay. That, uh, that could be good. I'll think about it." She offered Rayne the slightest of smiles before pressing her phone to her ear and turning away.

Celeste's genuine surprise stayed with Rayne as she reentered the pod of townspeople gathered near the gymnasium doors.

Rayne searched for Levi in the crowd, smiling as she spotted him lifting a small freckle-faced boy up to the water fountain spout, the boy's mother wrangling another young child nearby. But then her gaze locked on a familiar gray-haired farmer on the opposite side of the room. Her uncle. Ford. He stood with his back to her, facing a woman who looked a lot like . . . *Delia*? Rayne nearly bumped into a volunteer table full of personal-care packages.

Ford and Delia. Talking.

Just a mere twenty-four hours ago, the sight of the two of them together might have sent her into cardiac arrest. But not now. Not after all she'd learned. Now she hoped the rift that had splintered them apart eighteen years ago could be mended in time. Restored. The same hope she had for her family.

Gia breezed through the main doors of the high school, her dark curls a mane around her face. "Are you okay?" she asked, clutching Rayne's arms like a mother hen. "My dad said you helped evacuate the lodge."

"Yeah," Rayne said on an exhale. "Thankfully, there were only a few guests staying over."

"And what about Celeste? Did she freak?"

Rayne wasn't in the mood to gossip. Whatever had taken place in the hallway with Celeste had her feeling strangely protective.

An idea formed in her head, one she was certain Gia would balk at. "Actually, she's doing okay. Considering."

Gia narrowed her eyes. "What? What's that face about?"

"I'm wondering if . . . would you be willing to let Celeste stay at your place tonight?"

"Uh, last time I checked my hide-a-bed was occupied. By you."

Rayne raised her eyes to the man smiling at her from only a few paces away, and Gia's suspicious gaze followed, dragging from Levi back to Rayne.

"I'm staying here. With Levi." The statement was as bold as it was telling.

"You're not even trying to hide it anymore, then?" Although she'd asked a question, there was little inflection to her voice.

"I'm done hiding." From herself and from her family name. "I love him, Gia. And he loves me."

Her cousin winced. "Let's hope your love can outlast Cal's wrath."

There was so much Rayne needed to explain, so much Gia needed to understand about their family. About Ford and Grandpa Shelby. But not here, not tonight. The last twelve hours had taken too much of a toll on them already. "I've feared Cal's wrath for too long. He doesn't get to dictate my heart. Or my future."

"You discovered something, didn't you? What you've been trying to figure out about Cal and Grandpa's will."

"Yes." Far too simple an answer for eighteen years of missing family history.

"And?"

"I promise we'll talk about everything very soon. Just not tonight." Rushing such a revelation would cause more harm than good. Levi had been right about that. He'd been right about so many things.

"Fair enough." On the tail end of a sympathetic nod, Gia sighed. "And fine, let's go tell the blonde she can stay at my place tonight. But if only one of us comes out alive, that's on you."

Rayne looped her arms around her cousin and squeezed her tight. "I love you."

"I love you too, even if you do smell like a burnt marshmallow."

CHAPTER THIRTY-EIGHT

Levi's focus remained fixed on Rayne's shadow-draped face, even though she'd gone silent nearly twenty minutes ago. He memorized her: the arch of her eyebrows, the fan of her dark lashes, the heart-shaped pout of her lips. Studying her perfection was far more appealing than analyzing everything tomorrow might bring.

The cot groaned beneath him as he settled onto his side.

"You okay?" Her sleepy whisper made him all too aware of her nearness.

"I'm fine." He reached out and brushed his thumb across her cheek and then the indent in her chin. "Go back to sleep, beautiful."

She pillowed her head onto her elbow. "You're worried."

"Just thinking."

"Thinking alone can be dangerous."

"I'm not alone."

"No." She laced her fingers through his. "You're not."

Someone coughed near the bleachers, and he allowed his next words to simmer a few extra seconds. "I keep thinking of all the things I left unfinished. The paperwork I didn't sign on my desk. The warehouse

I didn't lock up. The e-mails I haven't returned." About the delay of Second Harvest's expansion plans.

"That's not all you're worried about."

Her ability to understand him was only one of the many reasons he'd fallen so hard for her. "No, it's not." But fretting over investors when the farm could be nothing more than two hundred acres of charred ground seemed petty by comparison. His gut roiled at the thought, calming only when he caught a glimpse of Rayne's searching expression.

Her presence bolstered a feeling of quiet strength inside of him, a reminder of a prayer he'd only just now realized had been answered.

In all the chaos, God had given him the gift of perspective. There was no setback that could destroy him. Not now. Not when everyone who mattered to him was safe.

Rayne flipped Levi's hand over and rubbed at the calluses on the inside of his palm. "What's your favorite memory of the farm?"

He stared at her, willing himself to follow her down that sentimental path. "I don't know if I can choose a favorite."

"Then just tell me about a moment that makes you smile anytime you think of it."

"Does you showing up unannounced in a golf cart count? 'Cause that makes me smile."

"No, tell me something I don't know about."

He pulled a memory up through the haze of unfinished business. "So, it was my second apple harvest at the farm. I was nineteen."

"Yeah?" She leaned closer, her cot springs squeaking.

"I'd talked Ford into hiring Travis for seasonal help, and we were supposed to fill the barrels for the fall festival. Ford had sent the other pickers home, and since Travis and I were the lowest men on the totem pole, and didn't have access to the farm equipment, we were chosen to sort the rest by hand." A loose grin twitched his lips. "Ford has this process when it comes to apple selection—it's tedious and time consuming, looking at every angle of an apple before adding it to the good barrel or tossing it into the reject box. He swore by the method; his reputation was staked on it. But after Ford turned in for the night, we decided if we couldn't speed up the stupid process, we could at least find a way to enjoy it a little more."

She bit her lip. "Uh-oh."

"Yeah. Travis paid a friend to bring us a few cases of beer."

The foreboding look on Rayne's face begged to be kissed, and he answered the silent request before continuing. "To be honest, I don't even know how we finished sorting that night, much less how we moved the good barrels into the delivery truck. We lost more than a few apples in the process."

She grimaced. "What happened?"

"Ford was waiting for us outside the barn the next morning, along with the trash can we'd carelessly discarded all our empty beer bottles into."

Her eyes rounded. "Was he furious?"

"We were sure he'd fire us. I'd never seen Travis so nervous, and I'm sure he'd say the same thing about me. We both had fathers who were deadbeats on their best day and violent drunks on their worst. We'd heard every possible four-letter-word combination to describe our level of worthlessness. So I knew whatever happened, Ford couldn't possibly say anything we hadn't already heard a thousand times."

The corners of her eyes and mouth turned down and he kissed her slender fingers.

"But Ford didn't fire us, and he definitely didn't give us the lecture we deserved."

"Then what did he do?"

"He told us he was taking us out for burgers."

"What?"

"That's what we said too, but we went along with it. After he dragged that trash can back to the side of the warehouse, he drove us to that old diner on Seventh. I think we held our breath the entire way there." He stroked the soft skin at the back of her hand. "He ordered for us and then asked both of us a question I've never forgotten: 'What kind of man do you want to become?'"

"How did you answer?"

"I didn't at first. All I could think about was who I didn't want to become—a man like my father. But Ford said, 'Good character isn't produced overnight; it's grown over many seasons. In the same way you sort the good apples from the bad, the marks of poor characters are just as easy to detect.'"

"Wow."

"Yeah, he loves to say, 'Character is built on every decision we make, especially those we make in secret.' The day Ford took me in was a new beginning, but the day he gave me a second chance when I clearly didn't deserve one—" He fought against the tightening in his throat. "That day changed the trajectory of my life. I could never hope to be a better man if I didn't make the choices of a better man."

"Amazing," she said on a breath.

"It's where I got the name Second Harvest."

"That's an incredible story." She rolled her lips together. "I still can't believe I'm related to him."

"I can." A higher compliment didn't exist.

Her sudden stillness sharpened his senses.

"I'm so grateful you've had him in your life, Levi." Tears compromised her speech. "Whatever tomorrow brings, I'll be forever grateful for what my grandfather's farm gave to you both—a family, the way family was meant to be."

He gripped the bottom of her cot and closed the two-inch gap between them. With a hand to the back of her neck, he spoke the words over her lips. "Whatever tomorrow brings, know that I love you, and I have no intention to stop."

CHAPTER THIRTY-NINE

The 9.2-mile drive had never felt longer.

Levi adjusted the controls on his dash, cutting the flow of outside air and saving their throats from the fumes of burning foliage. Careful to navigate around the orange-and-white road blockades, he tailed Ford to the fire marshal's designated meeting location.

Rayne stared out the passenger-side window, her fingers tangled into a worried knot on her lap.

"Hey." He reached across the console and squeezed her knee. "Whatever happens, okay?"

The tense smile that touched her lips mirrored his own, yet even still, she covered his hand and repeated the words they'd spoken nearly every hour since dawn. "Whatever happens."

Ford's turn signal flashed through the obtrusive haze. Like a desert mirage, the marshal's truck appeared in the gravel turnout a quarter mile out from the Shelby-Winslow property line. The smoke had settled below the treetops, hanging low enough to obscure the nature around them, and too dense to make out any structure beyond where they stood to meet.

Rayne's white-knuckled grip tightened on the door handle as a shiny black Mercedes came into focus on their left.

"Cal's here," she announced.

"I figured he'd demand a private consultation with the marshal." The words were sandpaper to his teeth. As much as he needed an update on the farm, the sudden desire to flip a U-turn pressed against his protective instincts. He forced the gearshift into park and regarded his passenger. "What do you want to do, Rayne?"

"What we came here to do." She popped open her door, not an ounce of hesitancy in her voice.

Once outside the truck, she slipped her hand into his and together they crunched across the loose terrain. Ford stood near the marshal while Cal paced in a fog patch nearby, his back to them all, a phone pressed to his ear. Levi searched for signs of the two other property holders in the area but found none.

"Where are the others?" Rayne asked.

His shrug was uncomfortably stiff. "Not sure."

"Levi." Ford's subtle gesture to approach made his gut bottom out. What did he know?

"Thank you for meeting with us today, Marshal Harris," Levi said as he shook the weathered hand of the county fire marshal and introduced Rayne, though she hardly needed an introduction. Marshal Harris seemed plenty well acquainted with the Shelby family. The man flicked an annoyed glare toward Cal's back and then glanced at his watch for what was apparently not the first time.

"Mr. Shelby," Marshal Harris boomed. "We need to get started here."

Rayne gripped Levi's hand as if to obtain strength from their unity. He squeezed back, wishing they could communicate through Morse code.

Cal swiveled on his heels and his shaded scowl slipped the instant he spied his niece—or rather, the instant he spied his niece's hand clutched in Levi's. Without a word, Cal plucked the phone away from his ear, tapped the screen, and stuffed the device inside the breast pocket of his suit coat.

"What's the report, Harris?" Cal demanded with no further acknowledgment of their existence.

No acknowledgment of his brother's existence.

"Shouldn't we wait for the Gourleys and the Kellers?" The sweet sound of Rayne's voice at his side tempered Levi's heightened irritability.

Marshal Harris set his gaze on Rayne. "We did everything we could, but the winds were too high. We weren't able to regain control on that side of the river until it was too late."

"And whose call was it to pull the ground crews out last night, Harris?" Cal's finger slashed through the polluted air like an aimless dagger. "If I lost so much as a shingle on my lodge, you can bet I'll be heading up a full investigation."

"It was my call." Harris's words issued a challenge.

Levi glanced at Ford before taking the reins. "Have you taken inventory of all the properties on this side of the river?"

The tension in the man's face held strong for another three seconds before he managed to shift his attention to Levi. "Yes. I have."

Whether Rayne's grip tightened in his or his in hers, he couldn't be sure. Whatever the case, they were in this. Together. *Whatever happens.*

Harris faced them, his gaze ticking from face to face like the second hand of a wall clock. "I called you here to personally commend and compliment the man responsible for digging the fire line along the old logging road. It not only preserved both properties on this side of the river, but it reinforced our efforts, which conserved resources and manpower. The water-suppression system he engineered to pump water into the fire line and wet the vegetation was better than anything I could have built myself. Using the river was ingenious." His revolution halted on Ford.

And though no words were exchanged, the conversation inside Levi's head was as clear as the river that belted Ramsey Highway.

All those extra trips off property with the tractor and backhoe.

All those random sketches and blueprint equations on Ford's desk.

All those bags of pipeline and irrigation materials in the warehouse.

All of it finally made sense.

Ford had been digging a fire line.

Every possible explanation for what Marshal Harris described contradicted the world Rayne had grown up in for the last eighteen years. A world where neighbors passed without acknowledgment of one another. A world where friendly mailbox meetings and cordial waves were obsolete. A world where there'd been no knocks at the door to borrow sugar, no front porch conversations, no contact whatsoever.

And yet . . .

"Please," she said, looking from the marshal to Ford, her voice hoarse and rough. "Explain."

The fireman thumped Ford's shoulder. "What I'm saying, Miss Shelby, is that that freshly dug fire line behind your property"—he cut his gaze to her uncle—"is the only reason why Shelby Lodge is still standing."

Less than twenty-four hours ago, she'd labeled Ford Winslow an enemy; now she labeled him a hero.

The concept of mercy had eluded her since childhood. Like a slippery substance she couldn't quite grasp, she'd struggled to accept why an all-knowing God would sacrifice himself for the souls of faulty people. People who strayed, people who doubted, people who didn't deserve a second chance.

People just like her.

The Shelbys had taken everything from Ford—a family that should have loved him, supported him, and cherished him. Instead, he'd been rejected, threatened, and disowned. And despite what her family deserved, Ford hadn't left their lodge to burn.

He'd been the one to save it.

For the first time in her life, the mystery of mercy had been unveiled.

She tasted the salt of her tears as she lifted her gaze to Cal, hoping this act of unmerited compassion would thaw the ice around his heart. Unfortunately, it wasn't gratitude she saw reflected in his eyes.

"I want to see it for myself." Her uncle's concrete tone scraped against her insides.

The marshal's hand slipped from Ford's shoulder. "See what for yourself, Mr. Shelby?"

"The lodge!" Cal pounded a fist to his chest. "*My* lodge!"

"The wind may have calmed, but it will be at least another twelve hours before we can safely reopen Ramsey Highway, unless, of course, God decides to give us some rain—"

"If you want to send the sheriff to arrest me, then send him, and while you're at it, remind him that he owes me a hundred bucks for dinner last night."

The stare down lasted only a few seconds, the marshal's face darkening by three shades. "I'll allow you thirty minutes but not a second more. I'll be waiting at the end of your driveway to escort you back to the blockade. Don't test me."

Her uncle bolted to his black sedan without a backward glance.

And something like static buzzed inside Rayne's chest, an unsettled tension that couldn't be ignored.

"I have to talk to him," she said, her words two steps ahead of her sanity.

Levi's incredulous gaze swept her face. "What? Why?"

"Because I need to." She couldn't explain it to him; she couldn't even explain it to herself. "Will you drop me at the lodge, please?"

At the sound of tires kicking up loose gravel in the turnabout, Levi threw out an arm, gesturing toward Cal's erratic exit.

"That man has done nothing but lie to you and manipulate you . . . he's a coward. He'll never own his part in this, Rayne. What good could possibly come from you talking with him?"

She rubbed her thumb over the back of Levi's hand, the vulnerability in his voice twisting at her heart. She'd planted the seed for his insecurity. She'd chosen Cal and the lodge over him time and time again.

But not this time.

"I'm asking you to trust me, Levi."

Though he said nothing, the fear of her corruptibility still lurked in his eyes.

Ford drew closer, his gait as steady as his gaze. "Let her go, son."

"That man wouldn't even look at you, Ford, much less *thank you* for what you did for him." The raw quality in Levi's voice pricked her throat.

"I don't need to be thanked." Ford placed a hand on Levi's shoulder. "Love isn't measured by what we gain. It's measured by how much we give away."

Levi released a tension-filled sigh and looked from Ford to Rayne. "You're sure about this?"

The anxiety in her chest eased. "I'm sure."

CHAPTER FORTY

Rayne padded across the deserted lobby, her footsteps cutting through a silence as eerie as the smoke outside. Her uncle's office sat vacant. So did the Great Room, the parlor, and the stairwell.

Cal wasn't anywhere to be found on the main floor.

She skimmed her fingertips along the barren wall of family history, no frames or portraits to warm the familiar space today. Instead, the stark hallway was a cold contradiction to her memory and, quite possibly, a true reflection of reality.

Empty.

On her second pass through the kitchen, her eyes were drawn to the window, to the silhouette of a man bent over the cedar railing of a wraparound porch. His gaze seemed transfixed on a horizon he couldn't possibly see—or perhaps, on a fire line much too distant, even on the clearest of days.

He didn't turn in her direction when the door creaked open; he simply spoke to the air in front of him. "This lodge is all I have left of my father."

It wasn't the first time she'd heard Cal mention her grandfather, but it was the first time she'd heard something close to sorrow in his voice.

The rapid thud in her chest fueled her courage and her compassion. "It would have been very hard to lose it."

He didn't respond.

She inched closer. "I can only imagine how painful Granddaddy's confession must have been for you."

He clenched his jaw and continued to stare out at the shapeless scenery.

"All those years the two of you were estranged . . . and then he confirmed your biggest fear just days before he died."

"You don't know anything." A halfhearted statement encased in denial.

"I know our family doesn't have to remain divided over Granddaddy's secret."

"Yes." The word slithered off his tongue. "We do."

"He's your brother, Cal."

"I have *one* brother!" He slammed his hand onto the railing, the vibration rattling the planked boards beneath her feet. "And anything that man told you is prosecutable!"

"Ford didn't tell me." A testament she would cling to. She'd been the one to speak the words, not him. "I just finally opened my eyes to what I'd been too blind to see."

"So that's your position, then?"

"Truth isn't a position."

"Do not preach to me about *truth*."

In the light of so many lies—her grandfather's, her father's, her own—how couldn't he see that truth was the only way to peace? To freedom?

"What exactly do you intend to do with this knowledge, Rayne? What is it you want?"

"Nothing."

A two-beat laugh. "Everybody wants something."

"I didn't come to fight with you."

"So why did you come?" His russet eyes narrowed. "The lodge?"

Two words that had measured her value and worth for far too long. The only place she'd ever felt wanted or needed or accepted. The only place she'd ever known approval. The only place she'd ever called home. But when she'd walked those desolate hallways only moments ago, she'd finally seen the lodge for what it was—a building with no pulse, no breath, no life.

Somewhere along the way she'd confused legacy with love. And position with purpose.

She prayed she'd never make that mistake again.

"No," she said. "I'm here to tell you that I won't lie for you or for my father. I won't keep your secrets and I won't deny the truth."

"Only a selfish brat would turn her back on her own family."

"And yet, you've turned your back on your brother time and time again. You've kept our entire extended family in the dark, spoon-fed us lies about how Ford weaseled his way into the will, stole our inheritance, and robbed our grandfather. You defamed his character and then encouraged us to do the same, all so you wouldn't have to own your shame."

"Your father's political image hasn't remained spotless by chance. Everything I've done is to protect him and to secure the future of our family name!"

How could anyone be so relentless in their denial? "Ford's the one who kept your lodge from burning to the ground!"

Cal's chest heaved as he shifted his stance. "If you choose him, you'll be making a grave mistake."

"What mistake is that? The same one Milton Shelby made by questioning your ethics? I used to pity him. I used to fear his fate. But now I fear yours. Now, I pity you." The swell of emotion inside her shook her voice as she thought of Delia and Celeste and Ford. "There won't be a family left for you to secure if you don't own up to your mistakes. If you don't stop lying."

A tear streaked down her cheek. *Am I crying?* She touched her face and felt another drop swipe across her forearm, carried on a wind gust. She tilted her chin skyward and stretched her palm into the open air. Two more drops in the span of three short seconds.

Rain.

Despite her uncle's scowl, a smile stretched across her face as she slipped down the uncovered porch steps onto the thirsty grass.

"He won't ever be one of us," Cal said. But the fear she heard in his voice revealed that he knew the opposite was true. Ford was already one of them. His influence had stretched beyond power, wealth, and fame. And more importantly, beyond Cal's control.

Ford had refused to allow Cal's hatred to corrode his soul. He'd refused to allow bitterness to corrupt his character. He'd refused to allow anger to taint his compassion.

And he'd chosen to forgive his enemies and to love them too.

A misty breeze rushed over her, sending goose bumps down her spine and a whispered reminder to her heart: the same choices awaited her now.

"I'm not taking sides. I'm choosing our family—even the part you don't want to acknowledge."

Cal froze at her declaration, his back rigid and tense. Saying nothing more, he shoved through the back entrance and disappeared into the vacant lodge. And unlike every interaction she could recall with her uncle in the past, the shame of failed expectations never came.

The drizzle of moments before intensified, and her pace quickened as she maneuvered through the Shelby grassland toward the farm. In only a matter of minutes, the weighty atmosphere had thinned, sharpening her senses to the world around her. The lenses on her glasses became smeared and sweaty, and she plucked them from her face. Her vision blurred, but her eyes didn't need to see the path ahead. Not when her heart had memorized the way.

She wove past familiar pine trees and thorn bushes, and much the way she'd done a dozen plus times this summer, she slipped through the slats of the fence.

A soaked Levi was waiting for her on the other side.

Precipitation poured from the heavens, her hair was as drenched as her dark cotton shirt, but the sight of him was as refreshing as the rain on their dehydrated valley. Without a word, he wrapped her in a hug and buried his face in the hollow of her neck. "Are you okay?"

How could she possibly explain it? "I'm so much more than okay."

He pulled back, a shadow of disbelief in his eyes. "And Cal?"

She reached up and touched his damp face, droplets of water balancing on the ends of his lash line. "I can't control the choices he'll make. I can only control mine. And I need to forgive him. The same way Ford did."

Levi smoothed a hand over her rain-showered hair. "I used to think Ford was some kind of superhuman anomaly. That the way he saw people, the way he loved people, couldn't possibly be matched. And then I met you."

She rubbed her thumbs along the day-old stubble of his jaw. "But Levi, you were the one who helped me see what I couldn't see before." Her lips trembled. "That I could be loved just as I am."

His arms encircled her waist and he pulled her close, speaking against her lips in a caress she wanted to taste. "You've always been enough, Rayne. Way before you ever met me."

His words resonated deep within her, exposing another kind of truth, one God had planted long ago. One she'd only just discovered.

Levi pressed his lips to hers, the taste of tears and rain mingling in their kiss. She could live here. In this moment. Forever.

His mouth curved into a smile as the downpour increased. She tipped her face skyward again, closed her eyes, and . . . and the most absurd thought struck her. For the first time in her life she had absolutely no clue what came next.

"What?" he asked over the hard plinking and pattering all around them.

A bit dumbstruck at the realization, she shook her head. "It's just, I'm homeless. And jobless. And—"

Levi kissed each of her cheeks and then the tip of her nose. "You're going to be just fine. This is your opportunity, Rayne. To take what's in your heart and bring it to life. And I have no doubt you will do just that." He inclined his head toward the large barn behind him—a barn befitting so many of the community events she'd outlined.

She smiled at him through her tears. "I love you, Levi."

A throat cleared behind them.

Ford stood only a few paces away, water rivulets streaming from the brim of his leather hat.

"Sorry to interrupt." His natural grin widened. "But I just spoke to Marshal Harris."

"Yeah?" Levi reached for her hand and interlaced their fingers. "Are they going to open up the road sooner because of the rain?"

"Looks that way." Ford tipped his head and opened his palm heavenward. "And if it keeps coming down like this, the crews will be able to get a much better handle on the fires, but still, he'd appreciate us clearing out for a couple hours until it's official."

Rayne studied Ford openly, her heart squeezing with nostalgia. She didn't know this man, not in the way she hoped to, yet there was no discounting his appeal. There was no discounting the magnetism of his humble spirit.

Levi started in the direction of his truck and Rayne tugged his hand. "Wait." She turned back to Ford. "Before we go . . . will you show me the tree?"

Ford smiled and gestured for them to follow. Levi held her hand as they trudged through the wet orchard. The invigorating smell of freshly soaked earth mingled with the sweet scent of ripening fruit. The orchard spanned farther than she'd realized. Hard droplets pinged against the shiny red and green apples, creating a nature chorus she hadn't heard in what felt like a lifetime.

Ford stopped just shy of the center of the orchard, a perfect grid of apple trees all around them. The soles of her sandals sank into the irrigated grass.

"This one here." Ford pointed to a tree with branches splayed wide, the leaves a vibrant, healthy green. Glistening apples peeked out at every angle. And even through sheets of pouring rain, the deep-purple words scrawled on a garden stone in childish handwriting stole her attention.

Rayne's Tree

Hand hovering over her mouth, she knelt, the knees of her jeans sinking into squishy soil.

Ford had kept it. After all these years. He'd kept his promise. He'd taken care of her tree.

The same way he'd taken care of her family.

She brushed her fingertips over the roughly painted letters and then reached out to touch the bumpy tree trunk in front of her, remembering the tiny start she'd planted nearly two decades ago.

Ford knelt beside her under the protective branches. "Your tree's produced a great harvest every year."

Overwhelmed, she released a sob-filled laugh. "*Our* tree."

He touched her damp shoulder. "God always takes care of his creation, Rayne. The same way He's taken care of us, and our valley." He tilted his eyes to the clearing skyline.

Tears dripped from her wet lashes as the steady tenor of Ford's voice soothed a piece of her newly restored soul. She didn't have a clue what the coming days and weeks and months ahead would bring, but maybe she didn't need to. If God could send rain to a parched land, if

He could reunite a family after two decades, then maybe He had a plan for her future too.

Ford helped her to her feet. Only, when he released her hand, she wasn't ready to let go.

In just two short steps, she bridged a gap of eighteen years and hugged the man who'd taught her more about life and love and promises kept than anyone she'd ever known.

"Thank you, Ford."

As the sky continued to spill tears of sweet renewal, Levi's loving gaze and Ford's solid embrace flooded her heart with the hope of new beginnings.

ACKNOWLEDGMENTS

God: Thank you for your unfailing promises and unending love.

My husband, Tim: Thank you for your unwavering commitment to loving Christ first, and me second. You are—and will always be—my greatest blessing this side of heaven. I love you, babe.

My boys, Preston and Lincoln: Your mommy could not be prouder of the men you are becoming. You make my heart smile on a daily basis. I love you deeply.

My family: Thank you for supporting the girl behind the pen so that her dreams could take flight.

Tammy Gray: I honestly cannot imagine (nor do I want to imagine) writing a book without you as my critique partner. I cherish our morning phone calls and the hundreds of hours we've spent chatting about fictional people and problems. Thank you for loving me enough to be a truth-teller—even when I really don't want to hear "You can do better, Nicole." Thank you. You've not only challenged me to be a better writer but a better friend. I love you dearly.

Amy Matayo: It would be an impossible task to summarize what your friendship has meant to me over these last three years. I'm so grateful for every sappy tear we've shed and every gut-laugh we've tried—*and failed*—to conceal. You're my person, my writer wife, my like-soul. Thank you for being a friend like no other. I love you. Also, please move to Idaho.

Conni Cossette: For being my favorite After Midnight Texting Buddy. Knowing you're awake writing or editing or researching has inspired and comforted me in more ways than I could name. Thank you for replying to all two billion of my "Would you mind reading this scene over?" texts, and for being generous and gracious enough to say, "Sure!" Every. Single. Time. I'm quite positive I owe you a pallet of huckleberry wine the next time I see you.

Kristin Avila: I don't know a single soul who can dissect a story the way you can. You have a gift, my friend, and I've been blessed to be the recipient of your insight many times over. Thank you for being a part of my life and my writing. I love and miss you.

Kacy Gourley: Thank you for twenty years of faithful friendship and for calling me at the 75 percent mark of every book I write to remind me that I'm not a quitter. I love you, sweet friend.

Joanie Schultz: You are the best neighbor a girl could ask for . . . especially since you geek-out over my favorite books. Ha-ha! Our long walks and fiction talks are the highlight of every sunny day. (Oh, and you totally get credit for Delia quitting the lodge. Good call on that!)

My agent, Jessica Kirkland: Thank you for being my fairy godmother and for granting so many wishes of my heart. I'm in awe of your tenacity and strength, and I'm so privileged to call you both my agent and my friend. Love you, Jess.

My editor, Jennifer Lawler: I so appreciated your expertise and editorial brilliance on *TPOR*. Your comment bubbles and carefully crafted feedback deepened the characters in Shelby Falls and elevated the story as a whole. I hope our paths cross again in the very near future. Thank you.

Amy Hosford, Associate Publisher, Waterfall Press: Thank you for believing in me as a storyteller and for encouraging me to stretch my wings wider with *TPOR*.

Erin Calligan Mooney, Acquisitions Editor, Waterfall Press: Thank you for being such a delight to work with and for keeping me on schedule. Looking forward to working with you more in the future!

To the team at Waterfall Press: Thank you for caring as much about your authors as the work they produce. I'm beyond grateful for you all.

My early readers: Christa Allan, Lara Arkin, Kristin Avila, Conni Cossette, Nicki Davis, Renee Deese, Kacy Gourley, Tammy Gray, Kim Keller, Sarah Monzon, Britni Nash, Sarah Price, Joanie Schultz, Amy Matayo, Amy Simpson. Thank you all for being the best cheerleaders ever!

Real Life Home Group Gals: Debbi McEnespy, Santha Yinger, Carmen Hendewerk, Jeannie Jesseph, Bryauna Hoertz, Cheri Backman, Sandi Willis, and Lindsey McKahan. I love living in community with you all.

My readers: Thank you for allowing the dream in my heart to find a place in yours.

ABOUT THE AUTHOR

Photo © 2014 Renee Deese

Nicole Deese is a full-time lover of humorous, heartfelt, and hope-filled fiction and is the author of the Letting Go series and the Love in Lenox novels, *A Cliché Christmas* and *A Season to Love*. When she's not writing sweet romances, she can usually be found reading near a window while sipping a LaCroix. She lives in small-town Idaho with her handsome hubby and two sons.